AN AIR FORCE SPECIAL AGENT AND A TIPSY BRITISH DIPLOMAT CHALLENGE THE CHINESE MOB FOR CONTROL OF A WORLD WAR II MEGA-WEAPON.

Global Hawk reconnaissance aircraft from the American Territory of Guam detect suspicious Chinese naval activity near an abandoned island airbase. Intercepted radio traffic suggests the Chinese are hunting for an Army Air Corps plane that disappeared in 1945. The Air Force Office of Special Investigations sends Agent Jack Quintana to find out why. Quintana teams up with tipsy British diplomat Thurgood Throckmorton (that's "*Sir* Thurgood" to you rabble) on Guam's seedy "Tumon Strip." There, they latch on to a Chinese mafia boss and chase a handful of clues to a private island, a Missouri farm, a London pub, and an uber-secret base in the Indian Ocean. Beautiful dames, island shamans, hungry sharks, Chinese paratroopers, and eighty years of history all lead to a forgotten mega-weapon and a super-power showdown in the vast Western Pacific.

Early Praise for Pacific Threat

FROM PAT BOONE–COUNTRY MUSIC SUPERSTAR AND AMERICAN ICON—

"THIS ONE IS A REAL GRABBER"

"'Pacific Threat' is a rare flight of fancy from a runway of historical fact. As the former Pacific Air Forces Command Chief Master Sergeant, I found the setting sublime; the story a bold fabrication upon the Air Force's enduring foundations in the Western Pacific. Fasten your seatbelts, ladies and gentlemen. We're comin' in on a wing and a prayer."—*Rodney J. McKinley, The 15th Chief Master Sergeant of the U.S. Air Force*

i

Jack shoved Throckmorton into the sand and popped two wild rounds back in Vitoli's direction. "You've disrupted an evening of absolute perfection, my boy," Throckmorton said. "I hope you've something to say for yourself."

"Get down!" Jack yelled. The helicopter swirled past the reef and approached the yacht. Vitoli made the mistake of firing on it.

7.62 millimeter rounds blasted from the open side of the helicopter on full automatic. Vitoli whirled, fell to the ground, grabbed the Kalashnikov, and resumed firing.

"That man is an idiot," Thurgood opined, lying on his elbow and brushing sand from his chest.

The helicopter gunner fired a long volley at Vitoli, and the Russian rolled behind a coconut tree.

The pilot hovered three feet over the beach. Jack shoved Throckmorton into the passenger hold. He looked back at the cottages and saw Xiao at her doorway. Jack moved to board the chopper and motioned for the pilot to scram.

The gunner helped him up. "You guys really know how to party!"

"Agreed," Jack replied, looking back at Xiao. She stood motionless as the helicopter lifted into the night.

PACIFIC THREAT

Matthew R. Matlock

Moonshine Cove Publishing, LLC
Abbeville, South Carolina U.S.A.
First Moonshine Cove Edition March 2022

ISBN: 9781952439308

Library of Congress LCCN: 2022905605

About the Author

Matthew R. Matlock is an Air Force Master Sergeant. He has enjoyed nine separate military assignments and executed missions in Afghanistan, Bahrain, Iraq, Oman, Kuwait, Jordan, Turkey, Djibouti, the Seychelles Islands, Singapore, Guam, and the mysterious British Indian Ocean Territory of Diego Garcia. He's languished in crypto vaults, schlepped secret packages around the Middle East, and maintained underground Minuteman III ICBM sites in North Dakota (yes, there are aliens, and yes, they screw with our nukes, but mostly because they dig the planet, man). The island of Guam, the tiny American Territory in the Western Pacific, owns a special slice of his heart. If the Chinese can refrain from nuking the island into oblivion, he hopes to revisit "Mac & Marti," the coziest bar on the Tumon Strip, for a few more brews and a shot of Jameson.

If you buy this book... yes, you there, wasting your time on this bio instead of plunging into the awesome story inside... he might even earn enough to buy himself a little beachfront shack. Tell you what. You buy this book, and you're invited to a barbecue at his Guam beach bungalow, where the grill will glow, the beer will flow, and some fumble-fingered boozehound will strum a guitar, badly, and sing Creedence, or Willie Nelson, or the Ink Spots. Or something.

Just buy the book.

Also, watch out for his ecological thriller, "Big Spring," and his forthcoming time travel trilogy, "The Resounding Recollections of Copernicus Jones"!

https://matthewrmatlock.com

PACIFIC THREAT

CHAPTER 1

Special Agent Jack Quintana took a drag on his cigarette and stared at the Chamorro Goddess of Life. Her statue stood illuminated before the airport terminal. The night air hung heavy with moisture and jungle aroma; it enveloped him like a warm lover in a hot shower. Speaking of hot showers, he would need one fairly soon.

The flight over the Pacific, from San Francisco to Honolulu to the American Territory of Guam, had taken over sixteen hours. His ass was numb, his mouth tasted bad, and he smelled like a vagrant. Beyond the airport sculpture, the lights of Tumon glittered on the coast.

The Air Force Office of Special Investigations, or O.S.I., had pulled him off a hot case in California after an urgent request from the Air Force Commander on Guam. Jack had asked for details and gotten airline tickets instead.

He lit a second smoke from the butt of his first and dragged his knuckles across a sandpaper beard. A taxi rolled to a stop in front of the Goddess. Jack lowered himself into the passenger seat and winced at the stinging sensation in his rear end.

"Hello, suh!" the taxi driver sang. "You mistuh Jack?"

"Guilty," Jack said.

The driver smiled and shoved the taxi into gear. "You want girls, I take you downtown. You want booze, I take you downtown. You want anything else, I take you downtown, and you find it yourself."

Jack laughed. "What's your name?"

"My name is Jerry, and this is Jerry Taxi."

"You're not from Guam, are you?" Jack asked, noting his accent.

"From Manila. I move to Guam five year ago. My family still in Philippines. I send money every month."

The ride from the airport to the Westin Hotel took ten minutes, slowed at the end by a sea of Japanese tourists jamming an intersection. Jerry waved at the passersby. "Japanese love this island like you

Americans love Hawaii," he said, waving twiddly fingers at a pair of young women.

"Seventy-eight year ago," he continued, "they bomb Pearl Harbor, invade Philippines, take over *this* island by force. You know all that, I'm sure."

Jack nodded and appreciated the legs attached to a slender Japanese woman in evening dress.

"You know they invade Philippines same time . they torpedo U.S. Navy on Oahu? Japanese Army kill both my grandfather in prison camp; rape one of my grandmother. Kill almost one million Filipino during occupation. Now, they the nicest people you ever meet."

"Is that so?" Jack said, still tracking the raven-haired beauty in the slinky black dress.

"They don't tip worth a damn," Jerry said, accelerating through a gap in the crowd, "but . they always pay, even when . they shitty drunk."

"Very conscientious," Jack said.

The hotel lobby yawned sparkling and elaborate. Two banks of glass elevators moved people, mostly Japanese, up to any one of twenty-one floors. The female attendant at the front desk wore a tasteful skirt and silk blouse. An elderly islander with a Spanish guitar crooned "Moon River" for drunken tourists.

His room, on the 17th floor, overlooked Tumon Bay and the downtown Strip. Still attuned to Pacific Standard Time, Jack's mind churned, and his legs felt restless from the extended flight. He showered, poured himself a short glass of Jameson Irish Whiskey from the mini-bar, and let the fiery liquid rest on his tongue as he opened a sliding glass door to the balcony.

The breeze from the giant Pacific pushed through his hair and riffled his collared shirt. He listened to the shushing waves and the human sounds from down in the street. A crescent moon rode high over the ocean. It cast a white beam across the water to the beach below. He took another jolt from the whiskey glass and wondered, not unpleasantly, just what the hell he was doing here.

The display on the bedside alarm clock indicated it was Thursday and closing in on 10:00 p.m.. If this trip was as important as the O.S.I. brass seemed to think, the Commander of the 36th Wing at Andersen Air Force Base would still be up worrying over it.

He removed a spiral notebook from his backpack and found the number his boss had provided. At this late hour, the secretary was out, but Brigadier General Michael Carter answered on the second ring.

"This is Agent Quintana," Jack said. "O.S.I. Headquarters sent me out at your request."

"Agent Quintana," General Carter replied. "I won't ask about your trip. I've flown it enough to know your backside feels like it's been assaulted with a meat tenderizer, your eyes are bloodshot, and you can't sleep because it's yesterday afternoon back in the States."

Jack grunted. "That's it exactly, sir."

"How soon can you be here?" General Carter asked.

"I can be there in an hour if my taxi's still available."

"Forget the taxi. I'll send my Executive Assistant, Lieutenant Johnson, to pick you up. Where are you staying?"

Jack told him.

* * *

"First time at Andersen Air Force Base?" General Carter asked. He sat in a leather office chair behind a wide desk. Historical paintings decorated the wall behind him. The B-29 *Superfortress* and B-52 *Flying Fortress*, both capable of delivering nuclear payloads, were featured prominently throughout the room. Along with various other aircraft, they provided a quick study of the base's past.

Jack seated himself on a leather couch opposite the General. To his right, several windows overlooked the flight line. It bustled with activity at the base of a sloping field. The runway lights glowed blue and red across the tarmac and stopped where the airfield terminated at an ocean-battered cliff.

"I've been here several times," Jack replied. "Just short refueling stops on my way to Okinawa and the Philippines."

"Johnson!" the General shouted. Jack heard the Lieutenant drop something out in the reception area. The young officer appeared and leaned through the doorway. "Pour us a couple of drinks, Lieutenant," Carter told him.

While Johnson hurried away for the booze, the General collected some papers and moved into a wingback chair, closer to Jack. He arranged his notes on a coffee table between them and appeared to collect his thoughts. The Lieutenant delivered the drinks, blended Scotch poured neat in heavy glasses, and closed the office door on his way out.

"The Japanese launched an invasion of Guam a few hours after they attacked Pearl Harbor," General Carter said, staring into his Scotch glass. "Our Navy held them off for three days. But with the bulk of the U.S. Pacific Fleet sunk in Hawaii, we had no choice but to surrender the island."

Jack hoped he hadn't come six thousand miles for a lesson in military history.

"In August of '44, our Marines took the island back from the Japanese." He gestured toward the window with his Scotch glass. "U.S. Navy Seabees built that airfield out there, just three short months later."

Jack sipped his Scotch and waited.

"In January 1945, Brigadier General James R. Andersen arrived on Guam and took command of this installation. About thirty days later, Lieutenant General Millard F. Harmon, commander of all Army Air Forces in the Pacific, asked Andersen to fly back to Washington D.C. with him. There was some squabble over ownership of long-range fighter groups. Apparently, Harmon wanted Andersen in his pocket while he duked it out with General Lemay.

"On 26 February 1945, Harmon and Andersen boarded an aircraft called a 'Consolidated C-87A Liberator Express,' Tail Number *41-24174*. They left that airfield," he gestured with his glass again, "for Hickam Air Force Base. They made it to the island of Kwajalein and refueled. Shortly thereafter, they busted out for the Johnston Atoll, last fuel stop before Hawaii."

He straightened, reviewed his notes, and read: "Pilot: Major Francis E. Savage. Co-Pilot: First Lieutenant Jack West. Navigator: Major Archibald Anderson. Radio Operator: Technical Sergeant Steve Geist. Engineer: Master Sergeant Douglas Anderson. Assistant Engineer: Private First Class Arthur Ofner. Additional passengers: Colonel William Bell and Technical Sergeant Charles McInerney."

He dragged a hand over his face. His eyes were bloodshot. "When Major Savage quit reporting their position and failed to arrive at Hickam Field, the Army Air Corps mounted a massive rescue operation, but found nothing. Shortly thereafter, the Air Corps declared the aircraft, crew, and passengers lost at sea."

Carter stood and walked to the window. "I'm getting somewhere with this, Quintana," he said. "This airfield has been invaluable to U.S. interests in the Pacific for a lifetime. It's my responsibility now." He was silent for several seconds, his eyes on a B-52 refueling on the tarmac.

"The final radio contact was between Major Savage and one of our ground stations in the Marshall Islands. A Sergeant Stanley H. Long received their last known position as: 11 Degrees, 15 Minutes North by 174 Degrees, 15 Minutes East.

"Some strange things have been happening around here, Jack. We've got *Global Hawk* surveillance aircraft in a hangar just five hundred yards from this building. Two days ago, the 69th Reconnaissance Group spotted Chinese Naval vessels in the same region where Harmon's C-87 Liberator Express was supposed to have gone down. The Chinese don't venture that far east without a damned good reason.

"What's more, the commander of Submarine Squadron 15, down at the Naval Base, paid me a visit yesterday. One of his Los Angeles class Fast Attack Submarines, the *U.S.S. Key West,* is performing a routine patrol in the area of Kwajalein Atoll, about 1,500 miles to the northeast of Guam."

11

As the B-52 on the flight line taxied into takeoff position, Carter turned back to Jack.

"About thirty-six hours ago," he said, "the *Key West* picked up several radio transmissions between the Chinese vessels in that area."

Jack straightened. Beyond the General's window and the sloping field, the B-52 lumbered up the runway toward the cliff, gaining speed.

"They've got a Chinese linguist down at the Naval base. After reviewing the chatter, the linguist pinpointed three specific details that make this thing interesting. First, they recorded multiple references to 'C-87 Liberator.' Second, the airplane tail number, *41-24174*, was repeated over a dozen times. Third, the Chinese vessels are stopping at various islands in the vicinity of Kwajalein and Johnston Atoll, deploying smaller boats, and dropping divers."

Jack rubbed his temples and wished the Lieutenant would reappear with a fresh glass. "General," he interrupted, "why would the Chinese be interested in a seventy-five year old Army Air Corps wreck?"

"Agent Quintana, I have absolutely no idea.

"However, I do know the Chinese have enough sense to take purposeful action where they see they might be able to gain an advantage, which is a practice we Americans might do well to re-learn. The goddamn Chinese Navy knows something we don't, and I don't like it.

"Even something so seemingly inconsequential as a downed VIP transport from World War II could hold import beyond our ability to comprehend. For Christ's sake, Jack, it's *our* plane! If there's something the Chinese want to know about it, I damned well want to know about it before they do."

Jack tapped a pen against the coffee table. "This is a bit beyond the scope of my experience, General. I might need some political strings pulled to get much further than you have already."

"Don't you worry about any of that. I've already informed the Naval base commander that you'll need a translator by tomorrow morning. Furthermore, he has forwarded my intentions for this investigation upward through the echelons of the entire Pacific Command.

"If you hit a snag, I want you to call me," he leaned forward and jotted a number on a piece of notebook paper, "directly. I'm not shitting around here, Jack. I don't care what time it is, where you are, or what the hell's going on. If you need support, you call this number..." He paced back around his desk and retrieved something from a drawer, "...with this phone."

Jack examined it. "Iridium satellite phone?"

"Use it," Carter replied. "You've got," he looked at his watch, "twenty-four hours to recuperate. After that, I need you to be on this like a pit-bull on a toddler. We've requisitioned a vehicle for you to use as long as you're on the island. The 36th Wing Headquarters will fund all of your above-board expenses."

Jack stood, drained the last of his Scotch, and listened to the B-52 rumble off the runway and climb out over the Western Pacific. "I'll do what I can," he said.

"Go to it, son," Carter replied, and offered his hand.

Jack shook it and left the office. Lieutenant Johnson waited in the reception area with a set of car keys.

He left the building by the main entrance, where a black Suburban sat in front of the base flag pole. Down the street, to his left, the 734th Air Mobility Squadron passenger terminal fronted the flight line.

He eased into the driver seat, started the vehicle, and pulled a pack of Camels from the breast pocket of his button-down shirt. He lit a cigarette, inhaled, and wondered what kind of puzzle awaited him this time.

Usually, he infiltrated drug rings, uncovered financial waste, and investigated fraud. This assignment was a damn sight more interesting than his usual fare.

He punched the Suburban into reverse, pulled onto O'Malley Avenue, and headed toward the flight line. He saw the 36th Communications Squadron building on his left. *Probably where this Iridium phone came from*, he thought absently. There was a single car in the parking lot: an orange Dodge Charger. Racing stripes decorated the hood and trunk. It gleamed under a sodium arc-lamp, all by itself.

On a whim, he pulled into the parking lot, passed the Charger, and parked the Suburban next to a smoking area. As Jack stepped out, a uniformed Staff Sergeant emerged from a set of steel exit doors at the rear of the building, removed his glasses, and pinched the bridge of his nose.

"Rough day?" Jack asked.

The sergeant jumped and peered at him. "You got that right," he replied.

Jack held out his hand. "Jack Quintana. O.S.I."

The sergeant looked briefly uncomfortable. Jack was used to this reaction. Investigators who investigated things always made people a little stand-offish.

Then, with a shrug, the sergeant replied, "Sergeant Scott Kirker. What's got you up so late on a school night?"

"Your boss's boss," Jack replied.

Sergeant Kirker laughed. "General Carter's still holed up in the HQ? I was wondering why they called me in at 9 p.m. to hunt up an Iridium phone. You got it on you?"

Jack pulled it out of his pocket.

"Know how to use it?" Sergeant Kirker asked.

"Not a clue," Jack said.

Sergeant Kirker smiled and gave him a brief tutorial. "Look," he continued, "if you need anything else, give me a call at this number." He punched a number into the phone, saved it to the "Contacts" listing, and lit another Camel.

"What would we do without you noncommissioned officers?" he asked.

"Not a damn thing, most likely," Kirker replied with a grin.

"I owe you a beer when I'm done with this case," Jack said, and climbed back into the Suburban. "Is that your Charger in the parking lot?"

Sergeant Kirker flicked his smoke into a sand bucket. "That's my baby. Try not to drool on her."

Jack laughed and rolled back out to O'Malley. He swung a left at the stop sign and motored down Arc Light Boulevard toward the front gate. The road rose gently, and he saw a traffic circle a quarter mile ahead. A sign before the traffic circle declared that "Beaches" and a "Scenic Overlook" were down the road to his right, while the main gate lay straight ahead.

It was almost midnight, but he felt sleep would elude him for hours, yet. He took the right-hand road, drove about two miles, and pulled up to the Scenic Overlook.

The Overlook was a simple, concrete pavilion with a steel guardrail at the precipice of a gravel-strewn approach. It ended at the edge of a drop-off into dark jungle. The jungle sloped down and away. Far below, he saw the beach, the coral reef, and the ocean.

The moon translated the sun's light onto the great Pacific. Rollers rippled to the shining beach and crashed past the reef with a thunder he could detect even from his distant vantage point.

From here, the island's northern extremity lay before him. He began to understand how people, like General Carter, could fall in love with the mission and history associated with this place. How many people had stood where he stood and appreciated the striking beauty of this South Sea sanctuary?

He lit another smoke and exhaled. His mind, foggy from sleepless travel, worked over General Carter's monologue. *General Andersen; General Harmon; Major Savage; the aircrew.*

God, he needed some down-time. His mind chased ghosts down unproductive avenues. He fixed his gaze on the moon. Had it been the last thing Major Savage saw before his Liberator Express corkscrewed out of the sky seventy-five years ago?

They had departed Guam for Kwajalein. They refueled in Kwajalein and then set off for the Johnston Atoll; another fuel stop before the long, island-free passage to Hawaii. Somewhere between Kwajalein and the Johnston Atoll, something had happened.

He tapped his left hand against the steel railing, and his wedding ring struck a tone through the metal. He didn't know why he still wore it. Ashley had been dead for years now, killed when the Blackhawk she was on went down in the desert.

Fourteen years ago, they had both been students at the Presidio of Monterey's Defense Language Institute. She studied Arabic. He studied how to get drunk and get laid on a consistent basis.

She had fine, porcelain features and auburn hair.

They married six months after they met. Shortly thereafter, the school staff shit-canned him for showing up to class drunk, and he was forced to retrain into a different career field.

They were together only six of their twelve years of marriage, but they made good use of their time together. They saw England in its entirety. They traveled Europe and savored Paris and Venice and Berlin. On St. Patrick's day 2006, they got drunk in Dublin and stumbled from pub to pub, guzzled Guinness with the Irish, and weaved through crowds of laughing, fighting, puking revelers until five o'clock in the morning.

During their last assignment together in Monterey, she deployed to Afghanistan with a special operations team. He saw her off at the little airport on Monterey Bay, where John Denver died in a plane crash.

That thought pulled him back to the present. *Hell of a time to hash up old memories. Hell of a time to choke yourself up over your dead wife, standing at the Andersen Air Force Base Overlook at midnight on a Thursday, with a mountain of work ahead.*

He cast his cigarette to the ground.

* * *

He made it back to the Westin hotel by 12:30 a.m. and decided to look for a drink. He left the SUV in the hotel's underground parking garage, mounted a series of steps, and headed for the Tumon Strip.

Tumon proved a bawdy collection of strip clubs, Asian massage parlors, bars, bars that doubled as Asian massage parlors, and novelty shops, mostly of the adult variety. Chinese and Korean girls posed in darkened doorways, backlit by neon signs. They called to likely prospects for "Massage? I give you good massage. Maybe more (moah), sail-uh!" They seemed to think every adult male on the Strip was assigned to the good old U.S. Navy.

Jack wandered through the working girls, the Japanese tourists, and the ubiquitous drunken sailors, searching for a quality bar. Ten minutes into his walk, he found a quiet place called *Mac & Marti*. Most of the clientele seemed either local or military. The bartender was young, beautiful, and Chamorro.

The phone behind the bar jangled as he entered. The bartender asked him to wait a moment while she took the call. Her brow creased at something the other party said. She shook her head and then stopped. Her eyes widened. She shifted them back in Jack's direction, bit her lower lip, and then looked away.

"Okay," he heard her say. "Okay, all right." She set the phone in its cradle.

"Hello," she said, and moved toward him behind the bar, graceful. She wore cutoff jeans and a halter top. "What can I get for you?"

"Jameson. Rocks. Please." He answered. "Better make it a double."

She flashed him a smile, and he thought it a bit forced. "Are you down at Big Navy?" she asked. He interpreted "Big Navy" to mean the U.S. Navy base at the south end of the island.

"I'm Air Force," he replied. "Just here temporarily."

"And what do you do for the Air Force?" she inquired. She leaned over the bar to better display her up-tilted breasts.

"This and that. How's that drink coming?"

She looked surprised that he hadn't devolved into a slobbering Neanderthal at the sight of her chest. She showed him that smile again, turned away, and poured his drink.

There were four other people in the bar at this hour: two Japanese businessmen, a black kid with an Afro, and an older Chamorro biker. The black kid and the biker discussed the merits of the Beatles song "Rocky Raccoon."

He noticed a pack of Camel Lights in the front pocket of her shorts. After a quick sip of Jameson, he put down his glass and said, "Let me bum a smoke. I'll up your tip by ten percent."

"Bring your drink," she laughed. "There's a table out front where we can sit."

She said her name was Isa Bordallo. She pulled a cigarette from her pack, lit it, and handed it to him over the table. A glass of brandy swirled in her left hand.

She had a Brenton Wood album on the bar's sound system, and the music piped into the street. Brenton crooned the song "Darlin'," and she swayed in her plastic chair. Her jet black hair covered her left shoulder and framed one exquisite breast.

Few pedestrians toured the street at this hour. A stray "boonie" dog trotted past the table, sniffed the bar's front door, and disappeared around the corner.

"Isa," he said. "That's an interesting name."

"It's the Chamorro word for 'rainbow,'" she answered. "Isa Bordallo. That's me."

The Jameson, compounded by the General's Scotch, did its work. He felt a little fuzzy and tried to steel himself against the sensation. "Darlin'" had given way to "I Like the Way You Love Me." She looked at the stars with half lidded eyes.

"Is this your personal playlist?" he asked.

"You betcha boots," she said, dreamy.

He smiled, liked her intensely, and tried to remember he had work to do in the morning.

"Where do you think we are?" she asked.

"Western Pacific Ocean," he said, and took another slug of whiskey.

"Not *that*," she laughed. She held her arms out to each side, palms to the dark sky. "Where the hell *are* we? Look at those stars. Look at the blackness in between them, where it isn't really black at all."

He looked at her doubtfully.

"Almost every point in the night sky is filled with light. We just can't see it all because most of the stars sending it can't be detected, even with our most powerful telescopes."

"Ah," he replied. "A follow-up to the oldest question in the world. 'Who are we?' That one's usually followed by: 'Why are we here?' Your addition: 'Where is here?'"

She sipped her brandy and kept her eyes on the sky.

"You must be either an astronomy student or a philosopher," he said.

"Neither," she said. "I'm studying archaeology at the University of Guam."

There was a commotion from inside the bar. Maybe the old biker had taken offense to something the kid had said about the Beatles.

"Excuse me," she said, and hurried back to her rowdy clientele.

The night was warm; the whiskey was warmer. The ocean breeze played through palm fronds. Swaying coconut trees lined both sides of the Tumon Strip. A stray dog chuffed somewhere in the darkness, making noise for the hell of it.

His thoughts drifted strangely. Isa's question was relatively deep; not something you'd expect the average college student to cough up on a whim. Coughing. The dog coughing, chuffing, barking. The breeze stirred and drowned the faraway sound of the dog. More raised voices from inside the bar, but in the final stages of argument. He looked over his shoulder. The kid with the Afro patted the old biker on the shoulder. Isa brought them a couple more drinks. She had the phone to her ear again.

Isa. Black hair, dark eyes, perky tits. Deep thoughts on a silky night in Tumon, with the Milky Way galaxy swirling above their heads. *Who are we? Why are we here? Where is here?*

He felt himself slide down into sleep, and he jerked himself awake again. He was tired, but he didn't think he was wiped to the point of falling asleep in a plastic chair outside a bar, like an old drunk that couldn't keep it together.

He tried to stand, but his legs wouldn't cooperate. He could lift himself by pushing off of the chair's armrests, but he couldn't feel anything below the waist. "That's a goddamn shame," he said, laughing. How was he going to lay this gorgeous Chamorro chick if he was numb from the waist down?

Fear struck him with sudden bluntness. He wasn't thinking clearly. For some reason, his legs had taken the night off. He had a lot more to worry about than whether he was going to be able to bed the bartender. He tipped forward, tried his legs again, almost overbalanced, and crashed back into the chair with a moan.

Isa emerged from the bar again. Her eyes didn't look dreamy anymore. They looked scared.

"Isah," he managed, pushing the word out over a tongue that felt three times too large. "Sahh!"

"Hush," she whispered. "Just hush now."

His head lolled back on the seat. He couldn't feel his arms anymore, either. Boy, was Isa going to be disappointed when she got him in the sack tonight. He chuckled and rolled his head back and forth on the back of the chair. The galaxy whirled over his head.

A police cruiser pulled up beside the bar. A local cop climbed out. He was short, stocky; mid-forties.

"Been drinking a little too much there?" the cop asked, and flashed strange glances up and down the Strip.

"Nah," Jack answered, unable to manage more than monosyllables.

Isa stood next to Jack and shifted her weight from one leg to the other, nervous. Sweat stood out on her temples.

"Help me get him into the cruiser, Isa," he said.

She whipped her pretty head right and left in a quick, negative motion. "I did what you told me. I'm not doing any more."

"Isa," he answered, feigning sadness. "You don't want to have anything happen to your grandmother, do you?"

"No!" she shouted, backing toward the door. "I did what you asked!"

"Help me with him. Make it quick."

Jack followed this conversation with lighthearted disinterest. Their voices melded with the sound of the palm fronds, the dog, the galaxy. And, hey! Brenton Wood had started in with "Where Were You." *There you go, Isa. Brenton Wood wants to know where you were. You were HERE. With me. Wherever the hell that was. Milky Way. Too damn big, baby. Too much SPACE!*

Rough hands grasped his arms, and the chair fell away beneath him. Isa had him by the ankles. They shuffled him over the sidewalk and into the cruiser's trunk. She started to cry. She looked pretty with those tears in her eyes. Mascara streaked down her cheeks, and he smelled her perfume as the breeze pushed it toward his face.

Then blackness presided, and he felt vague motion. They bucked and jounced over a neglected road. They turned left twice. They turned right once. He passed out.

* * *

When he awoke, he found himself tied to a straight-backed, wooden chair in a hotel suite. Silk tapestries lined the walls, silk rugs adorned the floor, and silk upholstered furniture sat around the room.

He tried to lean forward but could only incline his head. In his mind's eye, he saw Isa turn away from him to pour his drink, Isa on the phone, Isa with that crease in her brow. Isa possibly dropping something into his glass.

He stared at a wall of north-facing windows. The ocean churned on his left, and the bright lights of Tumon shone on the right, separated by the explicit coastline. An airliner banked over the city and then out over the ocean. He wondered if it was the same aircraft he had recently disembarked.

Behind him, he heard liquid tumble into a glass. He realized he could see someone in the windows' reflection. Their eyes locked through the night's mirror.

She looked Chinese. She wore a tight-fitting evening dress made of, surprise-surprise, silk. Sipping from the glass of red wine she'd just poured, she stepped out from behind an elaborate bar. Mother-of-pearl inlayed ebony gleamed behind her, and he thought the ashtray into which she tapped her cigarette might be ivory.

Leave it to the Chinese to hack off an elephant's tusks for something to catch burnt tobacco leavings. Come to think of it, weren't the Japanese just as bad about that sort of thing? He remembered Jerry's narrative and laughed out loud.

"Something funny, Agent Quintana?" she asked. Her voice was as smoky as her cigarette. He caught a whiff of it. It seemed like something classic. *Dunhill*, maybe.

"I was just thinking. You Chinese are almost as bad as the goddamn Japanese right before World War Two."

She watched him.

He coughed. "Actually, I guess you might be worse, what with all the nukes and intellectual property theft."

She smiled. "How do you feel?"

"Might feel a little better if you'd give me a drag on that coffin nail." He wanted her in front of him. She made him nervous standing around back there.

She walked around his chair and placed her own cigarette in his mouth. He inhaled and sighed a silver jet stream. "Dunhill?" he asked.

She brushed a lock of hair from his forehead. "I've got a thing for John Lennon," she said. "They were his favorites."

"You know, I've got a thing for Elvis, but I don't go around carrying Peanut Butter and Banana sandwiches everywhere."

She turned away and walked to the window-wall, well-muscled but feminine. She glided within the delicate fabric of her dress.

He rolled the Dunhill between his lips and expelled it onto the silk rug. She whirled and moved toward it. Then she regained her composure and sauntered to the spot where it smoldered on the rug.

She tipped her wine glass over the butt and put it out with a hiss.

"I'm disappointed. A boss-lady wouldn't give two shits about cigarette burns on the carpet. I thought you might be the head Chinaman on the island."

She raised her eyebrows and considered him. "You can cut the psychological games, Agent Quintana. My employer will soon arrive."

The double-doors behind him opened with a burst of light from the hallway. In the windows' reflection, he watched a tall, older Chinese man enter the room. The doors closed, and the man walked around Jack's chair to face him. He ignored the woman at the windows.

"Agent Quintana?" he inquired in perfect English, raising both eyebrows.

"The one and only," Jack replied.

The man knelt before him on the rug.

"Agent Quintana," the man sighed, pinching the bridge of his nose between thumb and forefinger. "Allow me to express my sincere apology for the way you've been treated."

His voice came deep and soothing. His suit might have cost less than the antique silk rug. It also might have cost more.

"Maybe I could find it in my heart to forgive you," Jack felt a tingling sensation in his arms and legs, "if you'd tell me what the hell is going on."

The man spread his hands and shook his head. "I informed the island authorities that I'd like to speak with you following your visit to Andersen Air Force Base, and I made the mistake of believing they understood the context of my request. These islanders," he said, "can sometimes be a bit obtuse, if you take my meaning."

"If you're talking about that dirty cop," Jack said, "'obtuse' is being generous." He tried to wiggle his fingers and toes.

"Then you understand," the man smiled, apparently relieved at having righted a social blunder. He looked around and located the silk-dress-lady, as Jack had come to think of her. "Bring a chair over here," he told her.

She grabbed a chair and positioned it for her boss.

He settled himself into it, snapped his fingers, and pointed to the floor to Jack's left. The silk-dress-lady frowned, cleared her face, and knelt beside Jack. "See what you can do about getting the feeling back into his arms," the man said.

Jack felt pressure on his left forearm as she massaged him. He thought this was probably the strangest meeting he'd ever had. Well, one of the strangest, anyway. The Chinese man caught Jack's expression.

"I know this must seem a trifle out of the ordinary," he told Jack.

A trifle? "Not at all. I'm frequently drugged, accosted, and massaged against my will. It goes with the job."

The tall man leaned forward and howled, wiping nonexistent tears from his eyes.

"Oh, Agent Quintana, that is good. That is so good."

He quieted, rose from his chair, and walked to the bar. "Can I make you a drink?"

Jack wondered about the consequences of more whiskey and UNKNOWN TRANQUILIZER. Then he found he didn't care. "Whiskey," he answered. "Jameson, if you've got it."

"Coming right up," the tall man said, bustling busily behind the bar. Silk-dress-lady made eye contact. She was not a happy camper. Jack winked at her.

"Xiao there is my personal secretary and head of my security," the tall man called from behind them, "among other things."

Her eyes darkened at this. She dropped Jack's left arm and worked on his right.

"I think I've got this figured out," Jack said, now able to twitch the fingers of his left hand.

"Really?" the tall man asked. "Do tell."

Jack watched as the tall man splashed Jameson into a glass, fussing over the ice cubes.

"You run Chinese organized crime on the island. You import drugs, prostitutes, and illegal gambling and export cash to your overlords in Beijing, retaining a sizable commission for yourself, I would imagine."

The tall man handed him his glass of Jameson, which Jack grasped in his newly revived left hand, and settled into the other chair. The man had poured himself something rather too sweet, Jack scented. Something like cognac or amaretto.

Jack continued. "Xiao is just what you say she is, your secretary, your security, your mistress..."

The tall man roared laughter once again, "Oh, my. Well. 'Mistress' might be a bit quaint, but—"

"You're Beijing's 'Premier of the Western Pacific,' aren't you?"

The tall man's nonchalant demeanor faltered; his eyes cooled.

"Yeah, you're the biggest deal in the boondocks, but your betters in Beijing told their boy to step-and-fetch, and you obliged with a smile."

"You have a very interesting way of putting things, Jack," he said, lighting a cigarette. "Ah, may I call you 'Jack'?"

"No," Jack replied.

"Well, Jack," he said, suddenly all business. "You're right about my being involved in organized crime, I must confess. But when everything everyone seems to want is criminal, it's rather difficult for someone in my position to be otherwise."

Jack sipped from his glass, aware for the first time that his left arm had become operational again. Xiao continued to massage his right hand, but she seemed more interested in the tall man's discourse than in restoring Jack's functionality.

"It's true, my 'betters in Beijing,' as you so charmingly put it, contacted me with a mandate when they learned you were en-route from San Francisco, some..." he looked at his gold watch, "twenty-eight hours ago. We collected your lodging details from the Westin Hotel staff. Oh!," he exclaimed, slapping his knee, "that reminds me. We took the liberty of upgrading your room. They had you in a horrid little hole on the second floor; absolutely no view. Were you happy with the accommodations as you found them?"

Jack pulled a pack of Camels from his pocket, remembered it was empty, and tossed it on the floor.

"Xiao," the tall man said. "Light the man a smoke, would you, dear?"

Xiao did as he asked. Jack pulled the smoke into his lungs and felt his head clear.

"So what's the deal?" he asked, rubbing his eyes. "What do your people want to know?"

"Yes," the tall man answered. "You want to... how do you Americans say it? You want to 'get down to brass tacks,' I imagine."

"Look, Shao-Lin," Jack began.

"My name is definitely not 'Shao-Lin.'" The tall man glowered.

"Shao, baby, I haven't slept in what feels like three years, I'm all done up on tranqs and whiskey, and I'd very much like to split this particular scene, so what the hell do you want?"

The tall man opened his hands again. "Why, I don't want anything at all. Not the tiniest little thing. Beijing wanted me to inform you that they're very interested in your assignment, and they want to help in any way they can."

Jack looked at the man blankly. Xiao finished with his right hand and stood behind him.

"You see, Jack, we Chinese don't like the damn, dirty Japanese any more than you Americans did back on the seventh of December, 1941."

He let this comment settle and dragged on his cigarette. Jack stayed mute.

"In fact, we're so wary of the Japanese that we managed to find ourselves a source that might be helpful to you, to *us*, I should say. We'd like to introduce you, if you're so inclined."

Jack dropped his cigarette into his whiskey glass, placed it on the floor, and leaned forward. "Don't keep me in suspense," Jack said.

"Tomorrow, Jack," he replied, waving his right hand. "You're in no condition to receive anything more engaging than Xiao's massage, if I read your state correctly."

Jack blinked and tried to banish the sting from his bloodshot eyes. "In fact," the well-dressed Chinese man continued, "we've already arranged a local flight for tomorrow afternoon. Four o'clock. We would very much like for you to join us."

Jack's head ached. He could feel his pulse behind his eyes. He wanted more information now, but his mind just wasn't up for it. He nodded.

"Very good," the man said. "It will be Xiao's pleasure to return you to your hotel and collect you tomorrow."

* * *

Xiao left him in the lobby while she retrieved a vehicle. As it turned out, the Chinese suite was on the top floor of the Tumon "Sheraton" hotel, some eight miles from the bar at which he'd been drugged and dragged by the dirty cop. A large map of the island hung on the wall. The Sheraton's location was marked with an illuminated glass pyramid, as if it were the center of the universe.

The Sheraton's lobby was more business-like than the Westin's. Although Japanese tourists patronized both hotels, the Sheraton housed a few Chinese as well. He hadn't noticed any at the Westin. Despite Jack's rumpled appearance, everyone was very polite. The Japanese smiled and nodded. The Chinese ignored him, but they were obvious about it.

Xiao appeared in her stunning, silken gown by the lobby doors and motioned for him. He walked to her, grasped her arms, and kissed her deeply. She twisted against him, delivered a jab to his lower abdomen, pulled a pistol from an expensive-looking clutch, and aimed it at his head.

Jack turned away from her and scanned the lobby. The Japanese tourists scattered, threw backward glances, and moved toward the doors. Every Chinese man in the lobby froze, some with hands in suit coats, some with weapons half-drawn. He counted seven security men, altogether.

He turned back to Xiao and put up his hands. "Nothing personal. Just wanted to see how many lackeys you had standing around."

27

She returned the pistol to her clutch and wiped her mouth. "That was ill-advised."

He flapped a hand at her. "You weren't going to shoot me. How can I attend your Daddy's meeting tomorrow with a hole in my head? It simply isn't done."

"He is *not* my father," she replied, waving off the security men.

"I did gather at least that much," Jack said and followed her out. "He doesn't have your delicate features."

"I do not understand you."

"Sometimes sarcasm is difficult, darling. I won't hold it against you." He opened the passenger door of a white Mercedes and dropped onto the leather seat.

"Don't call me 'darling.'"

"You people don't worry about keeping a low profile around here, do you?"

She started the car and whipped it out onto the road. "We have no need to do so. The local authorities are well compensated."

"How well is 'well?'" he asked.

"That depends on the position held."

"What about the dirty cop that delivered me to you lovely folks? How much do you pay him to perform those services?"

"Why do you want to know that?" she asked, glancing at him from the driver's seat.

"I want to know how guilty I should feel tomorrow morning."

"What do you mean?"

"Do you ever actually answer questions, or do you just ask more of your own?"

She smiled and returned her attention to the road. "We pay him the equivalent of his annual salary on the Guam police force."

"Which is...?"

"About thirty thousand U.S. dollars."

Jack considered this, drumming his fingers on his knees. The median income on the island couldn't be more than thirty thousand, and he assumed most of the locals were barely getting by. People thought money was the root of all evil, but he'd seen poverty breed plenty of corruption.

"Take me to his home," Jack said.

"I'm taking you back to your hotel."

"Take me to his home right now, or I'll get my people to pick up your Daddy this evening, right out of his penthouse apartment. They'll put him in a holding cell for 48 hours, incognito. Can your organization afford to have the Premier of the Western Pacific in a U.S. military holding cell for 48 hours?"

Jack was only partly bluffing. If it came right down to it, he thought he could wrangle a few of the O.S.I. agents on Andersen AFB out of their beds and into the Sheraton on a few hours' notice, but he wasn't sure. This jaunt to the cop's house was probably not worth the effort, but he didn't like the Chinese organization's arrogant attitude, he didn't like being drugged and kidnapped, and, damn it, he just didn't like dirty cops.

Xiao said something with the quality of a curse and turned the Mercedes around. "I'll take you, but make it quick. I like to sleep sometimes."

He nodded and lowered his window. The lights of Tumon behind them, they sped up a series of dark, narrow roads. Stray dogs dodged the car, and they passed within inches of several Carabao, a kind of tropical water buffalo, as the animals crossed the road in the moonlight.

For ten minutes, Xiao headed south down a four-lane highway that paralleled the ocean. Abruptly, she turned left at an unlighted intersection and pushed the Mercedes almost straight up a small mountain. They came to a pair of iron gates.

Xiao leaned toward a radio on a post and spoke into the receiver. A petulant voice answered. "Screw off."

"Open the gate, Teddy."

"Teddy?" Jack asked, incredulous.

"Teddy Calvo, the governor's nephew."

The gate swung open on an automatic lever, and Xiao pulled the car onto a long, brick-lined, palm-fronted drive. The house was modestly-sized but lavish and sported a lot of stainless steel and glass. An ultramodern pool, illuminated from within, jutted out on a platform over the side of the mountain and offered a broad view of the ocean.

"This guy makes sixty thousand a year, and he lives *here?*" Jack inquired.

"Who said anything about sixty thousand a year?" she answered. "We pay him thirty thousand every month."

Jack rubbed his temples. "And I was about to feel sorry for the guy. Just a poor, corrupt cop trying to get along in this bad old world on sixty grand a year. Maybe with a couple of kids and a wife to clothe and feed. He might even have had a sick mother."

Xiao stared at him from the driver's seat. "He has no immediate family."

"Fabulous," Jack said, throwing the passenger door open.

She walked him to the front doors, also made of stainless steel.

"Old Teddy doesn't have much in the way of taste," he said. "My refrigerator at home has doors something like these."

Xiao beat the butt of her pistol against the door, watching Jack. "Don't kill him. He's very useful to us."

"I'll try to be gentle."

Teddy Calvo opened his front door in a bathrobe he'd failed to secure, rubbing sleep from his eyes.

Jack shifted his weight to his left leg and pistoned straight out with his right. He caught Teddy square in the paunch. Teddy doubled over. Jack shoved two fingers into his nose and hauled him back into his own house.

Teddy backpedaled. "This is disappointing, Ted," Jack said, backing him into the living room. "I expected a little more resistance from a dirty cop."

Teddy tripped over his own feet and crashed into a glass table. It shattered, and shards skittered across the room.

Xiao pulled her pistol and held it on Jack. "Enough!"

Teddy sat in an accumulating pool of his own blood. He sucked air and shifted his eyes from Xiao to Jack and back again.

"Hope you didn't nick any arteries there, Ted, my man. That was a nasty fall."

Teddy took account of himself, dragged his legs out of the glass, and heaved himself onto a nearby couch.

"Anything spurting?" Jack asked, standing over him. "Or is the bleeding strictly venous?"

Teddy said nothing. "Well, Ted, if you're not worried, neither am I. Now, where do you keep the cash this good-looking lady pays you every month?"

"Screw off."

"Those are the only two words I've heard you speak since the bar, old Ted. You don't seem to have much in the way of vocabulary."

"Get out!"

"You're the king of the two-word sentence. I commend you on your grammatical niche and non-regional diction."

Teddy tried to stand, and Jack pushed him back down. "Where's the cash?"

He led Jack outside to the pool. A key dangled from a chain around Teddy's neck. He pulled it over his head, bent over the side of the pool, and inserted the key into a receptacle six inches below the water line.

A white panel popped open, and Teddy pulled twenty bundles of plastic-wrapped currency from the hole, scooping them off the surface of the water as they bobbed next to the open compartment. "That's everything."

"I'm sure it's not, but it'll do for now."

Teddy stood.

"Go get us a bag and load this inside," Jack said.

Three minutes later, Jack dropped back into the Mercedes' passenger seat as Teddy loaded the cash in the trunk.

Xiao shifted the car into gear, rolled past the open gate, and headed back toward Tumon.

* * *

"You're pretty good at making enemies," she said, braking to avoid another dog in the road.

Jack wondered at the discordance of a Chinese mafia Lieutenant taking pains to spare the lives of stray animals. He looked at her. She worked the steering and brakes, confident with the vehicle and the road.

"My father once told me a man without enemies is a man unworthy of friends."

"Sounds true. Was your father a law man too?"

He laughed. "I'm no 'law man.' I'm an investigator. I perform investigations and make recommendations to the people who make decisions about the people I investigate."

She downshifted and then accelerated into a right turn. "You investigated Teddy fairly hard."

"Yes, well. Teddy had it coming."

She said nothing, only jammed the accelerator and rocketed north on the beachfront highway. They passed a street-sign, and Jack noted the highway was called "Marine Corps Drive." Like "Andersen" Air Force Base, the name was another holdover from World War II. He appreciated the sense of enduring history.

He also appreciated the fact that if he didn't get some sleep, soon, he was going to die. Or, at least, that's what it felt like. "You know the bar, *Mac & Marti*?" he asked.

"Sure. But I don't want a drink."

"Stop there for me."

"Screw you," she said, slowing as they reentered Tumon.

"Now you're starting to sound like Ted. Thought you were a bit more educated than that."

"Fine. I'll drop you at the bar, but don't be late for the meeting."

"Yes, mother."

She pulled to the curb opposite *Mac & Marti.* Jack was pleased to see the bar was just closing down. "Pop the trunk, would you?" he asked.

She thumbed the button for the back hatch. "I'll be in the Westin lobby tomorrow at three o'clock. What you would call...," she hesitated, "fifteen hundred hours."

"I know what three o'clock is, but thank you for the translation." He pushed the door open and stepped onto the sidewalk.

Now, at 3 a.m., the Tumon Strip was empty. On the other side of the street, the old biker burst through the door of *Mac & Marti*, stumbled to a streetlamp, and puked in the gutter. The kid he'd been drinking with leaned out and cackled, "Whatsa matter, Jimbo?"

The biker heaved his guts again, and Jack winced as the splatter of the man's vomit reached his ears. "Can't hold your liquor?" the kid called.

The biker ignored his heckler, spat into the street, turned around, and hollered, "Isaaaa! I need another beer!"

Isa poked her head out of the entrance and made a shooing gesture with a bar towel. "No more beer for you, old man. I'm closing." She disappeared back inside.

The biker grumbled, unzipped his fly, and pissed into a large, ornate flower pot on the street corner.

Jack hefted the bag from the trunk, closed it, and smacked the back window. Xiao put the Mercedes in gear, did a tight 180 degree turn, and sped back toward the Sheraton. *Sleep well, dear heart.*

Perchance, to dream. But what does a young, female, Chinese mafia lieutenant dream about? Money? Power? Drowning kittens? *Money and power, yes. Drowning kittens, no.* That was too much. Kittens were helpless, after all.

Jack walked toward the bar. The biker heard him and whipped away from the flower pot, still pissing. Jack raised a hand to obstruct his view of a gigantic penis.

"Whoa there, hoss!" Jack called. "Put that shootin' iron back in the holster." Jack continued toward the front door and opened it as the kid came out, laughing at something Isa had said.

"Whatcha got in the bag, mister?" the kid asked.

Jack noticed the biker had sobered a little and was eyeing the bag along with the kid. Recognizing a rare opportunity to tell the truth, Jack stopped in the doorway, turned, looked at both of them, and said: "Two hundred thousand dollars. American."

The kid locked eyes with the biker and started to chuckle. The biker responded in kind, his johnson still in his left hand. Their chuckles turned into full-throated laughs, and then the kid noticed his buddy's acute state of exposure.

"Shit, man!" he said. "Put yo' dick back in yo' pants! What you think this is, a massage parlor?"

For some reason, this made the biker laugh even harder. He collapsed against a streetlamp and stuffed himself back into his jeans.

Jack walked inside and set the bag on the counter. Illumination poured from backlit liquor bottles. Isa was in the back. Jack heard empties clink somewhere and reckoned she was hauling a bag of trash to its rightful place.

A fresh beer waited on the counter. Jack imagined Isa had drawn a final draught for the biker in case he stumbled back inside. He grabbed the beer and wandered to the juke box on the wall. It was one of those new, satellite-connected, WiFi-enabled, L.E.D. illuminated pieces of garbage that had seemed to replace all the good old Jukes in almost all the good old bars in all the good old world. But it still took cash.

Jack slipped a five-spot into the slot and keyed up an old Della Reese song, "And That Reminds Me." When it came to slow, moody love songs, nobody but nobody could match the deep, resonant perfection of Della Reese. He followed the Della Reese song with "Hello Stranger," by Barbara Lewis, and then a little known gem from Percy Sledge called "Baby, Baby, Baby," from the 2006 album *Atlantic Unearthed - Soul Brothers.*

Della sang "...I hear the sound of music, your favorite kind of music... and that reminds me, dear, of you..."

Isa returned to the bar. She saw him. Jack turned from the Jukebox, beer in hand, and stared at her. They took each other in.

She walked out from behind the counter. "Who are you, really?" she asked.

He placed his beer on a table, put an arm around her waist, and was not surprised when her right hand met his left in traditional, slow dance form. "Just a guy who appreciates good beer, better music, and fabulous women."

She laughed a little at that. They swayed together as Della poured out her soul. "I'm sorry about earlier," she whispered. "My Nana's in a bed down at Memorial hospital."

"I think I passed that place on my way back up here," he answered, smelling the clean scent of her hair.

"She's got cancer, but that doesn't stop those bastards from threatening her life when they need me to do something."

"How'd you come by the tranquilizers?" he asked conversationally, wanting to keep her at ease.

"There's a Chinese man who comes in here about once a week. Usually, he just orders a Tsing-Tao and sits in the corner, giving everybody the stink eye."

Della finished up, and Barbara Lewis started singing "Hello, Stranger."

"I love this song," Isa said. She moved in closer.

"Keep talking," Jack told her.

"Sometimes, he wants information about the people who come in here. He usually waits for drunk sailors, follows them out, and then blackmails them when they visit the massage places. Other times, he shows me pictures of people and asks me if I've seen them in the bar."

"Has he, himself, ever threatened to harm your grandmother?"

"No. But if I blow him off, the local cops come in and hassle me about it, so I know they're working for whoever he works for. He gave me the pills a couple months ago. You're the first person I've had to..." she trailed off. "Teddy, the cop, called me when you showed up. He threatened to hurt my Nana if I didn't slip you the pills."

Isa began to cry. He let her. Isa was just a normal girl in a tough situation. If stuck between the Chinese mafia, dirty local cops, and a dying grandmother, he might well shed a tear himself. Probably not, he allowed, but he supposed it was possible. It would depend on how much he liked his grandmother.

He interrupted his own inner discourse and tipped her chin up with his hand. "Isa."

She held his gaze. Barbara gave way to Percy, who groaned out three "Baby's" in the first line of his overlooked but outstanding ballad.

"I left something on the counter for you. Don't worry about what happened earlier."

She tried to say something, but he shook his head.

"You're a nice girl in a bad spot. I can understand that."

She glanced at the suitcase on the bar, looked back up at him, and cried some more. He didn't mind.

* * *

He left the bar as Percy wrapped up his love song. His watch told him it was 4:00 a.m. His body told him he was an asshole, and if he didn't find a bed soon, it was going to initiate a labor strike.

The streets were deserted. No bikers pissed in flower pots, no Chinese henchmen stalked in the shadows, and no stray dogs scrounged for scraps. The ocean breeze favored him as he walked north toward the Westin hotel, and he decided that he actually liked Guam, dirty cops, enterprising hookers, and Chinese thugs notwithstanding.

Only a few of his previous assignments had approached this level of weird. He took stock of the evening. General Carter obviously didn't know he had a leak in the Wing Headquarters, maybe even a phone tap. Whatever intelligence he gathered was being fed straight to the Chinese. Jack made a mental note to report the breach.

He plodded up the sidewalk and rounded a bend on the Tumon Strip. The road canted upward a few degrees and reminded him how exhausted he was.

If the Chinese were sending divers into the water at islands near Kwajalein, they knew there was something of value to be located. But what? And what did this have to do with Japan? As far as Jack knew, the Japanese now made electronics, software, and weird comics, not war. What could possibly be so important three quarters of a century after World War II?

This "source" the Chinaman had mentioned piqued his interest. Obviously, the source knew, or claimed to know, what was so urgent about the ill-fated C-87 Liberator Express. And the Chinese believed him.

Then there was Isa, who claimed to be nothing but an abused civilian in the greater struggle between China and the United States, and *Jack* believed *her*. His head whirled with the disparate trails of thought. He turned left, off the Strip, toward the Westin Hotel lobby.

He stood at a safety railing beside the entrance and looked down at the ocean. The moon was still up, and it showed him the waves. He closed his eyes and listened as they washed through Tumon Bay and onto the sandy beach.

He was almost asleep on his feet when the muzzle of a pistol acquainted itself with his right kidney. He gripped the railing.

"My cash," Teddy Calvo breathed in his left ear. "Where the hell is my cash?"

Jack blew out a sigh and allowed his posture to droop. "Eddie. It's just you."

"It's *Teddy*. Whaddya mean, 'just you'? I got a .38 in your back, and you think you're safe?"

"I *know* I'm safe."

"Yeah?" Teddy jammed the pistol into Jack's lower back.

"Yes, indeed. Want to know how I know that?"

"Shut up."

"I know it because you're too chickenshit to pull that trigger. But I do give you credit for making this attempt. Shows you're not yellow all the way through. You're just a little stupid, as I believe we discussed earlier this evening."

"My *money*! Where *is* it?"

"I gave it to Xiao in return for a blowjob," Jack replied, turning to face him.

Teddy looked worse than he had earlier, if that was possible. He, or someone, had applied bandages to his lacerations from the glass coffee table, and he still had a blood mustache from Jack's double-nostril probe.

Jack watched Teddy try to process this reply as a legitimate answer and felt a moment of pity. Did people as dull as Teddy actually find their way through this world?

"Teddy, I'm joking, man. Do you think Xiao needs two hundred grand?"

Teddy stared.

"She gave me the blowjob for free. My kicking the shit out of you really cranked her into high gear, if you know what I mean."

Jack grabbed Teddy's shoulders and rammed his right knee into the man's midsection. Teddy dropped the revolver and doubled over.

While Teddy made choking sounds, Jack noticed a pack of cigarettes in the breast pocket of his shirt. Jack fished out the pack. "Mind if I bum one?"

No answer from Ted.

Jack lit a smoke and replaced the pack. Teddy would need them tonight, without a doubt.

He left Teddy to his misery and stepped into the lobby. The Chamorro crooner had vacated. A couple of drunken Japanese tourists hadn't made it back to their rooms. They snatched gusts of lobby air from awkward positions on a leather couch.

Jack entered the glass-paneled elevator, punched the appropriate number, and passed a hand over his face. He was fundamentally tired.

Back in his room, he returned to the balcony and gazed out at the moon-washed ocean. Lonely moments like this forced his mind back to Ashley. He wondered, for the thousandth time, if there could be life after death. He slept.

CHAPTER 2

"Quintana!" a voice urged. "Wake up, lad!"

Jack lunged from a bad dream, squinted into the drape-darkened gloom, and saw a wrinkled face framed in white hair.

He switched on the bedside lamp and winced at the too-bright L.E.D. bulb.

"Good God!" the face cried. "Do switch off that infernal spotlight. I shall open the drapes."

Jack tracked him groggily as the man crossed the room, threw open the heavy curtains, and suffused the space with sunlight.

"Much better, wouldn't you say?"

Jack blinked. At the balcony stood a deeply tanned older gentleman. His hair sprang wild and generous.

A bone-white mustache rode his upper lip. It spread across his face and tilted upward at either terminus, affording him a permanent jocularity.

"Have we met?" Jack asked.

"Rather stuffy in here, don't you think?" the man answered. He pulled the balcony door open and closed his eyes to the ocean breeze.

The gentleman produced a soft pack of Camels and tossed it to Jack. Jack snatched it out of the air.

"They told me you had an affinity for those, so I thought I'd go the distance with a bundle of non-filtered. Besides, filtered cigarettes smell bloody dreadful, wouldn't you agree? They may save the lungs, but they don't do a damned thing for olfactory ambience."

Jack peeled the package, extracted a tobacco-packed cylinder, and lit up.

"They, the more ambiguous 'they,' mind you, also say the ciggies will rot your lungs, in time. Of course, simply dying will rot your lungs with gusto, and cancer is only one avenue to the final thoroughfare we all must share, is it not? So, if everyone's lungs will rot when it's all said and done, I don't think a little fag smoke can make much difference one way or another."

Jack savored another drag and warmed to his unknown visitor's patter.

"But this line of talk is a bit depressing, isn't it? Why speak of death so early in the day? There's no cause for it." He swept a melodramatic arm over his head.

Jack coughed. "Look, uh, sir. I've got an important meeting in about two hours, so I think we'd better..."

"Yes! Yes, indeed. We'd very well better, hadn't we?"

He smiled. Jack was amused to see a sizable gap between the man's front teeth.

"I believe you have me at a disadvantage."

"Yes, well. Don't feel too badly about that, my man. It's no fault of your own, I assure you."

He wore a loud Hawaiian shirt, and his white cotton slacks expressed a preference for leisure.

"Allow me to introduce myself," he continued, striking a proud pose. "I am Thurgood Wintersley Throckmorton, the Third. Son of Thurgood, who was also the son of Thurgood, who, as it happens, was the son of one 'Rolfe' Throckmorton, eighth Earl of Nottingham. My Grandfather was the ninth Earl of Nottingham; my Father the tenth, and I, the Eleventh."

He finished with a flourishing bow and inclined his head as he rolled his hand in quick circles before himself. Jack raised an eyebrow and expelled smoke from both nostrils.

"But most of that, as they say, is neither here nor there," Throckmorton, the supposed Eleventh Earl of Nottingham, allowed with a sigh. "I'm afraid I was frolicking throughout the Marshall Islands and Micronesia when your delightful government hauled me away to a nondescript room on this island's Naval base. Asked me a lot of questions about my diplomatic status, what? Told me I'd be well compensated for my trouble, indubitably."

He seemed to ponder his own comment. "And that, my boy, was when they offered me a sizable sum in recompense for smearing metaphorical grease on the rails of your metaphorical track, Jack."

Jack stubbed his cigarette in a glass ashtray on the nightstand and stood by the bed. "And what track is that, Mr. Throckmorton?"

"Oh, I'm afraid it's *Sir* Throckmorton, if you would be *so* kind."

"Look," Jack said, eyeing the pack of Camels again, "we Americans have a deep appreciation for simplicity and brevity, which I'm sure you know."

"Forgive me," Throckmorton intoned, raising his head toward the ceiling. "I've disregarded your natural preference, and I shall rectify my deviation from your cultural protocol."

Jack nodded and grabbed a bottle of water from the nightstand.

"As I've explained, I've been floating about the Pacific on my yacht, *Her Majesty*, for some time."

"Your yacht is called *Her Majesty*?" Jack asked, smiling.

"Yes, *Her Majesty*, as in, 'The Queen of England.'"

"Go on."

"I was vacationing on the island of Majuro, in the Marshall Islands archipelago, and minding my own bloody-damn business, I assure you, when I was accosted by a number of your countrymen."

"Accosted?"

"Well, perhaps that's too strong a word. Let us say that they engaged me in conversation at the Marshall Islands resort when I was four or six glasses of Scotch to right of them. After a few hours, I was eight or ten glasses of Scotch to the right of them. Following that recollection, I cannot account for myself for a period of some duration. I found myself in that very efficient room on that very efficient Naval installation with the very devil of a hangover, and no memories of my transit from thither to hither, if you take my meaning."

Jack took his meaning.

"This morning, round about five o'clock, I gather, your U.S. Naval brethren fetched me out of bed, hauled me up to this Japanese tourist trap of a hotel, and instructed me to act as your liaison in some sort of hush-hush dealing with the damnable Chinese."

"Why would they ask you to do that?" Jack asked.

"Well, I do happen to be fluent in both Mandarin and Cantonese, don't I?"

"Don't you?"

"Indeed. I studied both dialects in the performance of my duties as British Ambassador to Hong Kong, back in the nineteen hundred and nineties, don't you know."

"That's lucky."

"Isn't it? I thought so myself, although I must admit I haven't the foggiest idea what it is we're actually supposed to do."

"I do," Jack said, turning toward the bathroom. "We're meeting with the Chinese Mafia in," Jack looked at his watch, "one hour and forty-five minutes. You're my buffer."

"Buffer?" Throckmorton asked, eyebrows flirting with this hairline.

"Yes, buffer. The good old U.S. of A. must be nervous about this whole thing. I'm supposed to accompany several Chinese to an undisclosed location in a few hours, and my government didn't want to be seen cooperating with the Chinese Mob.'"

"Chinese *Mob*?" Throckmorton repeated, shaking his head. "Good Lord, I've fallen into questionable company."

Jack stepped into the shower. "Don't worry, Pops," he called. "I won't let anything bad happen to you."

"I should hope *not*," Throckmorton replied in a worried voice. "It wouldn't do for the former British Ambassador to Hong Kong to be caught up in undesirable congress with the Chinese communists, would it?"

Jack snorted.

* * *

Throckmorton declared an intention to slip off to the bar for, as he put it, "a little drinky-poo before the hullabaloo," and Jack took the opportunity to dial the General. Half-dressed in khaki slacks with a towel about his shoulders, he stepped onto the balcony and put the Iridium phone to his ear.

"Goddamned bad news, Jack," General Carter said. "If I've got a leak in the Wing Command Section, it'll be hell trying to locate. All of my people have been vetted."

"It may not be your people that are leaking information," Jack said.

The General grunted. "What do you suggest?"

Jack squinted into the rising sun. "You'll need to get one of the agents at the local OSI detachment to sweep the headquarters building for electronic surveillance. If that turns up nothing, have them put a tail on everyone in the Command Section who knew about my arrival."

"Tail my own personnel? Isn't that a bit paranoid?"

"General, in my line of work, I've seen just about every kind of paranoia justified in one instance or another."

"Damn. What else have you got for me?"

Jack explained the events of the past few hours, leaving out the midnight rendezvous with the dirty cop. He'd found military officers could be curiously negative about physical violence when it wasn't strictly in the line of duty.

"And you intend to let this Chinese gangster haul you out to God knows where, on the off-chance that he has useful intelligence?"

"It's the only lead I've got." Jack pulled the towel from his shoulders and hung it over the balcony railing. "Oh, and thanks for the British babysitter."

"Yes, well," the General seemed uncomfortable. "We assumed this operation would involve direct conference with the Chinese at some point, and we... arranged to have the linguist transferred at the same time we called for you."

"He painted the situation a slightly different color when I met him this morning."

"Are you criticizing my methods, Agent Quintana?"

"No, sir."

"Good. We needed Crockmotton, or whatever his name is, and we got him, and that's that."

"Yes, sir."

"Call me when you've got another lead," the General muttered, distracted by a voice in the background. He cut the call. Jack tossed the phone onto the bed.

The door to his room burst open, and Throckmorton stumbled in with a drink in his hand. "What ho, the American hero. Dressed like a gigolo and dour as Maggy Thatcher."

Throckmorton downed the glass's contents in one, giant swig.

Jack cringed. "You'd better pump the brakes on that booze. What if I need you to translate something?"

"Bah! You've no faith in me. Dashes my feelings all to hell."

Jack grabbed a shirt and stuffed some supplies into a backpack. Thurgood flopped into a chair and put his chin in his palm, watching him.

"I take it you're under the impression we might be making a small journey?" he inquired.

"Didn't they tell you?" Jack asked, zipping his pack.

"They? *They?* Do you refer to the underhanded ruffians who rousted me from my tropical reverie, or the Chinese thugs down in the lobby?"

Jack shrugged.

Throckmorton put a hand over his eyes. "There had bloody-well better be some firewater on this trip. I shouldn't like to think a regrettable lapse into sobriety is anywhere close at hand."

"Come on, old man. We'll grab a bottle on the way out."

* * *

Shao-Lin stood in the Westin lobby to greet him. "Mr. Quintana," he said, inclining his head.

"*Agent* Quintana," Jack said.

"You're so right." The Chinese mobster took a long look at Throckmorton, from forehead to footwear, and asked, "Does this gentleman intend to accompany us?"

Throckmorton ignored him and turned to Jack. "This Communist speaks English. It doesn't appear my services will be necessary after all."

He tried to escape to the bar. Jack caught him by the arm and whispered, "You grab a bottle or two of whatever suits you and meet us outside in three minutes, or you'll never see *Her Majesty* again."

Throckmorton looked shocked. Jack handed him a piece of American money featuring Benjamin Franklin. Throckmorton looked appeased.

"Right-o!" he sang, and scurried toward the hotel bar.

"He's fluent in Mandarin and Cantonese," Jack explained, noting Shao-Lin's up-tilted eyebrows. "Best I could get on short notice."

"Xiao is waiting outside." With that, he turned on his heel and exited.

Jack trailed the man to the lobby doors. Xiao leaned against another Mercedes, a black convertible this time. She wore tight jeans and a white, shoulder-strap t-shirt.

He walked to the Mercedes and threw his pack on the hood. She said something harsh in Chinese. Where was that linguist when you needed him?

"I'm sorry, I don't speak Chinese gangster."

"Get that pack off my hood and get in," she glowered. "We have a plane to catch."

"Where are we headed?" he asked, lighting a smoke.

"Off island," she replied. "What are you waiting for?"

Throckmorton burst from the lobby doors with two bottles of Scotch, a satchel of freshly purchased underwear and socks, and a plastic bag that held toothpaste, soap, a toothbrush, and several varieties of deodorant.

A Filipino woman followed him out with her fists in the air. "He don't pay for underwear!" she shouted. "He don't pay!"

Throckmorton turned unsteadily and spilled deodorant onto the pavement. "My dear woman! When a man has purchased ninety dollars worth of Scotch in any given establishment, it goes without saying that underwear should be complementary."

"He don't pay!" she shouted, looking at Jack. Jack marveled at how quickly he'd become responsible for this bumbling old diplomat, and how apparent this responsibility seemed to everyone else.

"Room 1707," he told her. "Put it on my tab."

She looked satisfied and returned to the lobby. Throckmorton continued to spill items from his satchel and plastic bag in an attempt to avoid dropping the Scotch. Good thinking.

"Awfully generous of you, old boy." Throckmorton eased the bottles into the back seat of the convertible.

"Who the hell is this?" Xiao asked.

"Diplomatic necessity," Jack replied.

"What?"

"My translator," Jack said, and pushed his seat up so Throckmorton could make his way into the vehicle. Throckmorton scoffed, placed a steady hand on the side of the car, and surprised Jack by hauling himself over the side and into the back seat. "British gymnastics champion. Seventy-four Olympics. Munich. Bloody Arabs ruined the whole show."

Jack raised an eyebrow. "You forgot your deodorant, champ."

But Throckmorton was already popping the cork from a Scotch bottle. "Deodorant?"

"Forget it."

Xiao threw up her hands, got behind the wheel, and burned rubber all the way through the valet parking area.

* * *

They arrived at an airstrip fifteen minutes later. Xiao pulled a pack from the Mercedes, and they walked onto the tarmac toward a midsized, propeller driven aircraft.

The passenger compartment was utilitarian, but expensively so. Ten, widely spaced passenger seats were bolted to the floor in two rows, and no plastic or aluminum fascia covered the aircraft's various systems and components. However, the seats were plush leather, and a young Chinese flight attendant in a short skirt and sneakers handed him a coffee.

Thurgood ordered something in Mandarin. She brought him a screwdriver, and they chatted for a few minutes. He patted her backside and said something witty. She giggled and returned to the rear of the aircraft. Xiao rolled her eyes.

"What did you say?" Jack asked.

"A gentleman never does tell, does he?" Throckmorton answered, sipping the drink with raised pinky.

"You're no gentleman."

"You've found me out."

A rough-looking, middle aged man boarded the aircraft, stood in front of the cockpit, and faced the passengers with authority. He wore khaki pants, a tight-fitting tee shirt, and wraparound sunglasses. An impressive scar ran from the top of his right eye, over the curve of his scalp, and down the back of his neck.

"Hyello," he said in a thick, Russian accent. "I am Vitoli. I will be leading for your jump today."

Throckmorton snorted vodka and orange juice through his nose. "Did you say '*jump*?'"

"Please not to interrupt for safety briefing," Vitoli said.

Jack looked at Xiao, who stared out the window with a bored expression.

"Which one makes the jump before?" Vitoli asked.

Jack raised his hand. "Yo."

"How many times you make?"

"Eight or nine," Jack replied.

"Good-good," Vitoli answered.

"Ex*cuse* me, suh," Thurgood asked. "Am I to understand we shall be expected to exit this aircraft while it is still in *flight?*"

Shao-Lin, as Jack had come to think of him, boarded the plane, pulled up the stairs, and locked the door. "Welcome aboard, all," he called in that resonant, unaccented English. "One moment, Vitoli."

Vitoli nodded and sat in the jump seat.

"Before we take off, I'd like to explain a few things."

"Yes, I bloody-damn expect *someone* should," Throckmorton said.

"Beijing has directed me to coordinate an excursion, through which we hope to gain valuable insight into a matter that may be of some consequence to both China and the United States."

Jack raised an eyebrow.

"In order to make an initial inquiry," Shao-Lin continued, "we must first visit an isolated island just a few hours to the north."

"What island?" Jack asked.

Shao-Lin smiled and continued. "On this unnamed island live a wealthy investor from Hong Kong and his immediate family. This investor's father, a man of some ninety-seven years, is cared for on the island by the family and a personal physician."

Jack frowned. Throckmorton slurped at his screwdriver.

"Unfortunately, the elderly father is mistrustful of the Chinese government."

"Hear-hear!" Throckmorton praised, raising his glass.

Shao-Lin gave a thin smile and pressed on. "He has agreed to divulge his full story only to representatives from the American or British governments, so we haven't yet been able to... elicit... everything we need from him."

"And what is that?" Jack asked.

"I'm afraid I simply wouldn't do the story justice, Mr. Quintana. So," he clapped his hands, "we will proceed to the island with all haste and present you and this... Throckmorton...as emissaries of the nations that he trusts."

"Who gives a rip for any of that?" Throckmorton said. "What's this ridiculous *jumping* business all about?"

"Ah, yes!" Shao-Lin rubbed his hands together. "The island is surrounded by a treacherous reef with just one, shallow inlet. To save time, we must disembark at 10,000 feet and parachute to the beach."

"Why the hurry?" Jack asked.

"We received a call from the investor this morning. He fears his elderly father may reach his end at any time. It would take far too long to reach the island by ocean-going vessel. The old man is more or less on his death-bed, and we cannot afford to let him go with his story untold."

Throckmorton threw an arm over his face and either fell asleep or passed out. Jack couldn't tell which.

"And now, Vitoli will continue with your safety briefing."

Vitoli stood and pointed at Jack. "You make responsibility for drunk British?"

Jack sighed. "Yes. I make responsibility."

"Good-good. Under seat, you will be finding parachute."

Jack peered under his seat and saw the chute, complete with shoulder straps and waist harness.

"We will make preparation maybe one hour before jump. I am helping you secure parachute. When pilot makes readiness, we open rear door. First, you," he pointed at Jack again, "will make jump with drunk British."

"Okay." Jack glanced at Throckmorton doubtfully.

"After drunk British, you," he pointed at Xiao, "will following."

She nodded.

Vitoli turned to Shao-Lin. With greater deference than he'd shown to Quintana or Xiao, he said, "If you are acceptance, you will please to make jump after that one."

"Yes, yes," Shao-Lin replied, motioning for a drink from the miniskirted waitress.

"I will make final jump." He turned back to Jack. "How Americans say this, for 'last one'? Is 'caboose?'"

Jack grimaced at the comparison and pictured a locomotive falling from the sky. He gave Vitoli a thumbs-up. "Caboose. Sounds like a train-wreck."

"Yes?" Vitoli asked. "Good-good. I am jumping last jump for inspecting to see all open parachutes. Parachutes will make open on four-thousand feet, automatic. Your parachute is not opening, I will open him."

Jack was amused to discover parachutes had a gender.

"After open, you make follow on me for landing. You are steering with handle. Left handle. Right handle. You are pulling both handles down for earth contact. This will make soft landing. You don't pull hard, you are breaking your legs, maybe."

"What question you are having?" Vitoli asked.

Throckmorton had revived himself at some point during the briefing. "Is there a bar on the island, do you know?"

"I am not visiting this island before. End of safety briefing." He peered at Throckmorton. "You are maybe not drinking more alcohols until jump is conclusion?"

"Mind your own business," Throckmorton said.

Vitoli shrugged, sat, and buckled in.

Jack studied the scar on the back of the Russian's head. The man had a military attitude. Jack knew many Russian ex-paratroopers found post-service jobs either as mercenaries or itinerant skydiving instructors. This guy was probably one of those. Jack hoped for the latter.

Throckmorton snored, and Xiao stared out the window. Shao-Lin rose from his seat by the front door, caught Jack's eye, and motioned for Jack to meet him in the back of the aircraft.

Two jump seats folded out from either side of the fuselage, and the perky flight attendant stood as they approached. Shao-Lin said something in Cantonese. She fixed two drinks, a Jameson for Jack and a cognac for him, put on a pair of noise-canceling headphones, and sat herself in the last aisle, just ahead of them.

Shao-Lin called, "Hey, honey! How about a hand job?"

Vitoli and Xiao turned to stare at him. Throckmorton continued to snore. The flight attendant flipped open a magazine and did not look back.

Jack raised his eyebrows. "Is that her specialty?"

The Chinese man laughed. "I hope not. I wanted to make sure we could speak without being overheard."

"Speak on," Jack said.

"Beijing is interested in maximum cooperation between our two nations in this endeavor."

"I don't know what that means because I don't know what this endeavor is."

Shao-Lin sipped his cognac, closed his eyes, and said, "In World War II, China lost twenty million people in conflict with the Japanese. We were allied with the United States and Soviet Union. Our sacrifice and contribution is the primary reason we occupy a seat among the United Nations' Security Council and retain veto power in that forum."

"World War II was seventy-five years ago. A lifetime ago."

"Ah." Shao-Lin smiled. "An American lifetime, perhaps. You Americans value independence and individuality. In so doing, you free yourselves in the short term and doom yourselves in the long term. But in China, our lives are connected to the lives of our families. The memories of our families live for hundreds of years, so the Chinese remember what the rest of the world has forgotten."

"And what have we Americans forgotten?"

"That is what we will try to determine. The old man, either in a fit of dementia or an attempt to pass secret knowledge to his son, spoke of a 'great weapon in the Pacific' about which 'the Americans forgot' after the war."

"And you took this man at his word, dementia-driven or otherwise?"

Shao-Lin nodded. "I understand what you are saying. Normally, such a report would never have broken into significant circles in Beijing; would have been dismissed out of hand. At first, it almost was."

Jack motioned for him to continue.

"This particular investor's wealth has rewarded him with political connections that reach the very apex of Beijing. We Chinese attribute great importance to the preservation of mutually beneficial associations."

"Meaning, this investor told a friend in the Chinese government, and the friend felt duty-bound to investigate the claim."

"Exactly right," Shao-Lin said, swishing the cognac in his glass. "In fact," he chuckled, "we assigned one of your kind to look into the matter. Our very own 'Jack Quintana' of the People's Liberation Army. We dropped him onto this island a couple of weeks ago, the same way *we'll* do it in just a few hours. After speaking with the investor and getting no input from the old father, he returned to Beijing and executed a comprehensive investigation into the man's World War II history."

Shao-Lin paused in expectation of Jack's inquiry. Jack took a swig of Jameson and stared at him. Shao-Lin looked irritated and continued.

"Our agent found the man had, indeed, been a very young officer in the Chinese 'National Revolutionary Army' from 1941-1946. Furthermore, our investigator found copies of official, military dispatches associated with the old man's service. One of the dispatches directed the man, then a young Left-tenant, to accompany a prominent NRA official to a secret meeting with General Millard Harmon, who was the commander of all U.S. Army and Air Forces in the Pacific Ocean Area until his plane disappeared in February of 1945."

Jack shifted in his seat at the mention of General Harmon's lost C-87 Liberator Express, the same aircraft for which the Chinese Navy was currently diving in the vicinity of Kwajalein. He got the feeling the Americans were a little late to this particular game.

"The meeting took place on the island of Tinian, just north of Guam. Coincidentally, Tinian's 'North Field' was the launching point for your B-29 *Enola Gay*, which dropped the atomic bomb *Little Boy* on Hiroshima in August of 1945."

Jack thought for a moment. "Sounds like the old man may be dredging up memories from a meeting about dropping the bombs on Japan."

"Yes," Shao-Lin said, tapping the glass with his fingernail. "We thought of that, of course. But we would hate to overlook something important on a lazy assumption."

"What's China's interest in this, anyway? Why would you care if the United States had some old weapon rusting in the Pacific?"

At this, the Chinese man became evasive. "Why, despite what your American propaganda may indicate, the Chinese are immensely interested in maintaining peaceful continuity throughout the Pacific region. We simply want to ensure no threat exists that may harm the nations and peoples who call it home."

In his mind, Jack hurled up yesterday's in-flight meal at this political varnish. Outwardly, he thanked the man for the information and returned to his seat.

* * *

Two hours later, he dangled his legs over thousands of feet of nothing and felt his heart rate jump into the low 100s. No matter how many times he did this, it always felt like reluctant suicide. Throckmorton sat beside him, still mostly inside the aircraft. He didn't seem to want to violate the boundaries of the open doorway.

Also, he looked sober enough to be sick.

"Really nothing to it, I gather?" Throckmorton shouted. The sound of the plane's twin propellers nearly drowned him out. "Just fall forward, pull the handle, and steer toward the island?" Even as he said it, he looked dubious. Jack followed his gaze and saw the island was little more than a speck at this altitude.

"Wait about twenty seconds before you pull the ripcord!" Jack yelled. "Closing the distance will help you keep the island in view while you steer!"

"Jolly good." Throckmorton pitched forward and disappeared.

"Shit!" Jack yelled into the open space. He double-checked his straps, gave a moment's consideration to the possibility that Shao-Lin had found a novel way to commit murder, dismissed it as paranoid, and fell forward before he had a chance to reconsider.

There were, as always, about three seconds of absolute panic while his body told him he was an idiot in free-fall to a certain death. His heart pumped so fast he felt his fingers and toes pulsate. His eyeballs twitched and rolled in their sockets, an automatic response to an adrenaline-induced state of terror that helps the mind identify any possible escape from a fatal scenario.

Jack closed his eyes, shut his mouth to keep the wind from rushing down his throat, and breathed through his nose. Spreading his arms and legs into the "arch position," as skydivers call it, his body become a sail against the roaring updraft and slowed his plummet. There was no sound beside the rushing wind, and his heart rate diminished to a pace that no longer threatened the structural integrity of the organ.

He opened his eyes and saw Throckmorton deploy a bright pink parachute about two thousand feet below him, which put the "drunk British" at about four thousand feet of elevation. At the fifteen second mark, Jack tensed his body, pulled his own parachute, and groaned as his shooting-star descent slowed from 120 miles per hour to seventeen miles per hour in three seconds.

The island still seemed impossibly small. He looked away from the tiny scrap of land, and his vision almost "blue-washed." He saw nothing but the turquoise Pacific and it's twin, cobalt sky. Then he caught sight of Throckmorton's pink parachute again and grabbed his steering handles.

Something shot past him on the right and hurtled toward the ocean like a meteor. Vitoli, having waited to jump last, now sped to overtake Throckmorton so as to guide their descent. Jack decided maybe Vitoli wasn't too bad.

About fifteen seconds later, Jack saw Vitoli's canary yellow parachute pop open about 1,000 feet below Throckmorton. The old Brit, having caught the hang of steering himself, twirled in circles above the Russian before settling in for sedate pursuit.

Jack had battled a crippling fear of heights since childhood and refrained from any aerobatics. He guided himself after the two skydivers below him. Xiao swooped into his lane of travel from above. Jack cursed and yanked on his left steering handle to avoid a collision that would send them both swirling into the ocean, which he assumed was shark-infested. Why wouldn't it be?

Xiao gave him the finger. Jack focused on steering after the trio below him.

The island looked much bigger now than it had at 14,000 feet. He put it at 100 acres, all green, sloping hills leading down from a dormant volcano to a white border of beach. Beyond the circumference of the beach, bottle-green water formed a moat between a coral reef and the island itself.

Waves smashed into the reef. The spray wet his boots as he passed over razor-sharp coral. A thousand yards ahead of him, Vitoli landed on the beach, with Throckmorton close behind.

Xiao was still dead ahead of him. Jack effected a sudden dive, swung around her on the left, pulled his legs up to his chest to avoid dragging them in the water, and skidded in for a sandy landing on his knees.

Throckmorton, having witnessed the maneuver, applauded and hollered "*Bravo!*". Vitoli missed the whole scene. Xiao landed behind Jack and ignored him.

The Chinese mob boss came in last, wearing a faint smile, as if the risk associated with stepping out of an airplane from two miles high was a cause for mild amusement.

Jack hated him a little.

CHAPTER 3

Their host was a slight, nervous gentleman in his late sixties. He chain-smoked foul smelling cigarettes and seemed constantly distracted by his mobile phone.

What he lacked in personal grace, he made up for in style. The home he had constructed to contain his family and ailing father was solid, lined in teak, mahogany, and cherry, and somewhere close to 10,000 square feet.

Apart from the house, the guest quarters lined the beach of a tidy cove, where a sumptuous yacht floated at anchor. The cove fronted the western side of the island, which afforded Jack a front row seat to a knockout sunset.

He stood with his feet in gentle surf, watching parrot fish dart about in the shallows. Throckmorton had opted for a nap before dinner. Xiao made phone calls, and Jack took the opportunity to do the same.

He pulled the Iridium satellite phone from a zippered pocket and selected Sergeant Kirker's number from the "Contacts" menu. After an interminable period of satellite connection magic, it rang twice, and Jack heard, "Sergeant Kirker here. Is this my favorite spook?"

Jack smiled. "There's no accounting for taste, Sergeant. I need you to triangulate my position and get the coordinates to General Carter."

"Copy that," Sergeant Kirker replied. "The General called me earlier today and told me to expect this. I've got a Navigator here with an uplink to the satellite facilitating this transmission. Give me two minutes."

The horizon blazed blood red, flamingo pink, and fiery yellow. He wondered how much of that color was natural, and how much was a holdover from the United States's nuclear tests in the Pacific. How interesting that such destructive force could create these colors; this beauty. A flock of seabirds swept up, up into the radiant sky. Ocean waves frothed across the reef, rocketing foam to meet the birds.

He turned to find Xiao walking his direction from one of the guest houses. She was dressed casually in a sheer wrap, shorts, and a bikini top.

"How's it coming, Sergeant?" Jack asked.

"Almost done," Kirker said. Jack heard the Navigator in the background, pounding on a distant keyboard.

"Who are you talking to?" Xiao asked. She sidled up on his right.

"That's not your business, is it, doll-face?" Jack answered. He let her sidle. Hell, she smelled good.

"Fancy landing earlier," she said.

"Didn't want to get beat by a girl," he muttered, still appreciating the sunset.

"I didn't see anything in your dossier about jump training."

"Dossier? My inner narcissist is delighted."

She pulled away from him and scanned the sunset, brooding.

Sergeant Kirker came back on the line. "You still there, spook?"

"Yo," Jack replied.

"We've got your location. I'll pass it to the General."

"That's two beers I owe you now."

"Don't think I'm not keeping track," the Sergeant laughed. "One thing: The General told me he wants an update from you in three hours. He was pretty adamant about that."

"I'll do what I can. Out, here." He switched the Iridium phone off.

Xiao stood a few paces from him. "Ready for din-din, love?" he called.

She said nothing.

"Maybe afterward, I'll let you finish that massage you started last night."

"Let's go," she snapped.

* * *

The dining table was a massive slab of oak centered on an open air veranda that overlooked the guest houses, cove, yacht, and greater Western Pacific ocean. A dozen lanterns spread amber light in trembling pools.

The fare consisted of French wine and Polynesian seafood. When he selected a Pinot Noir to pair with his Ahi tuna, the waiter looked pained. "It does not complement, sir," the waiter said. "Would you like, perhaps, a chilled Sauvignon Blanc?"

Jack doubled down. "I would like the *Chateau De Cary Potet* from Bourgogne."

The waiter fidgeted mightily, started to protest, thought better of it, threw up his hands, and went to fetch the Pinot. Everyone stared at him. Jack smiled, popped an unrecognizable appetizer into his mouth, and chewed.

"A marvelous feast in a heavenly setting," Throckmorton said, raising his own glass of something very alcoholic. "To our generous host."

The slim Chinese gentleman smiled around a half-smoked cigarette, nodded, and sipped from his water glass.

Throckmorton asked him something in Chinese. The man looked surprised and then answered in halting English, "My father join us. After."

"Very good," Throckmorton replied. "We're keen to hear what he has to say, old boy."

"Yes," the host replied, and lit another cigarette.

Vitoli concentrated on the plate of appetizers and said little, despite Throckmorton's repeated attempts at conversation. Shao-Lin spoke with the host in Chinese, perhaps discussing topics Chinese mafia bosses find interesting: export tariffs, the price of oil, human trafficking ventures. Whatever.

The waiter returned with Jack's Pinot Noir, poured him a glass, and paused for Jack's approval before returning to the kitchen. The main course had not yet arrived, so Jack grabbed his wine and wandered to a stone balustrade. The sun was almost down, but he could still make out the shapes of old, Japanese pillboxes on the beach below.

He wondered what the soldiers who had once manned those entrenchments had thought about the war. Had they any personal feelings about it? They had been torn from their homes and families as roughly as the American troops. But most of them had been young. And young men tended to see the world in simple black and white, especially when the stark contrast was reinforced by propaganda and lives overseen by strict authority figures. Perhaps they were proud to be here on this 100 acre mountaintop in the middle of the largest ocean on the planet. Maybe they'd believed their posts and assignments important.

He turned as Xiao approached him. "You just can't stay away from me, can you?"

"What were you thinking about?"

Jack turned back to the view. "I was thinking of soldiers, and the faulty motivations of young men."

Xiao sipped her drink and considered him. "Come see me tonight, after our talk with the host's father."

Jack shrugged. "Maybe."

He expected her to be angry, but she nodded and returned to the table.

* * *

The host's father was not just old, he was positively ancient. The fussy waiter wheeled him out after dinner, and the remnants of his baby-fine hair twisted this way and that, moved by the slightest puff of breeze.

After post-meal coffee, Throckmorton made surprisingly sober introductions in Chinese.

The elderly man placed his cup on the table with a shaky hand. His son's mobile phone buzzed, and he shot the younger man a disapproving look.

Throckmorton's resonant tenor rolled across the table in English, following the old father's hoarse Mandarin. "When I was a young man of seventeen years," he said, "my father made it possible for me to receive a commission in the Army of China.

"Earlier, in the year 1937, after invading my country and sweeping through both Beijing and Shanghai, the Japanese launched an offensive against my home city of Nanjing. We were unprepared to resist the organized Japanese army. After a short struggle, the Japanese took the city.

"Something absent from commonly known history is the fact that the Japanese army did not simply *occupy* my city. My mother died of plague in 1932. I thought then that I understood the depths to which grief can drag a soul. I was wrong." Here, the old man's voice broke, and he halted. His hands shook as he brought them to his face and covered his eyes. After a moment, he continued.

"There was a young girl. For ten years, we walked to our classes together, and we came home together. We were inseparable. If a day passed that I did not see her, my spirit yearned for her in the way we long for something that is lost.

"When the Japanese invaded the city, we were together. I was fourteen years of age, then. She was a year older than I; a point of which she never failed to remind me on the rare occasion we came to some disagreement.

"We were playing a game on the front steps of my home when the troops came down the road. My father was in the city, trying to gather supplies that might last us a few weeks. Everyone had heard the artillery the previous day, and my father worried we would not have enough to eat if the Japanese broke through.

"We were so engrossed in our game, as children will be, that we did not realize what was happening until the soldiers were almost in front of the house. I wish I could say I tried to get her inside; that I took some action to protect her before they arrived.

"One of those dirty..." here, Throckmorton seemed to struggle as he encountered a slang curse with which he was unfamiliar, but the old gentleman did not notice, and Throckmorton caught up, "...hit me with the butt of his rifle. You may still see the evidence, here." He lifted his left hand to the side of his face, and Jack made out a faint scar that ran from the man's left eye to just below his earlobe.

"While I lay bleeding in the grass, the soldiers took my friend into the house and raped her 'til they could not rape her anymore. Then, they shot her in the head, and they left."

Throckmorton looked mildly shocked. Xiao and her boss watched the old man. Vitoli refilled his wine glass. The host, gazing into his empty dinner plate, held a cigarette in his hand but did not light it.

"This was the first time I knew hatred. I wanted to kill every Japanese I saw, but my father restrained me. He taught me the value of patience in the pursuit of revenge. For three years, we struggled under Japanese oppression. In that time, they raped and murdered three hundred thousand Chinese in Nanjing. In fact, in history books that still contain such truth, that part of the invasion is referred to as the 'Rape of Nanjing.' Can you imagine such devastation? More than a quarter of a million people, lying dead in piles in the streets, their sickly stench crying out the fact of this Japanese abomination.

"When my father and I escaped from Nanjing in 1940, I dedicated my life to the destruction of the Japanese empire. Before they withdrew, however, almost thirty million Chinese were dead. Thirty *million.*"

He sighed, gulped more coffee, and grimaced.

"In the city of Kunming, which we reached only with great difficulty, my father made connections with the organized Army and secured my commission. I had not much schooling after the age of fourteen, which was always a shame to me. But I found I could anticipate the needs of my superiors with much accuracy. This helped me to secure positions in the service of powerful men, which led me, eventually, to the meeting with," he met Jack's eyes "your General Harmon."

Jack leaned forward. Shao-Lin produced a mobile phone, ostensibly to record this next bit of narrative.

"My superior was very confused by the American General's plan. You see, at the time of the meeting, the United States had yet to drop the bomb 'Little Boy' on Hiroshima and the bomb 'Fat Man' on Nagasaki. I must confess those explosions brought me satisfaction. They still do."

Jack thought this a bit morbid, but understandable. Just then, Shao-Lin nodded to Vitoli, who lifted a semi-automatic pistol from under the table and leveled it at Jack. Shao-Lin said something apologetic to the host's father. The old man scowled.

"Please to stand," Vitoli said, pointing the weapon at Jack but glancing at Throckmorton as well.

"What the devil!" Throckmorton roared, pounding the table. "What in the bloody hell is this?"

"I think they mean to sanitize us before the old man gets to the good stuff," Jack said, rising from his chair.

"Sanitize? I've never heard of such behavior in polite company before."

"Don't bother with the wounded diplomat bit. Our Russian friend has us covered."

Throckmorton grumbled, drained his wine glass, and stood. Xiao approached and asked for his Iridium phone. Jack handed it over and felt a pang of regret. Then she patted him down, and Jack felt a pang of something else.

When she finished, Shao-Lin invited them both to regain their seats.

"I'm so sorry for this inconvenience. You see, we weren't exactly sure this was going to go anywhere. Now it appears we might learn something important, I couldn't take the chance you might reach back to your people, Jack."

"I get it. The old man wouldn't cough up the story without a Brit and an American in audience, and we were relatively handy."

"I knew you'd understand." Shao-Lin smiled.

"All I understand," Throckmorton said, "is that I'm not going to translate another word 'til I get some bloody Scotch."

Shao-Lin spoke a few words to the old Chinese man. The old man shook his head.

"Very well," Shao-Lin said to Jack. "He will not continue unless he knows you can understand what he's saying. He seems quite fond of you Americans."

"It's nice to have friends in strange places," Jack replied.

The waiter appeared with a bottle of single malt, and Throckmorton cooed like a new mother over an infant. While Throckmorton poured himself a brazen quantity, the old man began again.

"In late August of 1944, my superior and I flew from Kunming to an American base on the recently liberated island of Tinian. The Americans had captured Tinian in July of 1944 and immediately set about repairing and expanding the existing Japanese runways and infrastructure. Coincidentally, Tinian is only about 300 miles from where we are now.

"Once on the ground, we were driven to a large aircraft hangar beside the airfield the Americans called 'North Field.' Interestingly, it was from this 'North Field' the B-29s *Enola Gay* and *Bock's Car* departed for Hiroshima and Nagasaki the following year.

"I remember it well. The Americans had prepared the affair nicely. There was a large table with Bluefin tuna and all manner of seafood. There was chilled champagne and beer, and an entire table dedicated to wine. It seemed almost a celebration, although we knew we had been invited to collaborate on a project, and not to celebrate any specific victory. I was keen to know what had made the Americans so confident, but I did not learn it that night. Only later, after the bombs were dropped in Japan, did I make the connection.

"General Harmon had called my superior to the meeting in the hope that China might contribute to a specific undertaking. On one side of the aircraft hangar, the Americans had suspended a large, white sheet onto which an image of the Philippine Sea was projected.

"The islands of Palau, Yap, and Guam are all situated in the southern portion of the Philippine sea. To the northeast of these islands lies the Philippine archipelago, to the north is southern Japan, and to the northwest is the 'Izu-Bonin-Mariana Island Arc.' This 'Island Arc,' to the west, and the 'Kyushu-Palau Ridge,' to the east, are underwater geologic formations that effectively turn the entire Philippine Sea into a giant basin. In fact, there are two, distinguishable 'basins' in the Philippine Sea, the 'Parece Vela' and the 'Shikoku.'"

Throckmorton attended this narrative so closely that he hadn't taken a drink in at least the past 45 seconds. Besides, he was translating, so it was difficult. Jack strove to memorize the unfamiliar terminology.

"To simplify the picture," the old man continued, "imagine a bathtub filled with water. Guam, Yap, and Palau sit at the foot of the tub, and Japan sits at the head."

Shao-Lin stared at the old man. Vitoli kept his eyes on Jack. Jack watched the old man with Shao-Lin while trying to keep everyone in his peripheral vision and concentrate on the dialogue. Xiao watched everybody. Throckmorton brought his Scotch glass to his lips and then set it back on the table. The host still hadn't lit his cigarette. Jack figured it might go stale before he got the chance.

"What General Harmon asked was that my superior dedicate a team of our best engineers to accompany the Americans and the British in a joint effort to construct underwater...," here, Throckmorton hesitated again, "platforms... to be situated on the north end of each island. These... platforms... were to be designed to hold a large quantity of high explosive.

"The objective was to set off explosions on the north side of each island, in a specific sequence, and create a tidal wave that would sweep north, through the Philippine Sea, and destroy much of southern and eastern coastal Japan. Of course, my superior agreed to supply the engineers, but we could not understand how the thing could possibly work. In our minds, each of these platforms would not only have to be overflowing with high explosive, but the platforms would have to be as large as the islands themselves in order to generate the explosive energy necessary to create a tidal wave that would do any damage.

"I still remember where I was when I made the connection. There was a little bar outside Army headquarters in Kunming. It was the 7th of August, 1945. We had received scattered reports of Hiroshima having been destroyed by the Americans, but there was no clear explanation of how they had accomplished this. The bartender kept a radio in a window above the icebox. Following a broadcast of American 'big band' music, the radio announcer brought more news of the Hiro-shima explosion.

"When the voice on the radio explained Hiroshima had been ut-terly destroyed by *one bomb...*," the old man paused, "that was when I realized how the Americans could bring the Philippine Sea plan to bear."

"So," Jack cut in, "at the meeting on Tinian, when General Har-mon's people referred to 'high explosive,' they were really talking about nuclear weapons on the scale of Little Boy and Fat Man."

Throckmorton translated, and the old man nodded.

"Was the project ever completed?" Jack asked.

The old man listened to Throckmorton and then inclined his head to the left. "I cannot say for certain," he replied. "However, I do know the engineers requested by General Harmon were appropriated and deployed, as I arranged their travel myself. Less than a year later, the American bombs fell, and the war in the Pacific ended. Shortly there-after, I left the Army for somewhat more profitable employment."

"The engineers," Shao-Lin broke in, Throckmorton translating, "can you remember any of their names?"

"Even if I could, they are surely dead. I have now ninety-seven years. It is more life than a man can expect."

Shao-Lin was stoic. The host finally lit his cigarette.

"Where does the downed Liberator Express come in? The flight that never made it from Kwajalein to Hawaii?" Jack asked.

The old man's eyes flashed at this. For the first time, Shao-Lin looked uncomfortable.

"Yes. That is quite essential to the whole point of this meeting, is it not?"

Shao-Lin studied the table.

"I will soon die, and my capacity for hatred is quite extinguished. The Japanese are now a defeated people; a different people. I am con-cerned that there still exists a threat of death and destruction for a great many innocents, and I may be the only person left alive with enough information to reveal that threat. The first time I attempted to divulge it, Beijing refused to honor my request for American and British representation.

"Your man from Beijing was pleasant at first," he said, looking down his nose at Shao-Lin. "When I told him I would not speak without the Americans and British present, however, his agreeable facade crumbled, and I met the real man."

Now, both the host and his father stared at Shao-Lin, whose composure began to waver. Sweat beaded at his temples.

"You thugs with your strong men have dominated China for generations," the old man said. "But this is so in all nations, and always has been. I am proud to say I told your strong man nothing, until he produced the needle."

He shifted in his seat to address the entire table. "Look at my son," he said. "He is a small man, as am I. He tried to intervene when the Beijing *functionary*," he spat the word, "injected me against my will. Look at his face, and see the evidence of his bravery."

The host looked uncomfortable and expelled a long stream of cigarette smoke. Jack saw a healing laceration and shallow concavity in approximately the same place as his father's old scar.

"I am proud of my son, but pride and action are sometimes not enough, especially for the small. Fortunately, we have connections of our own in Beijing, who called off the trained dog before any real damage was done. I'm afraid I was induced to such an extent that the..." the old man uttered another curse that Throckmorton could not translate "...learned how important the aircraft is to the story, but not why.

"I can tell you," he pointed at Shao-Lin with a trembling finger, "that your position in this region is in great jeopardy after that regrettable incident. You selected the strong man, and his actions are your responsibility."

Shao-Lin nodded once and said nothing. Under the circumstances, Jack thought the response very wise.

"Now," the old man continued, "back to the matter of the lost aircraft, in which General Harmon and General Andersen are presumed to have perished."

The waiter appeared with a blanket for the old man. Another attendant produced a tray of dessert pastries and a bottle of Cognac.

As Jack sipped his digestif, the old man began again. "In early December of 1944, I received an important dispatch. An armed, American courier delivered the sealed document, having traveled all the way from Guam to Kunming. I remember him distinctly because of his insistence that he be allowed to submit the dispatch directly to General Harmon's intended recipient.

"As my superior was ensconced in a series of meetings when the courier arrived, the courier had to wait several hours. My superior invited the courier in to his office.

"While the American and I stood, my superior opened the dispatch and read it silently. He looked thoughtful for a moment, and then he read the dispatch again, which I found odd. Then, seeming to rouse himself, he stood, thanked the courier, and asked him a few questions about his travel, the usual pleasantries.

"When the courier departed, my superior handed me the dispatch, told me to burn it, and directed me to arrange travel to Honolulu immediately. I was not in the habit of reading correspondence meant only for my superior, but his reaction intrigued me. Before I burned the message, I read what it said.

"Though I cannot recall everything, I do remember certain elements. The message was from General Harmon himself. The first part was an expression of thanks for provisioning the requested engineers. After that, General Harmon wrote that the Philippine Sea Project was progressing on schedule, and that the control mechanisms were in place on Guam.

"After a few more details about various elements I cannot remember, General Harmon wrote something like: 'I plan to transport the detailed project files, as well as vital operational codes, to Hickam Air Force Base for safekeeping. I would like to invite you to attend a joint meeting at Hickam, with representatives from the Allied powers, on the 5th of March. Please do not send a delegate, as we cannot risk admitting anyone but you and your personal staff. I am eager to relay the specifics of our progress.'"

The old man hacked a wretched cough into his napkin and continued in a strained voice. "I believe there were a few additional notes concerning other efforts in the Pacific, as related to Chinese opposition to the Japanese.

"However, the last thing I remember about the dispatch is that it was not handwritten. It was a typed copy that General Harmon had signed in ink. At the bottom of the document was a handwritten copy number that read '2/3.' I understood this to mean General Harmon's staff produced three copies of this message, sent one to my superior, sent another, likely, to the relevant British representative, and probably kept one as a reference document at General Harmon's headquarters."

Jack mulled this over. "Thurgood," he said. "Ask him if he can remember the name of the American courier."

Throckmorton asked the question. The old man thought for a moment, and then he smiled. "I could speak little English at the time, but I was learning to write English letters. While we were waiting for my superior to return, the courier helped me to write his name in the headquarters log book for Western visitors."

He closed his eyes. "Give me a pen and paper," he said.

His son produced a notebook and a fountain pen. Jack rose and rounded the table to stand at the old man's side. Xiao did the same.

Gripping the pen with arthritic fingers, he spelled out in large, bold capitals: "L-O-N-G-I-N-O-T-T-I. T-O-N-Y. T-E-C-H-N-I-C-A-L. S-E-R-G-E-A-N-T."

"Old man," Jack said, "you've got one hell of a memory."

Throckmorton translated, and the old man laughed. "Ask me what I did yesterday, and I could not tell you. The old live in the past, and so, remember it well."

* * *

A gangplank rose from a beach pier to the starboard side of the yacht, where a pretty Micronesian gal tended bar. Throckmorton had sniffed it out like a bloodhound. Or a boozehound. Either one.

Jack asked for a Singapore-brewed Tiger Beer and then toured the deck. He stopped at the bow. Above him stretched the same blanket of stars he'd enjoyed with Isa the previous evening.

It had been three hours since his satellite call to Sergeant Kirker, and he wondered what General Carter would make of his failure to report in. Hell, he didn't work for Carter any more than he worked for Throckmorton, but the General had supplied him with this wonderful, tropical vacation, and he felt obliged to at least try to meet a few of his demands. Funny thing about Generals, they always expected people to step and fetch. Egomaniacs.

Beside Throckmorton's steady patter of conversation (Jack suspected the old diplomat was trying to get laid), the only sound came from the waves crashing on the reef, some thousand yards distant. No moon presided over this evening. The stars spilled their light on the ocean.

Jack sipped his Tiger Beer and thought about the old man's discourse. Three bombs, planted somewhere to the north of Guam, Yap, and Palau. Could there really be any danger? General Harmon's project had been unfinished in December of 1944. The old man had said as much from his memory of the courier's dispatch. And it probably could not have been completed in the two months between Harmon's dispatch to Kunming and his disappearance. Could the effort have continued after his presumed death in February of 1945? Jack thought so. After all, once manpower and personnel were appropriated and dedicated to a government project, whatever was cookin' tended to keep on cookin.' Even after it was burnt.

But even if the bombs had been built, transported to the three sites, installed, and readied for action, that had been seventy-five years ago. Were atomic weapons from the first moments of the nuclear age capable of withstanding the elements for a lifetime? Jack wished again for the satellite phone. He had a buddy at the National Security

Agency that helped him, from time to time, with the many technical questions Jack encountered.

The buddy's name was Josiah Supitski. Jack called him "Soup." An egghead supreme, Josiah had started out in the Army and then transitioned to a Defense Contractor position with the N.S.A. Throughout his career, Jack had met a lot of people who seemed to have an answer for everything. Soup was the only guy he'd ever known to have a *correct* answer for everything.

Jack drained the Tiger Beer and patted Throckmorton's shoulder as he passed the bar for the gangplank. The Micronesian chick seemed enraptured by whatever spiel the aged fox was laying out for her, and Jack wished him well. Everyone needed a little love now and again.

He walked straight to Xiao's room and pounded on the door. "Police!" he shouted. "Open up!"

She opened the slatted door wearing a bathrobe and a sour expression.

"Po*lice*!" he whispered. "I've got a warrant for your arrest."

"Is that right?" she whispered back.

"Yes, indeed, ma'am," he replied, conjuring John Wayne. He walked into the room and closed the door behind him. She looked startled.

He dropped onto the bed, and she relaxed.

"Sure feel naked without that satellite phone," he said, folding his hands behind his head.

She climbed atop the bed and allowed the robe to fall open. He pretended not to notice.

"You'd feel a lot more naked without your clothes," she said. "Vitoli wanted to strip you both down and lock you on the yacht as soon as the old man was finished."

"I knew he had a thing for me," Jack answered. "I could feel his eyes crawling all over me tonight."

"Thurgood's more his type," Xiao answered. She laid her head on Jack's chest.

"What's this?" Jack asked, incredulous. "Humor from the mirthless mafia lieutenant? It can't be."

She stroked his upper thigh.

"What did you think about the old man's story?" she asked.

Jack sensed an intelligence collection in the making. "Nothing to it. Even if this supposed 'Philippine Sea' project was ever finished, which it probably wasn't with Harmon dead, and even if his people were able to transport the bombs all the way across the Pacific and situate them in the correct places, and even *if* the bombs were properly prepared, there's no way in hell they could still be operational."

"Hmmm," she purred, moving her hand to his chest.

"I mean, good Lord, there's no way a seventy-five year old bomb is going to work the way it was intended to work, especially after having been under water all this time. How many typhoons have passed through here? How many layers of coral have encased it? How much shark shit is it buried in?"

At this last, her hand stopped, and she looked up at him. He thought he might have taken the act a bit too far.

"No way in hell." He grabbed her hand and moved it over his chest. "That feels nice."

She shed the robe and edged alongside him, her right thigh draped over his leg. She wore a pair of white, cotton panties to cover her womanhood. How chaste.

"Before we get started here," he said, "I'm going to need my phone." She stiffened against him. He stiffened against her. It was involuntary.

"I don't have it," she said, pulling away.

"You give it to the bossman? Shao-Lin?"

She raised her voice. "I wish you would stop calling him that. That is *not* his name."

"No need to shout, babe. Actually, I don't know *what* his name is. He never told me."

She considered this and then stifled a laugh. "His name is Bo Feng."

"You're kidding. You're sucking up to a guy named 'Beau?'"

"Not '*Beau!*'" she said. "Bo! It means 'older brother.' But not *my* older brother. Understand?"

"Bo freaking Feng," Jack said, pulling his pack of Camels from a pocket. "No shit."

"No shit," she answered, and bounced back onto the bed.

He lit the cigarette and blew smoke toward the ceiling fan as she started doing her thing.

* * *

About an hour later, he stepped out of Xiao's room and lit another smoke. The Camel tasted heavenly and accentuated the powerful scent of the open ocean.

He figured a visitor like Bo Feng would usually rate a room in the big house. After his little misstep, however, Jack surmised old Beauregard might likely be banished to a lowly suite in the guest cottages.

Over the surf, Jack heard the Micronesian bartender laugh from somewhere on the darkened yacht. *Way to go, Thurgood.*

Only one light was on in the whole line of bungalows. Jack approached it. He tapped at the door.

"Xiao?" a voice issued from inside. Jack heard someone move toward the door. He stepped back and waited.

Be Feng opened the door. Jack hurled is right fist forward and caught him in the belly. The older man expelled a lungful of air, slid backward, and crashed into a couch.

Jack entered the bungalow, closed the door behind him, and stood over Xiao's boss. "Sorry, fella. I just wanted to establish the relationship we'll need for this conversation."

Bo Feng gasped and held his stomach.

"Are we going to have any trouble?" Jack asked.

No answer from Beauregard.

"Bo, oh, may I call you 'Beauregard?' I've always loved that name."

Still no answer.

"I think I will. As long as you don't mind. Now, Beauregard, I need that Iridium phone you—"

Vitoli crashed through the front door. Jack winced. Russians were notoriously dirty fighters.

Vitoli rushed him like a bull. Jack sidestepped, grabbed a paring knife from the kitchen counter, and tried to trip him into a headlong sprawl.

Vitoli avoided Jack's leg by spinning away but caught an electrical cord and brought a lamp crashing to the floor. Incensed, the Russian yanked the cord from the wall, threw the lamp at Jack, and launched himself.

Jack caught the lamp full in the face, steadied himself, and then Vitoli was on him. The Russian scrambled for a headlock.

Bo struggled from the couch. The Russian was behind him now and had an arm around his neck, but Jack's right arm was free. Tightening his grip on the paring knife, he drove it upward, between his own legs, and directly into Vitoli's crotch.

The Russian's grip failed. He dropped like a sack of rotten potatoes. Unfortunately, Jack's maneuver had effected an unavoidable blow to his own testicles, and he was momentarily handicapped by ratcheting pain.

Bo snatched a candlestick from a nearby table and tried to bash him in the face. Jack tucked his head into his shoulder. The candlestick took him mostly in the upper arm. After another punch to the gut, old Bo dropped back to the couch.

Vitoli had yanked the paring knife out of his crotch but still lay on the floor, groaning. Jack kicked the knife away and turned back to Bo.

"The satellite phone. Where is it?"

The older man said something spiteful in Chinese.

"You're hurting my feelings, fella. And I thought we were pals."

Jack scooped up the paring knife and advanced on Bo. Bo cringed and held up his hands. "All right, all right," he said, shakily. "I'll get the phone."

Bo moved to a nightstand.

"Hold it," Jack shouted.

Bo made a move for the nightstand. Jack caught him with a right hook as Bo pulled a pistol from the nightstand drawer. The older man collapsed onto the bed, unconscious.

Jack ripped the pistol from Bo's limp hand and stuffed it into a pocket of his khakis. There were four lamps in the room. Jack yanked the electrical cord from each and tied Vitoli's wrists and ankles first, then Bo's. Vitoli began to shout. Jack wrapped an arm around his neck and held it. After thirty seconds, Vitoli went limp. Jack held the lock another ten seconds, and then released him. Vitoli was out.

"Jesus," Jack said, "what's a guy have to do to make a phone call around here?"

He found the Iridium in a desk drawer. He turned it on, and it vibrated immediately.

Jack pressed the "Answer" button. "Who's calling, please?"

"Agent Quintana?" a hard voice answered.

"Speaking."

"This is Lieutenant Commander Nielsen with Helicopter Sea Combat Squadron 25 out of Andersen Air Force Base."

"Pleased to meet you," Jack said, eyeing Vitoli.

"I'm en-route to your location now, at General Carter's behest."

Behest, no less, Jack thought. Very good.

"Do a lot of reading in your spare time, do you?" Jack asked, backing out of the room.

"What?"

"Never mind." Jack locked the door from the inside, drew it shut, and jogged back toward the yacht. "What's your E.T.A.?"

"Ten minutes," the Navy pilot replied. Jack heard the heavy chop of helicopter rotors over the phone, but the island air was still quiet.

"Copy that," Jack said. "There's a yacht in the island's only harbor. I'm going to crank up the lights on that baby. I'll need you to land on the beach, on the north side."

"Understood," the pilot replied. "How many PAX are we hauling?"

Jack considered this for a moment. "Three."

"I copy, three PAX," the pilot replied, and severed the connection.

Jack raced to the beach and up the yacht's gangplank. "Thurgood!" he called out. "Quit screwing around and get out here!"

No reply. Jack rushed into the yacht's cockpit and flipped switches at random. He found an intercom and turned it on. "Ambassador Thurgood Throckmorton! Attention! We are hauling ass in six minutes. Leave that cute thing alone, and let's boogie!"

Half a minute later, he found the toggle switches for the deck lights and shoved them all into the "ON" position. Mood lighting flooded the decks. To Jack's surprise, Chicago's "If You Leave Me Now," began to pour from the yacht's speakers.

Jack shrugged and ran back out to the bar. When he got there, Throckmorton was locked in a slow-dance with the Micronesian chick. He wore shorts. She wore nothing.

Jack grabbed a bottle of Jameson, poured himself a double-shot, and peered back at the beach. No movement from the guest cottages yet.

Jack heard the *whop-whop-whop* of rotors over the reef and drained the whiskey.

"Throck!" Jack shouted. "Head to the beach!"

Thurgood spun the young lady around, bowed deeply, kissed her, grabbed his wallet from the bar, and strolled down the gangplank after Jack.

Jack hit the beach at a fast jog. He figured he had just enough time to snatch Xiao from her room before the chopper arrived. A few hours of questioning under a hot lamp might set Guam's organized crime operation back a decade or two.

He pulled Bo's pistol from his pocket and stopped. Vitoli limped toward the beach with an AK-47.

"Shit," Jack breathed. Vitoli opened fire as Chicago sang "We've come too far to leave it all behind... How could we end it all this way..."

Jack shoved Throckmorton into the sand and popped two wild rounds back in Vitoli's direction. "You've disrupted an evening of absolute perfection, my boy," Throckmorton said. "I hope you've got something to say for yourself."

"Get down!" Jack yelled. The helicopter swirled past the reef and approached the yacht. Vitoli made the mistake of firing on it.

7.62 millimeter rounds blasted from the open side of the helicopter on full automatic. Vitoli whirled, fell to the ground, grabbed the Kalashnikov, and resumed firing.

"That man is an idiot," Thurgood opined, lying on his elbow and brushing sand from his chest.

"No shit," Jack agreed. Bo Feng leaned out of his room with a phone to his ear.

The firefight between Vitoli and the helicopter gunner continued.

The chopper descended as Chicago wound down. Dr. Hook took over with "Sharing the Night Together."

The helicopter gunner fired a long volley at Vitoli, and the Russian rolled behind a coconut tree.

The pilot hovered three feet over the beach. Jack shoved Throckmorton into the passenger hold. He looked back at the cottages and saw Xiao standing in the doorway. Jack moved to board the chopper and motioned for the pilot to scram.

The gunner helped him up. "You guys really know how to party!"

"Agreed," Jack replied, looking back at Xiao. She stood motionless as the helicopter lifted into the night.

The pilot yelled over his shoulder. "I thought you said *three* PAX!"

Jack shook his head. "No time for number three!" Jack replied. "Let's go!"

The pilot nodded, and they whirled into the warm Pacific midnight.

CHAPTER 4

Three hours later, Jack and Throckmorton sat on the couch in General Carter's office. One of the helicopter crewmen had given Throckmorton an extra flight suit that was too big for him, but no spare footwear had been available on such short notice. He lounged in a pair of thick, white socks.

General Carter sat on the edge of his desk. Jack laid out the details of their whirlwind trip to the private island while Throckmorton struggled to keep his eyes open.

The General consumed the story with interest and punctuated Jack's narrative with "Hmm," and "Really?" and "My God." When Jack was finished, the General massaged his temples, walked to the large window, and said, "To think there could be another 'Little Boy' or 'Fat Man' somewhere within a few miles of this base, staged to trigger a tidal wave across the Philippine Sea..." he shook his head. "It's incredible."

Throckmorton roused himself and stood. "Do you suppose there might be a little drink of Scotch handy somewhere in the vicinity, General?"

"In the outer office. My Lieutenant's off tonight. You'll have to get it yourself."

"Right-o."

"Bring us all a glass, would you?" Jack called. Thurgood grunted his acknowledgment.

Jack scribbled a note on a piece of paper and handed it to the General. It read: "Have you swept for bugs?"

General Carter dropped into a nearby chair. "Yes, indeed. Your local Detachment did a thorough job of it. As it happens, we did find two devices, one situated inside my desk, and another underneath the couch, there. That was just a few hours ago. When I think about the conversations I've had with my staff and my unit commanders in here..." he grimaced. "Makes me sick."

"You'll probably want to have them sweep this place every few days, from now on," Jack said.

"Don't you think I won't. Tomorrow, I'm replacing the entire staff."

Throckmorton returned with the drinks and lifted his glass. "May we be in heaven half an hour before the devil knows we're dead," he toasted.

"That's nice, Throck," Jack said.

General Carter sipped the whisky, swirled it in his mouth, and looked thoughtful. "We don't have much to go on, do we?" he said. "Sure, we could start combing the island for nukes right now. But if the damn things haven't been stumbled upon in the past seventy-five years, I don't think we're going to find them anytime soon."

"Only thing to do is find that downed Liberator Express," Jack replied.

"Which the bloody Chinese are already looking for," Throckmorton said.

"Yes," Carter mused. "And, according to our *Global Hawk* footage, the Chinese are still looking. Now, at least superficially, we know why they're looking for it, and we know we should be doing the same."

"What about the life-span of those bombs, General?" Jack asked. "Could we expect any of them would possibly detonate after all this time?"

Carter considered this. "That's tricky to say, for certain. As a B-52 pilot, I've been through some very technical nuclear weapons training. In the 1940s, we weren't sure exactly how long the bombs would last in storage. Some said, ten years; some said thirty."

He rubbed his eyes, excused himself, and continued. "However, recent inquiry into that subject area, generated due to our own, aging nuclear arsenal, indicates a plutonium bomb should remain viable for as long as eighty-five years. If that's what we're dealing with here, plutonium bombs like 'Fat Man'; they could very well still function, if triggered, anytime in the next ten years or so, depending on a host of contributing factors.

"In short, yes, the bombs could still detonate. Despite their age, they would be far too dangerous to disregard."

Jack stood. "I need some time to think about where we should go from here."

General Carter phoned the Base Defense Operations Center. Five minutes later, a Security Forces vehicle pulled up to the Wing Headquarters building. Jack and Throckmorton piled into the back seat, and the driver sped them back to the Westin Hotel.

Jack stumbled into his room, collapsed on the bed, and slept. He dreamed of Ashley, only Ashley was Xiao, and he'd gotten her into the helicopter as it hovered over the beach next to the yacht. The Sikorsky rose into the sky and turned toward the dark ocean, but one of Vitoli's AK-47 rounds struck something vital. The helicopter dipped, spun, and careened toward the yacht. She looked at him as the craft fell from the sky. "You killed me," she said. "I'm dead because of you."

Her face twisted into a slack jawed skull.

He screamed.

* * *

Jack started as the hotel telephone jangled through the silent room. He lay still for a few moments. When it became clear the caller was not a quitter, he sighed, rolled over, and grabbed the handset.

"Petrie's Parties and Birthday Gifts," he said. "How may I help you?"

The caller hesitated. "Is this the Westin Hotel, Room 1707?"

"Who wants to know?" Jack asked. He sat up and hunted for his cigarettes.

"This is Guam PD Lieutenant Nicholas Cruz," the voice answered. "I'm looking for a Mr. Quintana."

"You've got him," Jack answered, lighting up. "What can I do for you, Lieutenant?"

"I'm calling from the Tumon city jail. We're holding a 'Thurgood Throckmorton' on a drunk and disorderly."

Jack groaned. "Christ. What did he do?"

"Mr. Throckmorton was apprehended a couple of hours ago, after wandering onto the Tumon Strip in the nude."

Jack snorted.

"Apparently, he'd forgotten his clothes in one of the massage parlors. Two young Chinese women in bathrobes were following him around, trying to drape him in beach towels."

Jack laughed.

"That wasn't so bad," the Lieutenant continued, "but he wouldn't stop belting out that song from 'South Pacific.'"

"'Some Enchanted Evening'?" Jack asked.

"Nah," the Lieutenant replied. "'Bali Hai.'"

The police Lieutenant waited patiently for Jack's laughter to subside.

"I'll be down in an hour," Jack finally answered. He hung up the room phone, grabbed the Iridium, and dialed. Josiah Supitski picked up on the third ring. "I don't recognize this number," Josiah answered, "and I don't talk to people from numbers I don't recognize."

"Soup!" Jack exclaimed. "What unconstitutional crap are you pulling for the N.S.A. today, my man?"

"You insult me, Jack." Josiah replied. "I have a copy of the Constitution right here on my desk, and I reference it hourly."

"Bullshit. I need a favor."

"Another one, huh? What was it last time?" He recited: "'At 94% purity, when cut with ordinary baking sugar, how much heroin will kill a 200-pound man if injected directly into the eyeball?' Was that it?"

"California's over, Soup. I'm working a new gig out here in the Western Pacific."

"Jealous," Soup muttered. Jack heard him clack away on a keyboard.

"Soup, quit multi-tasking for two minutes and let me ask you something."

Soup sighed. "What's in it for me, Jack?"

"The pride of knowing you're helping the helpless and contributing to the longevity of the American way."

"You always say that."

"Its almost always true. I'd swing by and fill you in, but I can't seem to get back to D.C. as often as I'd like."

"Don't give me that. You hate D.C."

"Which is why you never get briefed on the heroic actions I undertake, which are occasionally based upon your advice."

"Okay, okay. Whatcha got?"

"It's a track-down job. There's someone I need to find and question. Might be the linch-pin to the case I'm working."

"Name?" Soup asked.

"Surname: L-o-n-g-i-n-o-t-t-i. First Name: T-o-n-y."

"Could he be an 'Anthony?'" Soup inquired.

"Could be. Probably is."

"What else you got? 'Longinotti' ain't exactly common, but I'm sure there are plenty around. And a first handle like 'Tony' doesn't help."

"Well..." Jack considered. "He's probably dead."

"Come again?"

"We came across his name while researching something that happened out here seventy-five years ago. He was a U.S. Army Air Corps Courier. Technical Sergeant. Stationed either on Guam or Hawaii, probably, in 1944 and 1945."

"You're probably right about the 'deceased' option, then. If he was a Technical Sergeant in 1944, he would have been active duty for at least five or six years, at a minimum, which may have put him anywhere between 24 and 30 years of age in 1944."

"Right," Jack answered, massaging his forehead.

"Which would mean he's a hundred years old, or older," Soup continued. "That actually helps. I'll start with all the Tony Longinottis, over 90 years old, that are still living. There can't be too many. After that, I'll search obituaries for WWII veterans. Obits almost always in-clude references about military service."

"How long?" Jack asked.

"Hey, man, gimme a break. I still got a day job, ya know."

"How about an estimate?"

"Ahh, I'll try to get you some initial results in the next 12 hours."

"Soup?"

"What else?" Soup sighed, exasperated.

"I appreciate you, man."

"Hey, it ain't free. Next time you're on the East Coast, I expect a steak dinner, with the works. You know, silverware and napkins and everything."

"You got it."

"And wine. Something expensive!"

"You could buy your own damn wine if you didn't spend all your money on cat food."

"My babies gotta eat," Soup said, distracted again.

"Talk later," Jack said, and hung up.

* * *

Throckmorton looked bleary and half asleep when Jack arrived at the holding cell, but he still had enough energy to hum the "Bali Hai" melody on a constant loop. He wore blue cotton slacks and a matching shirt that looked something like a nurse's uniform.

"What happened to your flight suit?" Jack asked. He led Throck-morton out to the Suburban General Carter had supplied.

"A delightfully nubile young female removed it for me," Thurgood slurred. "Ah, she was lovely. The very picture of sweet femininity." He slumped forward and then roused himself. "Where are we off to, my boy?" he shouted, rolling down his window.

"To the hotel," Jack said. "But we have to make a stop first. How much did you *drink* last night? You smell like a mismanaged distill-ery."

"Quite enough, I should say. Seems I blacked out for a period. I expect that's when the coppers snatched me away to that rank den of criminals."

"You were the only one in there."

"That is completely immaterial. Don't they know who I *am*?"

"How could they? You lost your wallet."

"Yes, well. That's a bit of a problem, isn't it?"

Jack drove slowly up the Tumon Strip. "The Lieutenant said he picked you up in the middle of the road, right up here."

Throckmorton turned to look at him. "Really?"

"Yes, really. I'm told you put on quite a show."

"I should expect nothing less of myself," Throckmorton answered, sounding satisfied.

Massage parlors lined the Strip on both sides of the road. "From which of these fine establishments did you emerge?" Jack asked, affecting a British accent.

"Mockery, I can do without." Throckmorton lowered his bushy eyebrows. "That one!" he pointed. "I remember the purple lettering and the guttering, neon sign."

"*The Lucky Sailor.*" Jack looked at Throckmorton and shook his head.

"Yes, I selected it because it applies to me, literally. What with my owning my own yacht, and all."

"Oh, yeah," Jack said, pulling up to the curb. "I'd almost forgotten *Her Majesty.*"

"Only, I'm not just a sailor. I'm the Captain." Throckmorton stumbled out onto the sidewalk.

A couple of Chinese girls peeked from the window. One of them smiled, apparently recognizing Throckmorton.

Jack led him to the door. "I think this is the place."

"Oh, it's the place, all right." One of the girls giggled, and he pinched her cheek.

Jack flashed his badge, and the lady at the front desk grew wary. "We need to collect this man's things," Jack said. "He left them here a few hours ago."

The older lady began to protest.

"You've got his wallet, and you're going to give it back. Don't make me shut this place down," Jack said, holding the badge out further.

Suddenly, the older lady was all smiles and affectionate touching. "Here, here (heeuh, heeuh)." She reached under the desk and pulled out Throckmorton's donated flight suit.

"Thank you," Jack said, and pocketed the badge.

Throckmorton continued to flirt with the Chinese girl.

"You take!" the lady said. "Take!"

"Where's the wallet?" Jack said.

"Inside!"

Jack rifled through the rumpled flight suit, found Throckmorton's wallet, and handed it over. "Hey, Casanova," Jack said, slapping the wallet into his hand. "Check this and make sure you've got what you're supposed to have."

Throckmorton peered into the wallet as if he'd never seen it before, recognized a few things, briefly lamented the missing cash, slapped the girl's backside, and exited the parlor.

Jack deposited him in his room with strict instructions to sleep off the drunk and stay away from massage parlors. "We may have work to do on short notice."

"Not to worry, Jacky boy!" Throckmorton yawned. "What do your Marines always say? Semper Paratus! I'm always ready."

"That's the Coast Guard," Jack replied, helping him out of his city jail smock. "The Marines are 'Semper Fidelis.'"

"That's what I said." Throckmorton rolled into bed.

* * *

Jack was halfway to the lobby, in search of breakfast, when the Iridium rang. He recognized the number as General Carter's office phone. "Agent Quintana," he answered.

"Need you up at the base in 30 minutes," General Carter said. "Meet me out in front of the Headquarters building."

Twenty minutes later, Jack pulled up to the flag pole. General Carter dropped into the passenger seat.

"Smells like booze in here," the General said.

"Throckmorton hit the bottle pretty hard this morning. Had a little trouble, but I smoothed it over."

"These diplomats are something else. You wouldn't believe the situations I've seen, and just in the past year."

Jack smiled. "Where to?"

"We're heading to the 69th Reconnaissance Group detachment," Carter said, and gave him some quick directions.

Jack pulled out onto the street. "The *Global Hawk* detachment?"

"Yeah. They've prepared a short-notice briefing, and I don't think I'm going to like what they have to say."

The 69th Reconnaissance Group, Detachment 1, was on the flight line. General Carter guided Jack through the airfield access gate, and they pulled up to a nondescript, beige colored building. An Air Force Major met them at the door and led them to a large conference room.

A mix of enlisted personnel and officers occupied the room. The Detachment commander, a Colonel, sat next to General Carter at the head of the table. An Admiral and a few U.S. Navy Captains, presumably from the Naval base at the south end of the island, sat around the sides. Somebody turned down the lights and brought up a large monitor on the opposite side of the room.

A Master Sergeant shuffled through a few papers, donned a pair of glasses, and began to speak. "General, at approximately 0400 hours this morning, our *Global Hawk* surveillance feed picked up some uncommon activity to the northwest." The Master Sergeant pressed a button on the slideshow remote, and a satellite image of the Western Pacific flashed onto the screen.

"Here," the Master Sergeant pointed, "you can see that a significant number of vessels associated with the Chinese Fleet have departed the South China Sea, via the Luzon Strait. While it's not uncommon for a few vessels to venture into the Philippine Sea from time to time, this particular development is extremely out of the ordinary."

The satellite image was time-stamped "0402L," which meant the image had been captured at 4:02 a.m., Guam local time.

The Master Sergeant switched to another satellite photo. "This next image was captured just one hour ago. As you can see, the Chinese South Sea Fleet vessels that were in the Luzon Strait earlier this morning have split into three distinct groups. This first group," he indicated the formation furthest east of the Luzon Strait, "is headed by the Aircraft Carrier *Shandong*. It is proceeding at full speed, or approximately 28 knots. While we cannot say where any of the groups might be headed, if the *Shandong* were to continue straight on its current heading and at its current speed, without deviating, it would arrive in the vicinity of Guam in approximately 49 hours."

This sparked a moderate uproar. The Master Sergeant waited for the conversations to subside before he switched to a different image. "Interestingly, despite the activity through the Luzon Strait and into the Philippine Sea, these smaller vessels we've been tracking between Kwajalein and the Johnston Atoll have made no noticeable course changes, although they've been wandering this 1,400 nautical mile stretch between the two islands, at considerable distances from each other, for the past few days."

Jack looked at the General, who nodded in return. One of the Admirals asked for a secure line and left the room with an escort. A Navy Captain turned to General Carter and said, "The National Reconnaissance Office called Pacific Fleet Headquarters this morning to report on this activity associated with the carrier *Shandong*. Admiral Leidecker," he motioned toward the door to indicate the Admiral who had just left the room, "is notifying 7th Fleet headquarters now. However, Carrier Strike Group 5 and the *USS Ronald Reagan* are only a few hours away, just north of Saipan."

This prompted further side conversations, and Jack had some difficulty following the Navy lingo. Admiral Leidecker returned with a notebook, scribbled a long passage, and guided himself back into a chair.

"Everyone who is not sitting at the table," General Carter said, "leave the room."

Nine or ten people streamed out, including the briefer. Carter picked up the slideshow clicker and backed up to the image that showed the three, Chinese South Sea Fleet groups on their southerly course.

"Gentlemen," Carter said, "Special Agent Jack Quintana has been on a special assignment for me over the past 36 hours. In the course of that assignment, he has gained intelligence that is specifically relevant to what is happening with these Chinese Strike Groups. I cannot divulge the full breadth of the information we've gained thus far. But I can tell you, with some confidence, exactly where those three Groups are headed."

Everyone at the table looked from Jack to the General, and Carter continued. "We have good reason to believe the Chinese Strike Groups are heading directly to the islands of Palau, Yap, and, finally, here, to Guam. We cannot say what they intend to do upon arrival.

"Fortunately, all three Groups are at approximately the same location, just now emerging from the Luzon Strait. That puts the first Group about 32 hours out from Palau, the second Group about 38 hours from Yap, and the third Group, as the Master Sergeant reported, something like 49 hours from Guam.

"The Chinese vessels between Kwajalein and the Johnston Atoll are searching for something related to this whole thing. However, from our earlier intel collection efforts, we know most of them are salvage vessels and do not pose any military threat."

Admiral Leidecker broke in. "Salvage ships? What are they looking for? And how is that connected?"

Someone else asked: "Is it a sub? Did the South Sea Fleet lose one of their nuclear subs?" An excited babble rose, and General Carter raised his hands.

"Gentlemen. Wait. Please. The intelligence related to the cause of these maneuvers is highly sensitive, and I cannot divulge anything at this table without permission from the Commander, INDO-PACOM."

"General," Admiral Leidecker stood, "I've got half the Chinese South Sea Fleet steaming toward U.S. Territory, and you can't tell me *why?*"

"Admiral, right now, you don't need to know why. All you need to know is that they're on their way."

Leidecker clenched his jaw. "I've notified 7th Fleet. The *Ronald Reagan* will be here in about six hours and will situate Carrier Strike Group 5 between Guam and the incoming South Sea Fleet vessels."

"What about Palau and Yap?" General Carter asked.

"We have no assets in the vicinity that can arrive before the Chinese. Besides, Palau and Yap are not U.S. Territories. If you want them defended, you'll have to do it yourself."

General Carter rubbed a beard-stubbled cheek. "You're right." Carter turned to the Major who had escorted them in. "Get the Ops Group Commander."

The Major stood and Carter said, "We'll meet him," General Carter looked at his watch, "in 20 minutes. And set up a secure video teleconference with INDOPACOM headquarters."

The Major nodded and left.

* * *

Abridging his earlier attitude toward the Admiral, Carter pulled Leidecker aside as they left the flight line and asked him to attend the classified teleconference. Leidecker, of course, agreed, and brought the Navy Captain with him.

In the bombardment squadron operations building, Air Force officers in flight suits walked back and forth through the reception area between an Operations Planning floor and their individual Squadron sections. A young Lieutenant took their identification, or "Common

Access" cards, to be returned upon exiting the building. A Staff Sergeant transcribed names onto an Air Force Form 1109 for entry control.

The Lieutenant whisked them all onto the Operations Planning floor. Raised tables dotted the room. A Senior Master Sergeant hollered from the front, where a large projection screen descended. "Everyone with the exception of General Carter's people and the unit commanders will leave the room now." He repeated the notification, and younger officers exited the room without a backward glance, apparently used to this sort of thing.

Once certain the appropriate personnel were in and the others were out, the Senior Master Sergeant went back to coordinating the teleconference. Three minutes later, the camera equipment was situated, and Jack saw an image of General Carter, Admiral Leidecker, the Navy Captain, and himself appear on the projection screen. A long series of digits popped up beside the image, and Jack realized the call was going through. After a moment, another image appeared, and a four-star Admiral and his staff were visible on-screen.

"Could someone out there in Hawaii give us a comm-check, please?" The Senior Master Sergeant said from the front of the room.

"We read you five-by-five," the four-star Admiral replied.

"Thank you, sir," he replied. "I have you same." He muted the microphone, handed the remote control to General Carter, and left the room.

"Here goes," General Carter said, and unmuted the microphone.

"Admiral Davis," Carter began, "thank you for accommodating us on such short notice. I have Admiral Leidecker and Captain Williams here, as well as Special Agent Jack Quintana, Air Force Office of Special Investigations."

Admiral Davis said something to his staff off-microphone, nodded to someone, and unmuted himself. "Thank you, General Carter. For everyone's situational awareness, General Carter updated me on the progress of Agent Quintana's investigation just a few hours ago."

The four-star Admiral, Commander of United States Indo-Pacific Command, or "INDOPACOM," proceeded to relay a play-by-play account of everything Jack had reported to General Carter since his arrival. Jack was impressed at the level of detail.

Admiral Leidecker looked incredulous, then amazed, and finally, worried.

"Do I have that all right, Agent Quintana?" the Admiral asked.

"Yes, sir," Jack replied. "Spot on."

With that, General Carter regurgitated the major points of the briefing they'd just attended at the 69th Reconnaissance Group head-quarters. Admiral Davis nodded. "Yes," he said, "7th Fleet HQ, at Yokosuka, has been feeding us hourly intelligence updates that pretty much mirror what you've just told us. I understand Admiral Leidecker has contacted Carrier Strike Group 5."

Leidecker spoke up, "That's correct, sir. The *Ronald Reagan* should arrive in just under six hours."

Admiral Davis considered this. "It's obvious to us that, whether or not these nuclear weapons exist at Palau, Yap, and Guam, the Chinese Navy either believes that they exist or sincerely wants us to *think* they do. In addition, the Chinese Navy is taking real action based on that perceived belief, although we do not yet understand what that action might be. They may not know yet, themselves, what they plan to do. I feel they're positioning these three Strike Groups in anticipation of decisions they expect to be made in the near future.

"Regardless of their ultimate intention, which we'll try to ascertain, we must react to their current actions, which are far outside the ac-cepted, routine behavior of the Chinese Navy.

"Admiral Leidecker," the four-star said, "I appreciate your quick thinking, and I agree Carrier Strike Group 5 should position itself in defense of Guam and the surrounding territory."

"Yessir," Leidecker responded.

"General Carter," Admiral Davis said, "we need your B-52s to pro-tect the entire region, starting with 24-hour alert rotations over Palau,

Yap, and Guam. I want those birds in the air within the next three hours."

"Understood, sir," General Carter replied. The Operations Group commander sat behind Jack, and Jack heard him scratching notes furiously.

"In addition, General," Admiral Davis continued, "I want B-52 overflight of the three, individual Chinese Strike Groups, as they approach. How soon can you achieve that?"

Jack did some quick calculations in his head, based on what he knew of the B-52's range and cruising speed. General Carter responded with something close to what Jack had imagined. "We can get B-52s out, in an oval pattern that begins and ends at Andersen Air Force base, to overfly the eastern-most Strike Group, in about four and a half hours from now. The B-52s would progress, in an arc, from one Chinese Strike Group to the next, on a continuous rotation, until such time as the Strike Groups stop movement. At that point, we would position aircraft in holding patterns above each Strike Group, and rotate aircraft in and out based on fuel status."

"How long could you keep up that kind of tempo?" Admiral Davis asked.

"My boys can keep it up as long as we've got the fuel, and we've got plenty of fuel."

Admiral Davis went off-microphone again. General Carter began an earnest discussion with the Operations Group commander and his subordinate commanders. The lower level squadron commanders dispersed to begin the overflight activity.

After a few more minutes, Admiral Davis came back on. "Gentlemen, I've just received a call from the Secretary of Defense. He concurs with everything we've discussed and is en-route to brief the President now."

Jack took a deep breath.

"Agent Quintana," Admiral Davis said, "we understand the Chinese are searching for the C-87 Liberator Express that went down between Kwajalein and the Johnston Atoll, taking General Harmon,

General Andersen, Major Savage, and several others with it. We understand your intelligence asserts the aircraft may have contained detailed information, to include operational codes associated with this World War II weapon system Harmon was building.

"What we need now, more than anything else, is that detailed information about the weapon system. In specific, we need the exact locations of the individual bombs, and the location of the Command & Control facility. Without at least one of those two elements, we have no way to defuse this situation. Does that make sense?"

Jack cleared his throat. "It does, sir."

"Good. Now, I don't want to risk an engagement with the Chinese vessels that are currently patrolling the area between Kwajalein and Johnston Atoll. That Liberator Express disappeared seventy-five years ago, and it's probably lying a few miles down on the bottom of the Pacific. The chances Major Savage crash-landed it on one of the islands between Kwajalein and Johnston Atoll are moderate, at best. The chances a downed aircraft on one of those islands could remain intact for a lifetime, out in the elements, and safely protect the documentation General Harmon was trying to transport, are exceedingly slim.

"That puts us in a bad position. We have no intelligence to collect besides what the Chinese Navy is already hunting. We cannot try to collect what we suspect is probably destroyed without an engagement with the Chinese Navy, which we cannot justify at this time. Do you have any separate leads?"

Jack thought back to his conversation with Josiah "Soup" Supitski. "There's nothing solid, Admiral. I am working a possible lead, but it's a long-shot."

"When will you have something actionable on that lead?" Admiral Davis replied.

"I have a contact that's tracking something down for me now."

"Who is your contact?" Admiral Davis asked.

"A defense contractor at the N.S.A. His name is Josiah Supitski. He's trying to track down a World War II courier that may have had knowledge of General Harmon's project."

Admiral Davis put a hand to his temple. "You're right, son. That's a long-shot."

"Agreed, but it's something."

Admiral Davis nodded. "I'll place a call to one of my contacts at the N.S.A. Your Mr. Supitski will get all the help he needs."

Jack winced. Soup hated outside interference. "We appreciate that, sir."

"General Carter," the four-star said. "I want a status brief every three hours until I say otherwise. Any questions?"

Nobody had any questions.

"INDOPACOM out," the Admiral said, and the image from Hawaii disappeared.

* * *

Jack dropped the General at the 36th Wing Headquarters building and got a stern reminder to cough up any new information. He assured the General he would do so and headed back down Marine Corps drive to the Westin Hotel.

He switched on the Iridium phone and received an immediate call from Soup. "What the hell did you *do*?" Soup groaned on the other end. "I've got the Director of the N.S.A. trying to give me teams of people to order around. I can't deal with this."

"Soup! I just left the briefing that precipitated your current tribulations. All I can tell you is this is important. You'll have to rise to the occasion."

"Damn it. I'm an *introvert*. I can't manage these people. They're lined up outside my office like a bunch of kids waiting for the ice-cream man. Only I got no ice cream."

"Soup, did you find my courier yet?"

"Not yet," Soup answered. "I've been digging through all these records, all this metadata, but I'm only one guy—"

"Task the people, Soup. Tell them what to do."

"Task the people?"

"The ice-cream is 'Tony Longinotti.'"

"I'm not cut out for this."

"Quit whining and get to work, champ." Jack hung up.

* * *

When Jack checked in on him, Throckmorton was still sleeping off his hangover. Evening approached, and Jack still hadn't heard anything from Soup. Goddamned records. Goddamned metadata. Goddamned Chinese Navy.

He wandered down the Tumon Strip with the Iridium in his pocket. Streams of Japanese tourists passed on both sides. These people had families and homes and lives back in Japan.

Would they return to find their lives destroyed?

A Japanese girl flashed him a smile from the other side of the street. She looked like the girl in the black dress he'd seen from the taxi. He looked away.

A Chamorro musician sang Bob Dylan songs on the sidewalk. Tourists stopped and clapped for him. Jack tossed a ten-spot into his guitar case. The tourists made with the donations. The Chamorro kid called out, "Hey, thanks, man."

Jack waved back over his shoulder. That kid might be dead in the next few days, depending on the breaks. *Depending on what I can do in the next few days; in the next few hours. What am I going to do?* Nothing original popped into his head.

Mac & Marti came up on the right, and Jack sat himself at the bar. Isa seemed to be off tonight, and another island cutie served him a local brew called "Minagoff." It occurred to him that he'd been able to drink at almost every location he'd found himself in the past 72 hours. He appreciated that.

Three hours later, he was four Minagoffs in. The Iridium remained silent. He weaved through the tables and accessed the Jukebox. He was in a Billie Holiday kind of mood, so he lined up an album, walked out to the street-side tables, and lit up a smoke. "It Had to Be You," sparkled from the external speakers.

Someone had abandoned a plate of pulled pork. He spied the same boonie dog that had been around the other night and set the plate on the sidewalk. The mutt helped himself as Jack puffed rafters of smoke into the night air.

People walked past on the street, laughing and talking amongst themselves. A pretty Chamorro lady stopped and looked at him and the boonie dog. She held up a camera and tilted her head. Jack winked at her. She snapped a photo as Billie moaned out the final lines of her song. The lady smiled, waved, and walked on down the street.

"It Had to Be You" was followed by "These Foolish Things." The first line went: "A cigarette that bears her lipstick's traces..." Jack looked at the ashtray and saw a half-smoked cigarette, still smoldering. There was no lipstick on it. But lip *gloss*. Yes. There was definitely gloss.

"You're pretty free about donating other people's food," a woman's voice came from behind him. He turned, and Isa stood, hands on hips, smiling.

"Didn't think you were gonna show tonight, doll face," he replied. She pulled a chair up beside him, put a hand in the crook of his elbow, and rested her head on his shoulder. Her hair smelled like roses.

"I told my grandmother what you did for us," she said.

"And what did she say?"

"She said you sound like trouble."

Jack laughed. "Don't kid yourself. I am."

Isa smiled and lit another cigarette. "Still on the job?" she said. "Or am I not allowed to ask?"

"Always on the job," Jack put an arm around her shoulders.

They sat like that for a few minutes, him staring into the street, her smoking, the dog lounging on the curb. It was nice.

"Got time for some love?" she asked.

"Yes, ma'am," he answered, and stroked her loose curls.

They left the boonie dog to his own devices, walked a couple of blocks, and arrived at her apartment. The place was small but orderly. The laundry was put away; the floors shined. Booze waited on the kitchen counter. Jack blessed her in his heart, fixed himself a drink, and dropped into a chair.

She racked up some music, and Jack was surprised to hear Al Hibbler break into "The Very Thought of You."

"Where did a young thing like you learn about Al Hibbler?" he asked.

She placed her knees on either side of his thighs, so she was on his lap without being *in* his lap. She massaged his eyebrows and wandered around to his temples. Tendrils of relief spread from his eyes to his cheekbones; from his temples to the back of his head.

Every few minutes, she brought his whiskey glass to his lips so he could take a sip. An angel.

"Don't fall asleep on me, now," Isa whispered.

"Wouldn't dream of it," he said, exploring the small of her back.

She removed her cotton shirt, and her bare breasts pressed against his chest. He brought his face up to meet hers, kissed her, and stood, holding her against him.

She let herself down, took his hand, and led him into the bedroom. She unbuttoned his shirt as Al transitioned to "I Was Telling Her About You." He slid out of his pants and made sure she did the same. Naked, they danced in the dark. He held his drink in his left hand. With his right, he twirled her in front of the bed. She laughed.

"Who can find a virtuous woman?" he murmured.

"What?" she asked, kissing him.

"Nothing. The universe thinks you're great."

* * *

The Iridium came alive at 3 a.m., and Isa rolled onto her side. Jack took a moment to appreciate the view, grabbed the phone, and walked out into the kitchen. It was a Maryland area code.

Jacked answered. "Soup, tell me you've got something."

"I got something, all right," he said, but sounded unsure.

"What is it? He's dead, isn't he?"

"For the past ten years."

Jack rubbed his eyes. "Well, you did find him."

"There's one thing," Soup said. "His widow is still alive. I guess she was quite a few years younger."

Jack stopped rubbing his eyes. "Oh, yeah?"

"Yeah. We actually got her on the phone."

"Well?" Jack said. "Don't keep me in suspense, fella. What'd she say?"

"That's the weird thing. She wouldn't."

"Wouldn't what?"

"Wouldn't *say*. Wouldn't say a damn thing, except that she had something for you."

"Something... for me?"

"Yeah. Something that her husband left her to give to you. Or to someone like you."

"Soup, man, you're giving me a headache. What did she say, exactly?"

"Hang on," Soup said. "I've got the recording. I'll play it for you."

Jack peeked back into the bedroom while Soup clattered around in his office. Isa was still asleep. God, she was pretty.

"Here we go," Soup continued. "You ready?"

"Go."

He heard someone pick up a phone. An elderly woman answered, "Hello?"

Soup introduced himself and explained he was calling from the National Security Agency, on behalf of the Air Force Office of Special Investigations, with regard to her husband, a Mr. Anthony Longinotti.

A few moments of silence passed as she digested this. "He liked to be called 'Tony,'" she answered, finally. "He never liked the name 'Anthony.'"

"Yes, ma'am," Soup said, nervously. "Well, I'm calling because an Agent with the Air Force Office of Special Investigations is looking for information about something that happened in the Western Pacific during the last year of World War II."

"Ya don't say. You quite sure about that?"

97

"Oh, yes. The O.S.I. is definitely interested in getting in touch with anyone who knew Mr. Longinotti well. If it's all right with you, could I have this agent call you?"

"No, I'm afraid not."

Soup's voice wilted. "No?"

"You tell him..." she paused. "It *is* a *him*, isn't it? I know they have women special agents nowadays, although I can't imagine why any woman would have a mind to go traipsin' all over God's earth, searchin' for this, that, and the other."

"Um, yes, yes, it's a him. I mean, he's a man."

The old lady hesitated. "All right, well. You tell him to come on down to my farm. I'll give you the address." She pronounced it *Address*.

"Ma'am, if you'll allow me to have him call you—"

"No, no. I can't tell him nothin' more than I can tell you."

There was a confused silence from Soup.

"I got somethin' to give him. Somethin' Tony left behind. And no, I won't tell you what it is, because I don't *know* what it is. Just a few months before he died, he said to me, he said 'Lucinda, I've got somethin' I want you to hold on to for me. This prob'ly won't happen, but, then again, it might. At some point, somebody from the Air Force might come around lookin' for information about a thing that happened toward the end of Big Two.' He always called it 'Big Two' instead of 'World War II.' I expect it was easier to say it that way."

"Yes."

"He said, 'Lucinda, if ever somebody from the Army or the Air Force comes around, tryin' to locate me, and I ain't around...'"

She sniffed a little. "I'm sorry," she said. "It's been a lot of years, but I still miss him somethin' terrible."

"It's no problem, ma'am. "

"'If I ain't around,' he said, 'you give the man this envelope, here. Now, I don't want you to open it,' he tole me, 'because it's got a lot of foolishness inside it that's got nothin' at all to do with you.'"

"I remember I asked him what it was that it had to do with, and he said, 'It's got to do with the princes and powers of this evil old world, is what it has to do with. But a whole lot of innocent people could be hurt, or worse, if I go on to glory and don't leave this bit of history layin' around behind me,' he said, 'for some young fella to come along and grab ahold of. And, maybe, fix a little bit of what's left to go wrong from that Christless mess.'"

"Now, I knew he was serious because he didn't never take the Lord's name in vain, less'n there was some serious reason to take it for. There's been a few times I got to missin' him and just wanted to read what it was he left to behind to be read. But I always put it right back in the top drawer of his dresser, unopened, like he asked (ast) me to. I feel I'd be breakin' my promise to him if I ever opened that envelope, and I expect I would be.

"So you just send that agent," she said, "or whatever it is they call 'em, right on out to my farm, and I'll hand over that letter."

"Okay, ma'am," Soup replied. "What's the address?"

"You tell him he can find me at 1325 Rockin' Horse Lane, in Ava, Missouri. Tell him it's right off the highway, but the road rambles a bit 'fore he'll see the house. Tony did all right after the war, and we got nigh on a hundred acres out here, not that I can work it no more. But I like to set and look at it from the porch and know it's mine, or will be, as long as I'm around to look at it."

"Yes, ma'am," Soup said. "1325 Rocking Horse Lane in Ava, Missouri."

"That's right, son. You have a care, now."

"I will, ma'am."

She hung up.

"Well, damn." Jack breathed.

"That's what I said."

"I guess I need to get on the next flight to Missouri."

CHAPTER 5

Jack left Isa's apartment, hailed a cab, and got back to the Westin in short order. After updating the General, Jack checked the flight schedule at Guam's "Antonio B. Won Pat" International Airport and knocked on Throckmorton's door.

"Hullo, my boy!" Throckmorton hailed with his usual flair. "What brings you to my humble hovel at this ungodly hour?"

Throckmorton looked haggard, but he no longer smelled like sour mash, and his eyes attended.

"We need to go to Missouri," Jack said.

"Got yourself a lead, I suspect," he said, twisting the cap from a plastic water bottle.

"Good to see you're hydrating."

"A regrettably necessary but temporary measure," the older man assured him. He downed the bottle, grimaced, held his stomach, and sat on the bed. "I don't believe I've ever heard of a substantial Chinese population out Missourah way," he said, tilting his head. "Why should you want to drag a sick old dog like me into the Ozarks?"

"We're going to see Technical Sergeant Longinotti's widow. I can't say for sure, but I may need your help in any number of ways. If this lead doesn't pan out, I'd like to keep you on here, anyway, just in case."

"Well, Jack, that's awfully pleasant of you. I can't say I'm keen to return to *Her Majesty* at the moment. What with all the recent ruckus, I should think sipping cocktails on the deck in Majuro would be rather a bore. I'm enjoying myself for the first time in years."

"Glad to hear it," Jack said.

"When do we leave?"

"We need to be at the airport in two hours."

"Right." Throckmorton stood. "Then I shall rouse myself, douse myself, and meet you in the parking garage."

Jack threw his things together, checked out, and proceeded to the garage. As he opened the Suburban's driver door, a small figure exited the luxury Mercedes beside him and placed a purse on top of the car. He turned.

She held a compact pistol, complete with silencer, to the left side of the purse, outside the view of passersby. She did not look happy to see him.

"Mornin', Xiao," he said. "I hope you're not banking on two kidnappings in one week. I don't know if I could take that kind of drama right now."

"I'll put one in your gut if I have to."

"Sweetheart, I know you're into me, but this is a little on the creepy side."

"Bo wants to see you," she told him, and held the Mercedes's driver door open. She motioned with the gun. "Get in."

Jack considered his options. He could get in the Mercedes and allow himself to be detained for God knew how long, possibly avoiding a bullet in the midsection, but he couldn't accept the delay. The next flight to Honolulu would be this time the next morning, and that would put the Chinese Navy a lot closer to their objectives.

"You tell Beauregard I'll give him a ring when I can."

Just then, a cracked, British voice traveled down the stairway to their level of the garage. The voice sang Willie Nelson's "On the Road Again," and sang it badly.

Jack shouted, "Throck! Stay where you are!" and tossed the Suburban keys into the stairwell.

The singing stopped. "Some kind of difficulty, Jacky boy?" Throckmorton called from the stairwell.

"Tell him to get in the passenger seat," Xiao said, racking a cartridge into the chamber.

"I think not."

She looked uncertain. He used the moment. "Throck! If I don't make it back here in one hour, I need you to push on without me."

"Right, Jacky," came Throckmorton's echoing reply.

Xiao rounded the car. A flock of Japanese tourists saw the pistol and scrambled for the exit. Jack raised his hands.

"You drive," she said, and held the pistol on him over the hood 'til he dropped to the driver seat. A wireless fob lay on the dashboard. Jack mashed the pushbutton start. Xiao slid into the passenger seat, pistol in her right hand.

"Where to, love?"

"Get us out of this garage."

I don't have time for this, Jack thought, and bumped the Mercedes into reverse. They backed out of the parking spot. Jack saw Throckmorton pop from the darkened stairwell to snatch the keys. Xiao raised the pistol and fired at him through the driver window. Jack tromped the accelerator and felt the bullet rip through the air in front of his face.

He swung out with his right fist. Her nose crunched under the impact. She jammed the hot silencer against his right temple and repeated, "Get us *out* of this garage." Jack risked a glance through the shattered window at the stairwell, saw Throckmorton was out of sight, and navigated toward the exit.

As they pulled into the sunlight, Jack flicked a glance at the rearview mirror and saw the big, black suburban leave its parking space. If the old man could drive, the old man was not dead. Not just yet, anyway.

Jack swung past the hotel's valet pavilion and made a right onto Palo San Vitores Road, also known as the Tumon Strip. Xiao dropped the pistol from his right temple and held it on his midsection. She produced a cell phone, said some things in Chinese, and told him to stay on the Tumon Strip. Her nose dripped blood on the upholstery.

They passed a bar called *Porky's* on the left. In the rearview mirror, Jack saw the Suburban swing onto the road. Throckmorton slalomed in and out of traffic, trying to catch up.

"Drive faster," Xiao demanded. Jack pressed the accelerator. They passed *Mac & Marti* on the right, and Xiao told him to get in the left lane. Throckmorton followed, three cars behind.

They came to a stop light. Xiao directed him to turn left before the *Pacific Islands Club* hotel. The road stretched uphill and away from the beach. At the top of the hill, they turned right onto Marine Corps Drive and headed south.

Two motorcycles, Honda 1000s, screamed north up the other side of Marine Corps Drive and swung U-turns. Jack was doing 50 miles per hour. Throckmorton flanked them now, a hundred yards behind. The bikes pulled up on either side of the Suburban. One of the riders pulled a pistol from a jacket pocket and brandished it at the driver-side window.

Jack saw Throckmorton smile.

Throckmorton whipped the Suburban to the left. The crotch rocket's front wheel hit the Suburban's front quarter panel. The bike flipped and launched the rider thirty feet over the highway. The other rider swung wide into the right lane as Throckmorton floored the heavy Chevy and brought it back to the middle of the road.

"I don't think this'll work out the way you'd hoped, my dear," Jack said. Xiao grimaced and shot him in the left leg. Blood spurted onto the steering wheel and dotted the window.

Pain hit Jack like a battering ram. He wrenched his left hand from the wheel and jammed it into the wound. Then he saw the exit wound was bigger than the entrance wound, and his head went fuzzy.

Xiao shoved the pistol into his right temple again. He was rather fed up with that pistol, but he didn't see what he could do about it just now. "Pull over," she shouted. Jack thought she was scared. *Scared enough to pop me in the leg, but not enough to put one through my head.*

With that, Jack realized she wouldn't kill him; didn't have the will or justification to kill him. Hell, if she blew his brains out, she could probably expect the same treatment from her own boss. The Chinese mob wanted him alive. Dead, he would be useless to them. And their ushering him into eternity would bring so much heat onto the Chinese mob they might as well leave the island permanently.

He laughed, and she screamed, "Pull this car *over!*"

He flashed another glance in the rearview mirror. Throckmorton played cat-and-mouse with the remaining bike a thousand yards behind them, ripping all over the highway. Jack stomped the brake pedal, swung the car around, and punched it back toward Throckmorton. "*What are you doing?*" Xiao cried.

Jack's vision faded. He slumped against the driver door, but he could still see the oncoming Honda and Throckmorton's behemoth SUV. The rider had his head turned all the way to the left. Throckmorton quit weaving and pointed the Suburban straight down the left lane.

Unaware of his onrushing doom, the rider steadied his left arm and leveled the pistol at the Suburban's passenger window. Throckmorton didn't flinch.

Jack plowed into the bike at sixty miles per hour. It flipped into the windshield. Xiao shrieked. The Mercedes slammed to a halt, and Jack saw Throckmorton get out of the Suburban. Just before he passed out, Jack watched the rider plummet into oncoming traffic on the opposite side of the highway. A northbound truck driver locked his brakes and swung sideways. As the biker struggled to his feet, the trailer hit him broadside, and a stream of blood splashed the white trailer.

It looked like raspberry jam.

* * *

Jack awoke to a low, constant rumble. He was in a hospital bed, but the overall environment was incongruous. "Incongruous," he said to himself. He felt like a stranger in his own head, like he had with the tranquilizers.

It was dark, and that was a bit wrong too. He remembered the impact with the motorcycle, in bright daylight. The rest of the scene blossomed backward into his memory.

Xiao had shot him. Yes, he could feel a deep, numbed burning in his left leg. He suspected that numbness would disappear if he failed to receive frequent doses of whatever was making his head feel like a high altitude weather balloon.

There was a circular window a few feet away, in the middle of a door. The door was marked "EMERGENCY EXIT" in black, capital letters against a yellow background. With a grunt, he sat up and looked out the window.

What he saw didn't make any sense.

A blanket of stars in a black sea filled the window. The heavy rumble continued beneath and around him.

I'm on an airplane, he thought dazedly. *Somebody's doped me up and stuck me on an airplane.*

A curtain surrounded the hospital bed. A hand pulled the curtain back, and a no-nonsense, thirty-something woman in a flight suit wrapped a blood pressure cuff around his arm.

"We're flying," he told her, still loopy from the pain medication.

"Damn right," the woman said.

"Holo-nulu?" he asked, failing to get his tongue around the word.

"Mostly right again," she said, and pumped the cuff by hand.

"Figured we'd miss the flight," Jack said.

"If you're talking about the commercial flight from Won Pat International, you did miss it," the lady answered. "You're on a C-17 Globemaster. We're halfway to Hawaii now."

She sat on a stool beside his bed. "Blood pressure seems okay. Could be better." She jotted some notes and looked at him. "Let me give you a rundown. First, the bullet that went through your thigh missed both your femoral artery and your femur. It blew a nice-sized chunk of meat out of your leg, but the wound was pretty clean."

"I'm lucky that way," Jack said, trying to keep her in focus.

"Second, your partner happens to share your blood type. The paramedics took you both up to Guam Memorial Hospital, and you got a little transfusion."

Jack winced. He wondered what kind of interesting social diseases Throckmorton might have. "Better than dying," he mumbled.

"What was that?" she asked, taking his pulse.

"Nothing. Where is the old man?"

Throckmorton poked his burly head through the curtains. "Did someone say 'old man'?" Throckmorton asked. "I am greatly offended."

Jack smiled. "Thanks for the juice."

Throckmorton grinned. "My pleasure, Jacky boy. This delightful creature," he put a hand on the nurse's shoulder, "says you're going to be just *fine*."

The military nurse plucked his hand from her shoulder, dropped it, and wiped her fingers on Jack's bedsheet. "Go back to your seat, please."

"But, Carla, there's not a drop to *drink* over there!"

She fought an involuntary smile and lost. "You go on back. I'll bring you something in a minute."

"Carla?"

"*What?*"

"You're an angel."

She raised the chart to swat him. He retreated behind the curtain. "That one's a real piece of work," she said.

"A piece of work who probably saved my life."

"Now you'll never be rid of him," she said, tapping a pen against her chin. "I've had you on a slow morphine drip for the past three hours."

"Thank you."

"I'm going to starting lowering the dosage."

"No, thank you."

"Yes, thank you. Can't have you turning into a junkie between here and Missouri."

Jack looked up at her. "You're taking us all the way to Missouri?"

"Not me," she said. "We'll swap out with another crew at Hickam Air Force Base, and they'll take you on to Springfield." The nurse peered at him and shook her head. "General Carter insisted you get in the air immediately. I don't think he's especially concerned about your overall health."

Jack laughed. "My new blood brother and I have a lot of work to do."

She turned to leave, and Jack caught her sleeve. "Yes?" she asked, eyebrows raised.

"The woman who was in the car with me," Jack said. "What happened to her?"

Now the eyebrows furrowed. "You mean the woman who aerated your leg?"

"The very same."

"Severe lacerations to the face and upper torso, but nothing life threatening. They had her in the bed next to yours, but they also had half the Guam Police Department in there with her. I think she'll be locked away for quite some time."

Jack looked back out the window. "Doubt it," he whispered, and passed out again.

When they landed at Hickam Air Force Base, a male technician replaced the nurse. Throckmorton was crestfallen.

Before he changed the dressing on Jack's leg, the technician gave him a heavy dose of morphine, which Jack appreciated. Three hours later, the C-17 lifted off again, en-route to Springfield, Missouri, some 4,000 miles distant.

For the first few hours, Jack bobbed in and out of consciousness. By the time the flight was half over, he started getting restless. Gradually, he realized lying flat on his back just wasn't going to work for him. "Hey." He called to the medical technician, who was dozing in a chair beside the bed. "Hey, I need to try to walk."

"Bad idea, sir. You've got to keep that leg elevated, or you'll start losing blood again."

Jack nodded. "I understand that, but I can't afford not to do it. As soon as we hit the ground in Missouri, I need to be on crutches and moving around."

The technician thought this over. "Well, I can give you a couple of bottles of Hydrocodone and some extra supplies. How long will you be on the ground in Missouri?"

"Can't say," Jack replied. "Could be hours; could be days."

"Okay," the technician replied. "I'm also going to give you several syringes of something called 'Tranexamic Acid,' or 'TXA.' If that wound starts bleeding through the dressing, dose yourself with TXA, and it'll help with clotting."

"Let's do it right now," Jack suggested. "I want to try to walk."

"Not recommended, sir."

"If you won't help me, I'm gonna crawl out of this bed on my own." He started to shift himself over.

"Hold it!" the technician shouted. "Just hold it a second. If it's like that, I'll give you a dose of TXA right now. Then I'll grab some crutches, and we'll try to walk."

"Agreed. And, thanks."

Jack was familiar with the C-17 and its cavernous interior from previous flights. However, when he drew the curtain aside, he was surprised to see no other passengers or cargo were aboard. INDO-PACOM seemed to have dedicated the entire aircraft to him and Throckmorton.

The diplomat lay spread-eagle on a heap of blankets beside the fold-out seats. Jack heard his snores over the plane's four, massive turbofan engines.

With crutches and a little help from the technician, Jack gutted out ten rotations from the rear of the cargo area, to the front, and then to the back again. By the last lap, his leg throbbed rottenly, but the TXA did what it was supposed to do, and they didn't need to change the dressing.

The technician offered another dose of morphine, but Jack refused. "Give me the Hydrocodone," he said. "I'll wait as long as I can between pills."

* * *

They landed in Springfield to a rising sun. The weather proved cool, and Jack was glad of it. Southern Missouri could be sweaty business, and he didn't want to re-dress the wound any more often than necessary.

A Colonel from Whiteman Air Force Base, about two hours to the north, greeted them on the tarmac with a couple of SUVs and drivers. "Agent Quintana," the Colonel said, "I don't know why you're here, but I want you to know we'll support you in any way we can."

Jack stood, grimacing, on the tarmac. "Thanks, Colonel. You could start by supporting me into one of those vehicles," Jack said, and downed a Hydrocodone.

The enlisted driver was silent. Throckmorton trundled into the second vehicle, and Jack stretched out his wounded leg on a rear bench seat. Despite having traveled over 7,000 miles in the past 24 hours, Jack actually felt pretty good, bullet wound notwithstanding.

"We're headed for 1325 Rocking Horse Lane in Ava," Jack told the Colonel.

Five minutes later, they rolled down US Highway 60 East toward Ava, Missouri. The Hydrocodone flooded his system, and he struggled to keep his eyes open. Jack had been through Missouri before, but never in the Spring. Dogwoods and wild roses bloomed on either side of the highway, and he wondered at the beauty in this rural section of America.

Thirty minutes later, the Staff Sergeant at the wheel called over his shoulder, "We'll turn onto State Highway Z in a couple of minutes, sir. That will lead to State Highway 14, and Rocking Horse Lane is just a few miles further. We'll be there in twenty minutes."

Jack squinted at the dashboard clock. It was almost 8 a.m. He grabbed the Iridium and dialed the number Soup had given him.

"Hello?" the Widow Longinotti answered on the second ring.

"Good morning, ma'am," Jack said. "This is Agent Quintana with the Air Force Office of Special Investigations. My friend, Mr. Supitski, has been in touch with you, I think."

"Josiah?" She asked. "Lord, yes. He's called me three times since yesterday. Said you was on your way from the South Pacific."

"That's right, ma'am. I landed in Springfield about an hour ago, and some people from Whiteman Air Force Base are driving me out to see you. We'll be there in about twenty minutes."

"Well," she said, "come on, if you're comin.' How many folks d'ya have along?"

"It's me, plus four other people. Five total," Jack answered.

"That'll be fine," she said. "I've got the coffee on. Take care comin' down the road to the house, hear? Tony planted apple trees back forty year ago, and some a' them branches come down in a 'lectrical storm we had last night."

"I understand, ma'am. We'll move them out of the way."

"You do that, son," she said, and hung up.

As Highway Z turned into State Highway 14, Jack found he liked Missouri quite a lot. Most of his work put him squarely in large population centers, where criminals thrived in the hives of the discontent. But out here, in the clean air, with spring flowers abloom, clear streams in rocky limestone bottoms, deer in the pastures, and sun in the sky, Jack felt at peace. He was quite sure it wasn't just the Hydrocodone.

"Coming up on the left, sir," the Staff Sergeant said.

Rocking Horse Lane was actually "Rockin' Horse Lane," complete with dropped "g" and apostrophe.

The Widow Longinotti hadn't been kidding about the tree branches. Blossoming apple trees lined the drive all the way to the old farm house. What winter hadn't pruned had, indeed, fallen the previous evening. The Colonel and the Staff Sergeant, along with Throckmorton and the other driver, took fifteen minutes to clear the branches from the lane.

Technical Sergeant Longinotti's wife greeted them in what Jack could only think of as a "dooryard," although he didn't think he'd ever used that word before. She bustled about in a blue dress and white apron and forced them into the house before she noticed Jack's bandaged leg.

"Good Lord and all that's Holy," she said. "What the devil happened to that leg?"

"Little hunting accident, I believe. Eh, Jacky?" Throckmorton said over her shoulder, smiling.

Jack opened his mouth to say something, but Mrs. Longinotti cut in, "Lord, Lord. My Tony knew a young fella what was hurt in a huntin' accident. Way back in '63, I think it was. Or maybe it was '64. I get so's I can't remember much in the way of details anymore." She hustled everyone into the kitchen, and Jack shuffled after them on his crutches.

"What was it you was huntin' out there in the South Pacific?" she asked. She had a keen look about her, and Jack thought the hapless old widow persona might be more act than reality. An eighty-something year old woman who could manage a hundred-acre farm for ten years, on her own, had to know how to handle herself. Jack thought this one did.

"Something that decided to hunt me back," Jack replied, and Throckmorton roared laughter. The Colonel and the two Sergeants smiled politely, as people will when they don't understand what the joke is about.

"Well, then," she said, "set yourselves down at the table, and I'll get you some breakfast." The Colonel tried to object and offered to wait outside with the drivers, but the old woman wouldn't have it.

She served them black coffee, scrambled eggs, home fries, bacon, and pancakes, which she called "hotcakes." There was fresh butter, raspberry jam, some kind of marmalade, apple juice, and more coffee.

Throughout the meal, she spoke to everyone at the table and injected bits of homespun narrative into each conversation. There were the cattle she didn't have anymore, "'...cept my two dairy heifers, couldn't let them go, no, I just couldn't. Had 'em since they was little calves, no bigger'n a Labrador retriever. Tony helped me pick 'em out from a herd my neighbor Audrey had back fifteen year ago..."

And the pigs she raised, "...no more powerful smell in God's whole creation than a dirty pig-pen. But I surely do love to see them little 'uns sucklin' at their mama's teat. I watch 'em grow and then sell 'em off. Tony and I never could bring ourselves to slaughter 'em. Why, it'd be almost like slaughterin' a dog you raised from a pup. Them piglets is awful smart. Does the bacon taste a little off from what yer used to? That's 'cause it's turkey bacon. Tony always did say pigs is close to people, but a turkey's naught more'n a stone's throw from a dinosaur. Whoever had feelin's 'gainst killin' a dinosaur, I'm sure I couldn't say."

And the chickens she tended, "...Now you take a good Rooster, and he'll protect them hens out there in the coop like they was the finest brood west of the Mississippi." Jack didn't know what geography had to do with the quality of brood hens, but he didn't interrupt. "...damned Roosters don't know no better, but the hens'll let you pick 'em right up off their layin' spot, and there's a pile of the sweetest brown eggs you ever did see."

When everyone was full, the Colonel begged off to make a phone call. The Sergeants went with him.

"Madam," Throckmorton said, stifling a burp, "I do believe that was the most profound breakfast I've ever consumed, eh, west of the Mississippi, that is."

She cackled and set a skillet into the wide, ceramic sink. "'Profound,' he says. Lord, Lord."

Jack's leg screamed at him. He took two Hydrocodone pills, washed them down with hot coffee, and decided to get down to the point of the visit.

"If it's all right with you, ma'am, we're on something of a short timeline. I wonder if we could see your husband's letter now?"

She dropped a dish in the sink and turned to him. The friendly grandmother look had not altogether departed, but Jack detected a deep sobriety and aching loneliness in her eyes. Her hands trembled.

"I reckon I been tryin' to put it off. That letter's been lyin' in the same drawer all these years. Almost feels like Tony's last words on this earth have yet to be spoke. Once the letter's open and I've read the words—I *am* gonna read the words, you can bet your everlastin' souls on that count—Tony will have said everything he ever had to say. Yes, I been puttin' it off. But now's the time for it, and I can't put it off no longer."

She trudged to a staircase that looked as if it had been hand-hewn from White Oak, and climbed it slowly. They heard a heavy drawer slide open up there. Thurgood walked over to the window and peered at a pair of Cardinals on a bird feeder. Jack rubbed the bridge of his nose and felt bad for her.

She took the steps down one at a time, careful to grasp the hand rail as firmly as her arthritic fingers would allow. She sat at the table and handed the yellowed envelope to Jack. Thurgood stayed by the window.

"You go 'head 'n open it," she said in a trembling voice. "I don't reckon I can."

Jack peeled the envelope open and removed a hand-written letter from a man who had been dead for ten years.

It read:

To Whomever the Hell It May Concern: I, Tony L. Longinotti, leave this letter as a matter of conscience, though I hope nobody never wants to see it. If somebody ever does want to see it, that will mean something's gone wrong out there in the Pacific, something with the Project. I seen plenty of action in Big Two, and I fought it out with a lot of Japs. I don't know if the Japs deserve what the Project had in store for them or not. But I do know there's a time for fighting and a time to stop fighting. I hope someday us people will figure out how to tolerate one another, though I can't imagine how that could be.

Anyway, when I was Technical Sergeant Longinotti, instead of just plain old 'Tony,' I had duty as a courier for the Army Air Corps, out of Hickam Field. In early 1944, the boss of the outfit, who was a mean old Master Sergeant, got himself shot down by a Japanese Zero somewhere in the Marshall islands, trying to make a delivery. That put me in charge of the whole Courier Station, as the Captain that was out there got himself some kind of social disease down to the docks and had to be put on bedrest for some time.

Well, one day in December of 1944, we got a call from way out on Guam. The big guy in the Pacific at that time was named 'General Harmon,' and he wanted the highest ranking Courier we had to speed on out to Guam and carry some high-toned classified material to somewhere for some reason. As I said before, that was me.

So, I got a flight out on a B-29 the very next day. Took me a godawful long time to get from Hickam Field to Guam. And when I got there, Guam was a mess. The island had just been liberated a couple months before. There was still Jap soldiers out in the jungle takin' shots at the Seabees who was tryin' to build up the airfields and the ports and whatnot. Anyhow, I found General Harmon after a few hours, and he tells me, he says, "Sergeant, I have an important mission I need you to execute." So I says, "Yes, sir." And he says, "I need you to deliver this letter to a representative in Kunming, China. I understand you're the most experienced Courier out of Hickam Field, and I need a man I can trust to see this through.'"

Now, that wasn't exactly true, about me being the most experienced, as there was a Staff Sergeant at the Station who had more experience than I did, but he'd got busted down for drinkin' on the job. So I just said, "Yessir, I can make the delivery." The General says "Good man," and he hands me a small package to take on out to China. At first, I was a little disappointed. I thought maybe there might be a whole bundle of classified. But then I realized a letter's a lot easier to haul around than a bundle, and it didn't really matter one way or the other. If the General thought a thing was important enough for a Courier to take and protect, from Guam all the way to someplace called "Kunming," well, that was his (the General's) business, and it wasn't none of mine.

So I says to him, "I'll get the job done, sir," and I saluted. He saluted back, and then he says, "When you come back through, come see me before you head back to Hickam Field. I may have another job for you." So I says to him, "Yessir, I will." And then I left and found the next crew headed west out of Guam.

I'll tell you, whoever you are what's reading this, that the trip from Guam to Kunming wasn't no damned "walk in the park." No sir. I had to fly from Guam straight to Kunming, overnight, which took almost fifteen hours. Mind, I hadn't had no sleep the night before, neither. With all the racket going on in a B-29, getting to sleep is nigh on impossible. I ain't belly-aching, but you try traveling for almost three days straight, and tell me how you feel about it.

Anyway, after we landed, I linked up with the navigator, drove into the city, and finally got to the place I was supposed to be. It was terrible difficult because nobody spoke English except one person in a thousand. But I got lucky a couple times, I guess, and I found the right office in this big army complex in Kunming. The navigator wandered off somewheres to get drunk.

I found the office where the Chinese big-shot was supposed to be, only he wasn't there, so I had to wait around with his secretary, or something, for a few hours. The secretary was a little guy, and he spoke some English, so we talked about stuff that had to do with the words he knew. "Lana Turner," and "Baseball," and stuff like that.

Finally, his boss came back from wherever he was, and I handed him (the boss, not the Secretary) the letter I came all the way across the Western Pacific to deliver to him. He read the letter, looked at me, and then read the letter again. I figured maybe he couldn't read English so good. But then, I never could read a lick of Chinese, so I reckon that's all about the same, and I couldn't hold it against him. But I did think it was strange that he read the whole thing over twice. After that, he asked me a few questions (he spoke better English than the secretary did), and then I left to look for the navigator I come with.

I couldn't find him right off. I was so dog tired and fed up with traveling I gave myself a day of leave, all by myself. Authorized it myself and everything. Since I didn't have no more classified to carry around, I felt free and easy to go out and get swacked. So I did. I think maybe I got robbed. But the next day, I was so hung over I couldn't remember if I had any money left when I was drinking or not, so maybe I didn't get robbed. But I spent the next day in some Chinese hotel, trying to boil water to drink, but I kept falling asleep while the water was boiling, and it was past four in the afternoon before I ever did get some water. And then it was hot, and tasted bad. But it was my own fault for carrying on the night before.

Well, it took me most of a week to get all the way back to Guam on account of engine trouble with the B-29. When I finally did get back to Guam, I tried to report in to General Harmon, but his "Exec" told me he was off-island for a meeting in Palau, which was funny because I was just in Palau a few hours before, for a refuel. But, of course, I didn't know the General was in Palau (how could I), so I came on to Guam. Anyhow, he came back to Guam the day after, and I reported in.

"You've done a damned fine job, Sergeant," he tells me. And I say, "Thank you, sir." And then he says, "I'm lucky to have found the best courier in the Pacific." I felt kind of ashamed when he told me that, on account of my having authorized myself liberal leave back in Kunming and getting "shit-faced." But I was still kind of proud, because I really had gotten the parcel delivered, and to the right person, and got all the way back, in not too much time.

"I've got one more assignment for you, Sergeant," he said, and then he opened a big safe in his office. There must have been something like a hundred-thousand dollars in that safe. I couldn't believe it. I guess that's where they kept the cash they needed to get things straight with the locals on the island, or something. But he didn't touch none of the cash. He pulled out a shiny, metal box. I think it was aluminum, because it turned out it wasn't too heavy. Might have been silver, though.

It had one hell of a big lock on the front of it, and he gave me the key. He said to me, "Sergeant, in this box may be some of the most important information ever to leave this island. I expect you to guard it with your life." So, I says to him, "Yes, sir. I sure will do that." And he says, "I need you to take this all the way to London. You're not to speak of it to anyone. If an officer asks you what it is, just tell them it's a special aircraft part prototype that needs to get to the European theater as soon as possible, on my orders. Speaking of that," he says, "I have a letter you can take with you, with an explanation about the aircraft part. This letter should get you priority on any bird flying east, from here to Great Britain."

So I took the letter, and the box, and I told him I would make the delivery, and I promised to call back to his office with a confirmation.

"Good man," he said to me, and then somebody needed him for something, and I left with the package.

Well, that night, I flew right through from Guam to Hawaii, and then on to Los Angeles, which I didn't like much. Oh, before that, I stopped over at the Courier Station at Hickam Field and showed the letter to the Captain, who was back from the hospital by then, and he told me "Good luck," and I left for Los Angeles.

After Los Angeles, I flew straight over to New York, which I didn't care for much either. It was the first week of January, 1945, and it was dreadful cold and snowy. Too many people running around, and not a one of them seemed to know where they was going nor why. But I got on a plane from New York to London, that was about a week after I left Guam, I think, and I found the place where I was supposed to be, and I was awful happy to be in London instead of Kunming because everybody there (in London, not Kunming) spoke English, but kind of funny, but I could still understand them most of the time.

I found the place in London, just off a nice spot called "Covent Garden," where I stopped to have a beer when I got out of the train station. There was a little pub across the street. You ain't supposed to drink when you got classified on your person, but I was terrible thirsty, and just one beer ain't really drinking anyway. Oh, I forgot to say the General told me exactly where to deliver the package, but he told me I couldn't write none of it down, that I had to memorize it, so I did, and he had me say it all back to him three times before I left his office, and then somebody wanted him for something, like I said, and I left.

I was thinking about those instructions on the flight over from New York, and I broke out in a "cold sweat" for a few minutes because I sort of forgot some of the details, but then I remembered, and I was able to find the place easily by asking for directions from some of the English folks in the street.

Anyway, in the section of London called "Covent Garden," if you come from the train station, up this long, winding staircase, and you come up to the street, if you take a right after you get to the top and go down that street toward the "Covent Square," and then you take a left onto that next street, sort of past the big square, you had to go into a "public house" (what the Brits called a "pub"), and this pub was called the "Coach and Horses," and then you had to go all the way to the back, where there was a curtain.

When I got to the curtain, the bartender gave me a look and asked me what the hell I thought I was doing. But I told him I was a Courier, and I was there on instructions directly from General Harmon, and he opened the curtain for me, and we walked down a little hallway that led back to a big, white door.

And now, I'm gonna tell you that I broke this letter up in two parts, just for security, like, in case somebody might be looking for this information that maybe shouldn't have it. So now you, whoever you are, tell my wife (if she's still alive, that is) that there's another letter hidden in the place where we found the kitten back in 1983. If she trusts you, she'll go to the place and get the letter. If she don't trust you, then I guess I'm putting her in kind of a bad spot, as you'll want her to get that letter either way. But I don't know what else to do about that, so I just hope you've got a good, official reason for wanting to know the rest.

Jack rubbed his eyes and handed the letter to Mrs. Longinotti. "He says that if you trust us, you should go to the place where you found the kitten in 1983. He has another letter hidden there, and that's got the rest of what we need to know."

She looked at Jack with wide eyes. "He said that? That's what my Tony wrote?"

"Yes, ma'am."

She started to read the letter from the beginning, saw how long it was, thought better of it, and set it aside. "Yes," she said. "I reckon I trust the both of you. Come along with me, and I'll take you to the place where we found the kitten."

They walked to the front door together. The Colonel approached, and Jack waved him off. "It'll be a little while," Jack said. The Colonel nodded, stretched, and made another phone call.

Jack and Throckmorton followed her down a path lined with raspberry and blueberry bushes. They walked about an eighth of a mile and came upon a sheer limestone wall about twenty feet high. Fifty feet down the face of the limestone wall was an opening. They followed her inside. "We heard that kitten cryin' in here for hours. It was in the middle of the winter, and Tony was worried it might've got lost in there, and we couldn't tell how old it was without seein' it anyway, but Tony thought it was pretty young from the sound of it."

There was an old, steel flashlight on a rock ledge just inside the depression. Mrs. Longinotti switched it on, and Jack saw they were entering a large cave system. "Sometimes, I'll drop my extra potatoes in here, when I ain't got no more room in the root cellar, 'cause it's cool. These caves go on and on through the side of these hills," she said. "Tony used to go down into these caves for hours, 'searchin' for Spanish treasure,' he always said. I thought it was a damn fool idea to walk around underground for God knows how long, but it never seemed to bother him. I used to worry somethin' fierce when he'd go and do that, but he always come back. If he ever found any treasure, he never told me nothin' about it, although we only owned about ten acres back in 1970, and by 1985, he'd bought the other ninety and paid off the house, with what money I don't know, and I never ast, 'cause it wasn't my business if he'd went and got the money to buy a bunch of land."

They turned right, down a small shaft, and then cut left into an open area with a large, cathedral ceiling. She pointed into a far corner of the cavern, where a puddle of clear water had formed from a stalactite in the ceiling. "That's where we found the poor little thing. It was young, just like Tony said, and thin as anything. We brought it back to the house and fed it, and we must've had that cat almost fifteen years before it died. Tony called it 'Spelunker,' because he said that was the word for a fella that goes wanderin' through caves. That turned into 'Splunker' later, and that's what we called that cat. 'Splunker.' Or sometimes, just 'Splunk.'"

She shone the light around above the floor, and Jack saw another stone ledge about five feet off the floor. On the ledge sat an old, black toolbox. Throckmorton took it down, and they opened it. In the toolbox was another envelope. Mrs. Longinotti suggested they take it back to the kitchen.

Once back at the kitchen table, Jack opened this final note. It read:

The Last Bit: Well, I guess you've found the second letter, and I surely hope you're on official business. Anyhow, I found this pub, called the "Coach and Horses," and the bartender took me back through the hallway to this thick, white door. I remember the door looked a little strange, because it looked like it was the only thing in the pub that had been painted in the last ten years or so, because the paint was glossy white.

So, he knocked on the door, and it was like a special kind of knock, like three knocks and then a pause, and then another knock, and then a pause, and then two more knocks, real quick. Well, somebody in a RAF uniform (that's "Royal Air Force") opened the door from the inside, and asked me to come in. I went in, like he asked, and we walked for what seemed like forever, down this metal corridor, all the way to a big, lowered floor, where a bunch of other Brits were looking at radar screens and writing reports and such. So, then, we went past that area to a big room that looked kind of like a records place. There was a whole lot of big, wooden drawers and shelves, and all kinds of stuff lying on the shelves, with reports and paperwork next to every-thing.

On one side of the room was a giant vault door, like in a big bank, like the one they used to have down in Springfield, at the First Bank of Springfield, back in the fifties. Of course, I didn't make that con-nection then, because the First Bank of Springfield never went up un-til 1956, after the war, and this was way back in December of 1944.

So the man walks me over to somebody that looks like maybe he's an officer, and he calls him "sir," so I follow suit and report in to him, just like I reported in to General Harmon back in Guam. I told him, I said, "Sir, I have a package for Field Marshall Sir Reginald Saxon, to be delivered directly, from General Millard Harmon." And he says, "I am Field Marshall Saxon." So I say to him, "All right, sir," and I took out the metal box, and I gave it to him.

He said to the other fella, the one who met me at the white door, he says, "That'll be all, Jim," like that, and the fella salutes him, just as smart as anything, and leaves me in that room with the Field Marshall.

"Have a seat, Sergeant," the Field Marshall says. So I did. And then he said, "Do you have the key?" And then I felt kind of foolish, because I set the box down on the table, but it was still locked, and I forgot to hand over the key, which was stupid, but I reckon I was tired, and maybe that one beer made me a little more tired than I would have been, but it (the beer) was good, and I wasn't sorry I stopped to get it. Except for the fact that maybe it made me forget about the key.

But anyway, so I gave him the key, and he opened the box. Now, I'm not sure I was supposed to see what was in the box, but the Field Marshall didn't seem to have no problem with it. I expect maybe he thought General Harmon had already showed me what was in it, or something.

He opened the box, and there was a strip of shiny metal in there, with a code on it. I couldn't see what the code said (and even if I did, I wouldn't write it down here), but I did see some of what was wrote on the other papers inside the box. I saw the words "Project Big Surf," and I saw the word "plutonium." I remember that, because I never had seen that word before, and I thought it was strange. But I heard about it later, in the news, after we dropped the bomb on Nagasaki. "Fat Man" was a plutonium nuke, I think. And the "Project Big Surf" thing sounded interesting, so that's why I remembered it, I guess.

The Field Marshall seemed surprised when he saw what was in the box, and kind of nervous, like maybe he didn't know if he should be involved in whatever it was. There was also a letter in the box, and he opened it, and it was actually the same letter I had already delivered to the big-shot way out in Kunming, only this one was a different copy, that General Harmon had signed.

What was funny was, when the Field Marshall read the letter, he kind of did almost the same thing the other fella in Kunming did. He read it once, then he looked at me, and then he read it again.

After that, he asked me something about how long I was going to be in London, and I told him I thought I had better get out as soon as I could. Not because I didn't like the place, but because I needed to get on back to Hickam Field, as they were a man short with my being out on special assignment for almost two months straight.

Then he thanked me for bringing him the box, and he called that guy, "Jim," back in to escort me back to the white door. Jim did that, and I went back through the white door into the pub, and I almost stopped to have another "pint," but then I thought maybe I'd better get on to some other pub for a pint, but I never did until I got back to the hotel, where there was a small bar. And I went to bed and never woke up until almost 10 o'clock the next morning. I left that night on a cargo deal back to Baltimore, and then all the way back across to San Francisco, where I got stuck for a couple days, but it was kind of fun, because I ran into this guy I went through training with, and we had some beers and some laughs. It was a good time.

Two days later, I made it back to Hickam Field.

Now, I know General Harmon's plane went down out there in the Pacific, somewheres between Kwajalein and Johnston Atoll, in February of '45. I remember because it was big news back then. And I kind of "took it to heart" because I'd just spoke to him (the General) a couple of months before, and I felt pretty badly about it. But then, work picked up again, and I was out on more missions for the Courier Service, and then the war ended just a few months later.

What I want to say is I think that package I took on out to London was something General Harmon was working on, "in a big way." I think maybe it was something like what finally happened to the Japs later that August, but something different, because I know the Chinese wasn't involved in the bombs we dropped on Hiroshima and Nagasaki. And I never did hear nothing at all more about anything else we did against the Japanese.

So, I figure whatever this "Project Big Surf" was, it might still be out there somewhere. Because, so far as I know, only General Harmon and the fella out in Kunming, and that Field Marshall Saxon in London, (and me, kind of) were the only folks that knew something about it. Besides the fellas who worked on it, whatever it was. But I think it might have been one of those "compartmentalized" jobs, where nobody working on it knows everything about what they're working on. Like what they did with the A-Bomb. Like that.

And then the war ended, and I seen what kind of things happened when the war was over. Everybody just kind of relaxed, like there wasn't nothing more to do at all. And maybe there wasn't, once the Japs surrendered. But I think maybe this one thing might still be out there somewhere, just waiting to go off and hurt somebody, like a "easy action" revolver laying around somewhere where kids might be playing, and they don't know nothing about it, but it's dangerous just the same.

Well, I reckon that's all I have to say. The rest is for my wife, who I always did love, because she was a fine woman and always took care of what needed to be done, even when I wasn't there to help her. I hope the rest of this damned letter finds her well, and you, whoever you are, can just butt out now, because the rest of this is for her.

Jack put the letter down and slid it across the table to the widow. Mrs. Longinotti started to cry, and Jack felt like an ass. His leg hurt, and he took another Hydrocodone.

Throckmorton pretended to watch the birds.

CHAPTER 6

Back in the SUV, Jack turned on the Iridium phone and called General Carter's office. "What have you got?" Carter asked, sounding harried.

"We've come across additional information that points to a location in the United Kingdom. I don't want to say more than that over this satellite link. Throckmorton has connections that may help us along the way."

"Well, I hope your information leads us to *something*," Carter said. "The first Strike Group is closing in on Palau, and the White House is releasing an official statement. Pretty soon, we'll have every goddamned ambulance chaser in the region trying to report on it."

"Understood. We're heading back to Springfield International now."

"Good. I called your pilots. This crew will stick with you until you hit a dead end or wind up back here. Or both. They understand you're laying out the itinerary."

"Thank you, sir," Jack grimaced as the driver caught a pothole.

"Out, here," Carter said, and hung up.

There were small television screens in the headrests of the SUV's front seats. Jack turned one on. The Secretary of Defense stood at a podium before a room of reporters. The White House Press Secretary hovered anxiously behind him, trying and failing to appear collected.

"Ladies and Gentlemen," the Secretary of Defense began. "Precisely 30 hours ago, three groups of Chinese Naval vessels entered the Philippine Sea via the Luzon Strait. While not considered an act of war, this activity is aggressive and outside the usual pattern of behavior. In response, the Commander, United States Indo-Pacific Command has positioned the carrier *U.S.S. Ronald Reagan* to the north of Guam, the eastern-most U.S. Territory.

"As we speak, one of these three groups of Chinese Naval vessels is approaching the island of Palau. While Palau is not a U.S. Territory, the Government of Palau officially requested U.S. protection some five hours ago.

"A second group of vessels is traveling to a point to the west of Palau and east of Guam. The two islands are separated by seven hundred miles of ocean, and a large portion of Micronesia lies between them. Consequently, we cannot say what the second group's ultimate destination might be.

"The third group of vessels appears to be headed for the vicinity of Guam, although it will not arrive in the region for another twenty-four hours, if, indeed, that is where the group is actually going. Out of an abundance of caution, I have directed the 515th Air Mobility Operations Wing, at Hickam Air Force Base, to begin evacuating military dependents and non-essential personnel from Andersen Air Force Base and Naval Base Guam. The first evacuees departed the island around twelve hours ago. More C-17 cargo aircraft, which can also airlift large numbers of personnel, are en-route to Andersen Air Force base from the 60th Air Mobility Wing at Travis Air Force Base, California."

Reporters began to shout questions at the man, and he raised his hands to quiet them.

"At this moment, we have no clear reason to believe the islands of Palau and Guam are under threat of violence. The Chinese ambassador called our State Department a few hours ago with an explanation that these maneuvers are part of a planned Naval Exercise in the region and should not be interpreted as hostile.

"While we investigate that claim, however, we will continue to move military dependents to Hawaii. In addition, the Commander of the 36th Wing at Andersen Air Force Base, Brigadier General Michael Carter, has ordered the B-52 Bombers on rotation there to initiate a continuous, 24 hour alert, which began some 20 hours ago. The B-52s, as well as a number of *Global Hawk* reconnaissance aircraft, will overfly these three groups of Chinese vessels until such time as their intentions are made clear.

"In addition, the President has authorized me to upgrade the U.S. Military's overall Defense Condition, or 'DEFCON,' from DEFCON 5, the lowest level of readiness, to DEFCON 4, while United States Strategic Command and United States Indo-Pacific Command have been elevated to DEFCON 3.

"I want to reiterate that, in the absence of a full mobilization of Chinese military forces, which we have not seen, it is unlikely these maneuvers pose a danger to Americans in the Pacific or on the Pacific Coast. I will now turn this briefing over to Press Secretary Omsted.

The Defense Secretary left the room without answering questions; the Press Secretary scrambled to the microphone.

Jack shut off the television and thought about Tony Longinotti's trip to London. How they were going to track down Harmon's metal box full of secrets, Jack didn't know. But hundreds of thousands of lives might be suspended between his ability to navigate this mystery and the intentions of the Chinese Navy, which were, as yet, unknown.

Forty minutes later, he and Throckmorton climbed back aboard the C-17 at Springfield. Someone had thrown down a cot for Throckmorton, but he didn't seem to notice. The old fellow appeared as though he could use a little liquid encouragement, a luxury that had been absent since Thurgood had consumed the two mini-bottles of wine from the original nurse.

Jack hobbled to the Loadmaster, who doubled as the Flight Engineer and then tripled as a hard-nosed Flight Attendant when passengers were a priority and cargo was absent. After a few words, the Loadmaster nodded, said something to the pilot, who gave him a thumbs up, and turned back to Jack. "We're taking on fuel now, so we can't go wheels up for another hour anyway. I'll be back as soon as I can."

Jack thanked him and walked over to Throckmorton, who wrung his hands and stared from the open loading ramp to the runway. Jack popped open his bottle of Hydrocodone and handed the old man a pill.

Throckmorton eyed it, took a glance at Jack's leg, and said, "Come off it, old boy. I'm quite all right."

"You don't look all right." Sweat beaded on Throckmorton's forehead in fine droplets, although it was only about 65 degrees in the aircraft.

"If you think I'm going to accept charity narcotics from a gunshot victim, you've gone daffy."

"Suit yourself, but sit down with me. We've got a lot to talk about."

Throckmorton shivered and trailed Jack to the dropdown seats on either side of the cargo hold. Jack extended his wounded leg, dropped onto a seat, and lay the crutches on the metal floor.

"Well," Jack said, "I suspect you know where we're headed next."

Throckmorton smiled despite the withdrawal symptoms. "I suspect you're right, Jacky. Old England lies ahead, anchored in the dark Atlantic, a kingdom unto herself."

"Sure," Jack said, repositioning his leg. "I'm hoping you've got some dusty old keys to that kingdom. We'll need to unlock a few doors that don't open very often."

Throckmorton stroked his mustache. "Right you are. All this travel has my old cerebrum in a bit of a fog, I'm afraid." He collected himself, smacked his lips, and asked, "Might I see that satellite phone?"

Jack handed it over and watched as Thurgood punched in a long series of digits from memory. As the phone rang, he activated the speaker option, and Jack hunched forward to hear the dialogue over the steady drone of the C-17's Auxiliary Power Unit.

Someone picked up on the second ring. "Office of Air Marshal Percival Downes," a female voice called out. "How can I be of help?"

"Liz, darling!" Throckmorton said. "It's Thurgood. I wonder if Percy is available at the moment? Something important's come up."

There was an awkward pause. "I'll just pop in and see if he's available," she said in a stilted rush.

Jack gave him a look.

Thurgood licked his lips, smoothed his mustache, and said, "Liz and I have something of an... association... you might say." He cleared his throat and held his hand over the receiver. "I promised to bring her along on my recent jaunt through the Pacific, but I'm afraid she's put on a bit of extra heft, and another lady made the cut instead."

Jack smiled. "Are you telling me you've got RAF secretaries lined up and competing for your companionship?"

Thurgood shrugged. "I have a natural sort of magnetism, I suppose."

"I'm sure the title, the money, and the yacht have very little to do with it."

Throckmorton looked peeved. "I should say *not*. And I resent the implication that—"

"Air Marshal Downes here," a voice burst from the satellite phone.

Throckmorton jerked and held the receiver up between them. "Percy, old boy. It's Thurgood. How've you been getting along?"

"Yes, yes. I thought it was you. Elizabeth looked positively depressed just now. I hear you've taken Gwendolyn out to the South Seas on *Her Majesty*."

Someone choked back a sob, and the Air Marshal called out, "Confound it, Elizabeth. What I have told you about listening in on my calls?"

Another sob preceded a sharp *click* as the heartbroken secretary gave them the line. "Ridiculous woman," the man said. "You simply must put a stop to all of this female drama with my office personnel."

"Sorry about that, Percy. You remember what it was to be a bachelor, I'm sure."

"Damn it, man. You know I've been shackled to the old ball-and-chain since I was twenty-three. I can't even recollect what it *means* to tomcat around."

Jack twirled his finger to indicate Throckmorton should move the conversation along.

"Look, Percy, something's come up, I'm afraid. Have you seen the news about the situation in the Pacific?"

Downes called for someone to bring him tea. "Yes, yes. I'm watching it now on the BBC. Looks to me like the damned Orientals have lost their bloody heads. What's all that noise in the background?"

"I've got onto an American transport, old man."

"What?"

"I say," Throckmorton shouted, "I've got onto an American transport out of Guam. We're to take off from southern Missouri in a flash, and we shall very much want to speak with you when we arrive at Heathrow in..." Throckmorton looked at Jack. Jack held up both hands, fingers splayed "...in ten hours!"

"What's all this about the Americans?" Percival asked. "What the devil is going on?"

"Can't explain over this line, old man. Very hush-hush, you know. But your office will want to be involved, I'm quite sure."

Like any competent bureaucrat, Downes smelled the opportunity to capitalize on a crisis. After a moment's hesitation, he replied, "Yes, well. Of course. We stand ready to aid in whatever way we can."

"Right. Then do this, would you? Have you got a biro handy?"

The Air Marshal muttered something, and Jack heard papers shuffle in the background. "Yes. Go ahead."

"Dial the control tower at Heathrow, if you would. Tell them they'll need to accommodate an American C-17, and we'll need transport from the aircraft to your office. The pilots will call ahead with all the relevant information, of course, but we'd like you to smooth it over, as it were."

"Not to worry, Thurgood! We shall be standing by."

"Cheers, then," Throckmorton replied and moved to hang up.

"And, Throck," Downes added, "make up with Elizabeth, would you? She's been moping about the office like a lovesick schoolgirl ever since you left with Gwenny, whom I would very much like to have back at work, by the by. She was supposed to have been back *days* ago."

"Right," Throckmorton answered, "I'll... see about that, old man."

"Is Gwendolyn right there with you?"

"Ah, sorry, Downes! Bad signal here. I'm losing you. See you at Heathrow." He hung up and blew out a sigh. "Good God, I could use a drink."

Just then, the Loadmaster returned with a brown bag and a handful of paper cups. "Special delivery," he said, handed the stuff over to Jack, and climbed up to the cockpit.

Jack pulled out a bottle of eighteen-year-old Chivas, poured them both a couple of fingers, and offered one to Throckmorton. "To the Royal Air Force and their melancholy secretaries," Jack said holding his cup aloft.

"To the very same," Throckmorton smiled, and downed the Scotch.

* * *

Ten hours later, after half the bottle of Chivas and a bit of sleep, Throckmorton seemed a new man. Jack felt like shit.

They landed at Heathrow in a drizzling fog.

Jack took down some contact information for the pilots, and he and Throckmorton climbed into a Rolls Royce limousine. "Lizzie!" Throckmorton boomed. Jack saw a plump but pretty woman in the opposite seat. "Elizabeth, dear! I've been desperate to get back to you."

Jack pretended to hunt for a seatbelt.

"Don't give me that, you old goat," Elizabeth replied. "I'm only here because Air Marshal Downes insisted upon my greeting you."

"But Lizzie, my darling, I've come back."

Elizabeth looked uncertain. "But you've left with Gwendolyn after promising *me*..."

"Shhh," Thurgood whispered. He clambered to the other side of the car to sit beside her. "All that's over, my love. It was a simple mistake."

He took her hand and patted it. Amazingly, Elizabeth smiled and moved closer to him. "Well, if you say it's over..."

"Without a *doubt*, my sweet rose."

Jack felt queasy.

While Throckmorton declared his undying devotion to the love-lorn Elizabeth, Jack closed his eyes and concentrated on the next steps.

Whoever this Air Marshall was, Jack suspected the chances of his being able to help them investigate Longinotti's story about the World War II intelligence operation in Covent Garden were not so hot. Before anything else happened, however, Jack wanted to find out what was going on back in the Pacific.

"Sorry to interrupt," Jack said. "How long until we arrive at our destination?"

"Shouldn't be longer than a half-hour," Elizabeth replied, gazing at Throckmorton, who fumbled with the Chivas and a paper cup.

Jack spied a television built into one of the leather side-panels. He switched it on. Elizabeth pried herself away from Throckmorton long enough to help him find Sky News.

"Olivia Knowlton, on scene just outside Andersen Air Force Base, Guam," a pretty anchorwoman said. Jack saw the installation's front gate directly behind her. It was dark, but he could make out the profiles of the Security Forces personnel inside the gate house.

"Behind me," she continued, "you can hear the thunder of B-52 bombers, some of which may be equipped with nuclear payloads," Jack doubted that very much, "as they take off and land on continuous rotation over the islands of Guam, Yap, and Palau."

So, the second Chinese Strike Group had arrived at Yap.

"We do not know why these Chinese warships have targeted Palau and Yap," she went on, "as there is no established U.S. military presence on either island. However," she was drowned out by a roaring B-52 on the flight line "...is a bastion of U.S. military power in the Pacific, hosting both Andersen Air Force base, at the northern tip of the island, and Naval Base Guam, at the south.

"According to reports from Palau, the Chinese vessels have not been deterred by the B-52 overflights, perhaps doubting American will to attack the Chinese Navy. We've heard nothing yet from the island of Yap, as there is little infrastructure there. However, the *U.S.S.*

Ronald Reagan, a symbol of the U.S. 7th Fleet's dominance in the Pacific, stands fast to the north of Guam as the third Chinese flotilla approaches."

Flotilla, yet.

"In just a few, short hours, we expect the Chinese Aircraft Carrier *Shandong* will approach the *Ronald Reagan*. At this time, I'll turn it over to network contributor, Dr. Ian Strong. Dr. Strong is a member of several Washington think tanks, and is the author of the recently published *To Win at Sea*, an in-depth look at the U.S. Navy's capability to fight a global conflict on multiple fronts. Dr. Strong..."

The camera switched to a thin man in a tweed jacket. He wore glasses that were too large for his face. "Thank you, Olivia," he said, in a startlingly deep voice.

"Dr. Strong," she asked, off-camera, "what can we expect to see as these two, giant aircraft carriers meet in the Pacific?"

"Traditionally," he rumbled, "what we've seen in this situation is a pitched aerial battle that begins and ends before the carriers ever catch sight of one another."

"Doctor," she broke in, "Doctor, I'm sorry to interrupt, but, are you saying we could see American and Chinese fighter jets go head-to-head over the Philippine Sea north of Guam?"

"Well," he replied, "what I'm saying is there is no way to know exactly *what* we'll see. The Chinese have not responded to U.S. demands to turn back to the Luzon Strait. However, the Chinese Strike Group situated north of Palau..."

"Strike Group?" Olivia broke in excitedly. "Is that what these are?"

Dr. Strong hesitated, "Perhaps I'm using terminology ill-suited to the situation."

But she sank into 'Strike Group' like a hungry dog into an under-cooked steak. "Do you think the people of Palau are in danger from this Chinese Strike Group? What kind of weaponry do you think is on board?"

"Hold on. What I was going to say was the Chinese vessels north of Palau have been in place for over ten hours now, and they have taken no aggressive action. They seem to be waiting for something."

"Could they possibly be waiting for the *Shandong* to make a move against the American carrier, Doctor?"

"Well, well," Dr. Strong stammered, frustrated. "We can't say what the Captains of these individual vessels are waiting for, or for whom they are waiting to direct them. Right now, it's a mystery."

"There you have it, ladies and gentlemen," Olivia's face panned back onto the screen. The doctor tried to contribute more information, but Olivia wasn't interested. "A mystery, and possible conflict with the Chinese Navy, developing before our eyes, just north of this easternmost American Territory. Right now, we need to move to the White House, where the Secretary of Defense is poised to make another announcement."

Elizabeth had started watching a few moments before, and Throckmorton tore himself from the Scotch to the television screen.

"...these developments in the Pacific," the Secretary of Defense began, "we are fully prepared to defend the American Territory of Guam, as well as the island nations of Palau and Yap. The Chinese have belligerently and ostentatiously intruded upon territory that is basically neutral. Chinese vessels have ignored repeated attempts to hail them, and there has been no further communication from the Chinese diplomatic apparatus.

"Consequently, I have authorized an upgrade in American readiness to Defense Condition, or DEFCON, 2. In this posture, America's nuclear arsenal will be ready for delivery at a moment's notice. China's leaders should think long and hard about their next move. That is all."

The Defense Secretary once more departed the stage without answering questions, and the Press Secretary dove for the microphone. Jack switched off the television.

"What a shit-show," Jack sighed. He squeezed his forehead between his palms.

"Keep your chin up, Jacky boy." Throckmorton splashed Scotch into his paper cup, and it started to leak. "Nobody's chucked any spears yet."

"Yes," Jack answered, "but both sides are warming up in the bullpen."

"I believe we've mixed our metaphors," Throckmorton replied, trying to kiss Elizabeth and sip Scotch at the same time. She giggled.

Ten minutes later, they arrived at a brick building labeled "Ministry of Defense." Elizabeth led them up a flight of stairs to an office entitled "Air Marshal." A short, rotund man in an RAF uniform met them in the doorway, introduced himself to Jack as "Air Marshal Percival Downes, at your service," and led the trio into his office.

The joint was lined in burnished walnut. "Lizzie" brought them refreshments and then bustled out to her desk. The Air Marshal closed the door behind her.

"Throck, you old dog," he began, eyebrows furrowed. "Gwendolyn's just called me from *Her Majesty*. Says you went out drinking some four days ago and haven't returned since."

Throckmorton looked dejected, tried to explain about the U.S. Navy personnel and the "kidnapping," saw the Air Marshal wasn't buying it, shut his mouth, and took another swig of Scotch.

"Anyhow," Downes continued, "what's all this tripe about that godawful mess in the Pacific?"

Throckmorton explained the situation to the best of his now limited ability, and Jack filled in the blanks. After a few questions, and despite a few incredulous frowns, Downes seemed to have the picture set in his mind.

"The U.S. Air Force Office of Special Investigations, you say?" Downes inquired.

Jack nodded, exhausted.

"Yes," Downes replied to nobody. "Yes, I believe I have it straight. Well, this Longinotti fellow was here quite some time ago, and the London of World War II has all but vanished from our modern metropolis.

"However," he tapped his chin, "I do happen to know a military historian who may be able to shed some light on your inquiry. What do you say we ring him up?"

Jack made the appropriate noises, and Downes directed Elizabeth to contact the man.

"I'm afraid you boys are done in," Downes said. "Unless you get some sleep, and soon, I don't believe you'll be able to investigate much of anything."

Jack struggled to his feet, grabbed at his crutches, missed, and caught himself on the edge of the Air Marshal's desk.

"That does it," Downes said. "Come with me."

Downes had Elizabeth fetch a wheelchair. Jack didn't want to use it, but he was wrecked. He sank into the chair with mixed disgust and relief, and Elizabeth wheeled him along. The Ministry of Defense building contained a set of guest rooms.

Jack rolled himself into a room, gave Downes a perfunctory "thank you," and shut the door. Once inside, he ripped the bandage and dressing from his wounded leg, filled the bathtub, and lowered himself into the water, his bad leg hanging out over the side.

His first bottle of Hydrocodone was nearly depleted. He popped the lid and swallowed two more pills. There was a bottle of rubbing alcohol on a shelf of sundries over the sink. Jack eyed it from the tub, anticipating the sensation it would inflict.

"What a bitch," he breathed, thinking of Xiao, who had almost certainly been sprung from jail at this point. "Too bad about your face, baby," he said to the empty bathroom. "You was a looker."

He realized he was getting loopy and forced himself out of the warm bathtub. He twisted the top from the bottle of rubbing alcohol, gritted his teeth, and dumped it on the wound.

Pain roared through his offended body, and he almost fainted. He gripped the edge of the sink, sucked air, and gutted through the interminable period between shock and relief. Gradually, the pain subsided. He applied a fresh dressing and bandage with all the care a six year old might take to slap a band-aid on a scraped knee.

With silent gratitude, he eased himself onto the soft bed, heard someone who could only be Elizabeth knock lightly on Throckmorton's door, and fell asleep.

* * *

He started awake some six hours later, after another nightmare about Ashley. He was going to need to see someone about that. Enough was enough, already.

He grabbed a remote control from the nightstand, pointed it around the room, and jammed the "On" button. A screen lit up in the right corner, just beneath the ceiling, and he saw the television mounted to the wall.

The situation in the Pacific was now the leading story on every network, but there had been no significant changes since he and Throckmorton had arrived the previous evening. The *Shandong* had halted some one-hundred miles north of Guam, ostensibly wary of the *Ronald Reagan*. Olivia's air battle had not yet begun.

Thank God for small favors, Jack thought, and dressed himself.

A common area was situated outside the guest quarters. Someone had lain out a breakfast feast for them. There was bacon (real bacon this time, and prepared the British way), baked beans, fried tomatoes and poached eggs. Jack consumed as much as he thought wise, gulped a cup of black coffee, and crutched himself back to the Air Marshal's office. He abandoned the wheelchair.

Air Marshal Downes was already in the office with a young man who introduced himself as "Jim, Jim Potter, suh." Jack shook his hand and lowered himself into a seat.

"Have you seen Thurgood?" Jack asked.

"The old goat's been up for hours," Downes replied. "I'm having him coordinate the return of my other secretary. He'll be back momentarily."

"Well, Mr. Potter," Jack began, "I assume Air Marshall Downes has explained what we're after."

"That's right, suh," Potter replied. "I've prepared a presentation for you, if you're quite ready."

Jack nodded. "Everything hinges on what you've got for us."

Potter pulled down a white screen. A projector hummed from overhead, and Jim Potter began.

"First, I'm going to show you a rough sketch of the Covent Garden area that your Sergeant Longinotti described. There are no remaining blueprints or plans of any Secret Intelligence Service facilities in that part of the city. That is, not so far as I can tell. However, I've heard a few things from some of the old S.I.S. fellows, and there may have been something there.

"The S.I.S.," Potter continued, "as well as several other intelligence organizations, had facilities all over London. Because of the intense German bombing and later rocket attacks, almost all of these facilities were underground. While there's not too much to go on, I'd like to start at this pub in Covent Garden, the *Coach & Horses*."

Jack stared at him. "It's still there?"

Potter laughed. "Oh, yes. We've got pubs in London that are hundreds of years old. This one, for example, was established in 1753, under King George the Second."

Jack was impressed.

"As a matter of fact, I've popped into the *Coach & Horses* for a pint or three on many occasions. It's a nice little place. Not too rowdy. A lot of older patrons. Quiet, like."

"Do you think we're actually going to find anything there?" Jack asked.

"Well," Jim answered, "in my experience, infrastructure's infrastructure. It's hard to change infrastructure. Most people just modify it or build around it. Only very seldom is it completely destroyed."

Jack nodded. "Sounds like an idea," he said. "When do we leave?"

"Tell you what," Jim said. "I'll get the number for the place and let 'em know we're on our way. They serve breakfast, I think, so they should be open now."

Throckmorton wandered in looking beleaguered. "Have I missed anything essential?"

* * *

Ten minutes later, they sped down a narrow road in the South of London. Throckmorton gave Jack the front passenger seat so Jack could stretch out his leg.

A police escort joined them and accelerated their progress. Jack wondered how anyone could ever learn his way around this city. It was a maze of one-way streets, blind alleys, office buildings, tube station entrances, housing areas, and industrial parks. They passed over the Thames. He caught a glimpse of Big Ben.

People were everywhere. People walking, people on bicycles. People on mopeds and motorcycles who Jack took for borderline suicidal. People in cars and loaded into buses.

Jack felt as though he had a small taste of what Longinotti must have experienced. The Courier had never been to London before. At least, that's what Jack had intuited from the letter. To have come through Los Angeles, New York, and then London, right after zooming across the Pacific Ocean, all the way from Kunming, Jack had to appreciate the man's flexibility.

But Jack knew how Longinotti must have felt. Many times, on various missions, Jack had been painfully aware of his ignorance of local customs, processes, procedures, and requirements. All of those things had to be navigated, and it took a skilled wanderer to find his way without serious incident.

The Air Marshal pulled up to the curb next to a Tube station marked "Covent Garden" and "Piccadilly Line." Jack hauled himself from the car and balanced on his crutches.

"Jim," he said. "How long has this Tube station been here?"

"The Covent Garden Tube station was opened in April of Nineteen Hundred and Seven," Potter responded, by rote.

"This station has been in place since before World War I?" Jack asked.

"That's correct. Actually, beside the streets and building fascia, little of this section of London has changed since that time."

Jack pictured Sergeant Longinotti, dressed in his Army Air Corps uniform, emerging from the Covent Garden Tube Station some seventy-five years prior. He could see him walk out onto the street, trying to recall General Harmon's directions.

Jack looked around. Across the street, he saw a pub called *The Nag's Head.*

"How about that pub?" Jack asked Potter. "Do you know if that was open in 1944?"

Potter referenced his inner library of historical information. "*The Nag's Head,*" he said. "Oh, yes. The *Nag's* has been open since Nineteen and Twenty-Seven. In Nineteen and Forty-Four, it would have looked much as it does now."

Jack felt an irresistible urge to walk in Longinotti's steps. "I think this might be the pub where the Courier stopped on his way to the *Coach & Horses.*"

Potter considered it. Throckmorton considered it heavily and then walked across "James Street" and went inside. Jack smiled and followed him in.

The Nag's Head proved gravid, with dark wood and low lighting. Jack slid onto a stool next to Thurgood and ordered something called "Landlord." Thurgood ordered brews for Potter and the Air Marshal, and they all sat at the well-worn bar together.

It was an interesting scene. Potter looked comfortable, as if he'd been there many times before. Probably, he had. Air Marshal Downes sipped a Guinness and talked to Potter about the pub's history. Throckmorton chatted up the pretty bartender.

Jack smiled as he thought of Longinotti. He, the Sergeant, navigator of oceans and cities and nations, lost as anything and asking directions from the locals. Maybe there had been another pretty bartender pouring drinks here back in 1944. Maybe Longinotti had sat right here, where Jack sat now. Maybe he'd asked her for directions to the *Coach & Horses.* Maybe she'd told him where to go.

He sipped his Landlord and basked in the feel of the old place, wondering at the multitudes that had occupied the same space in different times. There were so many stories here, buried one atop the other, all ready to be examined by someone who could appreciate the history, study the people, and draw the appropriate conclusions.

When all had consumed their brews of choice, they continued down James Street to Covent Square. From there, Potter led them down Russell Street, where they came to the intersection of Russell and Wellington.

There, directly across the road, in an ancient brick building with a crimson hardwood front, lay the *Coach & Horses* pub.

"This is it, mates," Potter said.

Jack was intrigued. "This pub has been here since before the American Revolution?"

"Sure thing, mate. But people 'round here don't like to talk about that much."

Jack frowned. "Really?"

"Nah, mate. I'm just takin' the piss out of you."

"Well, let's see it," he said, feeling slightly foolish, and hobbled into the cross-walk on his crutches. The others followed him across. Thurgood held the door for him.

Except for a television in the corner and a few bar games, the *Coach & Horses* looked just as it must have over a hundred years before. Hell, it may have gone largely unchanged for twice that period, for all Jack knew.

The carpet, a deep red that matched the crimson window front, spread before them into a pleasantly dark interior. An older woman with an Irish accent greeted them as they entered. Jack wandered through the pub as Throckmorton sat at the bar for another drink, and Potter spoke with the Irish woman.

Air Marshal Downes joined Jack beside the bar. Jack pointed. "Right back there is where the hallway was supposed to have been." Indeed, just as Longinotti had reported, there was a small curtain draped across what appeared to be a narrow hallway, on the side of the bar furthest from the entrance.

Downes nodded and showed the woman his credentials. "Madam," he began, "there is a matter of great importance that these gentlemen," he indicated Jack and Throckmorton, "are here to investigate. I am Air Marshal Percival Downes of the Royal Air Force. This is Special Agent Jack Quintana of the U.S. Air Force Office of Special Investigations, and Sir Thurgood Throckmorton, Eleventh Earl of Nottingham. Potter, I believe, you already know."

The woman looked partly impressed and mostly skeptical, but the Air Marshal was in his uniform, and he did have the credentials.

"Jaysus Christ above," she said, setting a fist on her hip. "We got Air Marshals, Earls, and Special Agents, all come for a pint before noon on a Wednesday."

Jack was interested to learn the day of the week, as he'd lost track some time ago.

"Well?" she asked. "What would ya like ta' see, then?"

Jack moved behind the bar, indicated the curtain, and pulled it aside. A very tight hallway led back, deeper into the building, from the front of the bar. Jack swung his crutch forward and followed it, the Irish woman close behind.

"P'raps ya' might tell me what it is yer lookin' for?" she said.

"We're looking for a wooden door," Jack answered, "at the end of this hallway."

"Ain't nuttin' back there but a brick wall."

As Jack reached the end of the hallway, he was disappointed to see the lady was right. His eyes adjusted to the gloom, and the hallway ended in (*ta-da*) a brick wall. "How long have you worked here?" Jack asked, turning to her.

"Been workin' here since me Da' bought the place in '79."

"Has that wall always been there?"

"What kind of a question's that? A 'course it's always been there."

Jack turned back to the wall and examined the brick, which was red, like the window front and the carpet. To the left was another brick wall. The wall on the right had been paneled in some kind of wood, and one of the owners had wallpapered over it. The brick on the left, however, had a different, older quality than the brick at the end of the hallway.

"It's false," Jack said to himself. Then, louder, "It's false!" He turned around, and the woman backed up in front of him as he crutched his way to the bar.

Downes and Potter went down the hallway to examine the wall, but Thurgood set his beer down and walked out. Jack frowned and went to the door. "Throck?" he called out.

Thurgood waved over his shoulder. "Be right back, Jacky boy."

Jack watched him walk over to a construction crew digging around a manhole. Jack heard one of them tell Throckmorton to "piss off." Throckmorton pulled cash from his wallet. The workers stopped what they were doing and lent him their full attention.

After a brief negotiation, one of them handed Throckmorton a sledgehammer. He sketched a little salute, rested the sledge against one shoulder, and walked back to Jack.

"My boy," he said, "as you are nothing if not indisposed, please allow me to do the honors."

Potter looked nervous. "Here, mate. You can't go doin' no demo-lition on a buildin' of this vintage without a permit."

The lady behind the bar narrowed her eyes at Throckmorton and jabbed a finger in his direction. "You take that hammer to one square inch a' my (moi) pub, and I'll see the London historical society bars ya' from enterin' the city for the rest a' yer everlastin' life."

Throckmorton raised the sledgehammer with a flourish and cried, "Step aside, woman."

She stepped aside.

Throckmorton stalked down the hall with the sledge raised over his right shoulder. As he approached the end of the passage, he pushed the sledge up, let it drop behind him, and swung it forward like a polo player, sans mount.

The sledge plowed through the bricks with a small, thudding explosion. Brick chips and dust peppered the air. Throckmorton backed up, kneeled, and peered through the hole.

"Jacky boy," he said. "Buy me a drink."

Five minutes later, Throckmorton sat at the bar with a water glass of the pub's finest whiskey. Potter, having forgotten all about city permits, whacked away at the rest of the false wall. Downes tried to tell him how and where to swing the hammer.

The Irish lady, intrigued, changed her tune and helped clear the fallen bricks. "Forty years I been here, and I never once suspected nothin' strange about that red brick wall. Now dat I see it, a'course, it's almost obvious it's false."

Gradually, as Potter swung and Downes directed and Thurgood sipped his drink, a white, wooden door emerged. There was a brass latch on the left side of the door.

"Potter!" Jack called from behind Downes. "Try the latch!"

"Try the latch, he says." Potter laughed. "That'll be locked, is what." He reached past the remnants of the false wall and pushed the latch down.

The door swung inward, into darkness.

* * *

Potter wanted to lead the way but deferred to Downes, who was, after all, a high-ranking military officer. Jack limped back out to the construction crew and paid them thirty pounds for a couple of battered flashlights.

"What'll you want with a torch, then?" one asked.

"What's goin' on in 'at pub?" the other asked.

Jack left them to their labors and went back inside. He gave one flashlight to the Air Marshal and another to Throckmorton. They proceeded inside in a line: Downes, Potter, Jack, and Throckmorton, who brought his drink along.

To Jack's surprise, the lady behind the bar found another flashlight somewhere and brought up the rear. "It's my place, now me Da's died, it is. I'll come along if I like."

Nobody wanted to argue with her.

The underground passage beyond the white door dropped sharply and then leveled out. They walked on a raised, wrought iron platform that hung several feet above brackish water of unknown depth. Rats scrabbled over stone in the darkness.

The iron platform seemed sturdy for the first hundred yards or so. Then it began to sway back and forth in sections that had detached from the wall but were still connected to the overall structure.

The Irish lady had been brave about the rats, but she turned back when the platform started to sway. Jack didn't hold it against her.

Perhaps two hundred yards further ahead, the passage widened into a cavernous space that reminded Jack of Longinotti's cave in the Ozarks. Jack stopped on the platform, leg throbbing, and Throckmorton shone his flashlight around. Down and to the right, he illuminated the lowered Operations Floor. A few wooden chairs poked up from three feet of standing water. Jack saw an old radar display on an upright table against a far wall.

Straight ahead, the platform led to an open doorway. Beyond the doorway, they found Longinotti's reported "big room." On the left wall of this room, a vault door loomed, now covered in cobwebs and dust. The vault was closed and locked.

From the corridor behind them, Jack heard a faint *pop* and then a scream. Throckmorton whirled, "What in bloody hell was that?"

Downes brushed past them and ran back toward the bar at a quick trot, Potter and Throckmorton close behind. Jack hobbled after them.

From far ahead, Jack heard Downes shout something unintelligible. "Throck!" Jack called. "What's going on up there?"

He saw Throckmorton's flashlight far ahead. "What the devil?" Throckmorton said faintly. Jack saw him take a swing at someone in front of him. The punch was a bit wild, and Jack didn't hear the impact. There was an "*Oof!*" sound, and Throckmorton dropped to the iron platform.

Someone picked up his flashlight, stepped over him, and shone the light straight down the corridor at Jack. Blinded, injured, and with nowhere to go but back to the vault door, Jack walked forward to meet Throckmorton's attacker.

The figure came toward him down the passageway. At about ten yards, the figure commanded, "Stop!" Jack heard an accent. "You will please to drop crutches."

Jack dropped the crutches and leaned against the metal railing.

"Good-good," the figure said.

"Vitoli?" Jack asked.

The figure approached and kept the light in his eyes. "Move to side, please."

Jack moved closer to the railing. The man had a pistol in his right hand, trained on Jack's stomach. He squeezed past Jack to get behind him. "Okay," the man said. "Pick up crutches. We walk."

Jack clung to the railing with his left hand, retrieved the crutches with his right, and started forward. Another dark figure emerged from the gloom ahead, helped Throckmorton to his feet, and led him back toward the bar.

"I am sorry for your wound," the man said from behind Jack.

"What?"

"I am hoping you are healthy when I am seeing you again."

Jack turned and got a look at the man's face. It was Vitoli.

The Russian shoved him forward. Jack's injured leg collided with the railing. He sucked a breath of damp air and kept moving.

"That's awfully nice of you to say, considering what I must have done to your family jewels."

"Damage was not so bad," Vitoli said.

"Sorry to hear that. I was hoping I'd eliminated your DNA from the human gene pool forever."

Vitoli laughed: a rich, baritone blast. It echoed through the passage.

"You are hurting my pride, maybe."

"I am hurting your pride, definitely. Unless you weren't proud of it in the first place, in which case, your ego would be questionable, but still intact."

"I cannot follow your sentence."

"Skip it."

"Now, you are wounded, and hand-to-hand combat would not be... how do you say... enjoyment?"

"Close enough."

"When you are feeling better, then I will kill you."

"Good to know."

That laugh came once more, and Jack smiled. Despite being a murderous bastard who worked for the Chinese mob, when you came right down to it, Vitoli wasn't such a bad guy.

Another surprise greeted him at the first section of the tunnel, where the floor pitched upward to meet the white door. There, in black tactical pants, white silk blouse, and stitches that tracked from her right temple to her left collarbone, was Xiao.

"Well, hello there, Frankenstein," Jack said.

She popped him squarely on the chin, and he crashed to the floor. "Get him into the bar," Xiao yelled.

Vitoli grabbed a handful of his shirt and dragged him the rest of the way into the bar. The pain in his leg had him groaning by the time Vitoli laid him out on the carpeted floor.

The Irish lady sat unharmed on a bar stool, mouth shut and eyes wide. Throckmorton helped Jack into a sitting position. Downes and Potter sat gagged and tied.

"Light me a smoke, would you?" Jack groaned to Throckmorton.

"Get up," Xiao said to Throckmorton, holding a pistol to his head. "Sit at the bar."

Thurgood looked at Jack, and Jack nodded. "I've seen her shoot people," Jack said.

Xiao knelt in front of him, found his cigarettes, lit one, and put it between his lips. "Thanks, Frankie," Jack said around the unfiltered Camel. "You're always so sweet to me."

She smiled and punched his wounded leg. He blacked out.

* * *

Some time later, he awoke to a setting sun. People walked up to the pub's doors, found them locked, and walked away again. Jack saw a "Closed" sign in one of the windows and curtains draped over all the others.

The Irish lady sat in one of the booths, smoking and looking pissed off. Downes and Potter were still tied to chairs, but their gags had been removed. Someone, probably Vitoli, had moved them to opposite sides of the pub so they couldn't speak to each other. Throckmorton sat on the floor next to Jack.

Xiao stood at the bar and watched the large television in the corner. Good old Olivia Knowlton was still on the scene, hair flying in the breeze.

Someone had admitted Olivia to the base, which Jack thought was poor judgment. She stood on a grassy incline that sloped upward toward the 36th Wing Headquarters building. Jack saw the windows that looked out from General Carter's office over the flight line. Carter had pulled the shades.

The camera panned around 180 degrees, and Olivia moved with it, careful to keep her well-tended face in the frame. Now, down the grassy slope and across Arc Light Boulevard, Jack saw a line of B-52s, a group of C-130s, and a contingent of F/A-18 *SuperHornets*, these last from the *U.S.S. Ronald Reagan.*

"From this incline," Olivia began, positioning herself so the wind would sweep her chestnut hair at just the right angle, "we can see the B-52 bombers, Navy Fighter jets from the *Ronald Reagan,* and some propeller driven cargo aircraft that are also used for what's known as "Close Air Support."

Jack was proud of her. She learned her terminology quickly.

"In a spirit of transparency," she continued, "Brigadier General Michael Carter, whose headquarters you just saw, has allowed us to set up our cameras here on this grassy slope. Thus far, the officials at

Andersen Air Force Base have been very transparent. They seem to want to communicate that the U.S. military has nothing to hide here. In just a few moments, a helicopter from," she looked at her notes, "Helicopter Sea Combat Squadron 25, will take us up and over the flight line, and out to sea, where we expect to catch a glimpse of the *Ronald Reagan,* and perhaps even the carrier *Shandong,* which lies fifty miles further out.

"The U.S. Air Force's 69th Reconnaissance Group detachment here has reported the Chinese vessels at Palau and Yap have deployed small boats. In the boats are teams of divers, who seem to be searching for something, although we don't yet understand what that might be.

"The overall situation has gotten very tense here, as a Chinese Fighter from the *Shandong* and a *SuperHornet* from the *Ronald Reagan* engaged in a short dog-fight over the open ocean, just three hours ago. According to the information we've been able to gather, neither jet was damaged in the dog-fight. In light of the risk of escalation, however, the *SuperHornet* pilot, who may have initiated the confrontation, has been grounded here at Andersen Air Force base. We have seen no further activity from the Chinese fighter jets, so some sort of compromise seems to have been achieved.

"The pilot of the *SuperHornet,*" she flipped through her notebook, "was reported as a 'Lieutenant Commander A.P. Rousey.' We've asked for a full rundown on Lieutenant Commander Rousey's flight history, but the Navy has not been forthcoming with those details.

"One further item that may be of grave importance: The U.S. Navy's Third Fleet, primarily responsible for defense of the Northern Pacific Ocean, has deployed Carrier Strike Groups Nine and Eleven, including the Aircraft Carriers *U.S.S. Theodore Roosevelt* and *U.S.S. Nimitz,* to the defense of Guam and Palau, respectively. The order to deploy these additional Strike Groups from the U.S. Third Fleet was given some time ago. They are now within four hundred miles of either location.

"This report comes on top of another we received, just a few moments ago, that the Chinese Navy's flagship destroyer *Nanchang* has entered the Luzon Strait. The *Nanchang* is reportedly flanked by four nuclear submarines, although we do not have the names of those vessels at this time. However, according to Open Source Intelligence, there are a total of five nuclear submarines stationed at the Yulin Naval Base on Hainan island, where the *Nanchang* originated.

"These nuclear submarines can carry up to twelve "JL-2" intercontinental ballistic missiles, or ICBMs. The "JL-2" ICBMS have a range of approximately 4,300 nautical miles. The U.S. Territory of Guam is over 6,000 miles from Los Angeles, and approximately 5,800 miles from San Francisco, putting these ICBMs just out of range of the U.S. mainland, if deployed from the vicinity of Guam. However, Honolulu is just 3,800 miles from Guam, and would be well within the range of a JL-2 ICBM."

Xiao had tossed Jack's cigarettes on the floor beside him. He pulled out a Camel, lit up, and continued to watch the intrepid reporter. She boarded a van with her camera crew and gave a play-by-play of her experience as the van rolled up Arc Light Boulevard toward Helicopter Sea Combat Squadron 25.

Xiao walked to the pub's front door, peered out into the darkening street, and twisted the bolt open. Bo Feng walked in wearing a three-piece suit. A slight, nervous Chinese man in coveralls accompanied him.

"Agent Quintana!" Bo greeted him. "And Sir Throckmorton. How wonderful to see you again."

"My luck just won't run out," Jack said, dragging on the Camel.

Throckmorton rose, poured two beers, and walked them over to the bartender. She was pretty in a rough kind of way. "Won't you assist me, good lady?" he asked. "Air Marshal Downes and Mr. Potter look positively parched."

She gave him a smile and took one of the pints over to the Air Marshal. Thurgood tended to Potter.

Bo motioned to Vitoli. "Those two can have one hand free," he said. "We are not barbarians, after all."

Vitoli shrugged and untied each man's left hand, leaving the other hand and both legs secured to either chair.

149

"You're a hell of a guy, Bo," Jack said.

"Agent Quintana, if you feel you are able to do so, please accompany me and my associate into the passage. I don't believe it is necessary to keep any secrets from each other."

Jack looked at the television. Olivia hammed it up while her crew unloaded next to a helicopter. Jack was amused to see the same helicopter gunner from their private island getaway give the reporter a long glance. She blushed. How sweet.

"Whatever you say, fella," Jack replied, and struggled to his feet. Bo did not offer to help. "Just answer me one question."

"And what is that?" Bo asked, gesturing for Jack to precede him into the passageway. The nervous little fellow in the coveralls leaned through the white doorway with a blazing flashlight in one hand and a large pack in the other.

"How in God's name did you people track me down?"

Bo laughed. "You Americans are so in love with your technology. You think that if you sweep for listening devices and GPS trackers, you are safe."

"Go on," Jack said, limping ahead on the hated crutches.

"Our people are more focused on Human Intelligence. That is, we use people to accomplish tasks, and do not restrict ourselves to technological gizmos."

"I'm not following you, Bo."

"Aircraft have tail numbers. Do they not?"

"As far as I can remember," Jack agreed.

"A tail number is something that is easily seen and recorded. Pilots are not careful about hiding a tail number, because it's right there on the side of the aircraft."

"Okay."

"We paid one of the paramedics who transported you to the airfield on Andersen Air Force base to copy down the tail number of your C-17 and then deliver it to us. While we were unsuccessful in our attempt to learn where you landed within the continental United States, we were notified of your C-17's flight plan to Heathrow shortly after it was filed. We have people in every major airport in the world who track such things for us."

Jack shook his head, grunted, and crutched forward after the nervous little man. The man stopped and started. He peered at the ceiling and the walls. He took photos of cracks when he found them, jotted notes, and continued forward.

"Planning a little something, are we?" Jack asked him.

The man glanced at Jack, adjusted his glasses, and went back to his inscrutable tasks.

They passed the area that opened on the lowered operations floor and then entered Longinotti's "big room."

The little man, whom Jack had come to think of as "the engineer," studied the vault door. A name was stamped into the steel atop the vault's giant, circular door: "Mosler." Jack recognized the name of the company that had constructed a vault for a Hiroshima bank. After the war, the vault had become famous for its having withstood the nuclear blast; the contents found safe and whole inside.

The engineer sucked air through his teeth when his flashlight found the company name. Bo said something harsh. The engineer cringed and replied in a deferential manner, but he did not seem hopeful.

Bo told him something else, and the engineer began to sweat. His head bobbed up and down. *Yes, yes. I can do it.*

"What did you tell him?" Jack asked.

Bo shrugged and examined his fingernails. "I told him we understand his family is very important to him."

Jack watched as the engineer scrambled around in front of the vault door, and pitied him.

"There's no way you're going to blow that door without bringing this whole tunnel down around us."

"We shall see, Agent Quintana," Bo answered. "Let us return to the bar."

* * *

Bo poured a glass of Jameson for each of them. Jack dry swallowed another Hydrocodone and pushed the whiskey glass back. "Now that we've gotten to know each other," Jack said, "I don't want to drink with you anymore."

"Now, now," Bo said. "Come, Agent Quintana. Don't let's be at odds. We're both after the same thing, after all."

"I'm not so sure about that." Vitoli shot billiards by himself on the other side of the pub. The ceramic balls clacked intermittently.

"But what, exactly, might we both be after?" Bo asked.

"If you think I'm going to tell you that," Jack said, "you're dumber than Vitoli."

Bo stiffened, sipped his Jameson, and then smiled. "Either way, Jack, we'll get it. We have hostages here, after all."

"Your hostages are worthless. Half the cops in London will swarm this place ten minutes after you blow that door."

"We're probably not going to blow it."

"No?" Jack asked, glancing at the television.

Olivia leaned through the helicopter door, looking heroic. The camera panned from her face to the ocean below. Jack saw the *U.S.S. Ronald Reagan* a few miles outside the reef, other helicopters approaching and departing, the carrier a hive of activity. He felt certain Olivia would win some kind of award for this coverage. He also felt certain she felt certain of the same.

Throckmorton pulled up a barstool, swiped Jack's whiskey, and drained it. Bo gave him a look. Throckmorton ignored him.

"When you're quite ready," Bo said, rising from the bar, "come see what we have planned."

"I'll do that," Jack replied, watching the helicopter pass over the aircraft carrier.

"I was in the Navy at one time," Throckmorton said.

Jack turned to him. "Really?"

"Oh, yes. I was a Left-Tenant on Her Majesty's Ship *Alacrity* during the 10-week 'Falklands War.' We swabbed the decks with those bloody Argentines, what? Glorious."

"Throck, you become more interesting with every passing day."

"Why, thank you, Jacky boy."

Jack watched Vitoli shoot bad Billiards and fought a wave of frustration. If only Xiao hadn't put this hole in his leg. Jack considered himself a man of action, sometimes even when the situation indicated patience and discretion the wiser choice.

Xiao stood at the pub doors with a pistol in her hand, surveilling both the street and the pub's interior. Mobile phones were heaped in a pile behind the bar. Jack spied his Iridium atop the jumble.

"Come on," he said to Throckmorton. "Let's see what that twitchy engineer is up to."

Vitoli fell in behind them as they re-entered the passage beyond the bar.

"I'm afraid you're not invited, old chum," Throckmorton told him without looking back.

Vitoli said nothing and strolled along, keeping pace as Jack struggled forward.

Bo turned a light on them as they approached the vault door. "So glad you decided to join us," he said.

The engineer had removed a pile of explosive charges from his large pack. They lay on the floor in an ordered mound, but it didn't appear as if he intended to use them.

To the face of the vault door, over the locking mechanism, the man had affixed a curious, spindly metal device. To Jack, it looked like a mechanical spider. Three, sturdy legs had been epoxied to the steel surface. These legs extended to the door from a central disk that was aligned horizontally with the locking mechanism, about twelve inches out from it. From this central disk, a straight piston extended back toward and affixed itself to the vault dial by a clamp.

"The explosives are a last resort," Bo said. "We will try to crack the combination first."

Jack felt keen interest and low dread. "I thought you Chinese weren't into the gizmos."

"Technology has its place."

The engineer ran a USB cable from a port on the disk to a laptop computer. Another, thicker cable issued from the far side of the disk,

153

and Jack recognized it as a 220-volt power cable. The little man plugged it in to a heavy battery pack, checked something on the laptop, and looked at Bo Feng.

Bo said something. The engineer selected an option on the laptop, and the piston connecting the central disk to the vault dial began to spin back and forth in a rapid sequence. One spin to the left, one spin to the right, another spin to the left, and then a sharp attempt at a final, right-spin rotation. Every time the vault failed to open, the laptop bleeped, signaling failure, and started a new combination entry.

Jack looked at Bo with raised eyebrows. "This is ridiculous," he said. "You could be at it for weeks with this thing."

"I think not," Bo answered. "The combination entry patterns are not random. The disk on the breaker interacts with a program on the hard drive, on which is loaded a comprehensive library of known vault combinations associated with British military operations, intelligence organizations, and even banks. Our organization compiled this 'combination library' by adding stolen combinations to a mounting collection, in the hopes that we could someday predict the kinds of combinations that a person of any given nationality might utilize, based on cultural influence and consequent, general tendency."

"Hogwash," Throckmorton scoffed. "I'm going back for another drink."

"This little fellow," Bo indicated the engineer, "lives right here in Soho. He's been cracking safes for us since the early nineties."

The engineer stared at the laptop screen. "The breaker is his design," Bo said, turning back to the doorway. "I'm afraid there won't be much more to see until we're in."

* * *

Vitoli helped Downes and Potter to the restroom on Bo's order. Xiao wandered back and forth between the bar and the vault and ignored Jack in an obvious way. Throckmorton threw darts at a battered board on the wall.

Bo sat in a booth and played cards with the Irish lady. Jack waited at the bar, eyes on the television. He nursed a Guinness and tried not to think about what might happen to Downes or Potter if the engineer wound up cracking the vault combination. If the objective was not immediately evident upon quick examination of the vault, which, Jack was sure it would not be, Bo would get violent in a hurry.

He would want to know exactly what Jack and Throckmorton were after. If they refused to cough up the information, Jack felt sure Potter would be the first man to eat a bullet. After that, if Jack and Throckmorton still remained mute, things would get complicated. They wouldn't want to kill Throckmorton because of his long-term status as a diplomat connected with China. Of course, they wouldn't want to kill the Air Marshal either, as executing high-ranking military officials tended to come with its down-side.

In that case, Jack figured, the Irish lady would be next to go. After that, who knew?

Olivia grasped a lanyard and effected a daring lean from the helicopter. Below them, dominating the ocean like a leviathan, lay the *Shandong*. Multiple "J-15" *Shenyang* fighters screamed around the carrier in a tight holding pattern. A Chinese search and rescue helicopter approached the U.S. Navy chopper.

Olivia's eyes gleamed.

"...approaching from the carrier *Shandong*," Olivia cried into the microphone. "They've positioned a small vessel directly below us," she continued, and the camera dipped over the side of the chopper to record the activity. "The Captain of the Shandong has invited us to board the carrier, but our U.S. Navy pilot cannot land on the Chinese vessel. Therefore," wind from the helicopter blades whipped her hair around her face, "we have agreed to disembark this aircraft and transfer to the Chinese helicopter by way of the boat waiting below us."

The cameraman pointed his lens at the U.S. Navy helicopter gunner, who prepared a rescue basket for the brave reporter. Olivia continued, "Our helicopter pilot did not want to allow this transfer. However, we called back to General Carter's office and explained the situation. If our reporting is accurate, we should see a civilian helicopter arrive at the *Shandong* within the next few minutes. On that helicopter will be the Governor of Guam and a Chinese Linguist from the Naval Base. General Carter has authorized us to transfer to the Chinese helicopter if..."

The cameraman pointed past Olivia as a white helicopter with the "Government of Guam" logo appeared and descended toward the *Shandong*. "This is it now!" Olivia shouted. The cameraman zoomed in on the white helicopter, which swooped over the carrier's deck and descended. Chinese Navy personnel on the *Shandong's* deck guided it in.

The gunner indicated Olivia should step into the rescue basket. She turned to the camera, eyes ablaze, and said, "I will now enter this basket, and the crewman will lower me to the Chinese vessel! My cameraman, Bill Warren, will follow me down, and we'll transfer to the Chinese carrier together."

Jack watched as the crewman loaded her into the basket. She seemed to want to take the microphone with her, but the crewman directed her to hand it to the cameraman, and she relented. The basket swung away from the helicopter, and Olivia grasped the handholds. She looked terrified, but she managed to keep at least half of her face exposed to the camera during the entire descent. Jack thought she'd make a terrific actress.

The cameraman followed. He was less interesting than Olivia and had nobody to keep the camera trained on him. The satellite video feed stopped, evidently to accommodate his transition from the U.S. helicopter to the Chinese vessel. The President of the United States, whom most networks had ignored in favor of Olivia, came on from the Oval Office in mid-sentence.

"...of utmost importance to America and its allies in the Pacific region. We will stand firm in our defense of Guam and the surrounding territory. However, we will take and create every opportunity to negotiate de-escalation through diplomacy and deliberate communication with the Chinese government."

Suddenly, from deep in the tunnel, the engineer gave a shout. Bo Feng slid from his booth and dropped his cards on the floor. Xiao stopped her endless pacing, and Vitoli stepped to the bar. Bo said something to Xiao, which Jack took to mean "stay put." She nodded in return.

Vitoli pointed at Jack and Throckmorton. "You will please to accompany."

Jack slid from the barstool, grabbed his crutches, and hitched himself toward the tunnel entrance again. Bo Feng walked in front of Jack, Throckmorton close behind. Once more, Vitoli brought up the rear.

Jack could no longer hear the rotating, ratcheting sound of the combination breaker. The engineer waited for them at the doorway beyond the lowered operations floor.

They stepped back into the room. The engineer had already removed the breaker from the vault dial, repacked his equipment, backup explosives included, and stowed the laptop.

Bo Feng had a word with the engineer. Throckmorton whispered a translation as Vitoli stood somewhere behind them. "The engineer says the breaker worked, and the vault is now unlocked. Bo is telling the man to open it. The man says he needs help with the wheel."

Vitoli started to come forward, but Bo waved him back. "Sir Throckmorton," Bo invited, "would you be so kind as to assist this man with the bolt retraction wheel?"

"Do it yourself, why don't you? What do I look like, your bloody valet?"

Bo produced a pistol from a shoulder holster.

"When you put it that way, old boy, it would be my pleasure."

Throckmorton positioned himself to the right of the bolt retraction wheel, while the engineer stood on the left. An arrow, stamped into the steel behind the wheel, indicated the wheel should be turned to the left in order to retract the security bolts inside the door. *Lefty loosey,* Jack thought.

Throckmorton grabbed one spoke of the rusty wheel in both hands; the engineer did the same on the other side. "One, two, *three.*" Throckmorton grunted, pulling the wheel upward on his side as the engineer pulled down on his own. With a grinding, shrieking rasp, the time-worn retraction mechanism responded to the pressure. "Keep going!" Throckmorton gasped as the engineer repositioned his hands.

The wheel made three complete revolutions, and stopped. Throckmorton stood in front of the wheel, took it in both hands, and tugged. The door slid forward an inch, rotating on hidden hinges to Throckmorton's right. Bo motioned for Vitoli to assist. The Russian trotted up and grabbed a handhold on the left side of the door.

With a gigantic yank from Vitoli, the door moved outward again. Throckmorton skipped away to avoid being forced aside by the mammoth, steel door.

An alarm sounded from inside the vault. Jack looked at Bo, who appeared surprised and newly anxious. As the door continued to swing, a flashing, red light and bright incandescent bulbs shone from inside the vault. The alarm, which sounded like an air raid siren, brayed continuously.

The vault lights blinded them. Jack saw a small figure standing deep inside. The figure appeared to be holding a rifle.

"Throck!" He cried out. "Hit the floor!" Jack tossed his crutches aside and went down on his face just as the first volley of bullets ripped through the air above them. Bo took a knee and fired back. Jack grabbed one of his crutches, swung it around, and hit Bo just above the eye. Bo went down.

Vitoli was out of Jack's crutch range, but Jack could tell the Russian was firing blind. His eyes slitted against the brightness emanating from the vault. The figure inside seemed to be wearing a dress. Jack wondered if maybe he'd ingested a bit too much Hydrocodone.

Vitoli took a round in the stomach, doubled over, and fell on his side, his hands smothering the wound. Blood oozed between his fingers in a rapidly accumulating puddle.

"Who's there, please?" a pleasant, older woman's voice called out.

Who's there, please? Jack thought, and stifled a mad cackle.

"Hold your fire!" Throckmorton bellowed importantly. Another shot rang out from the vault.

"I shall dictate the terms of your surrender, thank you very much," the woman said.

"Right."

Jack crawled over to Vitoli and grabbed his weapon.

"Ma'am! Please hold your fire!" Jack hollered. "I'm Special Agent Jack Quintana, with the U.S. Air Force Office of Special Investigations."

Jack heard a clatter on the metal platform outside the big room. The engineer sprinted back toward the bar. The lady fired a shot from inside the vault. She winged him. He gripped his shoulder and kept running. She cursed. "Throw your weapons into the vault!" she cried.

To Jack's right, Bo raised his pistol. He lay in a narrow shadow, outside the woman's view. Blood trickled from the side of his head. Jack racked the slide on Vitoli's pistol, aimed, and blew out the gangster's left shoulder. Bo screamed and flung his gun aside. Throckmorton snagged it and tossed it into the vault. Jack followed suit.

"Nicely done, Jack!" Throckmorton called out to him.

"Oh, pish-tosh," the lady said. "He was only ten feet away. Anybody could have made that shot."

Jack struggled to his feet and peered into the light. Rows of lockboxes, like safe deposit boxes, lined the walls on both sides of the rectangular structure. Jack had to squint to see the far end. An attractive, sixty-something woman in a flowered dress held a Thompson Submachine gun, complete with .45 caliber drum magazine and wood stock.

Vitoli groaned on the floor to Jack's left. "Blast," the woman said. "Is he still alive?"

"For the moment," Jack answered. He looked to his right. Bo Feng had passed out.

Throckmorton rose from his crouch on the other side of Bo. "My friend will appear to your left," Jack called out.

The woman came forward. Scarred wooden tables were scattered here and there, inside. She approached the vault door.

"Madam," Throckmorton said, "I hereby introduce myself as Thurgood Wintersley Throckmorton, the Third," he said with a bow. "This," he motioned to Jack, "is my colleague, Agent Quintana."

The woman smirked. "You two make quite a pair." She still wielded the Thompson, although she aimed the barrel at the floor.

From behind him, Jack heard the pound and rattle of heavy footfalls on the iron platform. "That'll be the backup," the woman said, keeping her distance. Throckmorton stepped forward. She raised the Thompson. Throckmorton stepped back.

Three men in plain clothes approached from behind. "Hands up!" one of them said. Jack and Thurgood obliged. After a quick pat-down, the men triaged Vitoli and Bo Feng. They moved Bo Feng first, hauling him through the vault and out the other side. "If that one's still alive when they return," she said, gesturing toward Vitoli, "they'll take him along as well."

"Well," she said, backing into the massive vault with the Thompson in front of her. "Make yourselves at home, won't you?"

Jack and Throckmorton found a couple of chairs and pulled them to a table. The lady backed away another ten paces, dragged her own chair to a different table, and placed the Thompson down in front of her, hand on the pistol grip.

"That's better, isn't it, lads?" she said, shifting her gaze between them. "What's brought you to the bowels of our fair city?"

CHAPTER 7

Jack explained the events leading up to this strange interview as quickly as possible, although it still took twenty minutes. In that time, the three plain-clothed gentlemen returned with a stretcher, hauled Vitoli through the vault, and disappeared. Jack found it difficult to acknowledge the sheer size of the place. Though perhaps only thirty feet wide, Jack put it at better than 200 yards in length, and the ceiling lofted twenty feet.

One of the men doubled back and reported Air Marshal Downes and Mr. Potter had been debriefed and sent home. And, oh! The *Coach & Horses* would be open for business come tomorrow night, and wasn't that just fine?

Throckmorton agreed that it was. The man left.

"That story smells like a load of horseshit," the woman said. But she removed her right hand from the pistol grip, and Jack took that as an improvement. "Right," she said, "I've been on shift here for the past twelve hours, and I've got a bloody-awful headache. The steel on that door is so thick I didn't even hear anything 'til the wheel started to move. You two stay put while I ring up the Command Post."

She hefted the Thompson with her, snatched an old-fashioned, up-right candlestick telephone receiver from it's side-mounted fork, and dialed a three-digit number. "Twenty-Seven, here," she said into the receiver. "Yes, day watch at Twenty-Seven." She listened to a response and then proceeded.

"One: What is situation in Pacific between U.S. and China? Two: Request short-brief on one 'Special Agent Jack Quintana, U.S. Air Force Office of Special Investigations' and one 'Thurgood Wintersley Throckmorton, the Third,' probable British citizen. Three: Verify arrival of one American C-17 GlobeMaster at Heathrow International, some eighteen hours ago."

She removed the cup receiver from her ear and pressed a button beside the phone. A few moments later, an elderly attendant stepped through the vault door behind her. "You rang, mum?" he asked.

"Kelly," she replied, keeping her eyes on Jack and Thurgood, "be a dear and bring us some tea, would you?"

"Right away, mum," he replied, and disappeared.

Jack heard a tinny voice from the telephone receiver. She placed it over her ear and replied, "Go ahead, Command Post." She listened for three minutes as whomever was on the other end of the line gave her the information she'd requested.

"Right, Command Post," she said thoughtfully. "Request immediate lock combination reset on Twenty-Seven vault door, west facing, *Coach & Horses* entrance." After a moment's thought, she added, "Detain and debrief *Coach & Horses* proprietress. Send the bricklayer. That is all."

She replaced the receiver, walked to the other side of their table, leaving the Thompson behind her, and said, "So sorry for the inconvenience, gentlemen. Security's not what it used to be, I'm afraid, but we do what we can."

"That's quite all right," Jack said. Throckmorton agreed.

"You may call me 'Sam,' if you like," the woman informed them. Kelly arrived with the tea.

As Jack sipped the hot beverage, he asked, "Sam, if you don't mind, could you tell me anything about this vault, why it's here, and why you happened to be in it this evening?"

She studied him and answered, "I started working here in 1980, after two years of intensive training with the Secret Intelligence Service. There are more than forty of these vaults, spread out over the city. They were constructed in the late nineteen hundred and thirties. Churchill found we had so much paper intelligence streaming into London that the military simply couldn't keep track of it all, much less keep it secure and make any sense of it."

"But why are the vaults still in use today?" Throckmorton asked. "Surely the British government has more efficient ways to process classified information."

Sam squeezed the bridge of her nose, sipped her tea, and continued. "Oh, yes. Absolutely, we do. What we do *not* have," she said, "is an excess of personnel whom the S.I.S., or 'M.I.6.,' as the public likes to call it, trusts to review, translate, quantify, prioritize, and action this incredible store of highly sensitive information.

"These vaults were in use 'til the nineteen hundred and ninety's. We had fresh intelligence coming in all the time, which we prioritized over the old intelligence. The old intelligence was stored until such time as we could allocate the personnel to review it. As a consequence, much of the old intelligence has never actually been fully examined. But," she said, plopping a cube of sugar into her cup, "it's all still here. Waiting."

Jack took a moment to wrap his mind around that. "Why would General Harmon have directed Sergeant Longinotti to deliver the box to this location, specifically?"

"Easy," Sam replied. "Twenty-Seven, that is, Vault Number Twenty-Seven, is reserved for all intelligence originating from the Pacific Theater, to include China, Japan, Southeast Asia, India, the Indian Ocean, etcetera. We had S.I.S. agents at the bar in the *Coach & Horses* 'til the end of Vietnam. After that, the hard-copy human intelligence deliveries through the *Coach & Horses* slowed to a trickle and finally dried up completely. They bricked over the white door in 1978, I believe. You lovelies were the first to come through in forty-two years.

"After '78," she went on, "any new hard-copy intelligence from that theater would have been processed through Central Receiving and stored here in Twenty-Seven. This, gentlemen," she gestured lavishly, arm outstretched, "is the single storehouse of all hard-copy British Intelligence from the Pacific theater of operations, from Nineteen Hundred and Thirty Eight to Nineteen Hundred and Ninety Four."

"You should lead with that next time," Jack suggested, smiling.

"Perhaps I will," she laughed. "We don't get much company down here. Lots of time for introspection, and not much practice for the old social graces."

"Madam!" Throckmorton said. "You are under no obligation to explain yourself. I consider your introspection admirable, and your social graces pristine."

Sam looked at Jack. "He's not very trustworthy, is he?"

Throckmorton blustered, and Sam cut him off. "So," she said, rubbing her hands together. "I expect you'll be looking for that box, then?"

* * *

Sam focused on the name "Longinotti" and narrowed the search area to a ten yard stretch of lockboxes, under a much larger section entitled "1944."

"All the entries are organized and filed by last name of submitting agent, or, in this case, submitting Sergeant," she explained. "Unfortunately," she said, "from 1939 to 1945, the rush of submissions was so bloody overwhelming that the whole period is moderately disorganized. Had a bunch of *men* in here trying to sort everything. The poor dears made an absolute mess of it, though I'm sure they did what they could."

The lockboxes were of varying sizes, from six inches by eight inches up to two feet by four feet. Inside, each entry was separated from the next by an aluminum divider. After half an hour of digging, Sam's replacement arrived. She looked to be in her early fifties and had the same air of competent efficiency. While Sam continued to help Jack and Throckmorton search through "1944," Nell reloaded the Thompson, opened a large section of "1952," and began poring over documents.

Finally, Sam reached into one of the larger lockboxes, yanked something from it's depths, and proclaimed: "Got it!"

They moved to an antechamber off the primary vault and sat around an old table. An antique lamp illuminated the space. Sam examined the box. "That's silver," she said. "No box of aluminum ever looked like that."

To a wooden handle atop the silver box, someone, the "Jim" of antiquity, perhaps, had tied a small key with a short, rough thread. "Well," Sam said, "it's an American artifact. Go ahead, Jack."

Jack could sense her excitement. Every day, Sam delved into the unknown and considered situations perhaps nobody else on the planet could evaluate. Even if only one file in a thousand ever led to actionable intelligence, it was her responsibility to find it, identify it for what it was, brief it to her superiors, and, maybe, learn of the fruits of her diligence. She was a true investigator.

Jack inserted the key. Even after seventy-five years, it turned easily.

Atop a pile of yellowing paperwork sat the dispatch copy referenced by the old Chinese gentleman and Sergeant Longinotti. It read:

Headquarters, U.S. Army Air Forces Pacific Ocean Areas

Asan, Guam Island

12 December 1944

To: General Xue Yue, National Revolutionary Army, Kunming China

From: Lt Gen Millard Harmon, Commander, Army Air Forces Pacific Ocean Areas

Subject: Project Big Surf

(1) General, it is my privilege to report that the engineers your government provided have spurred our progress greatly, with regard to the initiative we discussed on Tinian Island.

(2) The Philippine Sea Project, or "Big Surf," as we have come to call it, is progressing on schedule. The Control Center on Guam Island will be operational in a matter of weeks.

(3) Once the Guam Island Control Center is finished, I plan to transport the project schematics and vital operational codes to Hickam Field. I invite you to join me at Hickam Field for a meeting with representatives of the British government, who have aided us since Big Surf's conception. The meeting is to take place on the 5th of March, at the former headquarters of Admiral Nimitz, the Commander in Chief, Pacific Ocean Areas. Admiral Nimitz is in the process of moving his headquarters to Guam Island but may still be able to attend.

(4) Please do not send a delegate, as we cannot risk admitting anyone but you and your personal staff. Considering the situation, I am sure you understand our caution. I am eager to relay the specifics of our progress, in full detail.

(5) The allied expansion through the Pacific advances steadily toward Japan. Soon, General McArthur informs me, he will liberate the Philippines. From there, we could knock on Hirohito's door until it splits. When Big Surf is unleashed, however, McArthur may find the Japanese in Manila scrambling back to Japan, and in no mood to hold their Philippine position.

Respectfully,

Lt Gen Millard Harmon

2/3

Under the dispatch copy, Jack found a file folder labeled "Project Big Surf." Inside, General Harmon had organized a series of official memorandums in chronological order. The first was from the Office of Scientific Research and Development:

Office of Scientific Research and Development

1530 P. St NW

Washington D.C.

18 September 1944

To: Lt General Millard Harmon, Commander, Army Air Forces Pacific Ocean Areas

From: B. Hastings, Director OSRD

Subject: Bombs of Enormous Explosive Energy

General:

With regard to your recent inquiry, I can inform you that our scientists at the Office of Scientific Research and Development have indicated, with greatest confidence, that the supplies necessary for development of three bombs of enormous explosive energy, or "Atomic Fission Bombs," are well in hand. We understand you are developing a plan whereby Allied Forces might use these bombs in offensive action against the Empire of Japan.

In addition to another, ongoing project along those same lines, I am authorized to tell you we intend to apportion a sizable quantity of plutonium, from the Hanford Engineer Works, to your project directly.

At your earliest opportunity, please provide us with further details about your project. Our engineers will require an intimate knowledge of your intended method and goal before they will be able to design the bombs to fit your purpose.

Sincerely Yours,

B. Hastings

The second memorandum was a response from Lt General Harmon to B. Hastings of the Office of Scientific Research and Development:

Headquarters, U.S. Army Air Forces Pacific Ocean Areas

Asan, Guam Island

10 October 1944

To: B. Hastings, Office of Scientific Research and Development

From: Lt Gen Millard Harmon, Commander, Army Air Forces Pacific Ocean Areas

Subject: Project Big Surf

(1) I am greatly encouraged to learn that the necessary supplies are readily available. Whom should I contact in order to requisition the weapons?

(2) The details of Project Big Surf are being refined at my headquarters on Guam Island now. I have apprised Admiral Nimitz, who plans to move operational Pacific Ocean Areas Headquarters from Pearl Harbor to Guam in the very near future, and he has directed me to proceed with all haste.

(3) We would like to have all three Atomic Fission Bombs in place here on Guam Island no later than 31 January 1945. I recognize that this request may seem presumptuous. However, following a detailed operational planning session with a number of American scientists and engineers of the Royal Navy, Admiral Nimitz has full faith and confidence in the practicality and utility of Big Surf.

(4) I enclose with this memo a compilation of schematics, including exact bomb placement sites, latitude and longitude references, known submarine geography, detonation sequencing, and exact distances between each bomb site and the Japanese mainland. Furthermore, I have included a short briefing that will illustrate the overall concept of Big Surf. I trust your Office will find this technical information sufficient to inform the bombs' design and optimal explosive capacity.

(5) I will make every effort to return to Hickam Field within the next two weeks. When I have done so, I will phone your office directly, so that we may discuss the matter at length.

Respectfully,

Lt Gen Millard Harmon

Next, a memo from the Secretary of War:

War Department

Washington

29 October 1944

Lieutenant General Harmon,

Yesterday, I met with Dr. Hastings of the Office of Scientific Research and Development. Dr. Hastings informed me of your collaboration and recent telephone conversation with regard to "Project Big Surf."

I cannot condone the brash manner in which you have driven this project, almost to conclusion, with neither communication to nor blessing from the War Department. However, your initiative is beyond reproach, and Dr. Hastings has expressed great confidence in the project's viability.

In that light, I have authorized various elements within the War Department to coordinate directly with Dr. Hastings's office. Your Atomic Fission bombs will be manufactured before Christmas, and Hastings will select a trusted team to supervise their delivery to Guam by the end of January, 1945.

Finally, I cannot stress enough that these bombs WILL NOT BE DETONATED without express permission, either from me or from President Roosevelt himself. Initiative is encouraged; insubordination is not.

Yours,

Henry L. Stimson

Secretary of War

"Walking on thin ice, there," Sam said clucking her tongue. Throckmorton grunted his agreement. The final memorandum was from B. Hastings to General Harmon:

Office of Scientific Research and Development

1530 P. St NW

Washington D.C.

25 November 1944

To: Lt General Millard Harmon, Commander, Army Air Forces POA

From: B. Hastings, Director OSRD

Subject: Atomic Fission Bombs

General:

I am pleased to report that your plutonium bombs are complete. Design of the required watertight containers is underway, and I expect our engineers will have the finished products ready for shipment no later than mid-December.

The watertight containers will appear nondescript; ordinary. Essentially, they are simple aluminum boxes supported by steel skeletons. Inside, a rubber bladder of five inch thickness will encapsulate each bomb, preventing water intrusion. An insulated electrical cable will run from each bomb, through the rubber bladder, and out to the exterior surface of the aluminum container, whereupon a submersible antennae will be affixed to receive the relevant radio signal from your Guam Island control center.

I understand that your engineers and divers will affix the bombs to prepared, underwater platforms. I trust you will find the containers' construction complementary to your platform design, and you should have no trouble situating the devices at Palau and Yap. Incidentally, my engineers agree that placing the final bomb outside Guam Island's northern reef would be too disruptive to your airfield. Consequently, we recommend that you move the final bomb to the north side of Rota Island, which lies forty miles northeast of Guam.

My hand selected team, along with a contingent of Army security personnel, will accompany these boxes from their point of origin to Hamilton Field, California. From Hamilton Field, the bombs will each be loaded onto a separate B-29 Superfortress, and will follow the South Pacific Air Ferry route to Hickam Field. After refueling in Hawaii, the B-29s will continue to Midway Island, and then on to Guam Island.

Following delivery to Guam Island, the B-29 aircrews will, of course, be at your disposal for further transport, in accordance with the details

170

of Project Big Surf. My office will notify you when transport from point of origin has begun. Good luck.

Sincerely Yours,

B. Hastings

From under this last correspondence, Jack pulled a sheaf of technical papers, including diagrams, schematics, and calculations that none of them could decipher. Jack rifled through these documents as quickly as possible and tried not to damage them.

"Throck," he mumbled, spreading the remaining paperwork out over the old, scratched wooden table, "I'm not seeing any coordinates or activation codes."

Sam and Throckmorton stood and examined each page in detail, eyes narrowed for any indication of the missing information. Jack felt a drop of sweat run down his left cheek. Without the final details, this whole mission was lost. Had they come all the way from Guam to Missouri, from Missouri to Heathrow, from Heathrow to Covent Garden, from hostages to unwitting invaders of the Secret Intelligence Service's inner sanctum, only to reach a dead end?

"Damn!" Jack said, and slapped the table with his right hand. He left the antechamber and walked back toward the open vault door. S.I.S. security now lined the underground passage, from the vault to the bar, waiting for the vault combination to be reset and the false wall to be reconstructed.

He lit a cigarette and wracked his brain. *What happened to the coordinates and the codes? Were they still here, locked away in one of these metal boxes on the wall? If so, how would they find them without searching every last compartment? How long would that take? How many people would the Brits allow into Twenty-Seven to assist? When...*

"Jack," Sam called, pulling a small, manila envelope from the roof of the compartment. "I thought something like this may have happened," she said, grinning. "Sometimes, when S.I.S. thought that keeping an entire file together would be too dangerous, despite all of this," she spread her arms to indicate the massive vault, "they would tape a note to the inside of the compartment, indicating where the remaining portions of the intelligence had been transported. That way, in the unlikely event the physical intelligence we have here were compromised, another layer of security would lay between the enemy and the most important elements of the compilation."

She placed the envelope on the table. "I've seen this only once before," she said, and bit her lower lip. "It was something to do with..." she stopped and straightened, "well, something that I'm not at liberty to share with the likes of you, am I?"

Jack smiled. "Can I see the note?"

She pushed it across the table. Jack tamped his cigarette in a nearby ashtray and opened the envelope. The note read:

From the Desk of Field Marshall Sir Reginald Saxon

Dear Reader,

The contents of this intelligence packet, being what they are, have troubled me greatly these last few weeks, since the American Sergeant placed the damnable thing in my hands.

For that reason, I have removed the most sensitive elements and entrusted them to my personal assistant, Flight Sergeant James McPherson. I have issued Sergeant McPherson strict instructions to transport these elements to Royal Air Force Station Diego Garcia, which was activated in the Indian Ocean, in 1942.

RAF Diego Garcia, which I chanced to visit during a tour of the Chagos Archipelago, is sufficiently remote, in my estimation, as to guaranty the security of these few bits of information critical to the function of "Project Big Surf." I suspect General Harmon sent us these details as insurance against the possibility that he or his trusted agents, as related to "Big Surf," became incapacitated before the Project could be operationalized.

Because that eventuality is so desperately remote, I feel justified in my decision to separate these vital components from the overall Project documentation. However, if those details are ever needed, S.I.S. will be able to reach the Commander, 240 Squadron, at Diego Garcia, by encoded radio transmission.

I have instructed Sergeant McPherson to deliver the final elements of Project Big Surf to the 240 Squadron Commander, directly. Furthermore, I have ordered the 240 Squadron Commander to relinquish the elements to his successor, whomever that may be, and from his successor to the next, and so on, until such time as the matter is concluded or canceled. To gain access to the documents in question, the inquirer must pass the codeword "Elouise" to the responsible commander at RAF Diego Garcia.

I have the greatest confidence in Sergeant McPherson's ability to execute this delivery, as instructed. He departed London for Diego Garcia on the 25th of January, 1945.

With a little luck and God's providence, his travels will be a complete waste of time.

Sir Reginald P. Saxon

Field Marshall, Royal Air Force

Jack dropped the note to the table and sank into a chair with a groan. "Diego Garcia," he whispered. "What a goat-rope."

Throckmorton and Sam read the note together, silently. "Sam," Throckmorton said, "have you any further details on this Sergeant James McPherson? Any indication that he made the delivery and returned?"

Sam snapped her fingers and walked to a large filing cabinet on the other side of the room. Nell glanced over, interested, but returned to her own pile of intelligence.

"These are the personnel files for Twenty-Seven, from date of inception to present. I've not had much reason to review these in the past, but that name 'James McPherson' does ring a bell." She snatched a folder from deep in the drawer and slapped it onto the table.

Jack opened the folder and was greeted by a black and white service photograph of a hard-looking, mustached man in his middle thirties. At the back of the folder, Jack read: "Flight Sergeant James K. McPherson, Killed in Action, S.I.S. Operation Cosgrove Mill, April 1945."

"Well," Jack said. "He lived long enough to die in April of '45. That's definitely enough time to have made the delivery to Diego Garcia and return to London." Sam agreed, retrieved the folder, and gentled it back into it's place in the cabinet.

"How's about a pint, love?" Throckmorton asked Sam. "You're off-duty, I believe?"

Sam glanced at her watch and shrugged. "It's your money, after all." She turned back to her replacement. "Vault combination is to be reset within the hour, Nell. I see you've reloaded the Thompson; that's all right, then. Command Post is managing the security response, of course, and the bricklayer is set to replace the wall by four o'clock today."

Nell smiled. "Toddle off, then. I've got the stick."

"Right," Sam replied. "Now, then," she said, holding her arm out to Throckmorton, "take me out for a nip, why don't you?"

Arm in arm, they strolled through the vault and traversed the dank passage toward the *Coach & Horses*. Jack followed a' la crutch.

* * *

Security personnel guarded the front door, awaiting the bricklayer. As Sam had reported, Air Marshall Downes, Mr. Potter, and the Irish lady had been whisked back to whatever safety awaited them, amongst heaps of non-disclosure agreements, no doubt.

Jack approached one of the guards. "Did you apprehend an attractive young Chinese woman, about yea high," he held his hand at chest level, "white silk blouse; black tactical pants?"

"I'm afraid not," the security man replied. "CCTV recorded both her and the little man with the large pack leaving the building. We're trying to track them down now."

Jack thanked him and shuffled to the bar.

Throckmorton and Sam had found themselves a cozy booth and a couple of drinks, so Jack poured himself a Guinness, sat down on a leather-cushioned bar stool, and rested his bad leg. Olivia was back on the television.

She stood on the deck of the *Shandong* as the Governor of Guam addressed the world. "The Captain of the *Shandong* has expressed his deepest apologies for having caused the people of Guam any unintended distress. According to the Captain, his superiors directed him to proceed to this location without providing any specific reason. He expects that reason to be communicated in the near future. However, he cannot depart this area until he is ordered to do so."

Jack sipped his Guinness and blew a raspberry at the television. Sam glowered at him. Jack turned back to the television.

"According to the Captain," the Governor continued, "his government is prepared to make an official statement, which he says is forthcoming. In addition, the Captain reports there is absolutely no reason the citizens of Guam should feel threatened by the *Shandong's* presence in the region.

"Finally, the Captain has asked that B-52 overflight of the Chinese vessels here at Guam, to the north of Yap, and to the north of Palau cease, as, according to him, the Chinese Navy intends no hostile action."

"Fat chance," Jack mumbled, and popped another Hydrocodone. Xiao had left the bottle on the bar for him. What a gal.

"At this time," the Governor concluded, "I will return to the island to assist with the ongoing evacuation."

The camera swung to Olivia, who's hair and makeup had been retouched in the very recent past. "There you have it. The Guam Governor unable to sway the Captain of the *Shandong*, who has cited his obligation to remain in these waters until ordered otherwise."

She pressed a manicured finger to her earpiece. "I'm getting something... just a moment." She tilted her head to the left and looked off-camera.

"The..." she began, "network has just informed me that the Chinese Government has issued an official statement. We don't have that visual for you, but I will relay it as it is dictated to me.

"This... this from the Chinese Embassy in Washington D.C.: 'Seventy-two hours ago,'" she said, finger to earpiece and eyes on the camera, "'the Government of the People's Republic of China uncovered reliable intelligence indicating there exists a threat of grave harm to the people of Japan.'"

Olivia looked confused as she said the last word, turning it into an unintentional question: "'Japan?'"

She continued. "'According to unimpeachable, non-partisan sources, the Government of the People's Republic of China has concluded that the United States military has lost control of multiple weapons of mass destruction at key points in the Philippine Sea. These points,'" she continued, "'are reported to be in the vicinity of the Islands of Palau, Yap, and Guam.'"

Jack heard the thrill in her voice. She was in the vicinity of the Island of Pulitzer.

"'If accidentally detonated," she continued, "'Chinese Naval intelligence indicates the detonations could set off a tidal wave.'"

The Captain of the *Shandong* appeared a few yards behind her, looking responsible and concerned.

She went on. "'According to our intelligence,'" "that's the Chinese Navy's intelligence," she editorialized, "'this tidal wave would sweep northward, through the Philippine Sea, and destroy much of southern, coastal Japan, and any islands in between.'"

Jack appreciated the staging. Sure, the network could simply have cut back to a desk in Washington D.C., and they probably did have a visual narrative for the statement. But, oh, how much more riveting to have the statement recited by the plucky journalist, from the deck of the Chinese aircraft carrier.

"'For that reason,'" she continued to parrot the audio coming through her earpiece, "'the People's Republic of China, and the Chinese Navy, are embarked on a humanitarian mission to help the

United States recover the lost nuclear weapons. In this way, the People's Republic of China will secure the Western Pacific from the irresponsible United States military and save the lives of countless, innocent Japanese.'"

"That is the end of the official statement," Olivia said, bright-eyed. "Amazing."

The Captain of the *Shandong* walked up beside her. "Captain," she said, "can you give us a few words about the official statement from your government?"

The Captain smiled, nodded, and said, "It is good that we should now understand the reason we have been ordered to this region. As Captain of the Aircraft Carrier *Shandong*, I commit my vessels and resources to the recovery of these lost nuclear weapons, so that the people of Guam, Yap, Palau, and Japan can once more be safe."

"Captain, if you should locate these nuclear weapons before the United States military can recover them, will you turn them back over to the U.S. military?"

"We will do whatever is necessary to protect the people of this region," he replied, smiling. Then he turned and walked off-camera.

"Well," Olivia said to the camera, "historic developments off the northern coast of Guam. We have yet to validate this information, and we do not expect the Chinese government to provide us access to these unnamed sources. However, if this is true, the U.S. military will certainly have a lot to answer for.

"As you know, the U.S. military has had several blunders with nuclear weapons. The most recent incident, in 2007, occurred between Minot Air Force Base, North Dakota, and Barksdale Air Force Base, Louisiana, when six "AGM-160" cruise missiles with 'WG-160 variable yield' nuclear warheads were mistakenly loaded onto a B-52, the same jets that are overflying these Chinese vessels now."

As if on cue, a B-52 screamed over the deck of the *Shandong* like a smoking dragon and rumbled into the distance.

"The warheads were mishandled and unaccounted for over a thirty-six hour period.

"Thankfully, an Airman at Barksdale Air Force base identified the nuclear warheads for what they were, and the incident was addressed before the situation could go further awry. Regardless of consequence, both the Secretary of the Air Force and the Chief of Staff of the Air Force resigned over the incident.

"Whether we have another nuclear incident on our hands remains to be seen, but we do not believe the Chinese Navy would venture this close to U.S. Territory without a verifiable reason.

"This is Olivia Knowlton reporting from the deck of the Chinese Aircraft Carrier *Shandong*." The video switched back to the network's D.C. station for more coverage from the Chinese Embassy.

Jack drained the last of his Guinness, struggled to his feet, and walked over to Throckmorton and Sam. "I'm sorry to interrupt, love-birds, but me and this old buzzard are late for a date with a C-17."

Sam nodded. Throckmorton pouted. Jack snatched his satellite phone from the heap behind the bar.

"Sam," Jack asked, "I know you're probably exhausted. But would you drive us out to Heathrow?"

"Have you there in a trice. It's on my way home."

* * *

Throckmorton fell asleep as soon as they boarded. Jack used the fifteen minutes between boarding and take-off to call General Carter.

"You'd better have something good for me, Quintana," Carter roared. "I've got the Secretary of Defense breathing down my neck, for Christ's sake. They're sending a special team out here to hunt for those ancient nukes, and I need to be able to tell them where to look!"

"I understand, sir. We're closing in on the intel you need."

"How much longer is it going to be?"

"We have to fly out to Diego Garcia from here. It will take us about seven hours to get to Bahrain International, a couple of hours to refuel, and then another six hours from Bahrain to Diego. After we arrive in Diego, I can't say. But seventeen hours, minimum."

"Well, it'll take the team longer than that to get out here from the States, so we might be all right on that count."

"We're making all the headway we can, sir," Jack said, running a hand through his hair.

"I know you are," Carter replied. "But this shit is getting hairy, and these Navy pilots are getting restless. I don't know how much longer I'll be able to keep them out of the air."

"Roger that, sir. If the intel still exists, we'll get it to you."

"Copy," the General replied, and hung up.

Jack strapped in and prepared for the giant aircraft's sudden take-off thrust. He snapped sideways in his wall-mounted seat as the aircraft screamed down the runway. His leg throbbed like a bad tooth.

He tried to sleep, but his mind darted through questions and possibilities. What would they find when they got to Diego Garcia? If he remembered correctly, the damned RAF base had been shut down right after the war, and nobody but the locals had inhabited the island between 1946 and 1965. What had transpired in that 19-year British absence?

Had one of the RAF commanders destroyed the remaining intelligence when the base closed in '46? Had the information been stuffed into a locked drawer and forgotten? Was it sitting in a safe under three feet of sand at the bottom of the lagoon? There was no way to know.

The lack of continuity scared him the most. Organizations had a way of forgetting what happened six months ago, let alone seventy-five years ago. And that lapse in British presence... that really was a bitch.

Who could expect the first RAF commander that returned to the island in the mid-sixties to pick right up from the last commander? *Stodgy, old boy! I'm headed out to Diego Garcia. I understand you had that command back at the end of the second world war. Have you got anything for me that I need to know? You do? Well! Special dispatch from a Sergeant James McPherson, you say? Stored in the second drawer of the blue safe in the old headquarters building? The combination's what? Wait, let me take it down. Don't give it over unless the inquiring party gives the code word 'Elouise?' Right. Anything else, then? No? Easy peasy, Japanesey.*

Right.

He thought of Isa and their night together on Guam. He thought of Xiao and the engineer. Finally, after an hour of drowsing, Jack fell asleep.

He was jarred awake six hours later as the C-17 landed at the U.S. Naval Airfield at Bahrain International Airport.

"Two hours to refuel," the Loadmaster reported. Jack nodded.

He wandered off the C-17 and walked over to the Navy terminal. There was a small, covered area outside, and he pulled out his cigarettes. His watch told him it was three o'clock in the morning. He lit a smoke and watched the airfield activity.

Little trains of airport cargo cars hauled luggage to and fro. A Navy UH-60 landed, and some enlisted guys pushed it into a hangar. A small C-12 passenger plane took off and disappeared over the Persian Gulf.

Jack remembered having been here many years before, on a much different mission. He'd been working a methamphetamine case in South Dakota, of all places, when he got the call from his commander.

Ashley had deployed to Kandahar, Afghanistan a few months earlier. Splitting up had always been difficult, but both of them were professionals, and the job was the job. Each of them had found a certain fulfillment in hard, brain-and-body-busting work.

"There's something you need to know," his Commander had told him. "We just received word your wife was involved in a helicopter crash outside Kandahar."

"Okay," was all Jack had been able to say.

"Nobody made it off that bird, Jack. I'm calling to tell you she's gone."

Jack had been sitting in a rented car outside the "Independent Ale House" in Rapid City, cell phone mashed against his ear. He and two other agents had been waiting for a drug deal to go down a few buildings over. Most of his brain had wanted to cancel the phone call and go back to the drug bust. *Why did you have to call me and tell me that? That's not something I want to know. Let's just take the last twenty seconds back, shall we?*

"Jack?" his commander asked. "You still there?"

"Yes," he responded slowly.

"Get back to the Detachment as soon as possible. Drop what you're working on. Smitty and Kevin can handle it."

"Right." He seemed able to reply only one word at a time.

"Tonight, Jack."

That seemed to smack him out of his daze. "Yes," he said. "I'll be on a plane tonight."

"Good," his commander answered. "Send me the flight details. I'll pick you up at the airport."

"Will do."

After that, he floated through a series of interactions on auto-pilot. Yes, he was doing okay. No, he didn't need anything, thank you. Yes, he wanted to meet the plane with the remains, of course. Where was it? Still in Kandahar? He'd meet it when it landed in Bahrain to refuel.

And so, he had. Eight years ago, he'd sat here in this abandoned waiting area, smoking cigarettes, waiting for Ashley's remains, and wishing he had a drink. Wishing he had a bottle of something that would knock him out for a few days. Sure, he'd feel worse when he woke up than he did now, but boy did he want to not feel what he was feeling, and start not feeling it ASAP.

The Human Remains, not just Ashley's, but all the remains collected from the crash site, had arrived on a C-17. Since then, he had experienced an emotional connection with that aircraft that was not anger or hatred or sorrow, but something akin to melancholy.

As the plane had refueled, Jack boarded, found Ashley's metal coffin, and sat down in the closest seat he could find. He didn't leave the aircraft until the coffins were off-loaded at Andrews Air Force Base, some 17 hours later. The President was there. Jack hadn't really cared.

He buried his wife in her family's plot in West Virginia. The Coltons were poor, but they had a big spread of land, over two-hundred acres. Property taxes were cheap in West Virginia. Otherwise, they would have been pushed out decades earlier.

The plot was in a pretty spot. He remembered that's what he'd thought when he saw the place. *The plot is in a pretty spot.* It stuck in his mind all through the ceremony. *At least the plot is in a pretty spot. I'm glad she'll be buried here, because the plot's in a pretty spot.* It was too bad she would never draw another breath, see another sunrise, walk another step, feel another raindrop, but at least *THE PLOT WAS IN A PRETTY SPOT.*

He tossed the cigarette and tried to fixate on something else.

Throckmorton stumbled around the corner and plopped down on a bench. "Give us a fag, Jacky."

Jack handed him the pack. "What's got you down, my son?" Throckmorton asked, lighting up.

"Not a thing. Just concerned about what we might not find out there in the Indian Ocean."

"Not to worry, not to worry." Throckmorton waved his hand. "In my experience, if a thing that has always been outside your span of control is going to happen, or not going to happen, there's not much you can do about it."

Jack was silent.

"Of course," Throckmorton continued, expelling smoke from his hairy nostrils, "that's a load of fatalistic shit, and you know it."

Jack smiled.

"Dash it all, Jack. I never was much good at giving advice. All my brains have been scrambled up here," he twirled a finger at the side of his head, "since I contracted syphilis down in Darwin back in '79."

Jack smirked.

"It's true, it's true. Swear it on my sainted mother's grave in Sussex. I was down in Darwin with a couple of mates, right before the Falklands, it was, and one of them said to me, 'Thurgood, look up at that window across the street.' We'd been drinking since ten in the morning, and it was 'round about ten at night by this time, and I couldn't very well identify my own hand in front of my face, but I told him I saw the window."

"'That window, there,' the drunken fool said," 'the one with the Christmas lights strung up around it.'"

"I looked again, and this time, I actually did see the window. I remember thinking how nice it was that someone had taken the time to decorate. In February."

"'Go on, then,' he told me. 'Get on over there and give 'er what for.'"

"Now, I don't know if I knew what he meant or if I thought I'd just go over and find out, or if I really crossed the street just because of the Christmas lights. Anyhow, I crossed the street, knocked on the door, and was greeted by the most beautiful blonde I'd ever seen. My god, she was a bloody knockout.

"Well, she led me inside, and I took out my pocketbook. The little tramp had my pants down around my trousers in ten seconds flat. Then, I blacked out."

"You... blacked out."

"Right you are, my old son. Next thing I remember, my mates were pounding at the door, I was in the bed, and this beautiful blonde was hollering at them to go away. Then, one of the fellows, a big fat Welshman, put his shoulder through door, and the blonde hopped off."

"'*She's got the syph!* "they shouted as I lay there with my flag raised to the ceiling. 'Thurgood! Get outta that bloody bed and come have another drink.'"

"Well, I left her a twenty pound note, because I didn't know if I'd had a good time or not, or if anything had happened at all. I was completely bloody numb, you know, but I blew her a kiss goodbye."

"'Throck!' "they yelled, half laughing and half concerned, the way people will talk when they've seen their mate take a face-dive into cobblestone," 'You didn't put it to her, did you?'"

"'Sure, I did,' "I said. 'What do you think I am? Some kind of nancy boy?'"

"'Aww, *God*, Throck!' One of them cried. 'An old barkeep walked by soon as you went into the house! Told us the whore had bloody syphilis!'"

"I stopped dead in the street. 'Syphilis?' I said, dazed." "'I don't remember seeing any syphilis.'"

"'Throck!' they laughed, fit to split their stomachs. 'You can't always *see* syphilis. You just *get* syphilis.'"

"'Well,' I replied, swaying on my feet, 'If I remember my literary history, Oscar Wilde had syphilis, so I'm in bloody fantastic company. If Oscar Wilde can die of syphilis, so can I.'"

"At this, one of my mates doubled over and fell in the street, he laughed so hard. We hauled him into the nearest pub and settled him down with a pint of something, but nobody could stop laughing. Best night of my life, the night I got syphilis."

"Throck," Jack said.

"Hmm?" he asked, twirling the cigarette.

"There's no way you have syphilis."

"No?"

"No. If you'd contracted syphilis in Darwin, forty years ago, you'd be dead."

"Fabulous news, Jacky!" he replied, eyeing the burning cherry at the end of the camel.

"You're not listening to me, are you?"

"What?"

"Never mind."

CHAPTER 8

Seven hours later, the C-17 lined up with the runway on the remote island of Diego Garcia. Jack climbed the steel ladder from the cargo bay up to the cockpit, hopping the rungs on his good leg. The pilots handed him a cup of coffee, and Jack peered out the cockpit window at the sight below.

The Indian Ocean sparkled deep blue. Diego Garcia traced a slim, emerald outline around an aquamarine lagoon, shaped something like a footprint. It wasn't so much an island as a limestone-reinforced sand-bar that had emerged from the water a few thousand years ago. Every-where the land rose more than a few inches from the sea, there was bright, living green. The rest was white sand about that gorgeous, tur-quoise lagoon.

"Welcome to the middle of nowhere," one of the pilots joked, ad-justing the flaps in preparation for landing.

The island rushed up to meet them. His view of the lagoon trans-formed to a view of coconut trees as the aircraft descended, and they touched down on the deserted runway.

Jack and Throckmorton stepped out into raging sunshine, occa-sionally relieved by flocks of clouds over the lagoon. A middle-aged Filipino gentleman approached in a Toyota pickup truck.

"You go terminal," he told them. "Put your bag." He indicated the bed of the truck. "I gonna take you over."

They threw their bags into the back of the pickup. Jack sat in front with the little man, and Throckmorton hopped into the bed.

With no official warning of their impending arrival, the British of-ficials in the terminal received Throckmorton readily but wanted Jack to wait around for a Customs briefing. While Thurgood went to find whomever was in charge, Jack wandered the small waiting area and stared back out at the tarmac.

Filipinos seemed to be everywhere. The man who'd brought them from the C-17 passed by, and Jack flagged him down. "What's your name?" Jack asked, smiling.

"Benedict, boss," the man replied.

"How long have you worked here?"

"One year so far, this time. I am coming here for two year."

"Why two years?" Jack asked.

"The Byott gonna hire for two year, then they gonna send us somewhere, back to Pilipeen. Sometime, if you working hard, they gonna get you visa for U.K. Sometime U.S.A., maybe."

Jack looked around for a definition of "Byott." There, on a terminal customs sign, he read "British Indian Ocean Territory: BIOT."

"Nice to meet you, Benedict," Jack said. "Thank you."

Benedict smiled, waved, and continued about his business.

Throckmorton returned with a British Customs official. After coughing up his Official Passport and Air Force O.S.I. credentials, the Customs official waved him through to the other side of the small terminal.

"Your diplomacy skills seem to be in order," Jack told him as they exited the terminal.

"Never better. Got us a lorry as well."

Jack raised his eyebrows as Throckmorton opened the door of a new Nissan pickup truck. "You seem to know your way around this place."

"Right-o!" Thurgood replied, tossing the bags in the back. "I was stationed here from '85 to '87, wasn't I?"

"Weren't you?"

"Oh, yes. The Royal Navy gives the burgeoning diplomats all the cruddy assignments. Two years, I was here, and nothing to do but lie on the beach and chase Coconut Crabs and tip the bottle and get laid."

"Sounds like a real hardship tour."

"Don't you doubt it." He threw the Nissan into gear. "I'll take us 'round to the BIOT headquarters building, and we'll see what we shall see."

Jack smiled. With Thurgood handling the logistics, he could let himself think. There seemed to be only one road, which made sense when Jack remembered the island's aerial view. There was only *room* for one road, and nowhere to go but one way or the other. The strip of land around the lagoon was that small.

As they rolled past palm-lined beaches, Jack noticed signs for "villages" on the side of the road. "What are these 'villages,' Throck?"

"The Flips live in those places," he answered.

"Flips?"

"The Filipinos. After the government forcibly removed the Chagossian residents back in the mid '60s, named for the Chagos Archipelago, the government found they'd deprived themselves of all the available cheap labor. So, naturally, the government had to import the labor. They decided on the Filipinos because so many of them speak English, and they'll work for next to nothing, so goody for the Queen."

"What happened here during World War II?"

"Well," Throckmorton replied, frowning a little, "we Brits had enjoyed substantial influence throughout India for some time, and that influence naturally extended to the Maldives and the Chagos Archipelago. We simply claimed it all, for the Crown.

"So, we had some units operating out of Chennai, India, at a place called 'Red Hills Lake,' back in the 1930s. When the second world war broke out, we had a couple of flying boat squadrons stationed at Red Hills Lake, on the east coast of India, that is. We also had a refueling stop in the Maldives called 'Kelai.'

"While there wasn't much activity from the Japanese this far into the Indian Ocean back then, the powers that were thought it would be wise to push one of those flying boat Squadrons out to Diego Garcia, sort of as a forward base to detect Japanese Naval activity before the Nips could reach the Maldives or India.

"As well as I can remember, the Nips took down a few British and other civilian ships in the vicinity of Diego Garcia, but they never threatened the island itself.

"After the war, we abandoned the island to the few Chagossians who chose to remain here. From 1946 to 1965, Diego saw very little activity from outsiders. However, in 1965, the British Government formally constituted the British Indian Ocean Territory, paid the Maldives government something like three million pounds for use of the island and surrounding area, and moved back in.

"After the Chagossians were all removed, we partnered with you lot," he looked at Jack, "to build the place up as another check against the Soviet Union, as we'd have been able to launch aircraft from Diego that could overfly Russia and return."

"Since then, both of our governments have used the place to various ends, as I'm sure you know."

They pulled up to a two-story, rectangular building that sported poles for both the American and British flags.

"Used to be my office, Jacky boy." Throckmorton grinned. "How I've missed this place."

They walked past the flag poles and into the air conditioned building. Throckmorton took a left, and Jack followed him down a long, central hallway. On the right, Throckmorton found what he was looking for.

The placard on the door read: "Lionel Cuthridge, Commander, Royal Naval Forces, Diego Garcia."

Throckmorton read the placard, laughed, and entered without knocking, "Lionel, you old Donkey!" Throckmorton called.

Jack followed him into the office. From behind a heavy old desk rose a balding man in his sixties. "Good God," the man said. "Thurgood, is that you?"

"Right you are, Commander," Thurgood replied.

The other man flapped his hand at him. "Let's have none of that 'Commander' business, shall we?"

"Whatever you say," Thurgood said, sitting on the edge of the desk. "Commander."

Cuthridge grabbed a coffee mug and made as if to sling it at Throckmorton, which got him off the desk. "Lionel," Thurgood said,

188

"this is Special Agent Jack Quintana, of the U.S. Air Force Office of Special Investigations."

"Pleased to meet you," Lionel said, offering his hand. Jack shook it.

"I'm afraid we're here under rather strained circumstances," Throckmorton continued. "I'm sure you've seen what's going on at Palau, Yap, and Guam."

"Indeed, I have. Strange goings-on, what?"

"No doubt. We've come on urgent business from Brigadier General Michael Carter, Commander of the 36th Wing at Andersen Air Force Base. In addition," he continued, "our activities have been sanctioned by the Commander, United States Indo-Pacific Command, and the Royal Air Force."

"Really?" Cuthridge asked, interested.

"Yes," Throckmorton said. "You remember Air Marshal Downes from last year's gala in the Seychelles, don't you?"

"Percy Downes? Of course, of course. Good sort, that one."

"Right. Well, you see, old chap, we've just come from London, where we happened upon some intelligence preserved by the S.I.S. since World War II."

Cuthridge motioned for Throckmorton and Jack to sit in a couple of cushioned chairs facing the desk. He called over his shoulder into an adjoining office. A young female officer appeared. "Bring us some tea, would you, Left-Tenant?"

"Of course, Commander," she said, and flashed Jack a brilliant smile.

Cuthridge grinned as she left the room and looked at Jack. "Oh, she's got it bad for you, my son. Did you see that smile? She hasn't smiled at me like that since I gave her three weeks Christmas leave."

Jack nodded and motioned for Throckmorton to continue.

"So," Throckmorton went on, "this intelligence the S.I.S. had maintained since 1945 indicated a portion of sensitive information related to a joint U.S. and British operation from World War II had been transported here for safekeeping. As far as we can tell, this transfer was extremely unusual. We'd hoped its outlandish nature would have helped to preserve it, lo these many years."

"Yes," Cuthridge mused. "You know, it's quite interesting. It's not the first time something out of the ordinary has happened here, at the end of this lost archipelago."

"Is that right?" Jack asked.

"Indeed, yes. I remember old Commander Covington, uh," he hesitated and looked at Throckmorton, "you remember Covington, don't you, Throck?"

"Indubitably," Thurgood said, craning his neck to ogle the Lieutenant as she clattered around in the next room. "He was Commander here from eighty-four to nineteen and eighty-six, if my recollection serves me. The man was a drunk."

Jack shot Throckmorton a look. Throckmorton winked at him.

"Yes, I believe that's correct," Cuthridge said. "Well," he continued, "we were down at the pub one night... You know the one, Throck, right down the road, on the beach."

"I know it well," Throckmorton said, still distracted by sounds of the lovely Lieutenant in the office next door.

"It was just he and I. There had been some difficulty with a shipment of fuel, some bloody barge run aground on a sandbar a few hundred miles distant, but it was wreaking hell on our operations here, and it took weeks to get the ship out to sea again for delivery.

"Well, he'd had the very devil of a time with the whole business, but, at that point, the barge had been freed and was on its way here. He decided to celebrate a bit, and I was the only officer left in the building, it having been a Friday evening when he got the good news.

"Naturally, I agreed to accompany him; what good officer wouldn't? It was during those few drinks when he mentioned something I thought very strange."

The Lieutenant returned with hot tea on a silver serving arrangement. Jack thought hot tea a bad idea in the middle of the day, with the sun blazing and car tires sinking into baked asphalt in the parking lot outside. But he knew the British would have their tea, regardless of the weather conditions, and damned if it wasn't hot enough to scald the skin from your tongue.

She gave Jack a wink as she bent forward to serve. She was well groomed and strikingly pretty. Jack thought she may have been locked up on this island a bit too long.

As Throckmorton visually recorded her every movement, for posterity maybe, the Commander sipped his tea and looked out the window behind him. "'Line,' Covington said—he always called me 'Line' instead of 'Lionel'—'when I was stationed here back in the middle seventies,' he told me, 'there were some strange doings on this island.'"

"'Strange doings?' I asked him."

"'Oh, yes,' he said. Quite strange, in fact.' I remember he looked out over the lagoon and pointed. 'Do you see that buoy out in the lagoon?' he asked me. 'That orange bastard way out toward the other side?'"

"'Yes,' I said. 'I see it.'"

"He took a swig of his ale then, and I knew he was done in because some of it slopped onto his uniform, and he was always fastidious about such things. But he paid no notice."

"'Back in seventy-seven,' he went on, wiping his mouth absently, 'I took a little kayak out there to investigate a few odd lights that were bobbing up and down. I hadn't ever noticed them before,' he said. 'It was nigh on to midnight, I think, and I'd been drinking at the bar since eight o'clock, but I was still right enough to paddle 'cross the lagoon, so I know it wasn't any kind of silliness like a hallucination or a dream or anything like that.'"

"'Go on, Commander,' I told him," Cuthridge said.

"'I paddled across the lagoon, and when I got close to the lights, I heard voices on the water. They weren't speaking at high volume, but they certainly weren't whispering, but I couldn't make out any of the words they were saying.'

"'I paddled a bit closer, and that's when I realized they were speaking a language that wasn't English. I couldn't recognize it, but I knew it wasn't English.' *Now, there's a problem,* I thought to myself, *that isn't English and that isn't Tagalog, what the Flips speak, and there's nobody but Brits, Americans, and Flips on this whole bloody island.'*

"'Being slightly drunk, as I was,' Cuthridge continued, reciting Covington's words from memory, 'I called out, 'Ho, there! Identify yourselves!'

"'They didn't identify themselves, but they didn't stop talking, either. One of them started toward me. And you know what was strange,' Cuthridge recited, "was the bloke wasn't on a boat. He bloody *walked* toward me, through water that must have been six feet deep at the shallowest point.'"

"Now," Cuthridge said to Throckmorton, "I know that sounds insane. The both of us know, in that part of the lagoon, the depth has always been six to eight feet. Covington said the same, but assured me he'd actually seen the figure wade toward his kayak, in water that would have been over Covington's head.

"Anyway," Cuthridge said, "Covington went on to say, 'the bloody figure was coming toward me at a rate of speed we would consider a normal walking pace on dry land. It moved through the water like it wasn't slowing him up a bit, although I could see the wake it was making. I call it an *it* because I can't think what kind of man would be that godless tall and be able to move through the lagoon like that, but it looked like a man to me. Just, you know, immense.'

"'Well, when I saw him walk toward me like that, my courage left me. I paddled the kayak 'round and shot back toward the beach like a man afire. But before I reached the other side of the lagoon, I looked back. Something big, and I mean bloody *big,* mind you, rose up out of the lagoon behind me. It was jet black against the stars. That's how I knew how big it was. You've seen the stars out here at night, Line,' he reached out and punched me in the shoulder then. 'When an aircraft moves across they sky, you can see its black outline against the stars.'

"'Right you are,' I agreed, wondering just how drunk the old man could have been."

"'Line,' he went on, 'this bloody jet-black behemoth was the size of a goddamn Cricket field. It came up out of the water. I could hear the displacement it made when it rose. It hovered for a few moments, and shot up into the sky, in a blink.'"

"I was a bit taken aback by the story," Cuthridge said, "but the man was my Commanding Officer, and I didn't want to offend him, so I just nodded my head and agreed it was all very queer."

"'And that's not all,' Covington said. "Two days after that, a couple of plain-clothed gents arrived in an unmarked aircraft. Yanks, they were, asking if anybody had seen anything strange in the past few days. Well, I kept my mouth shut, and tight. They took some samples of something or other from the lagoon, and then they left. But I'll never forget what I saw that night. I've had the bloody devil of night terrors about that big, dark figure moving toward me through the lagoon.'"

"He finished his drink then, and stood. 'But maybe somebody slipped me a little something in my drink that night. I was quite a fetching young stud back then. And there were plenty of nurses with access to all kinds of interesting medications.'"

"We laughed, and he bid me good night. I'll never forget that strange story."

Throckmorton looked unimpressed. "Right," he said to Cuthridge. "Well, I'm afraid our situation is a bit more tangible than that, thank God."

"What've you got?" Cuthridge asked.

"According to the intelligence we located in London," Jack answered, "in either January or February of 1945, a Flight Sergeant named James McPherson made a delivery of some critical information associated with the joint operation Thurgood mentioned. He was supposed to have delivered the files to the Commander of 240 Squadron, which was operating PBY Catalinas from this island during World War II."

"Ah, yes!" Cuthridge exclaimed. "The 240 Squadron. One of their Catalinas washed up on the beach here during a typhoon in '44. Still right where the storm left her. 'Kate' she's called."

"Yes," Jack said, trying to keep things on track, "well, what we need to know is whether you have any insight into what may have happened to any wartime intelligence deposited here for safekeeping during the war. I understand the British left the island in 1946 and didn't return until '65."

Commander Cuthridge spread his hands. "I'm afraid anything deemed important would have been transported back to London when the 240 Squadron and remaining British support elements departed."

Jack looked at the floor. *No files. He has no idea what the hell we're talking about. This whole thing was a waste of time.*

Throckmorton leaned forward and fixed his eyes on Cuthridge. "Lionel, does the word 'Elouise' mean anything to you?"

Cuthridge frowned. Then he said, "You can't be serious."

Jack looked up.

"Serious as the grave."

"But that was just a... just a bloody joke."

"What?" Jack asked. "What was a joke?"

"Well, 'Elouise,' man. 'Elouise.' It's been a running joke on this island for years."

Jack looked at Throckmorton, who had looked away from Cuthridge and appeared to be trying to remember something. "Yes...," he whispered, deep in his own booze-addled mind.

"Will someone please tell me what this 'joke' is about? If it's something connected with 'Elouise,' we need to find out what it is, and pretty goddamn quick."

"'*Elouise!*'" Throckmorton cried, "I'd forgotten all about it!"

Jack looked from Throckmorton to Cuthridge and back again.

Cuthridge laughed and then said, "Forgive us, Agent Quintana. I'll explain. It's a story most of us old codgers remember from way back."

"Please go ahead," Jack said, frustrated.

"When the Commander of 240 Squadron left the island in '46, there were, perhaps, three hundred Chagossians that wanted to remain. They'd been here all their lives, working the old coconut plantation. Well," Cuthridge's eyes glazed, and then he came back, "actually, this ties in with your intelligence nicely, although I didn't realize it 'til just now."

"Go on," Jack said.

"Well, in nineteen and forty-six, the 240 Squadron Commander had cleared out everything that needed to be returned to India, Kelai, or London. There was one little safe, however, that he said had arrived with strict instructions to *never leave the island*, under any condition. Apparently, whomever had delivered it, perhaps your Sergeant McPherson, had communicated this draconian requirement to the Squadron Commander. For whatever reason, the Squadron Commander took it literally, and followed that stipulation to the letter.

"Before he left on the last PBY Catalina—besides 'Kate,' that is, she's still with us—he had a little ceremony with the leader of the Chagossians, whom some bloody idiot had nicknamed 'King Solomon,' for what reason I couldn't say. Anyhow, the nickname stuck, and everyone referred to him as such.

"During the ceremony, the 240 Squadron Commander entrusted this small safe to King Solomon. As the Commander had no doubt hoped, King Solomon took the safe as a token of British respect for his people, and promised to maintain it until such time as the British returned for it. Atop the safe, the Squadron Commander had painted the word 'Elouise.' He referred to the safe as 'Elouise' throughout the ceremony.

"When the departure ceremony concluded, the Squadron commander climbed into his Catalina and left for Kelai. I'll bet you're wondering how I could possibly be privy to these details," Covington smiled, leaning forward.

"I'll bet you're right," Jack said.

"Well, every year, on the anniversary of the date the 240 Squadron Commander departed the island, the remaining Chagossians have themselves a little ceremony, complete with the original safe and it's original contents. They call it the 'Ceremony of Elouise.'

"They always invite the Royal Naval Commander and his staff, so I have attended these ceremonies personally."

"I thought the Chagossians had been removed from the island in the mid-sixties," Jack said.

"They had. However, a small band of them, perhaps a hundred, in all, managed to return in their native, ocean-going vessels. We didn't have the heart to turn them out twice, so we let them remain. There are only about sixty left, I'm afraid. King Solomon's grandson runs the tribe these days. We call him 'Young Solomon.'"

"And they still have the safe?" Jack asked, struggling to his feet.

"Elouise? Of course. That bloody safe is the mainstay of their entire culture, I'm afraid."

"We need to get to that safe," Jack informed him. "As soon as possible."

Cuthridge held up his hands. "Whoa, now. Things are a bit sensitive when it comes to relations with the Chagossians. We're trying to be good stewards of the remaining population, so we treat them, more or less, as equals. We can't just barge in to their village and demand they hand over Elouise. It would be like Young Solomon walking into Buckingham Palace and demanding the Crown Jewels."

Jack massaged his temples. A headache threatened.

"Tell you what, old sock," Throckmorton said. "Why don't you arrange a summit with this 'Young Solomon,' and tell him we have urgent business to discuss. As a matter of fact, tell him emissaries of the 240 Squadron Commander have returned to ascertain whether Elouise has been properly maintained, and, if it has, to formally recognize Young Solomon and his people for their diligent watchfulness over the past five decades."

Cuthridge belted laughter. "Anything for you, Throck. Anything for you. Tell you what. I'll meet with him directly and try to schedule something for this evening. You two are welcome to accompany me later, if Young Solomon proves amenable."

"Might work," Jack said.

"Of course, it will work," Throckmorton said, and clapped him on the back. "Now, Lionel, is the Seaman's Center still open? I'm famished."

* * *

The Seaman's Center turned out to be a bar in the American district of the island installation. It featured tiki hut decoration, and a cute Filipina waitress served them.

"I'll have the grilled mahi-mahi," Throckmorton told her, "and three Coronas, please."

The waitress looked to Jack. "That sounds good," he said, avoiding the small print on the menu. His head really throbbed now. "I'll have the same."

She laughed. "Six Corona for two people? Okay." She bounced back to the kitchen, and Throckmorton rubbed his hands together.

"I used to eat here almost every day. Lovely menu."

Jack looked out a window on the back wall of the restaurant. Beyond a parking area, the land rose to a small hill, where a picnic bench overlooked the water.

The waitress brought their six Coronas. Jack snagged one and excused himself. "I'm going out for a smoke."

Throckmorton, who had already begun to flirt with the waitress, paid him no mind.

Jack walked the incline to the picnic bench and looked out over the lagoon. It was now late afternoon, and the sun came down behind him. The clouds on the horizon blushed pink and scarlet.

He took a swig of the Corona, found it was good, and took another, which was even better. He lit a camel and considered Cuthridge's story about old Commander Covington.

Throughout his years with the O.S.I., Jack had come across a number of incredible stories. Covington's ranked up with some of the most bizarre. Jack remembered an investigation in North Dakota's Intercontinental Ballistic Missile complex. During the course of the inquiry, seven trustworthy individuals, including two Security Forces members, two ICBM launch officers, two County Sheriff's deputies, and a tactical squadron commander all swore they'd seen an Unidentified Flying Object.

According to their eerily similar but individually collected statements, they'd witnessed a large, triangular object descend over a Minuteman III ICBM launch site, blast a series of pulsing lights down over the launch facility's steel-reinforced concrete hatch, and disappear into the night sky, all in a span of fifteen seconds.

The following day, an ICBM maintenance crew deployed to the launch site. Upon opening the hatch, the maintenance crew discovered vital electrical elements within the underground launch facility had been melted, as if someone had invaded the secure area with a blowtorch and selectively sabotaged the components that would facilitate a launch.

Small waves from the lagoon rolled to the sandy shore before him. The pink in the clouds had deepened to purple.

"Jacky!" he heard from behind him.

He turned and saw Throckmorton lean out the bar's back door. "Supper's ready, lad!"

Jack waved and put out his cigarette.

A television hung from the wall, and Jack asked the waitress to switch it on. She tossed him the remote control for the satellite dish, and he channel-surfed until he found the news.

General Carter had lost his argument over the F/A-18s. Footage from Olivia's team showed one of them buzz the *Shandong's* control tower.

"We don't have much time left," Jack said.

Throckmorton grunted and concentrated on his Mahi-Mahi.

Olivia piped up after a few more frames of video. "Intelligence from the 69th Reconnaissance Group's *Global Hawk* surveillance aircraft has shown the Chinese Strike Groups north of Palau and Yap are still in place. Of note, however, is the activity of the Chinese dive teams.

"At first, and according to their own reports, we believed these divers were trying to locate supposed 'lost' nuclear weapons. However,

Global Hawk surveillance footage, which the Air Force has allowed us to broadcast, shows these divers merely swimming next to the vessels from which they've deployed. None of them appear to have actually descended underwater to search for anything.

"More on this. Here's a recorded video of an interview with Brigadier General Michael Carter, from just a few hours ago."

In the video, General Carter stood in a conference room while the *Global Hawk* video rolled on a screen behind him. "As we suspected, this farce about 'lost nuclear weapons,' is just that. The Chinese Navy is using this fabricated scenario in order to test our resolve in this region."

On the screen behind him, Jack saw an aerial image, ostensibly from a *Global Hawk*, that showed two Chinese divers flip forward from their small vessel, into the deep waters outside the coral reef at Yap Island. Instead of diving, however, the two men simply bobbed next to the boat.

"This situation has progressed far enough," General Carter said. "If the Chinese vessels fail to depart from the areas surrounding Palau, Yap, and Guam, my B-52 crews and the *SuperHornet* pilots from the *Ronald Reagan* will have no choice but to take drastic action."

A babble of voices followed this last proclamation. Jack tuned it out. Something about that video nagged him. The Chinese were not diving. The Chinese knew, or thought they knew, that the nuclear bombs were there, somewhere, close at hand. But they had not yet made any attempt to locate or retrieve them.

A thought tried to surface in his mind, and then Commander Cuthridge walked in.

"We're all set, lads," he said, clasping his hands together. "Young Solomon has agreed to meet with you, whom I've identified as representatives of 240 Squadron, in one hour's time."

"Good news," Jack replied.

"Is there anything Young Solomon... appreciates?" Throckmorton asked, eyeing the bottles lined up behind the bar.

"He's a Scotch man," Cuthridge answered.

* * *

Forty-five minutes later, as the sun dipped below the blue horizon, Jack, Throckmorton, Cuthridge, and the female Lieutenant pulled up to a clearing on the beach. The clearing was dotted with palm huts, and a number of what Jack took for Chagossians gathered around a growing fire.

The Lieutenant introduced herself to Jack as "Lydia Chambers, pleased to meet you again." She gave him an encore of that smile.

"Now, remember," Cuthridge briefed as they exited the vehicle. "*Elouise* is a solemn talisman for these people. We must all remember to appear polite, interested, and engaged throughout the ritual."

"How long do you think—" Jack started to ask.

"Shhh!" Cuthridge interrupted. "Here's Young Solomon."

A tall man of about twenty-five years strode forward to greet them. He had large white teeth, sharp eyes, and the musculature of a professional swimmer. His skin burned a deep, bronze color. He wore cut-off jean shorts and nothing else.

"Commander Cuthridge," Young Solomon said. "You have brought da emissary of 240 Squadron!"

"Young Solomon!" Cuthridge said, matching the young man's pitch and enthusiasm. "I invite you to greet the messengers from 240 Squadron. This," he indicated Throckmorton, "is Sir Thurgood Throckmorton, Eleventh Earl of Nottingham."

Thurgood pitched a fulsome bow, as if Young Solomon were the Queen of England.

"And this," Cuthridge clasped Jack's shoulder, "is Special Agent Jack Quintana, United States Air Force Office of Special Investigations, here on behalf of 240 Squadron."

Young Solomon approached Thurgood, embraced him, stood back while holding Thurgood's hands in his own, and proclaimed: "Sir Thurgood Throckmorton, my people keep da promise."

Thurgood closed his eyes and bowed again, which looked a bit silly with his hands still clasped in Young Solomon's. Lydia smothered a laugh. Cuthridge elbowed her.

Young Solomon released Throckmorton, sidestepped, and embraced Jack in the same fashion. "Special Agent Jack Quintana," he said. "My people keep da promise."

"Thank you," Jack replied. "240 Squadron thanks your people for their many years of dedication."

Young Solomon seemed to appreciate this. He grinned. "The ritual of *Elouise* gonna begin!"

Several Chagossian women ran forward, took their hands, and led them to the fire. A naked child passed everyone warm cans of Budweiser. The Chagossians opened their beers. Throckmorton, Jack, and Lydia followed suit.

When everyone but Young Solomon and Cuthridge was comfortably seated, Cuthridge produced a bottle of Glenfiddich and a couple of glasses. He poured about two fingers into each glass and said, "For many years, the people of King Solomon, the people of his son, The Man Solomon, and the people of Young Solomon have guarded a special secret on behalf of 240 Squadron and the Royal Navy."

"Da 240 Squadron!" Young Solomon shouted, and drained his glass of Scotch. Cuthridge followed suit.

"240 Squadron!" the Chagossians replied, and chugged mouthfuls of warm Bud.

Cuthridge refilled the glasses. "On this day, the emissaries of 240 Squadron have returned in order to honor the secret of *Elouise*."

"Dat secret of *Elouise*!" Young Solomon cried, and drained another two fingers.

Cuthridge did the same.

"The secret of *Elouise*!" Jack and Lydia answered with the Chagossians. More Budweiser.

"And now," Cuthridge said with a slur, "the emissaries of 240 Squadron are prepared to witness the ritual of *Elouise*."

"Ritual of *Elouise*!" Young Solomon cried, and made more Scotch disappear. Jack began to worry about the man's liver.

Jack, Lydia, and the audience echoed Young Solomon and downed more tepid Anheuser-Busch.

From somewhere to Jack's left came the scratch of a record needle. Then, amazingly, the first few notes of electric piano from "This Guy's in Love With You," by Herb Alpert and the Tijuana Brass, echoed from speakers hung in coconut trees around the clearing.

Young Solomon shuffled his feet slowly, rolled his hips, and snapped his fingers, eyes closed. Around him, the Chagossians stood, Budweisers in hand, and began to slow-dance.

Jack looked at Lydia and smiled. "Shall we?"

"We shall," she said. Jack took her in his arms.

Herb sang, " *When you smile, I can tell, we know each other very well. How can... I show you... I'm glad... I got to know ya 'cause...*"

Lydia leaned close and whispered in his ear. "This is ridiculous."

"Yes," Jack said.

"I love it."

Jack smelled her hair and tried to keep an eye on Young Solomon. The half-naked romantic waltzed his way to an imposing, stone altar.

Jack held Lydia and watched him retrieve something from the altar. It looked heavy, but the man continued to dance. Gradually, he brought it back to the fire.

The people swayed while Young Solomon held the thing over his head and moved to the music.

"This may prove the most memorable dance of my life," he told Lydia. She laughed and put her cheek on his shoulder. Chagossian kids danced around them, mimicking their posture.

Somebody switched Herb and His Tijuana Brass out for Percy Sledge, who belted "Warm and Tender Love" over a crowd of Indian Ocean islanders, a Royal Navy Commander, a British Diplomat, an Air Force Special Agent, and a friendly Lieutenant, until they were all thoroughly engaged in the ritual.

Dogs ran in and out of the crowd, chasing each other. Jack watched the sun gain the horizon over Lydia's shoulder and wondered how it was possible that he could be here. It was weird and beautiful, and he would remember it forever, but he really didn't have time for it.

The kids came around again with more Budweiser, and Young Solomon set his burden, bundled in a blanket, on a large slab of limestone before the fire.

The people stopped dancing and watched him. He raised his arms skyward, lifted his head, and rumbled, "*Elouise* is da Secret."

The crowd gave it back to him: "*Elouise* is da Secret."

"*Elouise* is da promise," he said, unfolding the blanket.

The crowd agreed that Elouise was the promise.

"*Elouise* is dat sacred bond!" Young Solomon shouted, hands still upraised.

The people confirmed that Elouise was, indeed, that sacred bond.

Young Solomon said something in Chagossian, and everybody sat again.

"We gonna honor da sacred bond here tonight," he said. "We gonna gib 240 Squadron emissary da blessed assurance dat *Elouise* gonna be safe wit Young Solomon and his people."

"Blessed Assurance!" the people cried.

"Secret! Promise! Sacred Bond!" Young Solomon wailed.

The people gave it back to him.

With a flourish, Young Solomon threw a section of blanket aside and revealed a small, steel safe with a large, rolling combination lock. It was not unlike the massive vault door lock back in London.

In fact, Jack made out a stamp near the base of the safe. "Mosler," it read.

The people gasped as if they'd never before witnessed this particular hunk of steel.

"*Elouise*," Young Solomon intoned, "we gonna open da sanctum sanctorum for to show da 240 Squadron emissary dat secret.

"My people!" Young Solomon called, "Recite for me dat sacred number."

"Forty-Seven," they answered.

Young Solomon twisted the dial to 47. Jack heard the ancient tumblers grind inside the mechanism.

"Recite for me dat blessed number!"

"Sixty-three!"

He twisted right to 63.

"Recite for me dat holy number!"

"Thirty-two!"

He twisted left to thirty-two, and then twisted sharply right. With a sharp *CLACK!*, the safe door swung open.

Jack leaned forward to see what was inside.

Young Solomon pulled a tattered bundle of papers from the safe's interior and laid them atop the limestone slab. Jack thought they were awfully close to the fire.

"Tonight," he said, "we gonna say da numbers. We gonna speak da words. We gonna keep dem safe in our heart for 240 Squadron."

The crowd did not answer back this time. Jack figured that part of the show was over.

Young Solomon reached into the safe again and retrieved a strip of silver that had been stamped with a few words. Jack couldn't make them out.

The Chagossian grabbed the paperwork with his other hand. What followed was a stream-of-memory delivery that was testament to the ritual's cultural significance.

"Island of Palau," he said, paper held before him but eyes closed, "Thirty Kiloton Plutonium."

The crowd sighed, "Eight Degree, Zero Minute, Twenty Second North..."

Jack scrambled to retrieve a notebook from a zippered pocket.

"...by One-Hundred Thirty-Four Degree, Thirty-Six Minute, Thirty-Five Second East."

"Praise be to Jesus and 240 Squadron," Young Solomon said. Jack scribbled the coordinates.

"Island of Yap," he declared, eyes shut. "Twenty-Eight Kiloton Plutonium."

The people answered, "Nine Degree, Thirty-Nine Minute, Thirty-six second North..."

"What the hell is going on?" Lydia asked him.

He ignored her and continued to transcribe the coordinates.

"...by One-Hundred Thirty-Eight Degree, Eight Minute, Forty Second East."

"Bless dat Sacred promise of *Elouise*," Young Solomon chanted. "Island of Rota," he said. "Twenty-Six Kiloton Plutonium."

The crowd replied, "Fourteen Degree, Ten Minute, Forty-Five Second North..."

Jack looked around and saw children trying to follow along with their parents.

"...by One-Hundred Forty-Five Degree, Eleven Minute, Twenty-Two Second East."

"Da blessed saints gonna protect us people, and keep safe dat sacred promise of *Elouise*," Young Solomon assured the crowd, just as he had likely been assured by his father, and his father before him.

"Control Center," he called.

They responded en-masse, "Thirteen Degree, Twenty Minute, Fifteen Second North, by One-Hundred Forty-Four Degree, Thirty-Nine Minute, Fifty-Nine Second East."

Finally, the young man snatched up the metal strip, ran his fingers over it, and held it out to the crowd. "Together we say dat sacred scripture of Elouise."

From every voice in the crowd came the same sentence: "Now I am become Death, da destroyer of world."

Jack wrote it down. Lydia grasped his arm. "This turned rather dark in a hurry, didn't it?"

"Look at them," Jack said. "They don't know what they're saying."

Lydia looked around, and Jack saw the confusion on her face. The Chagossians were elated; smiling. The ritual had been performed and the magic had happened. They were safe.

* * *

More canned Budweiser flowed, like, well, Budweiser. Throckmorton joined Young Solomon and Commander Cuthridge for another slug of Scotch. With Young Solomon thus distracted, Jack snapped photographs of the coordinates and the curious, stamped strip of metal. It was silver after all.

Jack recognized the verse as the line Robert Oppenheimer had quoted after detonating the first atomic bomb. It was a verse from the Hindu text Bhagavad-Gita.

Jack didn't know thing one about the Bhagavad-Gita, but the line was obviously important. They'd put the bomb coordinates down on paper, sure, but the Oppenheimer quote they'd stamped into a hefty hunk of pure silver. Why? It meant something. On the other side of the silver strip were a series of dots and lines. Those probably meant something too.

When he was sure he'd gotten photographs of everything, he stuffed the phone into his pocket and approached Commander Cuthridge, who'd wandered away from Young Solomon to take a piss in the bushes.

Jack walked up beside him and unzipped his fly. "Jesus Christ, man," Jack whispered. "These people have been reciting the coordinates of three nuclear weapons for the past seventy-five years, and nobody thought to check up on it?"

Commander Cuthridge looked at him. "You mean to say you expected us to believe the United States would just leave three nuclear bombs lying around at Palau, Yap, and Rota?"

Jack saw what he meant. The oversight *was* unbelievable.

"Of course," Cuthridge said. "We supposed the information had been of some operational value at some point. Why else would the S.I.S. have sent it all the way out here?

"The first time I attended one of these, it was with that boy's Grandfather, 'King' Solomon. You think the kid's got charisma," Cuthridge shook his head, "his Grandfather was a bloody superstar."

"Anyway," he continued, zipping his fly, "when I first heard what they were saying, I was blown away. But I looked around at the other Naval officers in attendance. They smiled and winked and joked about it. I asked the same question you did, and they gave me the same answer I just gave you."

"Jesus," Jack muttered.

"Right," Cuthridge confirmed. "But around here, the Son of God is on the same pedestal as Elouise, so you just watch your language, mate."

Jack thanked the people for the Budweiser and gave Young Solomon a grave handshake. "Two-Forty Squadron is satisfied you and your people have served *Elouise* with distinction."

Young Solomon beamed at this. Throckmorton gave him an equally reprehensible line of bullshit, and they returned to the vehicle.

* * *

Cuthridge dropped them back at the Seaman's Center, where Throckmorton had parked the Nissan pickup. "Going to be here a while?" Lydia asked.

"Could be," Jack replied.

"I might be around later."

Jack gave her a quick smile, "Okay, Lieutenant."

Cuthridge pulled the vehicle back onto the road.

"Say Jacky-boy," Throckmorton said. "I believe you put some ants in that girls pants back at the dance."

"That's enough of that," Jack told him, dialing General Carter.

"But she hasn't a chance."

"Throck." Jack warned him.

"'Cause you won't spare her a glance."

"Let's get a drink, Throck," Jack encouraged, pushing him through the entrance.

"Praise be to Elouise!" he shouted, and made for the bar.

Jack paid for a bottle of Tiger Beer while the satellite phone tried to connect. He walked out to the abandoned picnic table and lit another smoke.

"Carter," the General said. He sounded shot.

"Quintana here. I've got what you need."

Silence yawned from the General's end. Then, "You'd better not be yanking my crank, Quintana."

207

"I wouldn't do that, sir," Jack assured him, and took a drag on the Camel.

"Hold on!" Carter replied. Jack heard papers shuffling in the background. "Just hold it a sec.

"Johnson!" Jack heard Carter yell. "Get your ass in here, Lieutenant, and take this goddamned phone."

"Lieutenant Johnson here," Jack heard a nervous voice say on the other end, "I'm ready to transcribe, Agent Quintana."

Jack gave him the coordinates, as preached by Young Solomon to his island congregation and guaranteed by the sacred promise of *Elouise*. Also, as validated by the photos Jack had taken of the paperwork and silver strip.

"Gimme that phone, Lieutenant," Jack heard Carter say in the background. "Jack?"

"Yessir."

"That special team is set to arrive at Won Pat International in three hours. Your timing is impeccable."

"Thanks," Jack replied, watching the moon rise over the ocean.

"You need to get on back to Guam as soon as possible," Carter demanded. "You and that Crockmotton, both."

"Roger, sir. We'll do that."

"I expect you've been watching the news?"

"Off and on. Whenever I get a chance."

"These hot-shot Navy boys from the *Ronald Reagan* are out here trying to kick off World War III, and the Chinese aren't diving for the bombs. Now, if those Chinese were actually diving for the bombs, I'd say to myself 'Okay, Mike, those bastards are trying to find those old nukes before we can get to 'em. Trying to scare up a mess of radioactive news coverage to validate their role in 'securing the region,' and we all know just what the hell that means.'

"Now, at this point, my ass is in a sling. I can't tell the media we actually *did* lose three nuclear bombs, but that it wasn't my fault, that it wasn't my daddy's fault, that it was actually my granddaddy's fault, because everybody thought everything was good to go when the war ended, and we just kind of forgot about these three plutonium bombs that were ready and set to detonate out in the Pacific. That's just something I cannot say.

"On the other hand. I can set this special team on the hunt for this one bomb off the coast of Rota. I sure as hell can do that. What I can't do is airdrop teams on Palau and Yap to go search for those other two bombs.

"Now, you and I know that the Chinese know that they've got control of the north end of both Yap and Palau. So why aren't they looking for those bombs? Why are they just sitting out there, floating around, preventing us from—"

"That's it," Jack said, in a flash of inspiration. "That's it!"

"What?"

"They are preventing us from accessing the weapons. They expect us to find the coordinates, but they don't want us to disable the weapons."

"What? Why?"

"That's what we have to find out, why the Chinese Navy doesn't necessarily care about finding the bombs, and why they don't want us to be able to find them, ourselves."

"Doesn't make sense," General Carter said. "The best thing they could possibly do for themselves would be to dredge up one of those nukes, show the world the American markings on it, label us as irresponsible, and get global sympathy for taking over the Western Pacific."

"So they've got a different angle on exploiting this situation. They want more than control of the Western Pacific, or they want more out of this crisis than they know they can get at this moment."

"You'd think they would *ask* for something," Carter told him. "You'd think they would be at the negotiating table right now, demanding non-reprisal for military takeover of Taiwan."

Jack had an idea. "General, what are those Chinese vessels between Kwajalein and Johnston Atoll doing?"

"They're still doing what they've been doing since the beginning. Wandering around and sending out divers."

"Why would the Chinese be diving at islands between Kwajalein and Johnston Island, and *not* at Palau and Yap?"

"You tell me, Jack."

Jack thought a moment, took another drag on his Camel, and continued. "They're *not* diving at Palau and Yap, which means they're not interested in recovering the nukes and cashing in on the publicity."

"Okay."

"They *are* diving between Kwajalein and Johnston Atoll, which means they're still after General Harmon's Liberator Express, despite the odds against their being able to locate the wreck after all this time."

"All right," Carter said.

"The only reason they would still be interested in the Liberator Express is because they know the Liberator Express held the coordinates for the Control Center, and the operational codes."

"Christ! They want to detonate those nukes."

"Right you are," Jack said, staring at the moon. "Finding the nukes at Palau and Yap doesn't really matter. It's the location of the Control Center and the operational codes..."

After several seconds, Carter said, "Jack? You still there?"

"Yes, I just realized something."

"What?"

"The operational codes are not 'codes.'"

"I'm not following you."

"There's only one code...." Jack paused again. Then, "The code!" Jack flipped to the photos on the satellite phone and forwarded the image to General Carter. "Look at that image, General. That's a strip of pure silver with an Oppenheimer quote on one side, and a series of dots and dashes on the other."

"Morse Code," Carter said.

"That *is* the activation code. 'Now I am become Death, the destroyer of worlds.' That is the code, only it has to be transmitted by radio, from the Control Center, which is somewhere on Guam. I just gave the coordinates to Lieutenant Johnson."

General Carter came to grips with this new information. "We have to secure that Control Center ASAP."

"Maybe yes, and maybe no. At this point, it's probably a great idea, but the biggest thing is making sure the Chinese do not gain access to that Oppenheimer verse."

"Johnson!" Carter yelled. Jack took the phone away from his ear, "Get back in here with that transcription!"

"General," Jack said. "If the Chinese want to detonate those nukes, then they want to accomplish the same thing we wanted to accomplish seventy-five years ago."

"Jesus Christ. They want to wipe out the southern coast of Japan."

"Probably so. If I were you, General, I'd demand all the surveillance I could get of coastal China. Look to see if the People's Liberation Army divisions are moving toward the coast."

"You're thinking... what? Invasion?"

"I can't think of a better way to stage an excuse for invading Japan than to hide it under a flag of humanitarian assistance," Jack said. "They could blame the nuclear detonations and tidal wave on the United States, send ships and paratroopers across the East China Sea and Sea of Japan, and seize control in a matter of weeks."

"Jack, you get back here. In the meantime, we'll dedicate every available resource to throw off those search vessels between Kwajalein and Johnston Atoll."

"Understood."

The General hung up, and Jack walked back to the bar.

* * *

He didn't see her at first.

Throckmorton had found another other old chum from yesteryear, and Jack sat at the bar alone. The news channel continued to broadcast images from the ocean north of Guam, mostly B-52s and F/A-18 *SuperHornets* buzzing the *Shandong*. Jack had first tuned it out and then turned the volume down.

211

She walked past Jack to the antique jukebox against the wall. He noticed the scent of her perfume and turned to watch her. She caught his eye and then turned away, reviewing the options on the juke.

She wore a simple black skirt, heels, and a sleeveless blouse. Her blonde hair had been put up when she'd been in uniform earlier. Now, it swept back from her forehead to rest on either shoulder.

She pumped a couple coins into the slot. The Andrews Sisters' "I Can Dream, Can't I?" began to play.

She didn't come toward him. She just leaned on the juke and looked at him. She bit a fingernail, and a lock of that golden hair fell across her face.

Jack rose from his barstool, wincing at the stiffness in his leg, and walked to her. "Come on," he said. "Let's go out to the beach."

He held the door for her. She took his arm and said, "You can lean on me a little, if you like."

Jack smiled. "I think I can manage."

They limped to the beach, arm in arm, as the song from the jukebox floated behind them. A crescent moon hung over the lagoon like a muted searchlight.

"This is quite a place," he said.

"Quite a lonely place," she whispered.

"How long have you been here?"

"A little over a year, now."

Jack nodded. "But a pretty girl like you shouldn't have any trouble finding company in a place like this. It's ten-to-one men out here."

"I like to be selective."

"And you've selected me." It wasn't a question.

"I have. I hope you don't think that's terribly forward."

"No, I think it's wonderfully *straight*forward. One thing, though." He chuckled. "I'm a bit of a wounded duck."

"I noticed," she said, turning to him in the moonlight. "We can work around that."

He cupped her chin in one hand and kissed her. Little waves lapped the shore, and a seabird called from across the lagoon.

* * *

Six hours later, a half-drunk Throckmorton woke him with a knock at the Lieutenant's door. Jack rolled out of bed and tried not to muss the new bandage she'd applied for him.

"Got to get airborne, Jacky!" Throckmorton said. Jack shushed him and told him he'd be down in a moment.

She sat up as Jack blundered around in the dark, looking for his pants. "On your way, then?"

"The Chinese won't give me a moment's peace."

"Too bad, that." She found his shirt, fished his Camels out, popped one into her mouth, lit it, and stuck it between his lips.

He took a drag and handed it back to her. "You finish it for me, sweetheart. I gotta run."

"No, you don't. Not before you've brushed and washed up."

He grinned at her. "You sound like my mother."

"There's a spare toothbrush on the sink," she shooed him away with her hands. "Your breath smells like stale beer."

He laughed and limped into the bathroom. "I like you, lady," he called over his shoulder.

"You're not so bad yourself."

He emerged from the bathroom fifteen minutes later, but she wasn't around. With a little difficulty, he got into yesterday's clothes and ventured out into the hallway. She lived on the second floor of a co-ed dormitory. It was basic but featured the standard creature comforts.

Throckmorton sat behind the wheel of the Nissan pickup, dead asleep. Jack knocked on the window. Thurgood started.

"Did you see her come outside?"

"Who?"

Jacked glared at him.

Thurgood smiled. "She's gone up the terminal. Said something about hot breakfast."

"Slide over. You're drunk."

213

Fortunately, the Nissan was an automatic, so Jack's wounded leg was not called upon to work a clutch. He sped down the island's single thoroughfare, back toward the BIOT Air Terminal. Jack tried to ask Throckmorton what time the C-17 would be ready to take off, but the old fellow had passed out in the passenger seat.

Early morning washed over them. Jack rolled his window down and raised an arm to greet the humid ocean breeze. A thin line of pink marked the eastern horizon, though he could still see a few stars.

A gray Egret swooped from a jungle perch and glided next to the truck. Jack hailed it. It swung back toward the beach to do Egret things.

Five minutes later, they arrived at the little terminal. Lydia was there to see them off. Understanding they were in a hurry, she'd taken the liberty of ordering hot ham, eggs, and oatmeal for them.

"What manner of angel are you?" Throckmorton asked, digging into the eggs.

"The manner that knows drunken fools are hungry in the morning," she said.

"I resent your condescension, Lieutenant," Throckmorton said, spraying scrambled eggs back onto the table. "But your thoughtfulness redeems you."

"How wonderful." She watched Jack as he scooped oatmeal into his mouth. "It's been awfully dull around here. You two are the first excitement I've had in ages."

"Yes," Throckmorton said, spilling his coffee. "Ever since I took up with this lot," he elbowed Jack, "I've been air-dropped over an island, shot at, airlifted out, apprehended by the police..."

"That one was your own fault," Jack reminded him.

"Yes, well," Throckmorton fussed, "don't interrupt. Where was I? Oh, yes... Apprehended by the bloody coppers, involved in a high speed car chase, flown 'round the world, introduced to a lovely S.I.S. agent..."

"She had the hots for you," Jack said, refilling his coffee cup.

"Of course she did!" Throckmorton cried. "I've been called the Sean Connery of my generation, you know."

"Sean Connery *is* your generation."

Lydia laughed and rose from her seat. "Enough, enough. I want to tell you that meeting you was fabulous. If ever you should find yourself in need, Jack," she said, bending to kiss him, "you just give me a ring."

"I'll do that, Lieutenant."

The C-17 pilots walked into the terminal. "That's my cue," Lydia said. And she was gone.

"Ready in ten minutes," the Senior pilot informed them. "Any coffee left?"

"Help yourself," Jack said. He craned his neck to get a last look at Lydia, but condensation had formed on the windows. He couldn't see a thing.

Twenty minutes later, they rose from the island's runway, and Jack wondered if he'd ever see it again. He wondered if he'd ever see *her* again. His eyelids drooped, and he fell asleep.

CHAPTER 9

A concussive explosion shook the aircraft. Jack sprang from sleep to his feet in half a second. The C-17 fell into a sharp dive, and Jack slid down the empty cargo bay toward the cockpit.

The Flight Engineer looked alarmed. Jack thought that was probably bad.

"Get to a seat and strap in!" the Flight Engineer shouted.

Jack heard flares deploy from the rear of the aircraft, and another pounding blast rocked the plane.

"What the devil is going on?" Throckmorton said.

The Flight Engineer climbed the ladder to the cockpit. The C-17 executed another sudden dive and then a hard left bank. Jack and Throckmorton had both buckled in and narrowly avoided being thrown against the far wall.

The Flight Engineer emerged from the cockpit and stumbled down the ladder as the plane swung into a right bank. He grabbed a couple of packs that looked suspiciously like parachutes.

"Unbuckle and put these on!" he shoved the packs at Jack and Throckmorton, and then put one on himself.

Jack examined the pack as the plane rocketed almost straight up, causing his stomach to plunge.

"Is there some... trouble?" Throckmorton asked the Flight Engineer.

"You bet your ass," the Flight Engineer said. "A Chinese *Chengdu* J-20 just chucked a couple Air-to-Air missiles at us."

"*Chengdu...*?" Throckmorton asked, dawdling with the parachute.

"The Chinese Air Force's answer to the F-35 *Joint Strike Fighter*," the Flight Engineer said. "Hurry up with that."

A third detonation ripped a gash in the far wall. Shrapnel ricocheted through the cargo hold.

"That's it!" the Flight Engineer shouted. "You!" He pointed at Throckmorton. "Help me position the life raft!"

Throckmorton pointed to his own chest. "Me?"

"Yes, you!" He pointed at Jack, "His leg, remember?"

"Ah, yes," Throckmorton nodded. "What can I do for you?"

The Flight Engineer led him to a large yellow box. Together, they hefted it into position in the middle of the cargo bay. The Flight Engineer situated the life raft container's parachute to face the rear of the aircraft, locked the container into place, ran to a handheld control unit, and opened the cargo bay door.

Cold air howled through the aircraft. Jack saw blue sky. The Flight Engineer deployed the drogue parachute—designed to deploy a larger parachute when in full descent. The drogue parachute whipped and swung in the open air.

He ran back to Jack and Throckmorton. "The raft goes first! You'll find it as long as you jump right after I let her go!"

"What's our altitude?" Jack shouted.

"Something like 18,000 feet! You jumped before?"

"We've had some very recent experience," Throckmorton answered, cleaning his fingernails.

"Good!" the Flight Engineer said, and turned away.

"Wait!" Jack yelled. "Where are we?"

"South China Sea!" he called back. "Just west of Manila!"

Jack stood and walked to the center of the cargo bay. The Flight Engineer held up a gloved hand and screamed, "Three!"

"Two!"

On "Two," he released the life raft.

"One!" The life raft scooted from the cargo bay like a dragster leaving the starting line.

He swung his arm down and pointed toward the yawning exit. "Go! Go! Go!"

Throckmorton jogged to the open bay door and executed a perfect swan dive out into nothing. Jack limped after him and fell from the aircraft.

As he plummeted out of the sky with his back to the ocean, Jack saw another Air-to-Air missile scream in from nowhere. The pilots pushed the giant plane into a third combat dive. The missile detonated under the C-17's right wing. Half the wing disintegrated. The C-17 went into a slow spin.

The accelerating speed of Jack's fall whipped him around so he no longer faced the sky. He lost sight of the C-17, but he saw the life raft, still in free-fall far below. Throckmorton was closer.

Jack watched the life raft. He didn't want to deploy his parachute 'til he saw the raft's chute open. Otherwise, he might lose both the raft and Throckmorton.

Jack craned his neck for another glimpse of the C-17. Instead, he saw the *Chengdu* fighter pass overhead, in pursuit of the mangled cargo plane.

About 30 seconds later, at somewhere close to 5,000 feet, the life raft's parachute deployed. He yanked his ripcord an instant later. Throckmorton did the same. The parachute slammed Jack into a gentle descent, and he decided this was his best opportunity to coordinate a rescue, while the satellite phone was still dry.

He unzipped his shirt pocket and pulled it free, only to fumble it over a carabiner. He had a bad moment when he thought he was going to drop it, but he pulled his legs up and caught it between his knees.

"Jesus," he breathed, holding the phone in both hands. He punched the "ON" button and waited for the phone to acquire a signal. Thankfully, this close to the Philippines, it took only a few seconds. He dialed the General and got nothing but a steady ring and then a polite, recorded female voice that informed him... "the recipient's voicemail box is full."

"Damn!" he cursed, and took another look below him. He was off-track. With a few adjustments to either steering handle, he got himself back in line with Thurgood and the life raft. His altitude was running out.

He dialed the only other number he'd saved to the phone. Sergeant Kirker picked up on the second ring. "Kirker here," the Sergeant said.

Jack heard loud voices in the background. *"Get that COMSEC over to Ops, right now!"* and *"...in the Headquarters briefing room getting ready for..."*

"Sergeant Kirker!" Jack shouted. "I need you to listen carefully. I only have a few seconds."

"Go."

"I was on a C-17, en-route from Diego Garcia back to Guam. We took three Air-to-Air missiles from a Chinese fighter. The C-17's going down over the South China Sea. Somewhere just west of Manila. Are you tracking?"

"Tracking," Sergeant Kirker replied.

"The crew was still aboard when we bailed out with a life raft," Jack continued. "I'm going to hit the water in about fifty seconds, and then this phone may be useless. I need you to communicate all of this to General Carter, ASAP."

"Will do," the Sergeant responded. "Now you listen to me."

"Okay."

"On your sat-phone, there's a cover on the top right corner of the handset. Remove it, and press down on the red button."

Jack followed the instructions. A prompt appeared on the satellite phone display: "Entering Emergency Mode in 20 Seconds. Deploy the antenna and make sure it is oriented towards the sky."

Jack yanked on the antenna; it was fully deployed. A green indicator reading "SoS" glowed brightly beneath the red button.

He mashed the phone against his face again. The water rushed toward him.

"Kirker!"

"Yes?"

"Thanks, man."

Jack shoved the phone back into his pocket, pulled up the zipper, and pulled both of the steering lines. His bad leg hit the water first, and he screamed.

* * *

While Jack tried to stay conscious, Throckmorton swam to the life raft. Jack watched him activate a pressurized canister. The raft inflated, and Throckmorton threw him a nylon rope.

Jack pulled himself to the raft, and Throckmorton helped him up and over the rim. The raft was roomy, intended for many more than two people. Jack wondered what had become of their flight crew. He pulled the satellite phone out of his pocket. It was drenched, but the green "SoS" light still flickered. He hoped that meant something positive.

"So, Jacky," Throckmorton said. "Here we are in the good old South China Sea, emphasis on the word 'China.' How long do you suppose it will be before the damnable Chinese Navy absconds with our persons for a long session of 'What Do You Know?'"

"Cut it out, Throck. My leg is killing me." Jack found the dregs of his Hydrocodone and popped two, soggy tablets into his mouth. They felt like slime-coated pellets.

"Sorry, Jack," Throckmorton replied. "Look!" he cried. "There's a compartment in here." He rifled around behind a yellow flap and produced a case of plastic water bottles. "We'll live for a while," Thurgood said, "but we shan't do it in style."

Beside the water bottles and a few "Meals Ready to Eat," or "MREs," Throckmorton found a powerful radio with a solar battery charger. "Awfully good of them to leave us a little entertainment," Thurgood mumbled, and rifled through the MREs.

Jack looked at the western horizon. The sun was half buried in it. "Not much chance we'll be rescued or absconded with tonight," Jack said. "It'll be dark in twenty minutes."

"Right you are, Jacky," Throckmorton said, and handed Jack a water bottle. Jack wished he'd waited a few minutes before dry-swallowing those pills.

"Throck," Jack said, feeling the Hydrocodone start to work, "I want to thank you for maintaining such a positive attitude."

"My pleasure, Jack. Really nothing to it, though. When you've had the women, success, money, and influence that I have, it comes quite naturally."

Jack laughed. "One of God's chosen, then?"

"You could put it that way, I admit. I do have my little problem." He mimed tipping a glass. "But life wouldn't have much depth without a dash of addiction and flawed character, would it?"

"I guess it wouldn't."

"After all," he continued, opening a bag of chocolate candies from an MRE, "we're all just a bunch of semi-intelligent monkeys, building on the success and failure of the semi-intelligent monkeys that came before us. You know, Darwin once said that..."

Jack rested his head against the side of the life raft and stopped listening. The first few stars twinkled in the eastern sky. The shirt pocket in which he stored his cigarettes was water resistant and usually protected his smokes against rain and sweat.

He unzipped the pocket and found only a few smokes in his remaining half-pack substantially wet. In fact, he had a veritable wealth of not one, not two, but three untouched cigarettes. After drying his lighter by whipping it through the air in front of him, he got it to produce a flame.

"...and that's why people from Norway have blonde hair and blue eyes," Throckmorton prattled, prying open a tin of sardines. "It's got to do with the Deoxyribonucleic acid, you see, that's the stuff that..."

Jack lit a Camel and drew the smoke into his lungs. The back of his neck tingled, and he released the smoke in a silver stream. The air stilled, and the smoke raftered to the sky. Jack watched it dissipate among the stars.

"...falsification of the fossil record is the most heinous crime anyone could ever perpetrate upon the history of this ancient earth," Thurgood said, indignantly, between bites of sardine. "Like a bite, eh, Jacky?"

Jack shook his head and continued to appreciate his cigarette. It was almost half gone now. He stared at the burning tobacco and thought how strange it was to smoke a North Carolina crop in a big rubber life raft on a foreign sea on the other side of the world. He wondered about the farm where the tobacco was grown. Was it a big, complex, industrial operation? Or was it worked by a holdout from the old Carolina tobacco families, by a man who loved his job and knew how to do it right?

Jack shook his head and realized he'd almost fallen asleep. The Hydrocodone was good stuff, but he thought his exhaustion a consequence of the pace at which he and Throckmorton had executed their investigation. And the investigation was far from over.

"Filaments!" Throckmorton said, nodding his head and searching for something in the food case. Crackers, maybe. "Little filaments of tungsten. He tried everything before discovering the light bulb could only be truly viable if he used filaments of tungsten, which burned continuously in a vacuum..."

They still had to get back to Guam and find that Control Center. Sure, they had the coordinates. But even if the coordinates were accurate, there was seventy-five years' worth of dirt, trees, grass, shrubs, and debris to clear from the site. The place had to be underground. Otherwise, somebody would have found it already. Or it could have been demolished by a typhoon. Or by accident, maybe.

Jack considered that. Maybe all the danger was already gone, erased from the equation by some post-World War II demolition crew. That would certainly give the old Chinese a kick in the head. With no Control Center, there would be no way to deliver the Morse Code transmission to the bomb receivers.

He supposed the Chinese could try to deliver the transmission with a modern radio, but who knew to what frequency the receivers were tuned? The Chinese would have to try them all. And how many frequencies were there? Jack didn't know, but he knew there were enough to keep the Chinese transmitting long enough to guarantee the American Navy and Air Force would push them out of the Philippine Sea before they found the right one.

If Jack's guess was right, the Control Center equipment would already be set to the correct frequency for transmitting to the bomb receivers, or there would be instructions readily available to that end. The most important element, now, was to find and secure that Control Center before the Chinese could locate it.

General Carter said the ships between Kwajalein and Johnston Island were still wandering, still searching. But that had been some fourteen hours ago. A lot could happen in fourteen hours. If the Chinese did happen to find that old Liberator Express, there could be trouble at the Control Center site, regardless of whether Carter's Security Forces had it surrounded. The Chinese had dedicated significant resources and personnel to this effort. They might try to take it anyway.

"...flagellating themselves with whips in their distant, stone monasteries. What for? To effect a sort of physical and spiritual prostration before a God in which they believed wholeheartedly, but with no real reason..."

"Throck, toss me some of those sardines before I flagellate *you*."

* * *

They drifted for five hours before the ship arrived. Throckmorton shook him awake, and Jack heard it plowing through the water, somewhere in their immediate vicinity.

Jack peered over the rim of the life raft. He could see only a murky outline. It was about a thousand yards off, but someone aboard worked a searchlight over the sea.

Their chances were fifty-fifty, Jack reckoned. If it was looking for something in the middle of the night, it was looking for them. Fishermen didn't hunt for tuna with a searchlight, and commercial vessels didn't sail in circles. It was either Chinese or something friendly, but the odds threw too much risk into revealing themselves.

Throckmorton looked at him and shrugged. "We'll wait to see if it gets any closer," Jack said. "Maybe we'll hear something."

Passing clouds broke the light from the waxing moon, which was lucky. If this were a clear night, they would already have been spotted.

Five minutes passed. Then the vessel turned and chugged almost directly for them.

"Damn it," Jack breathed.

"What's to do, Jacky?" Throckmorton asked.

"Grab a safety line," Jack told him. "We'll have to slide over the side and try to pull the raft out of the way."

"That leg might present a problem," Throckmorton said, scratching his beard stubble. "The South China's full of sharks, you know."

"No time to worry about sharks," Jack said. "Let's get over the side."

They both grabbed a line and slipped over the rim of the life raft, opposite the approaching ship. "Dog paddle," Jack said. Salt water invaded his wounded leg. It stung like a thousand angry hornets. He gasped and began to paddle.

Throckmorton was a strong swimmer. In thirty seconds, they'd pulled the raft far enough to avoid being run over, but the vessel would surely run right past the raft.

At a hundred yards distant, Jack heard voices from the deck. "Can you make them out?" Jack asked Throckmorton as they huddled in the water, grasping the safety lines.

Throckmorton tilted his head and listened. "I can hear the voices, but not the words. However, the cadence does not sound English." He listened a few moments more. "Tagalog, spoken in the Philippines, is rather guttural, with lots of soft consonant starts and stops. What they're speaking seems to include many long vowel sounds."

"What does that mean?" Jack asked.

"Means it's likely a Chinese vessel." They bobbed at the surface on the far side of the life raft.

The searchlight roved. Jack watched it bathe the ocean in front of them. Suddenly, the light pulled up closer to the ship and illuminated their raft. Jack and Throckmorton hid in shadow.

Excited voices, now clearly Chinese, babbled from the deck. "Throck!" Jack whispered, "The food!"

"Threw it back under the storage flap, didn't I?" Throckmorton whispered.

The vessel pulled closer, and their protective vein of shadow grew thin. "When that spotlight is directly overhead," Jack said, "we'll have to dive under the raft."

"Right," Throckmorton replied.

A Chinese sailor snagged the raft with a gaff hook, and Jack nodded to Throckmorton. They both inhaled and dove beneath the surface.

Jack hadn't fully realized the danger they were in.

Sometime in the fifteen minutes since they'd slipped over the side, his leg had begun to bleed. In the ambient, subsurface glow from the spotlight, Jack counted seven sharks circling the life raft. He recognized one of them as the aggressive "Oceanic Whitetip," the shark that had wiped out over 150 sailors when the U.S.S. *Indianapolis* sank between Tinian and the Philippines in July of 1945.

His heart rate spiked. His lungs screamed for more oxygen. Jack forced himself to look up at the bottom of the raft. The salt water stung his eyes.

From the search vessel, a debate started in Chinese. Throckmorton looked at Jack and bobbed his head from left to right, indicating there was some kind of back-and-forth between two of the crew members.

Jack imagined the conversation in his mind in order to distract himself from the sharks. *Get that life raft up on the deck!* What for? There's nobody in it. *There could be something we need to see.* Like what? *I don't know, but it's better to be safe than to miss a trick.* If you want that life raft up on the deck, you can haul it up yourself. It's heavy. *Look, I outrank you, and I'm telling you to drag that sucker up here.* Do it yourself. *Blah-blah-blah.*

Jack's body ached for a fresh breath. He looked down at his thigh. A bloody tendril twirled from his pant leg like crimson smoke. One of the sharks ventured closer to the raft. Jack pressed a hand against his leg, trying to stop the bleeding.

At last, the searchlight moved away from the raft, and the Chinese sailors did not attempt to haul it into the ship. Throckmorton yanked his arm, and they swam toward the edge of the raft.

The sudden absence of bright light disoriented him. Throckmorton disappeared, and inky darkness plunged him into confusion. Jack kicked his legs 'til his head touched the bottom of the raft, and then followed the slick material in what he hoped was a straight course to the outer edge.

Something bumped his good leg. He tensed. His body throbbing for oxygen, he inched along the underside of the raft 'til he felt the slick material bend up and away.

Jack surfaced and whooped a great lungful of air. Throckmorton heard him and scrambled in his direction. Jack threw an arm up and over the rim of the raft.

Something slammed his bad leg, hard. "Pull me up!" Jack cried.

Throckmorton grabbed his arm and yanked him up. At the same instant, one of the smaller sharks, it might have been a Mako, lunged after Jack's bleeding leg. It landed halfway over the rim, thrashing and gnashing.

Thurgood pulled Jack to the center of the raft and then slid toward the splashing shark. Jack sucked air and struggled into a sitting position.

Throckmorton kicked out with his right leg and caught the Mako in the eye. It crashed back into the water.

"Throck," Jack gasped. "I owe you one."

They looked at each other and Jack broke into hysterical laughter. "Jesus Christ! I was two seconds from being fish food."

Throckmorton saw the dread on him and scrambled over. "Hold tight, there, Jacky," he said, gripping him by the shoulders. Jack laughed and laughed, but his face held an ugly grimace. "All right, now," Thurgood said. "Danger's passed."

Jack got himself under control.

"Nothing but smooth sailing, now," Throckmorton said. Jack looked at him, and they both laughed, real laughter, at the same time.

"Smooth sailing!"

"Smooth sailing. Right..."

A few minutes later, when their guffaws had subsided into chuckles, Throckmorton pulled the solar powered radio from beneath the storage flap. He switched it on, got a blast of static, and rolled the channel selector under his thumb. They picked up a couple of Tagalog stations, presumably out of Manila, and Jack was encouraged. If they could pick up FM radio stations, they couldn't be too many miles from land.

"I'm sorry to admit I don't know a single word of Tagalog," Throckmorton said. "But it's definitely Tagalog, and that's a hell of a lot better than bloody Chinese."

They found an oldies station, and Throckmorton stopped fiddling with the dial. Gilbert O'Sullivan sang "Alone Again, Naturally," in his patently Irish voice. Jack lay on his back, sure to stay away from the sides of the raft. He watched the moon as they bobbed on the water, all the bright universe above, and circling death below.

* * *

As the sun flirted with the eastern horizon, Jack pulled the satellite phone back out of his pocket. The SoS indicator still gave a feeble blink every few seconds.

Throckmorton snored on his back in the center of the raft. Jack ventured a glance over the side. He couldn't see any sharks, but they might still be there, just a few feet below the surface, waiting.

Then, over the gentle splash of water against the sides of the raft, he heard something. He couldn't be sure at first, but he thought it might be a helicopter.

"Throck!" he called, rising to this knees.

Throckmorton snorted. "What? What's the trouble?"

"You hear that?"

Throckmorton stilled himself, listened, and said, "That's a bloody whirly-bird, it is."

They scanned the horizon. Jack spied an infinitesimal black dot. It was difficult to see through the bursting sunlight behind it, but the dot expanded.

Five minutes later, an orange-and-white Philippine Coast Guard Air Bus H145 swooped over them and circled the raft. Jack waved his arms. The side door opened, and a man waved back. He stepped from the side of the helicopter in a rescue harness and descended to the life raft.

"You Jack Quintana?" he called.

"You gonna leave if I'm not?"

The man laughed, now at eye level with Jack and Throckmorton, "Staff Sergeant Kyle Hooper, Air Force Pararescue."

Staff Sergeant Hooper secured Jack in the harness, and Thurgood steadied them as they ascended. "Sorry it took us so long to find you," Hooper said. "We only got two good position readings from your satellite phone, and you seem to have drifted pretty far from the first position."

"Don't apologize," Jack told him. "We're glad to see you."

After loading Jack aboard the hovering aircraft, Hooper went back for Throckmorton, who decided he wanted to keep the radio.

Once situated, a Filipino technician slammed the chopper's door shut, and they whirled back toward Manila.

"Quite a lot's happened since you took off from Diego," Hooper said, removing the rescue harness.

"Do fill us in, Sergeant," Throckmorton said. He opened another tin of sardines from the raft.

"Well," Hooper said, planting himself on the floor, "something happened out near Kwajalein last night. Some kind of standoff."

Jack bumped his leg against a piece of equipment and winced. Hooper saw the blood. "Hey," he said, "we should do something about that."

Jack shook his head. "Tell us about the standoff first."

"I got a quick briefing back in Okinawa before I flew out to Clark Air Base, just outside Manila. Apparently, General Carter redirected a few of those B-52s on the alert route from Guam to Palau and Yap. He sent three or four to reconnoiter the Chinese vessels near Kwajalein.

"The Captain of the *Shandong* sent a couple *Chengdu* fighters after the '52s. It looked like the Chinese vessels near Kwajalein might have found what they were looking for on one of those uninhabited, no-name islands in the Kwajalein archipelago. They'd stopped wandering, I guess, and that's why General Carter sent the B-52s.

"Those *Chengdu* fighters harassed our bombers all the way out to Kwajalein, trying to get them to turn back, probably. As the '52s approached their destination, one of the *Chengdus* fired an Air-to-Air, and one of our bombers went down. The crew survived, I think, but they were picked up by the Chinese.

"Basically," he said, "we're now at war with China."

Jack ran a hand over his face. "That's why the Chinese fighter took out our C-17," he said. "They're trying to clear all American presence from the unoccupied Western Pacific."

Sergeant Hooper nodded. "Probably so."

"Any news about our crew from the C-17?" Jack asked. "The Flight Engineer was wearing a parachute, but he told us to bail out first. Right after we jumped, the C-17 took a hit and started going down."

"We're still searching for the wreck, but it doesn't look good for them."

They were silent for a moment. Then Sergeant Hooper said, "General Carter wants both of you back on Guam, and he wants you there yesterday. We can get you out of Clark Air Base on a C-130 within the next three hours."

Jack nodded. "That'll work."

"In a C-130, it'll take about six hours to get back to Andersen. I'll ride back with you and take care of that leg."

Forty minutes later, they landed at Clark Air Base, transferred onto a waiting C-130, and took off again. The C-130 sported red, nylon webbed seating over aluminum tube framing. Fortunately, Hooper had called ahead and got them a couple of medical cots.

Once they reached an appropriate altitude, Hooper cut Jack's pant leg off and examined the wound. "Looks like it was starting to heal and then reopened," he said, preparing to swab it with alcohol.

"Mako shark rammed it a few hours ago. Throckmorton pulled me out of the water just in time."

Hooper whistled. "Sounds like a rough night."

"You don't know the half of it," Jack said, steeling himself against the sting of the alcohol.

Hooper saw him tense and produced a syringe. "I'm gonna stick you with a local anesthetic, and then you're gonna get something to put you out for a couple hours. You'll need a clean leg and a clear mind when we land in Guam."

"Thanks, Hooper," Jack said.

CHAPTER 10

Jack awoke in an ambulance. Throckmorton sat beside him. "Headed back to HQ, Jacky," Throckmorton said.

Jack looked out the ambulance's rear windows and saw coconut trees. "All the way around the world," Jack mumbled, coming out of his drug daze.

Somebody gave him a new set of crutches when they reached 36th Wing Headquarters. General Carter met them in front of the building. "Quintana," he said. "You look like dog shit."

Jack smiled and saw the bags under his eyes. "You don't look so hot, yourself, General."

All around the building, people hurried back and forth. Little meetings happened everywhere: outside, in the hallway, on the staircase, even in the Command Section. General Carter led them through all of these and into his office, which was vacant.

"Sorry I missed your call, Jack," Carter said.

Jack dropped onto the couch. "Think nothing of it. It probably worked out better that I got Sergeant Kirker instead."

"Yes, he ran right over and passed me your message. They shot you down right after splashing one of our B-52s over Kwajalein, the bastards."

"The Pararescue Sergeant filled us in," Jack said.

"Good," Carter replied. "So. We're at war with the Chinese."

Throckmorton wandered out into the Command Section area. Jack heard him ask the Secretary where the General had stashed his Scotch.

"I'm surprised you were able to keep things from escalating as long as you did," Jack said.

"Me too, but that doesn't matter now."

"No, it doesn't. What about the Control Center, General?"

"We think we've found it. The coordinates you sent indicated it was at the top of Mount Lam-Lam, which is the highest point on the island."

"That makes sense. General Harmon would have wanted to broadcast the signal from a high point."

"We've got a Civil Engineering crew up there now, trying to dig it out of a mound of jungle-covered dirt."

"What about security?"

"When those ships out near Kwajalein stopped moving around," Carter said, looking out the window, "we doubled the number of Security Forces Airmen we had up at Lam-Lam. The Navy base sent up a contingent of their own security personnel. We've got them strung out around the sides of the mountain like piping on an wedding cake.

"On top of that," he said, "Guam PD is controlling all vehicle access points to the mountain, so she's well covered."

Jack nodded. "Sounds pretty thorough. When can I get up there?"

Carter looked at him. "Son, you're in no shape to get up anywhere right now."

"Doesn't matter. We've got to head this thing off before somebody launches an ICBM. The faster we work, the less chance that'll happen."

Carter nodded. "Beside the downed '52 and your C-17, there's been no additional damage. When we heard about the '52, I authorized the F/A-18 pilots to retaliate. We got two of their Chengdu J-20s. I wouldn't call that even, but it's a good point to take a breather."

Throckmorton strolled back in with a glass. "General," he said, "allow me to congratulate you on your splendid selection of intoxicating libations."

"Drink up fast," Carter said, as he put a phone to his ear. "We're on our way in five minutes."

Thurgood slammed the Scotch, smacked his lips, and set the glass on a table. "Where to?"

* * *

They bounced and rolled through five separate checkpoints on the way up to Mount Lam-Lam. The first stop was controlled by Guam PD, which reminded Jack about Teddy Calvo.

As they powered up a dirt trail in a four-wheel drive Sport Utility Vehicle, Jack borrowed the General's mobile phone and dialed Guam PD headquarters in Tumon. "This is Special Agent Jack Quintana with Air Force O.S.I.," he said. "Let me speak to Cruz."

"Which Cruz?" the voice answered. "Half the guys on the force are named 'Cruz.'"

Jack wracked his brain. "Hold on," he said to the desk Sergeant. "What was that police officer's name, the one who held you for Public Nudity down in Tumon?"

"It was 'Drunk and Disorderly,'" Throckmorton corrected him, "and you know it."

"Whatever, Throck," Jack said. "What was his name?"

"His name was 'Nicholas,' I believe," Throckmorton said, looking out the window. "Charming young man."

"Nicholas Cruz," Jack told the Desk Sergeant. "Lieutenant."

"Hold on," the Sergeant said.

Lieutenant Cruz picked up. "What is it?" he said, sounding none too happy.

"Lieutenant Cruz, this is Agent Quintana."

"Should I know that name?"

"Last week. Naked Brit on the Tumon Strip. Bali Hai."

"Ahh, yes. Have you lost your diplomat again?"

"No, but listen. I know you're aware of what's going on with the Chinese."

"Yep."

"One of your boys, an Officer Teddy Calvo, is on the Chinese Mob's payroll."

Cruz said nothing.

"Look, Lieutenant," Jack said, "I'm not trying to get into your business. General Carter, who's sitting right beside me at the moment, has asked that Guam PD help secure a certain landmark. You've done that, and thank you. All I want is to make sure Officer Calvo is not on-duty for that effort."

"I hear you. Only our most trusted officers are on that particular job. Calvo is not one of our most trusted officers."

"Then we understand each other."

"Yes. Good luck, Agent Quintana."

Jack hung up.

"One less thing to worry about?" General Carter asked.

"One less thing."

They rounded a stand of tropical grass, throttled up an incline, and stopped. They'd reached Lam-Lam's apex. Through the windshield, Jack saw a large excavation a little way down the other side of the mountain. Jack spotted a crumbling concrete wall beside a deep trench.

General Carter pointed. "That wall makes up one side of what we think is the Big Surf Control Center. The excavation crew has avoided the top of the building for fear of collapsing the structure. We just need to excavate around it, and we should be able to get inside."

"Let's go," Jack said.

They passed a final checkpoint on foot. The Security Forces sergeant snapped to attention and saluted General Carter. A Civil Engineering Captain jogged over to meet them as they approached.

General Carter introduced him as "Captain Dean."

"You can see an entire wall unearthed on this side," Captain Dean said. "We've got about half the other side cleared now."

"What would you say the dimensions are?" Jack asked.

"It's exactly twenty feet deep and twenty feet wide. Not a large structure at all."

Jack nodded. "Just large enough to serve it's purpose. Once."

"I wouldn't know about that, but I can tell you we'll have it unearthed and ready for entry in two hours."

"Thank you, Captain," General Carter replied. To Jack and Throckmorton, Carter said, "I need to get back to Andersen, and I need you two to dismantle the guts in that Control Center as soon as you can."

Carter pulled another satellite phone from his pocket and slapped it into Jack's hand. "I understand your last sat-phone got a little soggy. All of my numbers are pre-programmed. We threw in Kirker's number as well, just in case."

"Thank you, sir."

Carter walked back to the SUV, hopped in, and drove away.

Jack crutched down a trail toward the Control Center. From what was probably the front of the building, an impressive view of the western side of the island spread before him.

He sat on a rock and lit a cigarette. Another day had passed. The sun chased the horizon. Behind him, the team of civil engineers exposed the structure with hand tools. They had a couple of Bobcat Skid-Steers, but Captain Dean didn't want to risk damaging the building. Jack thought his caution wise.

Although the building was concrete, concrete tended to last only about a hundred years. After that, it began to weaken and disintegrate. This building had seen only seventy-five years, of course, but it had endured the scores of typhoons that had eventually buried it, and who knew what damage had been done by mud, water, and tree roots?

He took a final drag on his cigarette and thought about the Chinese. How long 'til the nuclear missiles started to fly? He threw the cigarette into the dirt, picked up a shovel, and limped toward the structure.

* * *

Throckmorton joined him twenty minutes later. Jack's shovel made a sound that was something between a scrape and a thud against the old, softening concrete. He was working on a section toward the middle of what he figured was the front of the building when the implement made a different sound.

Everyone stopped when the jarring *clang!* rang out. Jack couldn't see anything yet. The dirt was thick, and the sun was almost down, but he thought he might have found a metal door.

"I need some light over here!" he shouted. One of the civil engineering airmen started up a Bobcat, punched the lights on, and positioned it before the structure.

Everyone moved to Jack's spot and helped clear the area. Gradually, the outline of a door emerged from the soil. An old monkeypod tree sat directly atop the building, and large roots draped either side of the entrance.

Somebody brought a bucket of water and a brush. Jack splashed the metal door and used the brush to remove a layer of mud.

An aluminum placard was riveted to the steel door. The placard read: "Proj Big Surf Control. Restricted Access."

"This is it!" Jack cried, scrambling to reveal the latch and clear the remaining dirt. Ten minutes later, they had it clean enough to start puzzling over the door.

Captain Dean inspected it. "Looks like it opens inward," he said.

"Can we force it open?" Jack asked.

"I wouldn't," Dean replied, running a dirty hand through sweaty hair. "It may be helping to hold up the structure. Of course, there's no way to tell unless we open it. But if it has become a load-bearing element, the whole building could come down without it wedged into its spot."

Jack considered this. Maybe they *should* just go ahead and destroy the structure. That would definitely keep the Chinese from using the equipment. On the other hand, what if the building's contents held information they would need? What if it protected an old "continuity of operations" plan that contained the location of some backup facility? What if?

"What options have we, then?" Throckmorton asked, leaning against a shovel.

"We'll have to cut our way in with a blowtorch," Captain Dean answered. "Depending on the quality and thickness of that steel," he continued, "it could take another couple of hours."

"Come on, Throck," Jack said. "Let's get some water."

"There's beer in the cooler under that truck," Dean gestured without taking his eyes from the door. "Help yourself."

Throckmorton threw his shovel to the ground. "It's true what they say about American officers!"

Dean looked back, "What's that?"

"That you are also *gentlemen*." Throckmorton trundled off to the pickup truck to investigate the contents of the gentleman's cooler.

"Where'd you pick *him* up?" Dean asked Jack.

"The Navy brought him C.O.D.," Jack answered and followed Throckmorton.

Captain Dean shrugged and turned back to the steel door.

* * *

Jack and Throckmorton sat on the pickup's tailgate and drank Busch from a can. "I take back what I said about that officer being a gentleman," Throckmorton grimaced. "This beer is awful."

"It's not that bad."

"Are you joking? It tastes like someone took a thimbleful of actual beer and dumped it into a can of mineral water."

"It'll keep you hydrated, then," Jack answered, opening a second can.

"Awfully dark out here, Jacky. Do you suppose those Chinese between Kwajalein and Johnston Atoll actually found Harmon's copies of the files?"

"They might have."

"And if they did find them, what do you think they're going to do?"

"Can't say." The moon loomed fuller tonight. It gleamed on the ocean below them.

"Yes, yes, but *think*, Jacky. They wouldn't escalate anything now because they still don't have what they need."

"And that is?"

"The bloody tidal wave, man. Big Surf. They need it to justify further action against you Americans. After all, I don't think they really want a war just yet. They want to occupy Japan first. They want to take the Pacific one bite at a time, not blow it all in a nuclear Armageddon."

237

"That's probably right," Jack said.

"Of course, it's right. I said it, didn't I? Anyway, if you were Chairman of the Chinese Communists, what would you do next?"

"They might try to set off the bombs at Palau and Yap without the Control Center access," Jack said. "I mean, they're in possession of that territory at the moment."

"That's true, but those bloody bombs are encased in seventy-five years' worth of coral. Even with the coordinates, it could take them weeks to find those antiques and dig them out without damaging them; probably even longer."

"Well, they could set off their own weapons at those locations and blame the explosions on the old, American bombs."

"I'd thought of that," Throckmorton replied, taking another swig from his can, "but I don't think it would work, and I think the Chinese know that. They don't need 'explosions.' They need the viable, properly timed series of precisely placed *detonations* that will set off the tsunami that will destroy coastal Japan.

"Remember what the old, Chinese fellow said. He said that Harmon enlisted teams of engineers to construct 'platforms' for these bombs. The official memorandums between Harmon and the Office of Scientific Research and Development contained that word as well."

"Right."

"But the old man didn't really say 'platforms.' That was just the best translation I could produce at the moment."

Jack looked at him.

"I've been thinking about that word he used. It's arcane. I don't know if I've ever heard it before, but it's more complicated than 'platform.'"

"I'm not following you, Throck."

"The word is very old but also very technical. It means something like a concave wall, like half an oyster shell stood up on its side."

"You're saying the construction of these platforms was as essential to the functionality of Big Surf as the explosions themselves."

"Exactly. If you set off a nuclear bomb in the middle of the ocean, even in the middle of the Philippine Sea, which has that basin-like quality, the energy would be distributed more or less evenly, in all directions. Now, the fact that each bomb is positioned on the north side of an island means that most of the resulting wave energy would be directed north, toward Japan, with the island of origin acting as a backstop."

"I see what you're saying," Jack said.

"But it's still not enough. The energy would dissipate into a fan shape as it moved north over hundreds of miles of ocean. It might produce a tidal wave, but I don't think it would be terribly destructive. However, if the bomb were detonated inside an underwater structure that was large enough and strong enough to direct that explosive energy into a focused cone that would dissipate only slightly along its course toward Japan, and you reinforced the explosion with complementary detonations along the way, I imagine you could produce a tidal wave that would be immensely destructive."

"So, you're saying Palau would go first, the explosion blasting out of this 'concave wall' construction, and be strengthened by a second explosion at Yap, which is northeast of Palau, and then a third explosion at Rota, which is northeast of Yap."

"Yes," Throckmorton said, staring out at the ocean. "If the detonations were timed properly, each explosion would build on the one before it, intensifying the wave to such an extent as to turn it into a ... forgive the tired term... weapon of mass destruction."

Jack drained his beer. "Okay, so that might have been the plan. But we have the Control Center," Jack gestured, "obviously."

"Yes," Throckmorton said, sounding troubled.

Jack looked down to where Captain Dean's team worked on the door with blowtorches. The light from the torches was blinding, and Jack looked away.

* * *

A shot rang out, and Throckmorton fell forward from the tailgate.

"Throck!" Jack cried.

More shots ripped through the night, and the pickup's rear window exploded. Jack jumped to the ground and pulled Thurgood under the vehicle. Jack looked down at Captain Dean's team. They continued to work on the door, unaware of the gunfire.

From the darkness above the mountain came a sound like rippling silk. Gunfire rained down around the truck. He jumped into the cab, thumbed the radio, and shouted: "All stations, all stations! The Control Center structure is under attack! All units deploy to the top of the mountain!"

A bullet punched through the windshield, and the radio exploded on the dashboard. Plastic shrapnel sliced a channel in Jack's forehead. He rolled out of the truck and crawled underneath it. Throckmorton lay unconscious. From what Jack could see, he'd taken a round in the back, just below his right shoulder.

Black shapes fell from the the black sky. Black parachutes hung above them. Jack snagged a tarp from the bed of the truck, spread it over Throckmorton, and limped down the hill toward Captain Dean's team.

Halfway down, he heard boots strike the earth behind him. He looked back and saw figures detach themselves from parachutes. The figures fired on the Control Center building.

One of Captain Dean's people took a bullet in the leg and screamed. Both of the blowtorches went out. "We're under attack!" Jack shouted. "Take cover!"

Dean's team huddled against the building. Jack, caught in the open between the attackers and the Control Center, could do nothing but continue toward the structure.

More gunshots cut the island night. Jack recognized the hearty *pop-pop-pop* of the American M-4 assault rifle set to semi-automatic fire.

Someone screamed in Chinese behind him. He stumbled a final twenty yards to the cover of the concrete structure. Captain Dean pulled him down.

"What the hell is going on?" Dean asked, applying pressure to the leg wound his troop had sustained.

"The Chinese found the coordinates for the Control Center. They're trying to take it away from us," Jack said, panting.

A gunfight erupted beyond the pickup truck. A Security Forces High Mobility Multipurpose Wheeled Vehicle, or HMMWV, roared up the incline and bathed the clearing in brilliant light. Some twenty Chinese paratroopers scrambled for cover.

Two Security Forces troops spilled from the vehicle and fired from behind its open doors. The Chinese paratroopers returned the barrage.

Between bouts of rifle-fire, Jack heard more rustling in the sky. "Shit," he said.

"What now?" Dean asked, fixing a tourniquet on his troop's leg.

Jack turned and saw more black parachutes descend onto the mountain. As they descended, the gunfire renewed in earnest.

Six parachutes came down on top of the control center itself. One of them caught in the monkeypod tree whose roots encircled the structure. Jack saw the paratrooper cut the nylon lines with a knife and then drop to the base of the tree, which was directly over their heads.

In the light of the HMMWV's headlights, Jack saw the black hair, slim figure, and scarred face of last week's violent affair.

"Xiao," he said.

* * *

Six Chinese paratroopers encircled them. Xiao dropped from the base of tree to the excavated area before the door. She kicked his wounded leg. He dropped to the dirt.

Xiao leveled a pistol at Captain Dean's head. "Please continue," she said.

"Take a hike, lady," Dean replied. She shot him in the midsection. He collapsed.

"You," she said, waving the pistol at one of Dean's civil engineering Airmen, "please continue."

"Do it," Jack told the Airman. "Or she'll shoot you and have her own men do it for her."

The Airman picked up the blowtorch, lit it, and went back to work. To his dismay, Jack saw the large square incision in the steel door was almost complete.

The battle raged on the hill above them. From the sound of the gunfire, Jack estimated more American troops than Chinese, but not by many.

The Airman finished with the blow torch. One of Xiao's paratroopers hefted a sledgehammer and swung it against the metal square. It popped from the door and clattered on the concrete floor inside the Control Center.

The new opening stretched four feet high and two feet wide, room enough for a small person. Xiao flipped on a flashlight and crawled inside.

From the ground outside the door, Jack watched her run the flashlight over some kind of control surface, a radio transmitter, and other support equipment.

The fighting continued above them. For the first time, however, shots came from the darkness on the slope below the Control Center. A team of Carter's Security Forces had climbed straight up the side of the mountain and commenced firing on the paratroopers outside the structure. The Chinese troops dropped and fired back as Xiao inspected the interior.

"So you found the old Liberator Express, did you?" Jack called to her.

"Found it."

"You look awfully sexy in that black leotard thing," Jack said.

She stepped back outside and glared at him. "Shut up."

A sharp-eyed Security Forces troop put a bullet through a Chinese head. The paratrooper fell backward and sprayed blood into the Control Center.

"This isn't looking good for your boys," Jack said.

She fired down the hill and then glanced around, searching for something.

"Of course," he continued, "looking good isn't really something you have to worry about anymore."

She fired another shot down the hill. One of Carter's troops put two bullets into another paratrooper. She backed toward the building.

"What with the Frankenstein scars and all. You know."

"Shut your mouth!" she cried. She grabbed two paratroopers, pointed them toward the pickup truck, and shouted something in Chinese. They abandoned the firefight and rushed up the trail toward the truck.

"You're not gonna make it," Jack said. "You're outnumbered here. This was a bold move, I'll give you that. But it won't pay off."

The paratroopers reached the pickup truck and jumped in. Jack saw Throckmorton shove the tarp aside, reach up underneath the cab, and cut the brake line. The pickup coughed to life, and Throckmorton rolled out from underneath.

Xiao's eyes widened, and she shouted something in Chinese. The men in the pickup failed to acknowledge her, dropped it into gear, and gunned it forward. The pickup gained speed down the trail. Jack saw the brake lights flash once, twice, and then the pickup barreled past them, down the hill toward a rock outcropping.

It smashed into the rocks at forty miles per hour, flipped end over end, landed in a grinding crash, caught fire, and exploded.

"There was half a case of *beer* in that truck!" Jack shouted at her. "Can't you do *anything* right?"

Another of her paratroopers took a bullet. Her little contingent was down to herself and two others. She grabbed one of them and pointed at a Bobcat Skid-Steer beyond a mound of freshly excavated dirt.

He sprinted for the Bobcat. While Xiao watched his progress, Throckmorton moved toward the Bobcat in a crouch.

Jack saw her put most of her weight on her left leg. From his prone position, he leaned back and rammed his fist into the back of her knee. She dropped in a heap and rolled away from him.

A second later, she popped up, pointed the pistol at his head, and started to squeeze the trigger.

Better this than sharks.

A bullet from one of Carter's troops caught her in the hip. She spun around and screamed. The Control Center wall held her up.

Jack looked back to the Bobcat. The paratrooper had reached it a few seconds before Throckmorton. Its diesel engine roared to life, and the paratrooper blasted it toward the Control Center.

She saw the vehicle coming and reached into a pack one of her men had dropped. With a painful grunt, she extracted a long, red cable with alligator clips at either end.

Power. Jack thought. *That's why she wanted the pickup. She needs to power the Control Center.*

Jack pulled himself to his feet with one of the tree roots. A bullet plowed concrete shrapnel out of the wall and into his face. He was going to look worse than Xiao before this thing was over.

Blood flooded his eyes. He wiped his face but couldn't clear his vision.

The Bobcat bounced into the cleared area and stopped in front of the Control Center entrance. The paratrooper jumped out. Xiao gave him one end of the red cable. He unlatched the steel engine compartment, found the battery, and clamped the alligator clips to either terminal.

Throckmorton sprinted from the trail and lunged at the paratrooper. They rolled downhill as bullets split the air over them.

Xiao leapt through the steel door with her end of the cable as five or six of the original paratroopers retreated down toward the Control Center from the top of the hill. Only a few remained, but they held the objective.

Jack squeezed through the opening in the steel door just in time to see Xiao rip the leads from an ancient terminal. The terminal was connected to a giant 1940s era battery covered in acid dust.

She opened the alligator clips, connected on the other end to the running Bobcat's battery, and snapped them onto the terminal connections. Several lights came on. A few incandescent bulbs exploded overhead. Jack saw an indicator light on a telegraph transmitter flash sporadically, and a hum of ancient electrical equipment filled the room.

He grabbed the red cable and yanked the leads from the terminal. The room went dark.

Xiao shrieked and shot him in the right shoulder.

Jack flew backward, cracked his head against the concrete wall, and slid to a sitting position. Blood spurted from the wound.

She reconnected the terminal. Another light bulb exploded, but two or three still glowed. From the floor, his vision fading, Jack watched her flip a switch. A two-inch diameter antenna rose from the Control Center floor, pushed through a hole in the ceiling, and then punched through the dirt above the building. For a moment, Jack thought the old electric motor pushing it skyward would blow itself out.

But good old-fashioned American engineering held tough. The motor smoked, the motor screeched, the motor caught fire, but the motor pushed that antenna all the way to full staff.

"Damn," Jack said.

Xiao whipped a silver strip from her pocket, sat at the telegraph, and started to send in Morse Code. Jack could hear only electronic noise from the telegraph, but he knew the message by heart: "Now I am become Death, the destroyer of worlds."

* * *

9:34 p.m. // PALAU LOCAL TIME

Three-hundred Chinese sailors off the north coast of Palau were vaporized in an instant.

Seventeen fishermen off the nearby Echo and Kayangel Islands burned to death.

Kossol Reef was destroyed.

A B-52 pilot overflying the Chinese vessels at Palau radioed news of a nuclear explosion back to Andersen Air Force Base.

The first wave of Project Big Surf began traveling north toward Japan.

* * *

Throckmorton wrenched himself through the opening a few seconds after Xiao transmitted the last coded letter. He drove a fist into the side of her head, and she crumpled to the floor.

"Failed!" Jack cried out to Throckmorton. "After everything, they've set the goddamned thing off!"

Gunfire continued between Carter's Security Forces and the Chinese paratroopers.

Throckmorton checked his pulse. Jack passed out.

CHAPTER 11

10:50 p.m. // YAP LOCAL TIME

Sixteen Minutes and Thirty-Four Seconds after the Palau detonation, two-hundred fifty Chinese sailors off the north coast of Yap were consumed in a nuclear blast.

Two thousand islanders living in the district of Rumung were set ablaze.

A B-52 crew in the area lost control of the bomber's avionics equipment, reported the nuclear explosion back to Andersen Air Force Base, and ditched in the open ocean.

* * *

Jack regained consciousness as they sped up Marine Corps Drive toward the Air Force base. He'd lost some blood, but he didn't think it was too bad. *Too bad we couldn't stop this. Too bad we couldn't cancel this Chinese horror show. Too bad...*

Jack sat up with a start.

"Lie back, Jacky," Throckmorton urged. "Well be there soon enough."

"No. It's not over."

Throckmorton stared at him. "We've heard by the radio, Jack. The bombs at Palau and Yap have gone off. Only Rota's left to blow. Must have something to do with that special timing. Things are ticking along just like clockwork. It's done. The fat lady's sung. I wonder if that's what one of them was actually called. 'Fat Lady.' They had a 'Fat Man.' Why not a 'Fat Lady?'"

"Throck, shut up and listen to me. We may still be able to stop this thing."

They reached the front gate. Their driver was one of Carter's Security Forces troops, and the guards waved them through.

"Take us to Carter's office," Jack told the driver.

The Sergeant raced down Arc Light boulevard, slid a drifting right turn onto O'Malley, and screeched to a halt in front of the Headquarters building.

"Get me upstairs!" Jack shouted.

Throckmorton and the Sergeant pulled him from the vehicle, slung Jack's arms over their shoulders, and walked him up to Carter's office.

Carter stood at the window with a glass of Scotch in his hand. A "Defense Red Switched Network" or "DRSN" phone waited on his desk. He looked at Jack and Throckmorton, invited them to sit, and then offered the Sergeant a drink.

"No thank you, sir," the Sergeant said, and left.

Carter's eyes looked vacant. "Thanks for swinging by the office," Carter said. "I was just about to call the Secretary of Defense."

"Don't do it," Jack said.

Carter laughed. "I *have* to do it, son. The goddamned Chinese have exploded two nuclear weapons in the Pacific. I'm supposed to be *protecting* the Pacific. Obviously, I have failed. It's time to turn the responsibility over to someone who can handle it."

"General, quit feeling sorry for yourself, and listen to me."

Carter stepped back as if Jack had slapped him.

"We were pretty careless seventy-five years ago, but everything was on the line, and we couldn't worry about being careless if it got results."

Carter opened his mouth and then closed it.

"In this situation, the Chinese got very, very lucky. But we can still stop this."

Carter laughed and drained his Scotch. "How in God's blue hell are we supposed to do that?"

"Listen to me."

Carter looked at him.

"We need to set off a counter-explosion in the path of the tidal wave, and we need to do it as soon as possible.

"Counter explosion?" Carter asked.

"You've got B-52s here," Jack said. "Now, I know they usually don't carry nuclear payloads out of Guam, but if you've got a nuke on this island, we're going to need it."

Carter said nothing.

"*Damn* it, General, is there a nuclear weapon on this island or not?"

"Two, actually."

"What time did the bomb go off at Yap?" Jack asked.

"2250 hours, twenty minutes ago."

A detailed map of the Pacific Ocean hung on the wall opposite the General's desk. Jack hobbled to it. His right hand dripped blood from the bullet wound in his shoulder. Carter didn't seem to mind.

Carter sat on the edge of his desk. "You've got five minutes," he said. "At the end of minute five, I'm calling the Secretary of Defense to inform him the Chinese have detonated nuclear weapons at Palau and Yap."

"You do that, and you risk a nuclear escalation that could wipe out all of civilization, General."

"Better convince me, son."

Jack pointed at Palau. "When did the Palau detonation happen?" he asked.

"2234 hours, local time," Carter replied. "It was 2134 local at Palau."

"All right," Jack said. "You say the detonation at Yap happened about sixteen minutes later, at 2250, Yap and Guam local time. Is that right?"

Carter nodded.

"Look, in deep water, a tidal wave travels at great speed, somewhere close to five-hundred miles per hour. Xiao," Jack hesitated, "that is, the Chinese, transmitted the operational code for Project Big Surf from the Control Center at either 2233 or 2234 local time. I can't remember which. I had just gotten shot."

Carter looked back at the DRSN phone. "General," Jack urged, "stay with me."

"All right."

"According to this map, Palau sits at about 7.5 degrees North latitude. Yap Island sits at about 9.5 degrees North latitude. If the second detonation, at Yap Island, occurred at 2250, then we know Harmon expected the tidal wave to travel very swiftly, covering the two degrees of North Latitude, or about 138 miles, in just about sixteen minutes.

"The Yap detonation was designed to reinforce the Palau wave as it swept north past 9.5 degrees North latitude."

Carter looked slightly more interested. "Go on."

"Rota Island," Jack said, "is where we believe the third bomb is set to detonate. If I'm right about Harmon's calculations, the Palau tidal wave, strengthened by the Yap detonation, will sweep north past Guam and Rota Island in about," Jack scribbled some calculations on a tablecloth, looked at this watch, and continued, "thirty minutes from now. That's fifty-three minutes to travel something like 441 miles between the Yap Island detonation, at 9.5 degrees North latitude, and Rota Island, at 14.1 degrees North latitude."

Carter stared at him. "The third detonation at Rota," he said. "I'd forgotten about that."

This revelation spurred him into action. Jack recognized the impetus. There might be something he could actually do about this, and he wanted to do it.

Carter picked up his phone and dialed a number. "This is General Carter," he said. "Get me the Governor, right now."

Jack went back over his calculations as Carter coordinated an emergency notification to the inhabitants of Rota. *All Rota islanders were to travel to the south end of the island immediately. No exceptions. The Governor of Guam would see to it. Yes, it was too late for an evacuation. Yes, it was the Chinese. No, it couldn't be helped...*

If Jack's math was correct, they had about twenty-five minutes before the blast at Rota. With any luck, one out of three detonations would fail, and Rota would be spared, but Jack didn't think there was much chance of that.

Carter put the phone down. Jack continued.

"Right after that third detonation at Rota, we've got to take action."

"You're talking about ordering a nuclear detonation on my own authority," Carter said. "Authority I don't have."

"Sometimes," Jack answered, "there's no time for authority, and men with ability must act of their own accord."

Carter considered this. "There's still time to ask permission."

Jack fixed his eyes on the General's. "Sure, there's twenty-four minutes to ask for permission, but I think you know what the answer will be, and I don't think you like it."

Carter walked back to his desk and stared at the DRSN phone. "If I ask for permission," he said, "the Secretary will tell me to go to hell. The Secretary will then advise the President to inform the world that the Chinese have detonated nuclear weapons in the Pacific, relatively close to U.S. Territory. The Secretary will further advise the President to publicize the fact that the Chinese Air Force shot down a B-52 and a C-17, and that we lost an additional B-52 at Yap, although the crew has been rescued."

Jack was silent.

"After the Rota Island detonation," Carter continued, "the Secretary will advise the President to retaliate against the Chinese People's Liberation Army with Intercontinental Ballistic Missiles. If the President declines, the United States will look weak, the Chinese may launch first, and there goes the country. If the President accepts the Secretary's advice, we may push the world into nuclear war and global holocaust."

Jack maintained his silence.

Carter moved behind his desk, picked up his regular phone, and dialed. "Tom," he said, "get over to my office with the best B-52 crew you've got. And make it fast," he looked at his watch. "You've got about twenty minutes."

* * *

Ten minutes later, Tom, who turned out to be the Operations Group Commander, showed up in the Command Section with a full B-52 crew. Throckmorton located the General's Scotch again.

In the time remaining until the expected detonation of the Rota Island bomb, Jack and Carter explained the situation to the crew.

"You want us to drop a nuclear bomb into the Philippine Sea," the pilot said, seriously, "just ahead of the tidal wave you say is headed north toward coastal Japan."

Jack nodded. Then an idea struck him. "We've still got about seven minutes until the detonation," Jack said. "I want you to see that tidal wave with your own eyes. I want you to know why you should do what we're asking you to do."

Jack and Throckmorton hustled everyone down to the entrance, where they piled into waiting Security Forces vehicles. "Take us to the Overlook!" Jack said, "And step on it!"

The Security Forces Airmen took Jack's guidance to heart. They made it to the Scenic Overlook in four minutes flat.

Throckmorton helped Jack out of the vehicle, and they walked up the short incline to the precipice. Below, Jack saw Tarague Beach and its placid, reef-locked bay. The moon shone over the water. Jack looked at his watch. They had about two more minutes.

"General Carter," he said, "what direction is Rota Island?"

Carter took his bearings and pointed out over the reef. "About forty miles in that direction," he said. "You can see it from here on a clear day."

The crew waited, respectful of General Carter but seemingly skeptical of Jack's promised tidal wave. As the seconds ticked by, Jack urged them to watch the moon on the water.

As two minutes turned to one minute, one minute to thirty seconds, and thirty seconds to ten, Jack counted down silently. "Watch the water," Jack urged them. "Watch where the moonlight shines on the surface."

At zero, Jack held his breath. Nothing happened. "Wait," he said. "Wait for it."

Fifteen seconds later, they began to murmur. General Carter looked anxious.

"Hold on, boys," Jack encouraged. "Keep looking at that water."

Ten seconds after that, someone gasped. The tidal wave, an immense ripple like God's ghost passing over space-time, barreled north past Guam's reef at amazing speed. Part of the reef collapsed as the tidal wave smashed it into the bay. Spray from the impact flew hundreds of feet into the air.

"Holy shit-balls," the pilot said. "That's headed for Japan?"

Four minutes and forty-eight seconds later, the Rota Island bomb detonated. A miniature sun rose silently over the distant island, which they saw superimposed against the flaming conflagration. The entire ocean illuminated. A few seconds later, a searing wind beat them back from the Overlook, and they heard the reverberating rumble and distant roar even from their forty mile distance.

A hellish mushroom cloud bloomed over the sea and blotted out the moonlight.

"I'm convinced," the pilot said. "When do we take off?"

* * *

In an abundance of paranoia, General Carter had already equipped two B-52s with nuclear payloads as an option for deterrence against the Chinese. He rode out to the first B-52 with the specially selected crew, gave them strict instructions, and then whipped the second crew into action.

The first B-52 left the runway while the second alert crew boarded and taxied. From the Rota Island detonation to the first bomber's takeoff, Jack counted thirty minutes. To the second, it was more like forty-five.

General Carter drove them to the operations building where they had briefed the Commander of INDOPACOM. Once inside, Carter directed several enlisted personnel to set up a mission tracking screen.

Because they had no way to track the actual tsunami, Jack helped a young Staff Sergeant build the 500 mile-per-hour underwater behemoth into a flight training program, which they displayed on a large monitor to the left of the mission tracking wall. They represented the tidal wave with the symbol for a Chinese Fighter plane. They programmed the simulated Chinese Fighter to fly slightly northwest from

Guam at exactly 500 miles per hour, and accelerated its progress to represent the time elapsed since the wave had passed the island.

On the screen beside the simulator, they watched the actual, live flight progress from the two B-52s in pursuit. Because of the thirty minute lapse between the passing tidal wave and the first B-52's departure, the tidal wave rolled some 250 miles north of the first B-52, and about 300 miles north of the second.

"What's the B-52's top speed, General?" Jack asked, watching both screens at once.

"Six-hundred and fifty miles per hour," Carter replied. "But most of them are over sixty years old, and we don't like to push them over six-hundred, if we can help it."

"Roger," Jack said.

"In the meantime," Carter continued, "I want all the goddamned insurance I can get." He ran over to a classified phone and dialed a number. "The *Ronald Reagan*," he said. "Put the Admiral on."

Carter hit the speaker button and placed the receiver in it's cradle. "Admiral Lofton, here," a voice answered.

"Admiral," the General said, "this is Carter."

"Carter!" The Admiral shouted. "I've been trying to reach you for the past hour. We registered that nuclear blast at Rota Island and got your reports about Palau and Yap. Tell me there won't be any more of those."

"That's why I called you, Admiral. I expect you registered that tidal wave as well."

"You bet your ass, we did," Lofton replied. "I've got twenty-two sailors overboard and two choppers destroyed."

"Listen, Admiral. We're going to stop that wave before it hits Japan. But we need your help. We've already had one '52 splashdown after an attack from a *Chengdu*. I'm asking for your protection."

There was silence from the other end of the line. Then, "Carter, if you're planning to do what I think you are, you're either dumber than a bush-pilot or a mother-loving genius."

"Let's go with Option Two."

"Hell, I'm with you."

Carter smiled.

"We saw your bombers creep past on the radar a few minutes ago," Lofton said. "The *Shandong* is about a hundred miles north of our location. My *SuperHornets* will escort your heavies all the way to destination, wherever the hell that is."

"Copy that," Carter said.

"And Carter!"

"Yes, Admiral?"

"You got a set of balls would sink a goddamn battleship."

CHAPTER 12

A Major from the *Global Hawk* detachment burst into the operations room. "General! We need to brief you immediately."

Two Captains and a Chief Master Sergeant ran in behind the Major, and he started talking.

"We just finished analyzing the imagery from our last *Global Hawk* reconnaissance flight over North Korea."

"Well?" Carter asked.

"We've identified massive Chinese troop movements through North Korea, to the coastal cities of Wonsan, Sinpo, and Chongjin. It appears as though the Chinese troops are preparing for an invasion of mainland Japan."

Carter looked at Jack. Jack nodded.

The Chief Master Sergeant unrolled a map and threw it over a nearby table. "The troops at Wonsan are accompanied by Chinese troop carrier aircraft associated with paratroop drops. Here at Sinpo and Chongjin, the Chinese have docked large cargo vessels, with which we believe they plan to move more troops to Japan."

"Thank you, gentlemen," Carter said. "I've got some calls to make."

They left the room. Jack watched the monitors and wished for a cigarette. Throckmorton located a stash of beer in a refrigerator somewhere, cracked one open, and groaned as a military nurse patched up the gunshot wound to his left shoulder blade.

A Security Forces Technical Sergeant stepped into the room and called for him, "Agent Quintana! You've got an urgent call out here."

Jack followed him out to the Entry Control desk. "I was checking in on my troops at the front gate when she called," the Technical Sergeant said.

"She?" Jack asked.

"I guess she didn't have a way to reach you, so she called the gate. I knew you were here, so I patched the call through to the building's Entry Controller."

"Who is it?" Jack asked, straining to keep up with the Sergeant.

"Said her name was 'Bordallo,'" he replied. "'Isa Bordallo.'"

Jack hustled ahead of the Sergeant, who looked surprised he could move at all, and snatched the phone from the desk.

"Isa!" Jack said. "It's me. What's going on?"

"Jack!" she cried. "I'm at the bar. Teddy Calvo came in and told everyone to leave. He pointed a gun at me. I ran into the back office and locked the door. He's trying to break it down!"

"Oh, man," Jack said. "Hang on! I'm on my way."

Jack hung up and looked at the Sergeant. "There's an old British guy on the ops floor drinking a beer and getting a gunshot wound cleaned. Grab him and meet me outside."

"Copy that," the Sergeant said.

Jack shuffled to the door and dragged it open with his left hand. He could barely move his right arm, but the bleeding had stopped. He'd directed the nurse to attend to Throckmorton first.

The Sergeant's security truck was parked in front of the building. Jack climbed into the passenger seat, took out the satellite phone, and dialed.

"Sergeant Kirker." The distant end answered.

"Kirker, this is Quintana."

"You all right?" Kirker asked.

"Never better. Where are you?"

"I'm sitting at the Comm Squadron with my thumb up my ass. Being a comm nerd kind of blows when the shit's going down."

"I imagine you're pretty handy with that Dodge Charger."

"I imagine you're right about that."

"We're leaving the base in two minutes, headed out from the Ops building." Jack reached over to the steering column and turned on the truck's Hazard lights. "We're in a blue Ford Expedition. Security Forces vehicle. You'll see the blinkers flashing."

"What do you need?"

"Not sure yet, but I know you're a good man to have around."

Throckmorton climbed in the back with a six pack of Stella Artois. "What's on the agenda, Jacky boy?"

The Technical Sergeant climbed into the driver's seat. "What's your name, Sergeant?" Jack asked.

"Slade, Chris Slade."

"Thanks for telling me about the call. Sergeant Slade, what I need to do may or may not be necessarily in the line of duty. I don't really know yet. If you stick with us, I'll make sure you're covered. If you'd rather drop us at our destination, that's fine too."

Slade turned to him. "I heard the Chinese just nuked three islands. Is that true?"

"More or less." Jack replied.

"Then all bets are off. Consider me your personal security attaché for the remainder of your stay on beautiful Guam."

"Good man!" Throckmorton yelled.

"Set that beer on the curb," Slade told him. "No drinking in the cop car."

"Damn." Throckmorton opened the door, set the beer on the concrete, and blew it a kiss as Slade rolled out toward Arc Light boulevard.

Halfway to the gate, an orange Dodge Charger swung in behind them. "The Dodge is with us," Jack told Slade. Slade turned the flashers off.

Together, the Expedition and the Charger roared out the front gate and swung a left onto Marine Corps Drive. "The girl that called," Jack told Slade, "she's involved with the case we're working."

"Okay," Slade said, slaloming around an islander on a moped.

"A dirty Guam PD cop has her trapped inside *Mac & Marti*. Do you know that bar?"

"I know it," Slade replied. "What's the angle?"

"Near as I can tell, they're using her to get to me."

"Looks like that's going pretty well for them."

Jack sighed. "I know. But we may have this China situation under control. If the Chinese are aware of that, they may want to use me as a bargaining chip later, which is probably why they're after my best gal."

"And this Guam PD cop is with the Chinese?"

"He's on the mob's payroll."

Slade turned his lights on when they hit the town of Dededo. Cars pulled to the side of the road. The Expedition and the Charger blasted south at eighty miles per hour.

Jack called Sergeant Kirker. "We're headed to *Mac & Marti.*"

"I thought this was an emergency," Kirker said.

"A girl who's associated with my case is being accosted there," Jack said.

"Check."

"A Technical Sergeant Chris Slade is driving us. He's got an M9, and that's the end of our firepower. Any ideas?"

Kirker thought a moment. Both vehicles swung wide around a mangy stray dog in the middle of the highway.

"There's a gun club on the Strip," Kirker said. "It's called *Shoot Em Up.* The place is a Japanese tourist trap, but they have plenty of weapons and ammo. I don't think I could get away with buying weapons on the spot, but your badge might do the trick."

"Copy that. I'll jump in with you at *Mac & Marti.*"

"Slade, I need you and Throckmorton to cause as much commotion as you can outside the bar. I'm talking lights, siren, burning trash cans, everything. We want the tourists to stay away, and we want Calvo to think he's got no way out."

"Is Guam PD already on the scene?" Slade asked.

"Probably not. But they will be."

Slade swung a hard right off Marine Corps Drive onto "Happy Landing Road" and screamed down a steep decline toward the Strip. Kirker followed close behind. At the bottom of the hill, both vehicles swung left.

259

Five seconds later, *Mac & Marti* appeared on the right. Slade slammed on the brakes, and they slid to a stop in the middle of the southbound lane of the Tumon Strip. Jack opened his door, limped around to Kirker's Charger, and dropped into the passenger seat. Kirker floored the beastly Dodge into a smoking, 180 degree turn, and they rocketed north toward the gun club.

Jack heard Sergeant Slade wind up his siren. In the rearview mirror, he saw Throckmorton urge tourists to turn around.

Kirker swung into the right lane, narrowly avoided a group of chattering Japanese, and then wheeled the Charger into a parking lot that fronted a two-story, concrete building with outdoor walkways on both levels. Up and to the right, a flock of strippers stood outside a club called "New Viking" and catcalled them.

"The gun club is down here to the left," Kirker said. They rushed from the car to the gun club and ran inside.

A group of young Japanese girls waited in line to fire a semi-automatic rifle. Kirker was still in his uniform. Half the girls broke away and rushed him for photographs. Kirker tried to resist, but Jack appreciated the distraction. While Kirker was being inundated, Jack slapped a credit card on the counter.

"What can I do for you?" the proprietor asked, ignoring Jack's bloody shoulder and shrapnel-scraped face. Jack flipped his badge open. "Special Agent Jack Quintana," he said quickly. "We're working a case and we're in a hurry."

The proprietor inspected the badge and glanced over at Kirker, who smiled awkwardly while Japanese girls draped arms around him and flashed the peace sign at any number of volunteer photographers from their group. "As long as this credit card works," he said, "I'll sell you whatever you want."

"Give me that Winchester 1894," Jack said, pointing at a western-looking rifle hanging on the back wall, "and a box of .30-30 shells." The man grabbed the rifle and the cartridges. Jack looked at the selection under the counter. He saw a Colt Single Action Army Revolver and a Ruger Blackhawk that seemed in good condition. "Those two as well," Jack said. "And cartridges."

The man put the revolvers and cartridges in a bag that read "*Shoot 'Em Up on the Tumon Strip!.*" Jack threw the rifle to Kirker and grabbed the bag with his left hand. The girls squealed and followed them out to the Dodge.

Kirker burned rubber out of the parking lot, sped south, and screeched to a halt behind Slade's Expedition. The whole jaunt had taken them six minutes.

Jack grabbed the Colt Single Action and tossed the Ruger to Throckmorton. Jack would have preferred the rifle, but he couldn't work it with only one hand, his left hand, at that. Slade held his M9 over the Expedition's hood, barrel leveled at the bar's entrance. Kirker took the same stance with the Winchester, over the hood of the Charger.

"Watch the crowd," Jack told them. "Calvo may already have called in for help. The Chinese may try to assist him if they feel they have something to gain."

Just then, a fleet of Guam PD cruisers approached from the south-bound lane. They halted behind Kirker's Dodge, and a handsome young Lieutenant stepped out into the street.

"Agent Quintana?" he called.

"Lieutenant Cruz," Jack answered.

"What the hell is going on here?"

"Your Ted Calvo has one of my people hostage in there," Jack said, tilting his head toward the bar. "We're going to get her out."

"This is Guam PD jurisdiction," Cruz replied, placing a hand on his service pistol.

"I'm going in, Cruz. You can either assist my team or get a beautiful young woman killed."

Cruz said nothing.

Jack shoved the Colt between his belt and the small of his back, pulled his shirt over it, and stepped inside the bar.

* * *

261

Teddy had Isa bound and gagged against the back wall. Tears streamed from her eyes. Jack winked at her. Teddy found this hilarious.

"Agent Quintana! You're pretty cocky for a man who's about to die."

Teddy had been drinking to keep himself entertained. Jack didn't know if that was good or bad.

"What's your play, Ted? This setup is no good for you."

"That's what you think," Teddy replied, slurring. He held a semi-automatic pistol over the table. "You carrying?"

"Does it look like I'm carrying?" Jack answered. He held out his left arm and twisted his right hand out from his side. That hurt.

"Guess not. Why don't you pull up a chair and have a drink?"

"What are we doing here, Ted?"

"Pull up a chair, I said! I got the gun. Not you."

Jack shrugged his left shoulder and sat down opposite Calvo. Isa was propped against the wall, on the floor to Calvo's right.

"Both hands on the table," Calvo said.

Jack grabbed his right hand with his left hand, grimaced, and lifted it onto the table. "There, old Ted. Satisfied?"

Calvo grunted and poured himself more booze. Jack saw he was drinking straight gin. "Have some," Ted said.

"No, thanks," Jack said. "Gin's not really my drink."

"If you're not gonna drink, then turn on the TV. I sure as hell don't want to talk to you."

Jack snatched a remote control from the table behind him and hit the "ON" button. The television behind the bar came to life, and Olivia Knowlton filled the screen.

Somehow, she had managed to get her news team onto the *Ronald Reagan*. The lady had more connections than a 1940s telephone switchboard.

"Two sailors are still missing after the giant tidal wave nearly capsized the Aircraft Carrier *Ronald Reagan*. The tidal wave was presumed to have been caused by the nuclear detonations at Palau and

262

Yap, and may have been exacerbated by the third blast at Rota Island, which is just forty miles northwest of Guam, some two and a half hours ago.

Cat's out of the bag now. Jack could only hope the President would keep the American ICBMs in their silos a little while longer.

"Concern is mounting that the behemoth tidal wave will continue sweeping north, through the Philippine Sea, all the way to the southern and eastern coasts of Japan. Hardest hit so far is the island of Okinawa. The wave impacted Okinawa just fifteen minutes ago, and, according to initial reports, inflicted horrible casualties. Local authorities predict tens of thousands will die on the heavily populated island.

"The island of Guam was spared significant damage because it lies at the far eastern edge of the Philippine Sea and caught only the wave's outer band. In addition, Guam is protected by a massive coral reef, although much of the island's southern reef is reported to have been destroyed by the advancing wave.

"Even the outer band, however, was powerful enough to tip the *Ronald Reagan* on its side, wrench two helicopters from their moorings, and toss twenty-three sailors overboard. Thankfully, the carrier's *SuperHornet* fighters were airborne when the wave swept beneath it."

Calvo chuckled and scooped more Gin into his mouth. "That big ass wave is gonna wreck Japan. Wreck it! And then the Chinese are gonna swoop in and take over, man."

"That's a lot of information for a brain like yours to handle. You sure you've got that right?"

"Don't insult me. You think you're such a big man. Mr. 'Special Agent.' Comin' out here to my island and tryin' to screw up the works."

"Is it your island, then, Ted? Or did you already sell it out to the Chinese?"

Teddy gave him the finger and poured himself more gin.

Jack turned back to the television. "Just over an hour ago," Olivia continued, "two B-52 bombers swept past the *Ronald Reagan*, ostensibly chasing the tidal wave. Now, we can't say why they would do that, but we can speculate it might be a last-ditch attempt to disrupt the tidal wave with a fourth nuclear explosion, detonated at the water's surface, near the wave's leading edge."

Ted stared at the television. "Can't do that," he whispered. "Won't work."

"According to our information, the wave is traveling at approximately 500 miles per hour. The B-52's top speed is 650 miles per hour. The first B-52 left Guam approximately thirty minutes after the tidal wave passed, which means it was already something like 250 miles behind the wave when it took off.

"If those numbers are correct, and if the first B-52 is flying at top speed, that first bomber should be catching up with the tidal wave just about now. Our sources indicate the B-52s left Guam loaded with several 'AGM-86 Air Launched Cruise Missiles,' which are equipped with 'W-80 Thermonuclear Warheads.'

"The W-80 Warheads are described as 'variable yield' weapons, which means the intensity of their explosive power can be dialed up or down, from five kilotons up to 150 kilotons. We don't know the yield settings associated with these particular warheads, but just one of these weapons has more capacity than the World War II bombs 'Little Boy' and 'Fat Man' combined.

"All of our hopes rest with these B-52 crewmen. If they should fail, or if the theory itself should fail, we predict hundreds of thousands of innocent Japanese will die within the next thirty minutes."

Guns blasted out in the street. Jack turned and saw Kirker work the lever action Winchester. He fired upward, as if returning fire from the tops of buildings on either side of the street.

The kitchen doors burst open. Xiao paced in with two beefy Chinese men in suits. Her right eye was swollen shut from Throckmorton's blow.

"You look worse every time I see you," Jack told her.

She looked at Calvo. "Give me your keys," she said.

Drunk and impudent, he replied, "You're not takin' my goddamn Cruiser."

She shot him in the face. Isa screamed through her cotton gag.

Xiao grabbed Teddy's keys and directed her henchmen to load Jack and Isa into the Cruiser. The suited thugs dragged them through the kitchen. They shoved Isa into the trunk. One of them took Jack's pistol and pushed him into the back seat.

Xiao jumped into the driver's seat and threw the Cruiser into gear. Jack saw Throckmorton huddled behind the Expedition, returning fire as bullets hailed from the rooftops. Guam PD scrambled for cover.

Kirker turned just as Xiao pulled out from a side street. Jack met his eyes. He heard Kirker shout something to Sergeant Slade, and then Xiao punched the Crown Victoria south down the Strip. It was the same route they'd taken the day she'd shot him in the leg. *Long time ago,* Jack thought absently.

Just as before, they swung left before the Pacific Island Club and scooted up the incline, back toward Marine Corps drive. Jack twisted his head around and saw Kirker's Dodge careen around the turn behind them, followed closely by Slade's Expedition.

"Where to, love?" Jack asked. She didn't answer.

At the intersection at the top of the incline, Xiao took a hard right and scooted into the left lane. Kirker floored his Dodge and sped up beside the Crown Victoria in the right lane. He worked the Winchester with his right hand, stuck the rifle's barrel out the driver's window, and pulled the trigger.

The Crown Victoria's right rear tire exploded. The thug to Jack's right rolled his window down and pumped four rounds into Kirker's door.

Kirker pulled back, and Slade's Expedition raced up to replace him. Just then, Xiao whipped the wounded Crown Victoria into a sliding left turn and stomped the accelerator. Sparks flew from the rear of the Cruiser as it rolled on the rim. Customers at a Circle-K gas station gaped at them.

Slade missed the intersection and locked up his brakes. Kirker tailgated the cruiser.

"Looks like we're headed for the airport," Jack said. "I've had enough travel, if it's all the same to you."

Xiao glared at him in the rearview mirror.

"Let's go back to *Mac & Marti*," Jack said. "I miss Ted."

They jumped a curb and smashed through the airport's chain-link fence. "I never listened to all those jokes about Asian drivers," Jack said. "Maybe there's something there."

The Crown Victoria rattled and wheezed. Kirker came up on Xiao's left and smashed the heavy Dodge into the Cruiser. Her window shattered. She pointed a pistol out with her left hand and fired blindly, eyes locked straight ahead.

"You missed him," Jack said. She snapped something at one of the goons in the back seat. He punched Jack in the shoulder. Jack's vision grayed, but he held onto consciousness.

Xiao pointed the Cruiser at a Lear jet on the runway. A line of Chinese men in suits waited in front of the plane.

"Christ," Jack whispered.

The men opened fire on Kirker's Dodge. He lost a tire and spun out behind the Cruiser.

Xiao pumped the brakes and jumped out of the driver's seat, shouting commands in Chinese. From behind, Jack heard the Expedition's 5.4 Liter V-8 scream up to maximum throttle. Slade pointed the SUV at the line of Chinese mobsters and ducked under the dashboard.

Distracted by Kirker's orange Charger, they hadn't seen the midnight-blue Expedition approach from the darkness. Some of them tried to scramble out of its path. A few opened fire on the big Ford, and the windshield disintegrated.

Slade plowed into the crowd like a two-ton wrecking ball. Bodies flew through the air. Men screamed.

Xiao's thugs yanked Jack from the Cruiser and shoved him aboard the jet. Xiao climbed on and pulled up the retractable staircase.

Jack watched from the window. Slade's Expedition hit a baggage cart and stalled out. A few remaining Chinese suits fired at the vehicle from around the little jet. Jack saw Throckmorton pop up and fire three rounds from the Ruger Blackhawk at the closest goon. The goon went down.

The jet started rolling. Jack looked back at Kirker. In a matter of twenty seconds, Kirker had snatched his hydraulic jack from the Charger's trunk, jacked up the side with the wrecked tire, and started twisting lug nuts from the wheel. There was a fresh spare on the ground beside him.

Slade spilled out of the Expedition and fired over the hood. Eight Chinese remained. They fired back from behind the totaled Crown Victoria.

Jack worried about Isa, locked in the Cruiser's trunk.

The jet taxied toward the runway. Airport security vehicles approached the firefight but paid no attention to the moving jet.

Come on, Kirker. Come on, man.

Kirker worked like a one-man pit crew. In fifteen seconds, he had the battered wheel off and the new one on the lugs. Sweat poured from his face as he spun the lug nuts back on, working the hydraulic pump at the same time to lower the car back to the ground.

The jet picked up speed and then slowed at the end of the runway. Jack lost sight of Kirker, but he could still hear Throckmorton and Slade trading shots with the Chinese.

The pilot turned the jet 180 degrees and ran up the engines.

Through the window on the jet's opposite wall, Jack saw one of the thugs notice Kirker and fire on the Charger. Slade blasted three rounds from his M9. The mobster fell to the tarmac.

Kirker threw down the tire iron, kicked the hydraulic pump out from under the car, and leapt into the driver's seat. Jack heard the Charger roar to life even over the jet engines.

Kirker dropped the Dodge into gear and punched the accelerator. The jet started forward. Kirker was a quarter-mile from the runway.

The jet picked up speed. The Charger covered the distance in twelve seconds and shot ahead of the jet. They rocketed down the runway together.

Xiao screamed at the pilot. The pilot gave the jet full throttle. Kirker slammed his brakes.

The impact was immediate. The jet's forward landing gear collapsed, and the nose went into the concrete. Kirker's Charger spun out and away from the jet. The cockpit caught fire. One of the big thugs started to cry.

Jack lunged out of his seat and grabbed the emergency release lever for the staircase. It flopped open and then sheared off as it hit the runway. Jack figured their speed at fifty miles per hour. The jet shrieked forward on the concrete without slowing, engines propelling it.

Xiao turned from the copilot's seat and fired a shot at him. It grazed his neck. He jumped from the doomed aircraft.

He almost made the grassy median between the taxiway and the runway, but not quite. His left knee smacked concrete. It didn't hurt at first. He rolled into the grass like a dud round from a Howitzer. The pain from his knee reached his brain. He threw up.

At the far end of the runway, the Lear crashed into an empty cargo plane and exploded. "Let's see her walk away from *that* one," Jack wheezed. He imagined a few of his ribs were broken.

Kirker pulled up in his Charger. The Dodge was missing its trunk now. Kirker pulled him into the passenger seat, and they drove back to the Expedition. Throckmorton and Slade had dispatched the remaining mobsters.

"Isa," Jack said. "Isa's in the trunk."

Throckmorton punched the Crown Victoria's trunk release. They pulled her from the vehicle and removed the gag and restraints.

She ran to Jack and threw her arms around him.

"Ow!" Jack cried. "Wait a second!"

She covered his face with kisses and ignored the vomit on his shirt. Jack thought that remarkably polite of her.

He retrieved the last, crumbling remnants of Hydrocodone from his pocket and swallowed them. "Let's vacate before Guam PD shows up. I'll have to explain myself at some point. But not tonight."

Isa jumped in the back seat of Kirker's Dodge. Throckmorton and Slade pulled out behind them in the Expedition.

"Where to?" Kirker asked.

"Let's go back to the bar," Jack said. "I'm thirsty."

* * *

When they got back to the Tumon Strip, it was mostly deserted. Jack tried to explain the complicated situation to Isa. She said nothing and clung to him.

Police tape sectioned off the southbound lane in front of *Mac & Marti*. Jack heard gunshots further down the road and figured Guam PD was still fighting it out with the Chinese.

Kirker and Slade helped Jack into the bar. Jack could hardly believe it had only been twenty-five minutes since he and Isa had been shoved into the police cruiser. Someone had removed Teddy Calvo's body. Jack was grateful.

Olivia was still on the television. By some miracle, *or by General Carter's political genius,* Jack thought, she had tapped in to live footage from a *Global Hawk*. The reconnaissance bird circled a large area of the northern Philippine Sea. On-screen, the footage zoomed in on the lead B-52.

All of them watched as the tidal wave, seen in moonlight as that same giant ripple across the sea, charged ahead of the B-52. The *Global Hawk* panned out. F/A-18 *SuperHornets* from the *Ronald Reagan* engaged *Chengdu* fighters from the *Shandong*. One of the Chinese fighters fired a missile at the lead B-52. A *SuperHornet* fired a missile at the missile and took it out.

The *Global Hawk* panned out again. The wave hit the southern Japanese island of Yakushima.

The *Global Hawk* zoomed back in on the B-52. The bomber now led the wave by five miles. A bright flash of light exploded from under the bomber's right wing. The Air Launched Cruise Missile shot ahead of the bomber.

A *Chengdu* fighter fired another Air-to-Air missile at the Air Launched nuclear warhead. Again, a *SuperHornet* pilot took the Chinese missile down.

The B-52 executed a slow, left bank, and the fighter pilots scrambled away from the warhead. One *Chengdu* and one *SuperHornet* remained.

The *Chengdu* pilot fired his last air-to-air missile at the speeding warhead. The *SuperHornet* pilot destroyed it. In desperation, the *Chengdu* pilot punched his afterburners and screamed after the warhead, trying to knock it out of the sky with his fighter.

The *SuperHornet* pilot pulled away and kicked in his own afterburners. He blasted almost straight up as the *Chengdu* closed in on the warhead.

A blinding flash erupted on the television screen, and Isa cried out. The *Global Hawk* feed stopped.

The camera switched back to Olivia, who, for once, had nothing to say.

Someone at the network redirected the video feed to the Kagoshima prefecture on southern Japan's Kyushu Island.

Olivia found her voice. "The... the American bomber... as you've seen... successfully detonated the Air Launched Cruise Missile over the Philippine Sea, just ahead of the racing tidal wave. Our video feed from the *Global Hawk* was cut off, likely from the Electromagnetic Pulse emitted by the nuclear blast."

"In one minute," she looked at her watch, "we will know if the American action was successful."

The camera switched back to a live feed from coastal Kagoshima. They could see the beach. The water in the live shot receded, and Jack breathed in. Isa gripped his hand hard enough to hurt.

"Thirty seconds left," Olivia's voice played over the video.

A dog ran down the beach, barking at the sky. Seagulls took flight and disappeared from camera view.

"It has to have worked," Throckmorton whispered. "It has to."

Olivia had the good sense to refrain from a 10-second countdown, but the numbers appeared on the screen.

On Five, the dog sprinted from the beach.

On Three, a large wave covered the horizon.

On One, it crashed onto the beach.

And receded.

They held their collective breath for a second wave. It did not come.

Throckmorton shouted in triumph. Kirker and Sergeant Slade echoed Throckmorton, and Jack nearly collapsed.

Olivia came back on camera, in tears, of course, and ran her mouth about deliverance and hope. A boonie dog woofed at them from the sidewalk outside the bar.

* * *

Kirker poured drinks while Isa cried on Jack's chest. Throckmorton and Slade walked outside and fed the boonie dog cold French fries.

"Sarge," Jack said. "Put something on the juke-box, and I'll buy those beers I owe you."

Kirker winked and strolled over to the wall unit.

"Quit it with the crocodile tears, would you, kid?" Jack asked, kissing Isa's forehead.

She looked at him with those bright eyes.

From the juke-box, Pat Boone started up with his superhit from 1957, "Love Letters in the Sand."